# Presidential Prey

JAMES F. HAMILTON, IV

ISBN-13: 978-0692044957
ISBN-10: 0692044957

For Carolyn
My inspiration and the love of my life.
Without your encouragement and support,
this book would not have been possible.

"The Southwest corner of the house faced the Pacific Ocean, but the fence just twenty-five yards away divided the compound from a public beach and the streets of a residential neighborhood. The fence was the closest point to the house from which an attack on the president could have been launched. Spotlights were trained on it throughout the night, and when Nixon was in the house an agent was always on duty at the corner beneath the study. Still, I often wondered as I stood at that post how I would stop a well-coordinated assault if it ever came."

*Secret Service Agent, Dennis McCarthy from his book*
*Protecting the President*

# PRESIDENTIAL PREY

## CHAPTER ONE

### MAY 16
### Atlantic Ocean

It was the *Cape Carol's* sixth day on station. The patrol boat, not large enough to be called a cutter, sliced effortlessly through four-foot swells, twelve miles south southeast of Myrtle Beach, South Carolina.

Despite the fervor and enthusiasm of her fourteen-person crew, The *Cape Carol's* sixth day on station, like the preceding five, was uneventful. No drug smugglers; no lifesaving missions; no boardings.

Even a few routine safety checks would have provided welcome relief to the monotony that continuous miles of empty water exacted on a crew averaging a meager twenty-one years of age.

Despite the boredom, three facts favored the moment. They were on their way back to their home port of Portsmouth, Virginia, it was Friday and it was the *Cape Carol's* last day on patrol. Before the night was over, most of the boat's young crew, several of whom were still in their teens, would find themselves at The Leaky Bucket, a favorite watering hole and pick-up joint situated a few short blocks from base.

It was shortly after nineteen hundred hours when a message from the bridge summoned Douglas Stream, the duty conscious Captain of the *Cape Carol*, from below deck. With his first gulp of fresh air, he was greeted by Chief Boatswain's Mate Thomas Tripp, and Second Class Petty Officer Terrance Grant.

Chief Tripp hurriedly briefed the young Captain on the developing situation.

"Sir, it's the tanker off the starboard bow."

Petty Officer Grant, eager in his inexperience and youth, pushed a pair of binoculars into his Captain's hands. Tripp continued his briefing while shifting his point of focus to a small white craft under full power headed away from both the tanker and the *Cape Carol*.

"That power boat, off our port side, just moved away from the starboard bow of the tanker."

Captain Stream shifted his binoculars from the smaller boat to the freighter.

"The tanker is the ... *Beograd*. It's operating under a Panamanian flag."

After lowering his binoculars, Stream turned to Chief Tripp.

"Not much we can do with the tanker, at least not out here. Let's see what's going on with the other one. She seems to know where she's headed. We're going to need full power Chief. Kick her in the butt!"

With a backward glance toward the bridge, Tripp caught the attention of his man at the wheel, First Class Petty Officer Anthony 'Tony' Carelli. A corkscrew gesture of the Chief's index finger motioned the boat to full power. The *Cape Carol* leaned hard to port. Her two thousand four hundred and seventy horses were unleashed to an immediate effect. The initial thrust of the engine pushed the boat's bow high in the water.

Eager to assume his command position, the twenty-three-year-old Captain scurried up the six metal steps leading to the bridge. It was there that he felt most comfortable.

With the ship's controls at his fingertips and helmsman Carelli at his side, Doug Stream was ready for any opposition a boat patrolling domestic waters was likely to encounter. In a thick Brooklyn accent, Petty Officer Carelli voiced the obvious.

"We ain't catchin' 'er, Cap'n."

The observation required no reply. Carelli continued his unsolicited commentary.

"They've got enough to stay in front, but they aren't that much faster than we are."

Chief Tripp walked through the door.

"When we hit it, so did they. They saw us and they're running."

Stream, with his binoculars fixed on their target, didn't hesitate, "Better hit the blues."

Tripp activated the flashing blue pursuit light situated on top of the bridge while Stream turned to address the radioman, seated behind him.

"Blake! Try to make contact!"

"Yes sir, Skipper! Have we got a name for her?"

"Can't make it out. Order them to cut engines and prepare to be boarded."

Tripp, wary of everyone and pessimistic by nature, offered a tactful suggestion in the form of a question.

"Think we should call for a chopper?"

"If there's no response on the radio, we'll have to. We sure as hell aren't going to catch her."

Blake hailed the unknown craft only twice before a heavily accented voice made an unexpected reply.

"Zoetrope to Coast Guard! Zoetrope to Coast Guard! We are cutting our engines."

"Looks as if they're going to do it!" exclaimed Tripp.

"Christ! I'd have bet a month's pay that we were in for a chase on this one."

"Maybe they thought they couldn't get away," offered Carelli.

Stream expressed his doubts, "You'd have to be dumb, blind or both not to see that we didn't have a chance."

Experience had taught Tripp well.

"This isn't the way it usually goes. I don't like it. Why take-off like you've got a firecracker up your ass, then suddenly stop and allow us to board. It's crazy."

After retrieving the microphone to the ship's P.A. system from its metal holding clip, Stream addressed his crew.

"Now, all hands to boarding stations! All hands to boarding stations!"

Helmsman Carelli voiced the obvious probability, "I'll bet they're dopers! A dollar to a dime those bastards are carryin' a million bucks worth of 'toot' on board."

It took the *Cape Carol* a scant few minutes to close the distance between herself and the stilled Zoetrope. At three hundred yards the patrol boat reduced its speed to a cautious four knots. The boarding party, wearing ballistic vests and blaze orange life jackets, scrambled across the deck. Armed with a combination of pistols, M16s, and twelve-gauge shotguns, the five-man detail was prepared to flex its enforcement muscle.

Stream ordered the *Cape Carol*'s small twelve-foot boarding boat, a rigid hull inflatable, placed at the rail. It would not be lowered into the water until he was sure their quarry was well within the range of the patrol boat's fifty caliber deck gun. With fewer than one hundred yards to go, the Captain instructed his radioman to contact the nearest Coast Guard Cutter.

"Let the *Medgap* know we're preparing to board. Describe the boat as a fifty-foot Chris Craft V-hull pleasure boat."

The Chris Craft bobbed as if it were a cork on the water, maintaining only enough power to keep her bow into the wind. A single individual, dressed in coveralls and wearing a beret, emerged as if prodded, through the door of the main cabin. After taking a few tentative steps, the bearded man stood motionless.

The *Cape Carol* continued her careful advance while Captain Stream made a last-minute survey of his men and equipment. The pivot mounted deck gun was pointed directly at the mysterious figure standing on the Zoetrope's rear deck. The five-man boarding party, weapons in hand, stood watch at the rail. Everyone was in place.

Captain Stream placed the microphone to his lips. His highly amplified voice was authoritative, sharp, and to the point, "Are you the Captain of the Zoetrope?"

The man's entire upper torso bobbed in the affirmative. Stream continued, "I want your crew and any passengers on board to step out on deck."

A noticeable shifting of attention between the bridge and the fifty-caliber machine gun betrayed the man's unmistakable fear. He gave no indication that he understood or comprehended the command.

"Do you speak English?" asked Stream.

A futile gesture of the man's outstretched arms answered the question.

"Ease us up on her port side," Stream ordered, "I want to be close on this one."

Before Carelli could react to his Captain's command, two figures burst through the partially hidden main cabin door. They were carrying something, but it took a split-second for Doug Stream to recognize the RPG-7 rocket launcher on their shoulders.

"Jesus!" he exclaimed.

Two rockets hissed brilliantly across thirty yards of water toward the *Cape Carol*. Stream, Chief Tripp, Helmsman Carelli, and Radioman Blake barely had time to comprehend the cause of their own death.

The first of two nearly simultaneous explosions reduced the forward portion of the bridge to confetti. Three of the five man boarding party, standing on the bow, were blown overboard by the ferocious impact of the second missile, which struck the body of the seaman manning the fifty-caliber deck gun.

Only one of the two Coast Guardsmen left on deck was conscious. The dazed nineteen-year-old, overcoming smoke, debris and her own shock rose to a kneeling position and emptied her M16 at the now fleeing boat. One of her shots found its mark. The man who was assumed to be the Captain of the Zoetrope fell to his knees, then, flat across the deck.

Before the young woman could jam another clip into her automatic rifle, the image of the fleeing Chris Craft dwindled to a speck on the evening horizon.

The *Cape Carol* and over half of her crew were dead in the water.

## The White House
## Washington, D.C.

President James Thomas Atwater, flanked and trailed by a minimal compliment of three Secret Service Agents, entered the elegant East Room of the White House with expected flare and predictable aplomb.

His abrupt appearance, calculated to highlight the evening's dreary itinerary, triggered a fiery Marine band rendition of *Hail to the Chief.* Even the more jaded among Washington's tread worn hacks were stirred by the president's predictable, yet thunderous entry.

At the sight of his tall handsome frame, the event-worn assemblage of Washington dignitaries and Ambassadors, obligated to attend such functions, were roused to a brisk and sustained applause.

The warmth of the chief executive's boyish grin melted through layers of callous indifference with amazing ease. Everyone's eyes were riveted on the man TIME magazine heralded as: "The most popular United States political figure of our time." Not since John F. Kennedy had the

American public been so enamored by the charm of a United States President.

Unlike all but one of his predecessors, James Atwater was not married. Not since James Buchanan (1857-61) had a bachelor been elected to the nation's highest office; a fact, according to most pollsters, that enabled him to pocket over fifty-seven percent of the female vote in both of his landslide victories.

At the age of 49, he could rightfully claim the most recognized face on the planet. His mastery of politics was legendary. He knew the game as if he were born to play. His country and most of the world rested neatly in the palm of his hand.

Six years in the White House had, by most accounts, made James Atwater a better man. A smattering of failures, a vicious news hungry press, and the seemingly unavoidable corruption of appointees had replaced the young chief executive's initial cockiness and much heralded ego with a proper sense of genuine humility

Through it all, and to the chagrin of his opponents, the Atwater name remained magic. The president's immense popularity allowed him a measure of political and legislative power unequaled since the glory days of Franklin Roosevelt. Any adversary he confronted knew that a probable majority of Congress and the better half of three hundred million Americans supported his position.

To avoid public scorn, even his harshest critics usually prefaced their criticisms with a personal acknowledgment of his true character and personal warmth. "I like and respect James Atwater, but ...," was an oft heard phrase.

Only politicians with kamikaze tendencies, dared to attack the youthful chief executive on a personal level.

His rugged features and charismatic presence inspired titillating correspondence from both sexes that would embarrass Dr. Ruth Westheimer. A full head of thick dark hair, almost black, was kept that way with Grecian Formula 16 hair color. It was one of the few things about James Atwater's image that wasn't what it appeared to be.

At six feet four inches in height, he towered over world leaders and most colleagues alike; an advantage he understood and exploited whenever possible. His many moods were reflected in his dark brown, nearly black eyes that regularly disrupted the concentration of those to whom they were directed. A disapproving stare from the president was never missed, mistaken, or more importantly, forgotten.

Despite his classic good looks, James Atwater was no pretty boy. A noticeable scar over his left eye and a rugged, slightly leathery complexion kept him a man's man. His voice was both low and soft at the same time. Its warm rich tonal quality demanded attention; he rarely strained to be heard.

Middle age and an always vigorous appetite padded the presidential waistline with an unnecessary ten pounds. Not bad in view of the fact that he lived his life only a finger-snap away from any snack or meal that might strike his fancy.

The president's life was pretty much an open book. His childhood was middle-class average. He shared his parents' considerable affection with one brother, Mike, who was four years his junior.

Through the course of a twelve-year Catholic education, James participated in a variety of activities, worked hard for good grades, and could throw a curve ball with the best of his peers.

When his father died of a heart attack, near the end of Jim's senior year in high school, the eighteen-year-old joined the Navy and served with distinction until a shipboard accident resulted in a heartbreaking medical discharge.

Yale Law School provided the brighter than average young man with a profession and a beautiful wife named Megan. The newlyweds made their home in Minneapolis, Minnesota. In his second year of practice, their nineteen-month-old daughter, Christie, died of leukemia.

Only three months after the death of his child, James watched his mother, a lifetime smoker, die an agonizing death from lung cancer. The untimely loss of his child, coupled with the egregious passing of his mother, drove an impenetrable wedge between James and his beloved Catholic church.

In the years following Christie's death, both he and Megan immersed themselves in a variety of community-based charities associated with childhood diseases. Their unselfish contribution of time and effort brought them considerable attention and eventually led to James Atwater's successful bid for a seat in the state legislature.

As a freshman in the Minnesota Senate, his impact and public appeal made it obvious that he was destined for greater things.

Two conspicuous terms in the United States House of Representatives bolstered him to national prominence. In a few short years he gained the reputation of Washington's "man to watch."

Pushed by a political party desperate to regain leadership, he sought and received his party's nomination to the U.S. Senate. In the wake of a successful campaign, his beloved wife, Megan, was killed in an automobile accident. Her burial took place four days before her husband was sworn into office. Six years later, at the tender age of forty-two, the charismatic Senator from Minnesota was elected President of the United States.

The whole Atwater package was a publicist's dream. The poor thought of him as their friend. The wealthy, while leery of nearly everyone, were experiencing unparalleled growth and prosperity under his administration.

The Hispanics and the Blacks all loved him and his efforts to improve their lot. In an age of relentless media scrutiny and criticism, James Atwater managed to tiptoe through the mine fields of adversity with the finesse and skill of a well- rehearsed ballet dancer.

Exhaustive investigations into Atwater's past invariably disappointed his adversaries. Iniquitous business dealings and lascivious affairs were not his usual style. Any prurient interest the American Public wished to attribute to their bachelor president was left to their collective imaginations.

Regardless of public perception and James Atwater's reputation as a "straight arrow," he bore the staggering weight of a single secret – a secret so volatile, that if revealed, would rock the nation down to its foundation. Every day brought with it a certain incalculable risk that it could be the day that the Atwater administration was brought to its knees; a staggering prospect in view of his unrivaled popularity.

The spontaneous applause, occasioned by the president's entry, subsided. With a warm and always ingratiating smile, he stepped forward to greet his waiting guests. They gathered around him eagerly, anticipating a hoped-for moment of recognition; they were not disappointed. Each individual and his wife, date, or companion, were greeted with a personal remembrance and usually addressed by name; an amazing fact, in view of the multitudes who passed through his life.

After everyone in the room was made to feel an important part of the evening, a gesture of the presidential hand slowed the band to a danceable tune. The swarthy chief executive then walked directly to Mrs. Lawrence Stewart, the sixty-five-year-old wife of the Secretary of the Interior, and asked her to dance; it was the perfect move. Had he picked a younger woman, as most would expect, the over-sixty crowd might have been reminded of their advancing age, as it was, he endeared himself to both young and old; a classic Atwater move.

At the conclusion of the dance, Vice President Sidney Holdridge and his wife, Robin, emerged from the crowd to greet the president. Sidney, as journalists had long surmised, earned his lofty position by virtue of the seventy-eight electoral votes he brought to the Atwater-Holdridge ticket. If James Atwater had known how unnecessary those votes would be, it is doubtful that he would have considered Sidney as his running mate.

In the presence of the president, Sidney Holdridge always felt inferior and colorless. It was as if the shadow of the president somehow obscured his own self-image. He never admitted to anyone, especially his wife that this dominance existed.

Despite his accomplishments, and there were a few, Sidney always felt as if he were an Atwater sibling; the brother that never quite measured up. This feeling of inadequacy, unfounded or not, always infuriated him when it occurred. It didn't help that he was more than six inches shorter than his boss, a fact mentioned in an issue of *Newsweek* that compared the vice president's rotund physical appearance to that of Lou Costello; a reference that went virtually unnoticed by everyone except Sidney, who was personally devastated.

Robin was the one person connected with the administration that both Republicans and Democrats could agree on. She was a full-blown, one-hundred percent, dyed-in-the-wool knockout.

Her cover-girl face was the center of attraction for the few who could tear their eyes away from her tall, slender, top-heavy figure. Tantalizing green eyes, shoulder-length blonde hair and full inviting lips, completed a near-perfect package.

At thirty-seven, Robin Holdridge commanded an arousing presence. Simply by being herself, she invited attention. She had a way about her; an intangible quality that made every man she met, young or old, want to be with her, want to touch her.

The president and vice president, despite their public image of togetherness, were never friends. Their relationship was business-like and professional, but never personal. They had nothing, outside of politics and the well-being of the nation, in common.

Over the past six months, Sidney had begun to call the president by his first name. He was only one of two men in Washington to do so. The other person, the president's personal aide, Sean MacDougal, was a life-long family friend and companion. And even Sean saved first name informality for occasions when he and the president were alone or in the company of other close friends.

The vice president's colloquial delivery of the word "Jim," concurrent with an irksome expansion of his brash behavior annoyed the president. There was no way he could know that Sidney's "chest pounding" was an involuntary and obviously futile stab at gaining the upper hand in their lopsided relationship.

With a big smile and an outstretched hand, Sidney approached the president. The informality of his greeting was consistent with the recent expansion of the more bombastic elements of his retooled personality.

"Jim! You throw a hell of a party! You know it's funny, but the Marine Corps Band never shows up at one of my get-togethers."

Sidney's laugh, as always, exceeded the impact of his humor. The president's impish reply rubbed salt in a far more sensitive wound than he realized.

"That's because you aren't the president, Sidney."

"I'm only a heart-beat away, Jim. That's close enough for me."

The game was tied. To avoid extra-innings, the president turned his attention to Sidney's wife, "How was Africa?"

"Very hot and very sad, Mr. President."

"The drought, or Macaba's government?" he asked

"Macaba has no empathy for his people. While he and his family bask in opulence, hordes of starving children beg for food outside the palace gate. Poverty and disease run rampant in every area of his country. It was extremely depressing."

Chief of Staff, Sean MacDougal, approached the trio, then waited patiently for Robin to finish her sentence before interrupting.

"Good evening, it's good to see that you and Mrs. Holdridge have returned safely, Mr. Vice President."

"Thank you, Sean. It's good to be back home," said Sidney

Amenities observed, Sean turned to the president, "I'm sorry to bother you Mr. President, but I must speak with you."

After excusing themselves, the president and Sean, trailed loosely by two Secret Service agents, stepped to the side of the room. Loud music and the surrounding clamor guaranteed privacy. Sean's somber mood foretold the serious nature of the subject at hand.

"Mr. President, the Israelis have bombed Jabal again."

"It must be bad, or you wouldn't be here."

The president's smile remained intact. He was always careful to avoid any behavior that might alert the prying eyes of curious onlookers to a possible crisis. Sean began with a shallow hapless sigh.

"Over one hundred – mostly kids. One of their bombs hit a school, a grade school we think. The State Department called a few minutes ago. Details are still sketchy."

"Are we sure?" asked the president.

"Yes. By tomorrow morning, the bodies of dead ten-year-olds will be strewn across the newspapers and television screens of the world. Kabazi's media blitz will enrage our friends and strengthen the resolve of our foes."

"As we've discussed, the world is already convinced that Israel is little more than America's fifty-first state." The president shook his head and leaned forward, placing his lips only inches from Sean's ear. "Get that cock sucker Pasha over here, now!"

"He's on his way, Mr. President."

Sean's anticipation of the president's request was not unusual. A thirty-year relationship had made him much more than a Chief of Staff; to the bachelor chief executive, he was family. The president's frozen expression melted into a more genuine smile, "You know me way too well."

The sixty-three-year-old Irishman's face lit up. "Yes, old friend. I do."

### The White House
### Oval Office

The West Wing of the White House was nearly empty, only the Secret Service and White House Police were left to prowl its empty corridors. In keeping with the style of his administration, one-on-one meetings with the chief executive usually took place in front of the Oval Office fireplace on plush thick-cushioned sofas and chairs.

Tonight's late-night meeting with the Israeli Ambassador would take place at the president's desk. It was no accident that the Israeli would be offered minimal comfort in the unyielding embrace of a straight-back wooden chair.

Zalman Pasha was a unique political figure. His quiet thoughtful demeanor conveyed wisdom and resolve without the tactless rhetoric that characterized many of his predecessors. The frail figure that Sean ushered through the Oval Office door moved slowly. He knew all too well why he was called to a late-night meeting with the most powerful man in the world.

Introductions were unusually formal. The president's distaste for the misdirected Israeli air attack was conveyed to his visitor without saying a word. Pasha's Hebrew accent lightly masked an otherwise excellent English-speaking voice.

"Good evening, Mr. President."

Unfazed by his guest's greeting, the president made no effort to hide his hostility. His voice was uncharacteristically cold and intractable.

"It was not a good evening for the children of Jabal and their families."

The Israeli waited for his host to sit before lowering himself to the questionable comfort of the rigid chair. After a moment of silence, the elderly diplomat lowered his head.

"It was so sad. My country was forced to launch a preemptive strike deep into the heart of Jabal. Unfortunately, the attack was unsuccessful."

"Your country seems guilty of the same irrational terrorism that it has spoken out against so vehemently for over fifty years. How can we continue to support your government's barbaric behavior?"

The president found it difficult to control his anger as he continued, "You kill children, then ask for increased military aide more bombs … more planes. The people of the United States, in fact, the people of Israel will not continue to support your policy of unbridled savagery."

Pasha looked up, into the president's angry eyes.

"The death of the children grieved us all. It was most unfortunate. Our enemies purposely place military targets near schools and civilian populations with the hope that any attack by us will result in world-wide condemnation."

The Israeli's choice of words irritated the President.

"Floods are unfortunate. Disease is unfortunate. Bombing civilians, especially children, is murder that prohibits justification. It cannot be absolved."

"There are circumstances, Mr. President." Pasha spoke with slow deliberation. "I am authorized to explain what only a handful of my own countrymen know. While you have been preoccupied with events in Iraq and Afghanistan, we have also been watching Jabal. Halim al-Kabazi's government has developed four nearly completed atomic weapons. They have labored day and night, for over six years on the project which has now reached the assembly stage. We estimate that Kabazi will have a deliverable nuclear package within the next sixty days."

"Explain," commanded the president, suspicious of Israel's reputation for paranoia.

"Our intelligence operations in Syria have been exceptional, allowing us, over the past ten years, to destroy three of their attempts to build a nuclear device. The Syrians, discouraged by past failures and the total defeat of the Iraqi army, have promised Syria they would surrender one of the two bombs the Jabalis expect to manufacture, upon completion. As you know, the so-called peace that exists between Syria and Israel is based on military superiority - not any willingness on their part to coexist. My government is convinced that both Syria and Jabal plan to use both of these weapons in a first strike against the Israeli people. We must find and destroy the bombs before they are delivered, or we are doomed. There is even sentiment among members of the Knesset to invade Jabal. There is also talk of using our own nuclear capability first! We are a tiny country, far too small to realize victory in retaliation. As you know, in our part of the world, the first nuclear strike will likely be the only strike."

"Is your intelligence accurate?" the harshness in the president's voice, so evident only moments earlier, waning, "many lives were sacrificed in pursuit of this information. The Mossad is an efficient organization. They are not culpable in this matter. Why have your bombing missions failed?"

"We are unable to confirm the precise location of the assembly plant. As the bombs near completion, we are becoming desperate. That is why today's incident occurred. Israelis also have many children."

Pasha continued, "Jabal is not Syria. Our intelligence in Jabal is minimal. As you know, Kabazi has sealed off his entire country. All travelers, foreign missions, even the press have been expelled. Jabal is a closed country of zealots and the fanatics who control them. Under the circumstances, Mr. President, you are the only man who can help us."

"United States military involvement, especially after tonight's fiasco, isn't a realistic option."

"No, no!" Pasha said, exhibiting a rare degree of enthusiasm. "Information, Mr. President. Information is what we need. We must know what your satellites can see. If we can identify the exact location where these bombs are being assembled, we can destroy them ourselves."

"You have a space program of your own," observed the president.

"Reconnaissance satellites, as we both know, must be equipped with state of the art electronic equipment or orbit at a low trajectory. Satellites forced to operate so close to the earth have an abbreviated life … as little as three or four weeks. Unforeseen technical problems have curtailed our launch schedule. Our last surveillance vehicle was placed in orbit nearly a year ago. It has long since burned up in the atmosphere," continued Pasha, "you must remember, our space program, relative to your own, is still in its infancy. Our capabilities are not as sophisticated as that of the United States. Barring a miracle, we will be unable to prevent what appears to be, an inevitable catastrophe. This project has taken the Jabalis six years by your own account."

"What about the information gathered by your satellites while they were operative?" asked the president.

"Useless. Rather than building one large complex, as the Syrians did, the Jabalis have built at least five small facilities, each charged with a specific stage of manufacture. We know where they were, not where they are," answered Pasha.

"Do you have intelligence operatives in Jabal?" asked the president.

"We did, but those who were in a position to gather pertinent information are now dead. This project is a carefully guarded secret in a country where secrets are a way of life."

The president rose to his feet.

"Mr. Ambassador, I understand your situation. I can't give you any answers without consulting with my own people. We will assess our capabilities and discuss an appropriate course of action. You'll be contacted within forty-eight hours. And as for the bombing, we'll just have to ride out the storm. You know that we cannot publicly support you. The world will undoubtedly demand an aggressive response from America. Rest assured, however, we will not consider an embargo or military action of any kind."

Satisfied with the effectiveness of his presentation, Pasha stood to shake the president's hand. "Thank you, Mr. President. The lives of many children rest on your strong shoulders."

## Atlantic Ocean

The twelve-man boarding party assembled on the deck of the medium endurance Coast Guard Cutter, *Medgap,* stood sullen and anxious in the cool night air. Lieutenant Roosevelt J. Baker, captain of the ship, stared with contempt at the Yugoslavian tanker, *Beograd*, anchored only a hundred yards away. The menacing silhouette of the aging hulk, hovering over the much smaller cutter, gave the mistaken appearance of a mismatch.

Light from the western horizon had faded to nothing more than a gray haze. Choppy water, that so recently swallowed three of the *Cape Carol's* crew, was now stilled to a near calm. An emerging moon dominated the evening sky, painting the surrounding ocean with a hint of romantic tranquility that contradicted the moment. The near continuous thunder of jet engines, searching the vicinity for any sign of survivors, curtailed most conversations and must have scared the hell out of the *Beograd's* crew.

Baker and his men waited almost an hour for permission from command in Portsmouth to board and search the huge ship. They were ready to go. Each person had checked and rechecked their weapons. Everyone on board, in fact, everyone in the Coast Guard, knew the fate of the *Cape Carol*. They wanted to know what connection the *Beograd* had with the death of their fellow Guardsmen.

Lieutenant Baker turned to Tom McGrane, his Executive Petty Officer.

"They've had plenty of time to destroy anything that might connect them to that boat."

"They should've let us board that hunk of shit when we caught up to her," snapped McGrane.

Baker knew the rules, "The Yugoslavian government will have to give us permission to board. You know how likely that is to happen. We took a hell of a chance just stopping her in international waters."

The twenty-three-year-old EPO wasn't satisfied.

"When these drug fucks figure out they can kill us and blow us out of the water with impunity, we might just as well dismantle the whole goddamn service and store these tubs in dry dock!"

"We're the good guys," reminded Baker. "We follow the rules. They don't. That's why we're out here."

The familiar snap of a keyed microphone, over the ships P.A. system, brought the conversation to an abrupt halt.

"Captain to the bridge! Captain to the bridge!"

Baker knew why he was being summoned. He also knew the probable outcome. As he trudged up the metal steps to the bridge, he resigned himself to hearing the explanation of why he and his men would not be allowed to board the *Beograd*.

The men on the bridge went about their business as if they were unaware of the call's importance. Stream grabbed the handset from its wall cradle, took a deep breath, then placed the receiver to his ear. For the next minute and a half, he listened to the caustic admonitions of his superior.

Two words were all he could utter without risking reprisal, "Yes, Sir."

There was no arguing his position. It would not surprise him if he were brought up on charges for illegally detaining the *Beograd* on the open sea. His "hot pursuit" contention was bullshit, and he knew it. The fact that he had even professed to believe such crap would probably curtail his career aspirations.

With reluctance, the disconsolate young lieutenant hung up the phone then returned to the deck and his boarding party.

"We've got to cut her loose," he said, avoiding eye contact, "the boarding party may stand down."

A cold caress of absolute futility enveloped him. No matter how hard he tried, it was difficult to rationalize the painful realities of their circumstance.

With his back to his crew, he stared across the emptiness of the open sea. The death of his friends played over and over in his mind. What happened in those final few seconds? How could it have happened?

McGrane stepped forward, positioning himself only inches behind his Captain's left shoulder.

"Doug Stream was one of your best friends. How can you walk away?"

Baker had never felt such contempt for the service and the system he so revered. He could only hope that his reply, however trite, would not betray the depth of his true feelings.

"Orders, we live by them, we die by them." Now notify the *Beograd* that she's free to go."

The men of the *Medgap* were shocked that they had been denied the opportunity to board the Yugoslavian tanker. If the vessel was released, they reasoned, the motives behind the attack on the *Cape Carol* would probably never be known for sure.

The disappointed young Coast Guardsmen returned to their regular duties absent the enthusiasm that characterized their service. McGrane, in particular, found it difficult to deal with his disappointment. Eight Americans were dead. Eight of his friends were dead. Almost certainly the *Beograd* had a part in the killings. The thought of letting them off the hook without a search was, in his opinion, cowardly. The U.S. military could easily force the *Beograd* to reveal the details of their involvement and intentions without any fear of a meaningful reprisal. The decision was no doubt political. One ambassador kissing another ambassador's ass. Some State Department flunky, unable to make a decisive move.

Baker, who had stubbornly refused to watch the Yugoslavian freighter leave, continued to stand at the railing. He had always thought of ocean air as an antiseptic. Breathe it, stare through it, smell it long enough, and your perceptions usually improved, or were they just dulled? He wasn't sure.

A distant object, barely noticeable against the Atlantic's choppy black facade, attracted the Captain's attention. Were it not for the presence of a half moon, he would never have noticed the tiny protrusion amid the to and fro motion of the ocean's countless waves.

His first thought was for the lost crewman of the *Cape Carol*. This might be one of the bodies that other Coast Guard craft had been searching for since shortly after the incident occurred. True, it was some distance from the point of attack, but there was a chance, and a chance was good enough.

With two spotlights trained on their target, the *Medgap* proceeded at little more than a crawl, avoiding the possibility of sinking the object in the wake of the ship's bow. A few yards from his target, Lieutenant Baker motioned to a nearby seaman.

"Kosio!" he shouted, "Grab a hook! Let's see what we've got here."

While he waited for Kosio's return, the young lieutenant asked himself how he would ever bring his crew back to life if they had to drag one of their own out of the ocean. Especially after releasing the ship that might have been responsible for the murders. In response to the commotion, Executive Petty Officer McGrane returned to the railing. His foul mood hadn't improved, "It's just garbage, captain. Shit floats!"

McGrane's insubordinate tone could not be tolerated despite their circumstance and the disappointment that everyone was experiencing.

"McGrane," Baker turned to glare at his EPO, "stow the attitude. I won't be spoken to in that tone."

Kosio's return saved McGrane from a further ass-chewing. With both hands, the skinny seaman extended the long gaff hook over the railing of the starboard bow. A prodding motion with the point of the hook revealed several bundles, bound together by rope. Slowly, with effort, the water-logged clumps of burlap were pulled from the ocean and slung over the ships railing.

At first glance, the sacks appeared to contain food scraps, tin cans, and a collection of normal ships refuse. Under the circumstances, Captain Baker determined that a cursory analysis was not good enough. As he assumed a squatting position, he began to initiate a grungy hands-on investigation. The *Medgap's* deck lights were barely adequate for the task.

With little or no wind to diffuse the odor, a foul stench began to engulf the entire deck area. Anticipating a call for assistance, casual onlookers, including Baker's disgruntled EPO, began to slink away.

As Baker tore into each sack and checked its contents, Seaman Kosio had the unenviable task of returning the slimy rubbish to the cold deep water of the Atlantic Ocean.

The meaningless contents of the first three sacks tempted Captain Baker to halt his messy inquisition. A tenacious streak that usually worked to his advantage kept him at his unsavory task.

His persistence was eventually rewarded. A tight wad of printed material, mired in the contents of the fifth sack, spilled to the deck. Continued effort revealed a stack of decomposing, nearly unreadable, fan-fold computer print-outs, assorted sketches, and hand-written notes.

Baker, his curiosity piqued, sifted through the soggy papers with care. Faint images of hand drawn streets and buildings were discernible among the many washed out pages. Each of the many drawings was noted with symbols and words written in a language that Baker tentatively identified as Arabic.

He continued to thumb through the remaining scraps of paper until he happened on a drawing that generated an involuntary burst of emotion.

"Shit!" he exclaimed.

A single image, complete and almost artistic in its thoroughness, remained intact. Captain Roosevelt Baker had no trouble recognizing a detailed drawing of the home of the President of the United States, The White House.

# CHAPTER TWO

## MAY 17
## The White House
## Oval Office

The president, accompanied by two Secret Service Agents, walked briskly down the red-carpeted cannonade that connects the Oval Office in the West Wing to the main building of the White House. Along the way, he acknowledged a consistent string of smiling faces who, employing little imagination, greeted him with redundant but sincere tonal variations of *Good morning, Mr. President.*

Upon reaching his office, the two agents assumed their regular posts, one next to the Oval Office main entrance, the other just outside the double French doors leading to the Rose Garden.

Within a few minutes of his arrival, a Navy steward served the president coffee with cream, no sugar, and a sweet roll, usually, a Danish. Against everyone's recommendations, including his own White House physician, the president seldom ate a *normal* breakfast. Most mornings, a sweet roll would be his first and only nourishment until lunch, his favorite meal of the day.

Everyone on the executive staff knew not to bother the president until the steward had finished his visit. This day would be an exception. Sean MacDougal entered the Oval Office through the staff door. He was one of three men who enjoyed true twenty-four-hour access to the president. The chief executive, absorbed by an editorial in the New York Times, was taking a sip from his first cup of coffee.

"Jim, we've got a problem, and this one scares the living hell out of me!"

Years of crisis living had vaccinated James Atwater against hype from anyone, even Sean. He spoke as he continued to read.

"Oh God, Sean! Is it nuclear? I hate nuclear problems before I have my Danish."

Sean didn't react to the president's sarcasm. He was determined to tell his story.

"There was an incident with the Coast Guard, last night off the Carolinas. We lost eight Coast guardsmen. At first, they thought it was drug related. Further investigation revealed a problem with much broader implications. It might even involve you."

"Me?" asked the president.

"Absolutely! At least that's the way the guys at State figure it. They've called in the CIA. Pinkle, one of their top men, is supposed to have pieced together the story. With Director Handelman's blessing, I've asked him to come over. He should be here in the next couple of minutes."

The president's humor remained undaunted. "A Pinkle ... in the CIA?"

"For Christ's sake Jim," Sean grinned, "everyone over there isn't named Rock. Matt says he's a hell of a guy, and a tough S.O.B."

Appointments Secretary Charles Bainbridge, who had full access to the president, during office hours, approached the chief executive's desk with a schedule of the days planned events and meetings. He handed a copy of the two-page itinerary to Sean as well as the president.

Following an exchange of pleasantries, Bainbridge informed the president of his first visitor.

"Representative Allen, from Colorado, is here to see you Mr. President. He's here to solicit your support for his conservation bill - HR-628. As you know the bill ..."

Sean interrupted, "Damn Chuck, I'm sorry! I should have told you. We've got a guy from the CIA on his way over for a special executive briefing. He's due here any minute. I think it's imperative that he speaks with the president."

The president, licking the remnants of a Danish from his thumb, nodded in agreement.

"Inform Congressman Allen of our predicament and make a luncheon appointment with him for next week. He'll prefer that anyway."

"Yes, Mr. President. Shall I cancel your morning schedule? You have a cabinet meeting at 10 a.m."

"Block out twenty minutes."

Bainbridge returned to his own office while the president leaned back in his chair and swung around to face the beautiful Rose Garden. The smile on his face had disappeared.

"The job's wearing thin, Sean."

"I told you this second go around would seem more like a sentence than a term."

"I hate to say it, but, I think you were right," replied the president somewhat ruefully.

A few quiet steps placed the Irishman at the president's side, where he could give his old friend a fatherly pat on the shoulder. "Look at it this way – today a president, tomorrow a postage stamp. How many jobs offer perks like that?"

The return of Appointments Secretary Bainbridge squelched the president's reply.

"Mr. President, David Pinkle from the CIA is here to see you."

"Bring him in," the president ordered.

Sean caught the eye of the president, who had anticipated his question. "Yes, Sean. I'd like you to stick around for this one."

Bainbridge ushered Pinkle into the office. The president was immediately struck by the agent's unusual size. He was huge, built more as a lineman for the Redskins than a stereotypical agent.

Sean, whose only previous contact with Pinkle was by phone, extended a personal greeting, then introduced him to the president. The Chief Executive's hand, large by most standards, disappeared in Pinkle's ham-like grip.

"Thank you for coming over this morning, Agent Pinkle. You look more like a representative of the WWE than the CIA."

"It's an honor, Mr. President," Pinkle replied.

The chief executive ushered the hulking agent to one of the two sofas placed on either side of, and perpendicular to, the Oval Office fireplace. He then made himself comfortable in a nearby recliner, only a few feet from his guest.

"Are there more at home like you?" asked the president.

"Family of six, Mr. President and at six feet five and two hundred and ninety pounds, I'm the runt of the litter," he grinned. "Even dad's bigger than I am."

Following several minutes of light conversation, the president asked Agent Pinkle to explain the circumstances that surrounded yesterday's incident involving the Coast Guard. The articulate young agent clicked off the known details of the attack on the Cape Carol with computer efficiency. The president's somber expression mirrored his concern for the young Americans who had lost their lives in the service of their country.

A brief chronology of ensuing events wound up Pinkle's presentation, "Following the attack, the Zoetrope headed for shore. We know this because early this morning the Coast Guard found the boat run aground near Surfside Beach, South Carolina. An unidentified body, probably the man shot by the crew person on the *Cape Carol*, was found dead on the Zoetrope's aft deck.

The material fished out of the ocean by Captain Baker arrived by helicopter approximately twenty-three hundred hours last night. F.I.S.H. (Forensic Information System for Handwriting) immediately rushed the material to their Cryptographers, lab specialists and forensic analysts.

Unfortunately, most of the likely suspects rarely write anything. Thus, our files are miniscule. We'll have the complete analysis sometime tomorrow. The State Department is still working on the evaluation. We've also given the material to the N.S.A. for their assessment.

Preliminary findings indicate that the insurgents consist of five to seven heavily armed individuals, representing at least four different nationalities – French, Libyan, Jabali and Cuban. There is compelling evidence to indicate that one of the perpetrators is the infamous Musa Abu Tabou, the most sought after international criminal in the world today.

It's almost impossible to examine the notes and drawings in the debris from the *Beograd* and avoid the conclusion that these men have been sent to assassinate you, Mr. President, in all likelihood, this is a 'decapitation' attack."

"How could the group you've described move about unnoticed?" asked the president.

"From our tentative assessment of the individuals we suspect are involved, we feel that foreign sponsorship is probably Mideast. Consensus opinion has it that they couldn't hope to pull this off without inside help. An individual or group within this country must be setting them up," answered Pinkle.

"What specific facts lead you to that assumption?"

"It's highly unlikely that the suspects walked ashore in South Carolina without prearranged transportation. These guys are pros. They'll have a contact that knows the ropes and can get them around. The director is working out a defensive plan as we speak. Everyone in the service is extremely apprehensive over the possibilities."

## Florence City, South Carolina
## Holiday Inn

Musa Abu Tabou exited the Edgetowner, a small standard fare restaurant, with a white unmarked sack clutched in each hand. The five feet eleven inch Jabali crossed Eighth Street and walked toward a familiar American icon – A Holiday Inn.

The building's shoe-box shape identified it as one of many built during the franchise's boom period – the sixties. The structure was a study in repetition. Every door and window were indistinguishable in appearance from the last or next – only the numbers changed.

When he arrived at room number 176, the dark skinned Tabou knocked, waited a few anxious moments, then, gave the metal door a thunderous kick. Before he had time to give it another shot, someone freed the lock, allowing the door to swing open wide enough to permit entrance.

Inside, nearly two-thirds of the ten most wanted terrorists in the world sat mesmerized by a children's cartoon show. While colorful figures pranced noisily across the screen of the room's poorly tuned television, the Jabali spilled the contents of his two white sacks across the worn bedspread atop the bed nearest the door.

In a matter of seconds, the harrowing pursuits of Road Runner were abandoned in favor of hot food. Small Styrofoam containers sailed back and forth until no one was any longer willing to surrender or exchange them.

The unsightly feeding frenzy that ensued was punctuated by crude jokes and occasional laughter. Even though each of the six men were fluent in English, they occasionally reverted to their native language to express a thought for which they could find no satisfactory English equivalent.

These men, ranging in age from twenty-six to forty-one, were the worst of the worst. A collection of misfits and sadists culled from the dung heaps of the world. It was more than their skill that made them the acknowledged best of their lot; it was their willingness to commit the unspeakable. They took life whenever and wherever it served their purpose. It was of no significance that their victims were nearly always unarmed, uninvolved, and unaware. Wide-eyed children with no agenda were easy targets. Innocence meant vulnerability, it meant attention. Blood was blood. Television newscasts and newspaper headlines were created by, and fueled with, the mangled bodies of the unsuspecting.

The Jabali, born Musa Abu Tabou, a man who could oversee any situation in which he chose to assert himself, was their leader. His heavily haired body was as dark as his soul. A mangy beard, a badge of masculinity to most Middle Eastern men, did little to hide the pock marks that scarred his tightly drawn face. His warped view of the world filtered through black, bloodshot eyes set deep under a fleshy overhang distinguished by uncommonly thick bushy eyebrows.

Tabou's looks were deceiving; he was in fact, a thinker in a bloody trade characterized by religious fanaticism and blind allegiance. Law enforcement agencies from around the globe had sniffed confidently along his wretched trail only to discover that their quarry had eluded them.

Individuals, willing to surrender information concerning the whereabouts of the elusive Jabali, had all but dwindled as the grisly fate of their predecessors became widely publicized. Lead after lead evaporated in the light of intensive investigation. In the end, it was the hunters themselves who were often made to look foolish.

The instinct of this uneducated terrorist, with little or no formal training, had served him well. He continued to survive while his contemporaries had, one-by-one, succumbed to the pressure of intensive manhunts and changes in political regimes that often tendered yesterday's hero for today's sacrificial lamb. Rare was the government that hadn't periodically purged a few trusting in-house executioners to enrich its military coffers from an always too grateful Western World.

Social amenities were given no priority in Tabou's chaotic life. He was brusque, primitive and uncouth in every way. His respect stemmed from the most basic of emotions - fear. He was lethal, and would kill at any time, for any reason, in any place. He was the Babe Ruth of his ghastly profession and probably the only man alive who could control the five men gathered in room 176.

After stuffing what remained of his sandwich into his hair-covered face, the Jabali swallowed, then rose to speak.

"We are here, in the home of our enemy. We have only to carry out our sacred mission and our place in history is forever."

With every word, small chunks of bread and tomato fled his whisker hidden mouth, peppering the immediate vicinity.

Miguel Bonilla, the only Cuban in the group, laughed.

"Piss on history. Give me my money and I will make my own history."

Mustafa Al Jaabir, a Libyan, rose angrily from the support of the far bed.

"You, Miguel Bonilla, are not Muslim! You are a mercenary! I do not trust you! I will watch you!"

Bonilla made a pumping motion with his closed fist next to his crotch, "Watch this, camel-fucker!"

Without hesitation or thought, the hot-blooded Libyan drew a knife from beneath his shirt and charged Bonilla, who was sitting at a small table adjacent to the front door. The headlong charge knocked the surprised Cuban to the floor. In an instant, the point of Jaabir's knife found his victim's throat. Weight and superior position gave the Muslim a clear advantage. Cold steel pierced the soft flesh covering Bonilla's windpipe. The flow of blood rapidly escalated from a drop to a trickle. Jaabir was not going to stop.

After removing his own knife from a scabbard taped to his ankle, Tabou rushed into the fray. In one facile movement, the Jabali stepped behind the Libyan, grabbing him by his long greasy hair. The razor-sharp blade of his stiletto pressed against the flesh of Jaabir's unshaven throat.

"Push it in Jaabir, and you will die right here in the land of pigs. There will be no glory for you."

Tabou's words had a glacial effect on the Muslim's fiery temper. The choice to live or die, even for Jaabir, was simple. He removed the six-inch blade from the Cuban's throat with dispatch. Satisfied that Bonilla's demise was at least temporarily postponed, Tabou released his own grip, allowing his humbled companion to slither toward the secluded confines of the farthest corner of the room.

Bonilla, the youngest of the group was accustomed to being the *tough guy*, the one who made the threats and did the killing. Among this gathering he was just another mouthy kid. Tabou, cast in the unusual role of peacemaker, growled a final warning.

"Keep your mouth shut, boy! The next time I will help him send you to whatever God you pray to!"

With his knife clenched firmly in his outstretched fist, Tabou turned to face his cohorts.

"We are here to kill a dog! Any man who would do anything that might keep this from happening is a dead man! Let any one of you who would not lay down his life for this mission stand before me."

Pierre Coutre, a Frenchman and the only Western European in the group, refused to be herded.

"Let us lay down James Atwater's life ... and keep our own."

Tabou interpreted the cheers that followed the Frenchman's statement as a defeat, since he had failed to secure the total commitment that he had hoped for. But rather than take issue with Coutre, the Jabali chose to exploit the positive aspect of his group's seldom expressed unity. A forced half-smile warmed his harshly featured face.

## The White House
## President's Living Quarters

It was nearly 8:30 p.m. when James Atwater stepped into the elevator that would lift him to his second floor White House residence. In the wake of a troubling day, an opportunity to relax away from the hubbub and escape the smothering presence of the Secret Service was always welcome.

38

As he entered the foyer, the absence of a greeting from his personal valet, William 'Benzy' Benzley, reminded him that his three-person domestic staff had been dismissed for the evening. The thought was more comforting than disturbing. He enjoyed taking care of himself and didn't mind tending to his own personal needs. Since taking office, the word privacy had taken on a whole new meaning.

A few feet inside the front door, the president was greeted by Riggs and Murtaugh, his two male golden retrievers. In defiance of their training, they placed their front paws as high on his chest as their outstretched back legs would allow. He hugged them both and led them to the expanse of his seldom used kitchen, where he proceeded to fill their bowls from the forty-pound bag of dog food that was kept in the broom closet.

In what had become a daily ritual, he used his short walk to the bedroom as an opportunity to distance himself from the crucial nature of his office. Early in his administration, he learned that life was intolerable if he lived the job twenty-four hours a day. Tonight, he mused to himself, it would be especially easy.

His bachelor bedroom was large, well-appointed, and decidedly masculine. Nearly every surface in the room was covered with wood, leather, or a dark fabric. Walking to his dresser, he turned and faced the long rectangular mirror that spanned almost half of the wall's considerable length. In the reflection, over his shoulder, he could see his bed and the secret that would shock the nation. The one revelation for which there could be no excuse.

The love of his life, the beautiful Robin Holdridge, wife of the vice president, was propped up on a pillow against the leather covered headboard of his king-sized bed. She was wearing a short, white, nearly transparent nightgown, trimmed in lace. Her legs were hidden by a silk sheet; the only remaining cover on the bed.

"How did you get away?" he asked wearily.

"It wasn't easy."

"I thought about you today, during the Cabinet meeting."

"Was that the only time?" she asked.

Piece-by-piece he dismantled his tailored suit. "No," he said as if that wasn't a possibility, "I thought of you many times. The Cabinet meeting fantasy just stood out in my mind."

"What were we doing?"

"You were masturbating. I was watching like the last time we were together."

"I remember. We should do it again. Did Sidney remind you of me?" she asked.

"Not hardly." The conversation was taking a wrong turn. He wanted to change the subject. "It's been a long two weeks."

"That's what presidents get when they send their lovers to Africa," she teased.

"I had to send Sidney to Africa, you know the problems. There just wasn't anyone else. I couldn't send my vice president and tell him to leave his wife at home."

"At least it was better than that God-awful trip to Afghanistan two months ago. Next time, do you think we could have a problem in St. Tropez?" she asked playfully.

After removing his last article of clothing, he turned and walked toward his lover. Her green eyes were riveted on his partial erection. He sat on the edge of the bed and paused to admire the most beautiful woman he had ever seen- the very thought of her excited him.

Ever so slowly, he leaned forward and touched her lips with his own. Their kisses stoked a fire that had raged for nearly two years. With sure hands and a passion born of a fourteen-day abstinence, he removed Robin's thin veil of a nightgown.

The unobstructed sight of her lovely body forced an appreciative pause. In response to his hungry gaze, her large nipples strained at the tip and deepened in color. By cupping his hands beneath her soft breasts, he was able to lift them and press her erect nipples so close to each other that they almost touched. With great care, he savored the taste and texture of her skin.

She placed her impassioned hands on either side of his face, guiding his hungry mouth across her warm flesh. Subtle flicks of his wet tongue, alternating with light brushes of his rugged face across the tips of her nipples were euphoric. Again, he lifted his head and sought the warmth of her lips.

"I've missed you so much, Jim," she whispered.

Their mouths pressed together. She tasted wonderfully familiar. Her scent was comfortable and intoxicating. James Atwater was a lights-on man. A man to whom seeing was as important as touching. He loved to savor the sight of Robin's body, especially if she was aroused. Her excitement was his spark. Eager to begin, he grabbed the shiny blue sheet and tossed it to the foot of the bed.

By reaching across his leg, she was able to grasp him in her hand. He felt long and particularly hard. With the tip of her index finger she coaxed the first drop of lubricant from the throbbing head of his now full erection.

Her fingers slid along the length of him several times before slipping underneath to his testicles. Her knowing touch caused him to jerk forward and twist toward her. In anticipation, she eased down flat on the bed. Her breathing was becoming quick and labored.

With his right hand he pushed gently on the inside of one knee and then the other, parting her legs as far as they would go. She was wet with anticipation. Her fleshy outer lips were tumid and rigid, exposing her very center.

Robin's smooth white hips rose in hungry expectation as her lover's hand skimmed back and forth across her inner thigh. Both of them surrendered any inhibitions that they might have harbored to the heat of the moment. Their recent separation had intensified an already strong sense of emotional need.

Guided by the experience of many nights, his fingers worked through her silky matted pubic hair and began rubbing the glistening area near her opening. With his thumb and forefinger, he tugged gently on her swollen lips, causing her to groan softly.

For a long time, he fondled and stroked the area between Robin's legs. At the height of her arousal, he entered her with his middle finger. Each stroke ended with a light brush against her now totally exposed clitoris. Every thrust was met with raised hips. Sticky sucking sounds filled the room, heightening their mutual level of excitement. Every breath ended in a muffled cry of pleasure.

His mouth, tracing a slow wet path across her breasts and down her stomach, prompted a renewed sense of urgency. With trembling fingers, she nudged his head toward the place most desperate for the warm wet pressure that only his tongue could provide.

Eager to please, he moved to a kneeling position, directly between her open legs. She invited him to continue his delicious work by drawing her knees up close to her chest. He feverishly consumed all that there was. His long tongue darted in and out of her repeatedly before concentrating on her most sensitive area - he left her with no secrets. Over and over again, his wet mouth circled and crossed that certain spot - he knew what worked.

Every crease, every fold of skin, every opening was fully explored. Robin responded to his movements with wild abandon. The time had come, she began to feel those familiar ripples that always preceded her orgasm. In an effort to delay the inevitable, she grabbed his head with both hands - it was too late. The ripple turned into a wave, then finally an explosion.

She pushed his face between her legs with all her strength. In a numbing spasm of ecstasy, she came and came, emptying herself in the president's eager mouth. His tongue never stopped its unrelenting pleasure. Gradually, the tide receded.

Robin lay on the bed, panting, while her lover leaned back on the sheets. His pulsing erection was a deep red, almost crimson. The sight of him stirred a need that she thought she had just satisfied. In a whisper, nearly every man she had ever met wished he could hear, she made an irresistible plea. "Please ... please put it inside."

He pushed her outstretched legs as far apart as they would go. The sight of her provided a mental snapshot that he would carry with him for months. Excited, wet, open, beautiful, his; they all described his beautiful lover.

After positioning Robin at an inviting angle, that complemented his own, he guided himself toward her moist pink flesh. Her swollen lips accepted him with ease. He pushed himself inside slowly, taking time to enjoy every inch of her depth. At the point of full penetration, he bent to kiss her gorgeous face.

"I love you, Robin. I love you more than anything," he whispered between gasps for air.

"I love you too," she panted.

Faster, then faster he buried himself inside her. His hands covered her breasts. In his final stroke, she felt him push in and hold. Every muscle in his body was suddenly rigid. Warm white liquid began to fill what was already full. Robin's second orgasm was simultaneous with her lover's. On the second floor of the White House, the president of the United States reached an earth-shattering climax with the wife of his vice president.

Secret Service Agent Thomas Speck, assigned to the president and Agent Ryan Pinder, delegated to watch over Robin Holdridge did what agents spend most of their career doing – they waited. It had been nearly two hours since the vice president 'swife entered the elevator leading to the president's private residence. Chairs, situated to either side of the elevator door, became objects of envy. Even when the president was in his private quarters, an alert hands-free agent must stand guard.

"How long do you think she'll be up there?" Pinder asked, searching for any subject that might break the monotony.

"Who knows? If it were you up there, I'd guess five minutes would be plenty."

"Maybe, but it would be the best five minutes of her life. God she's beautiful. Ya' know, if number two wasn't such a raving prick, maybe she'd stay home. You wouldn't believe where he spends his nights."

Speck yawned, then stretched.

"Yep, Mr. Vice President Holdridge is a real piece of work. There isn't a man in the service that hasn't had a run-in with him. If bullets ever start flying, I wonder which one of us will have to take one for that pompous chunk of shit."

The president and his lover were laying side-by-side on the bed. Still naked and breathing heavily, Robin looked at him and smiled.

"Do you think we could do it again and this time, maybe you could act a little more enthusiastic?"

The president rolled over and began to tickle Robin under her arms, "Any more enthusiasm and we'll stop traffic on Pennsylvania Avenue."

Robin howled in response to the persistent gnawing of the president's fingers against her ribs. Following a few playful minutes, the spent lovers mellowed-out on the smooth silk sheet covering the president's bed.

"Do you ever worry about the agents? Do you think they'll say anything?" asked Robin.

"I don't know," confessed the president, "I'm not worried about any of the men *in* the Secret Service, it's the ones who *retire* or *quit*. That's when the books start flying. I've made sure that all the agents assigned to the vice president and myself are career men who shouldn't retire in the near future. That's all I can do without drawing more attention to the situation."

Robin rolled over to face him with her head resting on her outstretched arm.

"Is that what we are, a situation? Most people have relationships."

"It's a situation if you're the president and you're in love with your vice president's wife."

"It had been a long time since I heard you say that," she said with a childlike inflection.

"Say what?" as if he didn't know.

"That you loved me. Or was that just a man about to have an orgasm talking?"

"Both. I love you and that was a man just about to have a fantastic orgasm talking."

He flashed a knowing smile and placed his hand on her cheek.

"I love you more than anything in this world. I love you so much it's embarrassing."

"What do you mean," she sounded upset.

"I mean I'm a forty-eight-year-old man and I feel as if I were a schoolboy. I think about you night and day."

"Will we ever be together?"

Her question brought another smile to his face.

"Why is that funny?" she shot back.

"I can just hear Tom Brokaw ... in a press conference held earlier today – President James Atwater announced his plans to marry Vice President Sidney Holdridge's wife. Sources close to the Pres ..."

A series of not-so light slaps on the stomach, forced the president to cease and desist. An ensuing period of play ended when Robin rolled seductively into his arms. Their frolicsome mood took a shadowy turn.

"Affairs, divorce, they happen every day. But they can't happen to me. I'm responsible for a country – people would lose faith. I can't do that to them."

"What about us?" she asked.

"Thank God for article twenty-two of the Constitution. I'm through next year. Then, my time and my life will be my own."

"Promise me we'll be together," she whispered.

"I promise that with all of my heart."

He cradled his forbidden love in his powerful arms – at best, their future was uncertain. It would take a small miracle for them to overcome their circumstances and establish a permanent union. Even in those rare stolen moments, when they were alone together, the prospect of her departure and return to an unhappy marriage, cast a mood dampening cloud over their loving relationship.

## MAY 18
### The White House
### Cabinet Room

An emergency meeting of the National Security Council was called by the president. Among those in attendance were: Secretary of Defense Mitchell White, Secretary of State Thomas Bertrand, and the Vice President Sidney Holdridge.

In view of the day's planned agenda, guests would include: Chairman of the Joint Chiefs of Staff, General Harold "Whipper" Overton, CIA Director Matthew Handelman and in a rare appearance, NSA Director, Laurence Hill.

Each person at the table was seated in a plush black leather arm chair. The chief executive's chair, though made of the same material, featured a higher back and was built to recline. The president, in the tradition of his predecessors, positioned himself on the window side of the room, near the center of the long octagonal table.

The Cabinet Room had remained essentially unchanged since the Roosevelt administration. White drapes, trimmed with gold rope, framed the large south window overlooking the Rose Garden. About half of the west end wall was devoted to a functioning fireplace; above, on the mantle, a detailed model of the famous American Frigate Constitution was displayed. Everyone but the president entered the room through the north entrance. The chief executive used the more convenient east door that connected through the Appointments Secretary's office to his own.

Meetings of the National Security Council were by nature less formal than most Cabinet meetings. At the request of the president, the six men in attendance spoke their minds in clear, often colorful, terms.

The final item on the day's agenda was a detailed account by the president of his earlier meeting with Israeli

Ambassador Zalman Pasha. CIA Director Matt Handelman then made his report to the Committee on what had already become loosely known as "the *Cape Carol* incident.

In his usual manner, once the problems had been tossed on the table, the president asked for discussion. His willingness to weigh and measure a variety of opinions before making a decision was an important strength. His first question was directed at National Security Agency (NSA) Director, Laurence Hill.

"Larry, what about these bombs the Israelis are after? What do we know about them?"

"Not much Mr. President. We've picked up some radio traffic that ..."

The president's voice boomed across the table.

"Not much! You people and your Communications Intelligence Group are sucking over ten billion dollars a year out of our budget. How the hell can something like this slip through your fingers?"

"I'm not sure that it has. Our intelligence volume has approached the saturation point. We're producing approximately fifty tons of classified material a day."

"For God's sake, Larry. What good is the intelligence if we can't access it?"

The president's eyes darted about the distinguished faces seated around the table When no comment was forthcoming, his mood darkened.

"It sounds like your so-called 'puzzle palace' is getting out of hand."

"I've asked our foreign instrumentation signals intelligence specialists to isolate and target the area. There won't be a communication in the region that we aren't aware of."

The president shook his head in frustration.

Secretary of State Thomas Bertrand, posed a question of his own.

"Since 1988, the Israelis have had their own satellite capability. Why do they need us? You'd think Jabal would be an intelligence priority."

The president, recalling his conversation with Pasha, offered an explanation.

"Their priorities aren't the problem. As Ambassador Pasha explained it, the Israeli space program is in its infancy. They did have a satellite in the area and lost it. In the immediate future, they find themselves unable to launch anything that would solve the problem."

Vice President Holdridge made the obvious inquiry. "What have *we* got up there?"

The question fell into Secretary of Defense Mitchell White's area.

"With the shuttle problems that we've had, we're down to one class seven reconnaissance satellite in orbit over Jabal. As luck would have it, this particular satellite is not operational. From day one, we've had trouble with the damn camera. My wife's Polaroid would have been more helpful."

CIA Director Handelman, conscious of the fact that he was a guest, entered the conversation with audible caution.

"May I make a suggestion?"

The president was quick to reply, "Yes, Matt. I want input, everyone's input. Don't hesitate to speak your minds."

"What about LEPERS? It's scheduled for a ride in three days if Discovery goes up on schedule," stated Handelman.

Glancing around the table, Holdridge asked for clarification.

"What the hell is LEPERS?"

Never shy and always ready with a comeback, General Overton laughed.

"Hell, Sidney, it's a guy with his fingers and toes falling off. Where the hell ya' been all your life?"

The group chuckled more at Sidney's reaction than to General Overton's rather insensitive remark. The vice president was not amused.

"I think this is pretty God damn serious!"

Aware that Holdridge could someday be his boss, Overton attempted to soothe the vice president's bruised ego.

"Relax, Sidney. Don't get your hair in a ball. I was just pokin' a little fun at ya'."

Sidney appeared uncomfortable at the mention of his own lack of humor. Before anything else could be said, Director Handelman displayed his excellent memory.

"LEPERS stands for Laser Earth Photo Enhanced Reconnaissance Satellite. In a low trajectory orbit, it's capable of defining objects as small as two inches across. Theoretically, under the right conditions and with the help of computer enhancement, it should be able to distinguish a silver dollar and tell you whether it's heads or tails ... There isn't a spy in the sky that can match it. It also operates in infrared. Depending on their method of concealment, this could be an advantage."

"What about LEPERS' orbit?" asked the president. "Will it pass over Jabal?"

"That's the catch," said White. "LEPERS planned orbit, in general terms, takes it over what was formerly Yugoslavia and Western Russia. I think we're at least five hundred miles off the mark."

"Can we alter our mission plan?" asked the president.

"Jesus Christ! Do you know what that would involve in three days? I don't know if we could do it," exclaimed White.

"We need that son-of-a-bitch over Eastern Europe roared General Overton. "Our involvement their demands better intelligence. We've counted on this ...."

"Priorities gentlemen," the president moved forward in his chair – pissed. "That's what we're talking about here. I think nuclear weapons in the Mideast take precedent over anything that I'm aware of in the Baltic States. Does anyone at this table know of a circumstance more crucial to U.S. interests than the situation at hand."

No one at the table moved a muscle. The president turned to Secretary White.

"Then find out if it can be done – and either way, do it. Our discussion on this matter is over."

"Yes, Mr. President," answered White.

A cautious silence preceded General Overton's next observation. His voice had lost its thunder.

"It looks as if both of our problems, the bombs and this *Cape Carol* thing, stem from the same source – Halim al-Kabazi."

Secretary of Defense Mitchell White was exasperated, "Just how much are we going to take from this guy? He's tried to provoke damn near every country in the world into a shooting war. I've seen just about all the dead kids in airports that I ever want to see. The man's record is reprehensible. Matt," he motioned to Handelman, "when I spoke to you earlier, you said you'd bring along some background on this guy."

After thumbing through a thick stack of papers, Handelman handed each of the participants a three-page summary of the Jabali's history.

"Over the past twenty years, we estimate that he has sponsored or helped plan forty-six bombings in Europe and the Middle East, resulting in the death of 327 people and those are only numbers that we can confirm," explained Handelman, "he's invaded or sponsored uprisings in Egypt, Sudan, Tunisia, Algeria and Chad, just to name a few. His government has given military aid to the Irish Republican Army, the Basque & Corsican Separatists, the Moro guerrillas in the Philippines and leftists all over Central America, even North Korea's pugnacious leader, Kim Jong Il, can't match his thirst for blood."

Handelman continued, "Those who know him, refer to him as the consummate deal maker. His under the table arrangements involve half of the world's known belligerents. He spins webs too complicated for spiders to follow."

"Hold on, Matt. The point is, the public's gone to sleep on this guy. We know he's made numerous attempts to kill various heads of state and succeeded in at least three instances."

"Yes," said Handelman, "The *Cape Carol* incident has a direct precedent. In 1989, Kabazi sent four men to kill

President Bush. The hit team had already reached America when their mission was inexplicably scrubbed. To this day, reasons for the Jabali's change of heart remain with the man himself."

"Bush tried to 'ice' the son-of-a-bitch in '90," Overton interjected.

"April 22nd, 1990 to be precise," Handelman continued. "Bush dropped twelve tons of explosives on Kabazi's personal headquarters. Kabazi, as it turned out, was sleeping below ground in a bunker and was spared. Sadly, his two years- old son, Kamil, was killed and one of his other children, including his wife was hospitalized.

"So much for a motive," White exclaimed.

"Since the bombing, Kabazi has continued his bloody work in a more private manner, with less rhetoric, and we are informed, with greater resolve.

"Is he vulnerable to a takeover?" asked the president.

Handelman tossed his report on the table. "Kabazi's own popularity with his countrymen rises and falls with the price of oil. His hold on their bank accounts is stronger than his hold on their hearts."

"Sounds like he's got hold of their balls," quipped Overton.

"Egypt's president recently told me that Kabazi is chaffing over Mahmoud Ahmadinejad's sudden rise to international prominence. The Iranian leader has seized the Mid-East spotlight that once belonged to Kabazi. Talabani claims that the Jabali and Ahmadinejad are bitter enemies who agree on only one thing – the imperative to destroy Israel. Those who know him say the probability that

Kabazi will mellow or modify his terroristic policies is zero."

White was visibly upset.

"I can't recall any leader in the world today who can match this bastard's penchant for senseless violence. What do you think, Sidney? You spoke with him a few months ago."

"Kabazi's a determined man," Sidney said thoughtfully, "I don't think he's as crazy as he is crafty. His vision of the Arab world is very different from our own."

"You might not want to hear this," General Overton thumped the table with his open hand, "but I'm going to lay it on the line. There comes a time, and by-God I never thought I'd be the man to bring it up, when free men should stop turning the other cheek and fight back. I would hope that this country might consider removing Kabazi from a position that allows him to kill and maim innocent people."

"What are we talking about here, Whipper?" The president wanted to hear General Overton state clearly what everyone at the table already suspected.

"We're talkin' about saving the lives of hundreds, maybe thousands of innocent victims. I think we should explore ways to neutralize the man."

"Neutralize?" asked the president.

"Kill the son-of-a-bitch," Overton exclaimed. "If Kabazi could lay his hands on the assets, and it looks like he's developing them, he'd be another Hitler. World peace is at stake here. If he has a deliverable nuclear weapon, there isn't a man at this table who should sleep a wink tonight. We've got trouble - big trouble!"

Handelman shook his head, "I don't see how I can ask any of our operatives to undertake such a task."

"That would pit us directly against the Executive Order issued by Carter in 1976," said Sidney. "That order forbids the government from authorizing assassination. There are also legal precedents to consider."

"May I speak frankly, Mr. President?" asked Overton.

The question brought a Cheshire cat smile to the president 's face.

"Does that mean you've been sweet-talking us so far, Whipper?"

Everyone, including General Overton, chuckled.

"I guess I've never been accused of being a shrinking violet. Bush affirmed the Executive Order that Sidney is referring to as soon as he took office. But when faced with the Kabazi situation, he himself tried to have the bastard killed. That's what you call it, isn't it, when you drop bombs on somebody's tent?"

Holdridge was visibly agitated, "The American people would never stand for it. The president would be an international outcast. We could all find ourselves standing before the World Court. I don't know about the rest of you gentlemen, but I wouldn't relish such a prospect."

"I think the majority of the American people would love to see Kabazi 'removed'," White injected with uncharacteristic enthusiasm.

General Overton seized the opportunity, "How the hell can any man sit at this table and not agree that the world community has a responsibility to act against this bastard! I don't think any true American who knows what Kabazi has done could examine the situation and condemn us for taking action! I think it's our responsibility to kill him!"

The president had heard enough.

"I appreciate your passion general, and even though I'd like to, this administration is not going to participate in or sponsor an assassination attempt on Kabazi or any other world leader. I simply won't involve America in that way."

White leaned back in his chair, "Why should Americans do it? Let the Israelis have the job. They want something from us. Let's get something in return, that will do us both some good."

Considered a dove on defense, Bertrand spoke, "Terrorist problems, gentlemen, most certainly will not go away if Kabazi is killed. But one thing's for sure. They won't get any better as long as he's alive. I like the Israeli idea."

The rest of the committee, including the president, were astounded by Bertrand's aggressive stance. Secretary of Defense White smiled.

"If Tom wants to kill Kabazi, I now believe anything is possible. Somewhere in the world cottontails are chasing Dobermans."

Further conversation did nothing to solidify a majority opinion. Both the president and vice president remained unconvinced. Bertrand continued to plead his case.

"Mr. President, the people of the United States and the world have lived in never-ending fear of what this crazy man might do. This isn't the problem of a specific nation or a particular region of the world. Kabazi's not like Amin and some of the other exterminators, who confined their atrocities to their own country."

"This is the problem of every European, every country in the Middle East, the Irish, the English, Africa and every man, woman, or child who sets foot on an international carrier. Ships, planes and buses have all been the targets of his outrageous barbarism.

"People are surrendering their lives for ideologies and conflicts they don't even understand. Three quarters of the people who have died at this butcher's hands couldn't even find Jabal on a map. If, through a second party, we can stop the killing, I feel we must do it."

The president addressed Sidney Holdridge; the only man on the council who failed to endorse the proposition.

"What's your final word on this, Sidney?"

The vice president tapped his fingers rapidly against the Walnut table's glossy finish.

"I don't like it. I think we're setting ourselves and this country up for a long fall. With a few reservations, I say no."

The president turned to the rest of the council, "I need to think about this, gentlemen. I also need to explore the Israeli position."

# CHAPTER THREE

## Washington, D.C.
## The Washington Post

While many of his fellow reporters scrambled to meet an 8 pm deadline, Henry Saperstein's day was drawing to a grateful close. He had spent the past few hours writing a gloomy column that left him depressed. Clayton Jennings, Virginia's thirty-eight-year-old representative from the third district, was lying only hours from death in nearby Bethesda hospital. He was one of the few politicians Henry admired; and no matter what kind of upbeat spin he attempted to place on the Congressman's short life, the result was little more than a dismal obituary. Platitudes and sage observations could not dull the impact of terminal colon cancer.

Briefcase in hand, the fifty-nine-year-old columnist shuffled toward the scarred maple door that held the outside world at bay. His anticipated departure was cut short by the familiar drone of a telephone, that as years past, he was learning to despise.

"Not now," he moaned.

The thought of ignoring the caller and making good his escape forced a hesitation. "Fuck me," he thought to himself. It might be my wife with some last-minute grocery pick-up or some other bullshit errand. He returned to his unimpressive gray desk, pushed aside a jumble of paper, and exposed the yellowish handset of what was once, a white telephone. Confident that he would hear his wife's voice, he picked up the handset

"Hello," he said, resigned to the inconvenience.

Silence on the caller's end gave him a welcome excuse to be on his way. The receiver of the telephone was several inches from his ear and dropping fast when a fragment of sound prompted him to reverse the movement. His second greeting bordered on rude.

"Hellooooo."

"Is this Henry Saperstein?" a reluctant voice asked. Henry had heard only his own name, but that was enough.

"This is Henry Saperstein. Who is this?" Again, there was silence. "Look, are we going to talk here or what? Who is this?" Henry inquired with characteristic impatience.

A male voice with the demeanor of a repentant sinner answered, ignoring his question.

"I'm close to the president."

"Aren't we all. So, what." Henry's sour mood wasn't making it easy for his caller.

"Look, I have something important to tell you. If you choose to berate me without even knowing the purpose of my call, I'm going to hang up. I don't need this."

Something in the caller's voice tweaked Henry's curiosity. He dropped his briefcase to the floor and slid into the butt-stamped seat of his threadbare chair.

"Hold on! Give me a chance to sit down. Who are you?"

"I can't say. And don't bother with any Caller I.D. nonsense. I'm calling you from a public telephone."

Henry fumbled for the tools of his trade and prepared to take notes. The caller's voice was suddenly stronger and more confident.

"Like I said, I am close to President Atwater. Something's going on that's wrong. Very wrong. Sins are being committed."

The word "sins" let the air out of Henry's tires. Flags went up, buzzers sounded; the guy was probably a nut case.

"Sins. What sort of sins?" He asked in mock alarm.

"The president is seeing a woman in the White House – in his personal quarters."

"So?" Henry replied matter-of-factly. "Does anyone seriously think the man doesn't have a private life? That he hasn't been laid for six years? Even I've been laid in the past six years – what's this woman's name?"

Anger added intensity to the caller's voice. "I thought you would understand. I picked you. I could have called anyone ... and I don't care for that kind of language! The president isn't married. He should be setting an example. If you don't understand that, then I've called the wrong man. And your question, 'Who is she?' is part of the problem. She's married. She's committing adultery."

"So is half the country. It's interesting, but it's not enough. I still need to know who she is."

"I don't think I should tell you." The door was left open a crack. Henry pushed. "Look, I don't know who you are. I don't know what you do. Now you tell me you won't reveal any names. Without names, your identity, her identity, this is a go nowhere dead-end call."

"Robin Holdridge," the voice blurted.

The accusation was so stunning that Henry could scarcely comprehend the implications. Mental pictures painted by this bizarre scenario charged through his reporter's brain like a runaway truck.

"Did you hear me?" the caller repeated, "he's seeing Robin Holdridge, the wife of the vice president."

"Yeah, I know who she is. How do you know about this? Who are you? If this is true, I'll protect you completely. No one will ever know who you are." Henry was ready to surrender his dignity and beg for this one.

"No, no. I'll never reveal myself. You're the reporter – report."

"A face to face meeting would solve everything. Just meet me ..."

The caller hung up; the phone was dead. Henry kept the receiver tucked between his ear and shoulder. Following a moment of thought, he punched in a seven-digit number. "Honey, I'll be late. Something's come up."

## MAY 19
## Florence City, South Carolina
## Holiday Inn

Empty food containers, beer cans and assorted debris littered the smoke-filled motel room where Musa Abu Tabou and his band of scoundrels had sequestered themselves over the past forty-eight hours. Amidst the clamor of a vintage western movie, the Jabali stood and walked toward the television.

A smack of his powerful right hand mashed the power switch to the off position. The resulting grumbles were silenced with a reproachful wave of his hand. In a gruff, heavily accented voice, he addressed his comrades.

"The incident with the American Coast Guard means nothing. As we knew, early detection was always considered a possibility. Our alternate plan will turn our discovery by the American authorities against them. I, as most of you, was in favor of the alternate plan from the beginning."

He turned toward the Frenchman, "The burden now falls on your shoulders, Coutre. We will travel to our destination and meet you there, when you are finished."

The Jabali removed then examined several folded papers from his pocket.

"Parker has secured a place of concealment. A place from which we can operate. It is there that we will meet you." He threw one of the papers in Coutre's general direction. "Destroy this when you have memorized the information."

The Frenchman's refusal to pick up the paper evidenced his own priorities, "Is it understood and agreed that I will receive $100,000 for this extra service?"

Tabou was visibly irked by Coutre's preoccupation with money. In his mind, this mission had nothing to do with dollars and cents. Mocking the Frenchman's accent, the Jabali made no effort to hide his contempt.

"Yes, you will get your money, Coutre."

## The White House
## Bowling Alley

In an effort to break the monotony of an endless string of meetings, the president chose to confer with the Supervisor of the Secret Service White House Detail in the bowling alley. This "perk" of the Presidency was situated in the basement of the main building.

Sean, ball in hand, took his place on the approach while the president and John Solis began an informal discussion.

"Shortly after I told Sean that I wanted us to meet down here, it occurred to me that I didn't know if you liked to bowl. I can see by your first strike that you do," noted the president.

"Well, Mr. President, I've never had a chance to do anything like this on duty. I'm enjoying the opportunity."

Sean returned to the bench elated with his pick-up of a five-ten split.

"By God Jim, it's like jacking off – you never forget!" he said with his usual enthusiasm.

It was the president's turn to bowl, but he remained seated.

"John, what have you put together?"

"Mr. President, we've doubled our outside people and increased our on-duty uniformed division by over ten percent. Four additional agents have been assigned to off-grounds surveillance, covering areas immediately adjacent to the White House.

Our Technical Security Division is going to make a bomb sweep of the building at 12:15, following the morning public tours. All rope-lines that were unattended will be manned by our uniformed division for the duration of any tour or public gathering in the building, such as a party or dinner. Canine teams will walk the grounds from sun-down to sun-up.

All White House passes are being reissued with current photographs and the necessity for each pass is being reevaluated. Only those with a valid reason to be on the premises will be issued a pass. To minimize the possibility of a missile attack, Counter Sniper Teams will be assigned to strategic positions throughout the immediate vicinity.

"You, Mr. President," continued John, "will have an additional agent assigned to you personally, 24 hours a day. For necessary local travel, three identical limousines will transport you to and from the White House. You will be placed at random in one of those vehicles.

On trips, your advance men will make security preparations with this new threat foremost in their minds. Our Intelligence Division has already stepped up their surveillance of foreign nationals who could be considered possible adversaries. Each individual will be thoroughly investigated and their whereabouts known. Everyone with past or present involvement in any Middle East protests or belonging to any organization with goals contrary to our policies will be sought out and ear marked for questioning.

Threats made on your life that fall into categories two and three are receiving special attention- particularly the one hundred and twenty names listed in category three. These are the individuals that we feel pose the greatest domestic threat to your security.

F.I.S.H, the forensic information system, has been pressed for all recent findings that might foretell of any conceivable assassination attempt. Outside the White House, the 'kill zone" will be filled with a wall of agents dressed in clothing similar to yourself. "In a nut-shell Mr. President, we're going to double our efforts and trust no one."

The president gave John a pat on the back, then stood to bowl.

"It sounds as if you've covered all the bases, John. I appreciate it. I really do ... and please convey my thanks to the director and your fellow agents. This isn't going to be easy on any of us."

## The Washington Post
## Editor's Office

Henry Saperstein walked briskly into the office of his friend, and Editor of the Washington Post, James Wingate. A sense of history permeated Wingate's office as thoroughly as the cigars he smoked. Autographed pictures and an assortment of memorabilia, primarily from politicians, covered the walls and nearly every square inch of each table top, bookshelf and flat surface in the room.

The surrounding clutter was in direct contradiction to the neat and well-groomed appearance of its sixty-five-year-old occupant. Jim Wingate, seated at his massive walnut desk, peered over the top of his thick spectacles while Henry made himself comfortable in an antiquated leather chair.

"Morning Henry. You sounded up when you called. What have you got?"

Henry shook his head and grinned.

"This is a corker, Jim. I got a call last night from an anonymous source."

Henry placed both of his raised hands in a palms-out defensive posture.

"Now I know that this gets off to a bad start, but hear me out ... this guy says he's 'close to the president.' After a little bit of back and forth he tells me the president's seeing a woman."

"Well, that old rumor's got whiskers on it. Over the past six years, we've heard that he's dated everyone from Kathryn Bigelow to Sharon Stone – and so what? But the guy goes on to say that the woman's married, so I perked up a bit, then he lays the bomb on me. He claims the woman is Robin Holdridge!"

Wingate stood, moved from behind his desk and walked to the door. With a gentle shove he pushed it closed.

"The vice president's wife?" asked Wingate. "Did you tell the guy he was nuts?"

"No chance. He hung up. But I started making calls. Maybe, just maybe he's not certifiable."

"Okay! Hold on! Do you mean to tell me that the President of the United States is screwing the wife of the vice president in the White House?"

"I know it sounds crazy," said Henry, "but listen. I called a half-dozen of the best people I have in town. Not one of them would say a word. Zero. But then, well you know, I've got a source that works as a domestic in the White House. This person has never clammed up on me before, but this time I got, and I quote, 'Just leave it alone. Why pry into something like that.' Now that wasn't a denial. That's the old Washington two-step"

Wingate ran his thumb and forefinger back and forth along his bearded chin.

"We've got to be careful with this. It could be, and I repeat 'could be' the story of the decade or it could be the biggest barrel of horse shit that's ever been rolled out of the barn. You're going to need help. Get Elizabeth Freeman on this with you."

The suggestion that Henry might need help from anyone angered the thirty-five-year veteran.

"Jimmy! Come on! I don't need Beth Freeman. I can handle this my..."

Wingate was adamant.

"I'm firm on this, Henry. I want absolute secrecy. I want speed. I want you moving like a three-armed paper hanger. I still don't believe it ... but, if it's true, you'll need more help than Freeman can give you. This isn't boring shit like Watergate and Whitewater. People can understand this. Everybody screws. If you can prove golden boy can't keep it in his pants, and with the vice president's wife- look out! You'll blow the lid right off this administration and the country."

## MAY 20
## Washington D.C.
## The Royal Haven Motel

Pierre Coutre struggled to fabricate a believable entry for each of the routine queries on the small registration card that had been thrust in front of him. A bright-eyed young desk clerk, unaware of the Frenchman's evasive effort, began to rattle off a list of familiar questions.

"Would you like a single, sir?"

"No, I need two rooms ... that are together ... for six people."

"You need adjoining rooms. Will two rooms with two queen size beds each, be all right?"

"Yes."

"Smoking or non-smoking?"

Coutre looked puzzled. The girl repeated her question in the manner of a first-grade school teacher querying a backward child.

"Will you be smoking in your room ... or do you want a room where smoking is not allowed?"

The Frenchman was anything but stupid. Her condescending tone irritated him.

"Yes," he nodded, with a surly snap to his voice, "we will be smoking."

"How will you be paying, sir?"

Coutre fished a fat wad of tightly rolled paper currency from his pants pocket and held it under the girl's nose. After achieving the desired effect, he peeled off a pair of one hundred dollar bills and tossed them on the counter.

"By the day. Each day I will pay you."

If the young woman was impressed, she gave him no outward sign.

"How long will you and your group be staying, Mr. ...," she snapped up the registration card and quickly scanned it for his name – "Moran?"

"I don't know. It depends on my work. I will inform you later."

For the first time, Coutre took notice of his inquisitor. Preoccupied with registering, he hadn't noticed the girl's natural beauty. Even her blue suit couldn't hide her lusty figure. Best of all, she was young. He had always been attracted to young girls. This one, he thought to himself, would make an exceptional trophy.

His eyes followed her to the cash register then to the board where she retrieved an oversize room key. Her return prompted a question, "What's your name?"

After handing him the key, she pointed with a smile to the brass plate on her jacket, "Monica," she smiled.

"Monica," he repeated, adding a French slant to the pronunciation. "What does it mean?"

"I'm not sure. It was my grandmother's name."

The young woman attempted to curb her customer's sudden personal interest by pointing to a diagram of the building, sandwiched between a sheet of clear plate glass and a time worn Formica counter-top.

"Your room is right here next to ..."

Coutre placed his hand over the drawing, blocking her view.

"Maybe you could show me," he leered.

Accustomed to flirtatious male travelers separated from their wives and a long way from home, the young woman simply backtracked far enough to make a complete sentence and continued her instructions.

"Next to stairway B. It's right in the middle of the building. Just walk out the front door and take a right. You and your party are in Rooms 164 and 166."

When she looked up from the counter, she made sure that her perky smile was gone. This would let her amorous customer know that he had stepped over the line. She could tell from the look in his eyes that the Frenchman had not heard a word she said. Instinct forced a step backward, so that only her outstretched hands touched the counter.

Coutre leaned forward on his elbows, "After work ... how would you like to go out tonight, Monica?"

"Aaaaa … how old are you, Mr. Moran?" she asked.

"What's the difference?" Coutre scoffed.

"About fifteen years, I'd guess," she said, smiling at her own cleverness. "I usually go out with guys around my own age. I'm only eighteen."

In matters of sex, which is the only context in which Coutre thought of women, the Frenchman never accepted defeat gracefully. No one had ever told Pierre Coutre that he was too old to be with. Wounded pride and a hair-trigger temper tipped the scales.

"You missed your chance, bitch. You look like a fucking tight-ass anyway! A cunt like you wouldn't know what to do with a real man. Forget it!"

In other circumstances, Coutre would have done more than shout obscenities. Paralyzed by fear, the soon-to-be high school graduate stood in wide-eyed disbelief as she watched the Frenchman snatch his room key from the counter and stalk toward the front entrance. The vulgarity of the stranger's verbal assault had terrified the unsuspecting teenager.

When the door finally closed, she looked down at her trembling fingers and moved with dispatch to the less public confines of the small office adjacent to the reception area. She had never been so scared of another human being. This was not just another dirty old man, she thought to herself. How could the simple mention of their age difference result in such a crude retort? Her miscalculation, she feared, could have done more than destroy her confidence. When the night was over, she vowed, she would not walk to her car alone.

## The White House
## President's Living Quarters

Israel Ambassador, Zalman Pasha, accompanied by the vice president and his wife, were enjoying an informal meal in the president 's private second-floor dining room. By White House standards the setting was warm and comfortable; two qualities the president had grown to appreciate.

Since he had no family in residence, the chief executive used his personal dining room as a frequent setting for small informal gatherings. Conversations held in this home-like environment were generally more substantive, resulting in accomplishments that could never be achieved in the distraction fraught environment of a larger, more grandiose, public arena.

Everyone, from the president of France to his sixth grade English teacher, had dined at the small but elegant table. Light conversation, punctuated by the occasional click of sterling silver on expensive china, took a serious turn with an unexpected comment by Ambassador Pasha.

"I understand a yet to be identified country, possibly from the Middle East, has sent a so-called 'hit squad' to assassinate you Mr. President. It is a terrible thing."

Robin, who knew nothing of this new threat to the president's life, was caught off guard. Her concern was all too obvious.

"What hit squad, Mr. President? Sidney, have you heard about this?"

Noting his wife's reaction, the vice president nodded his head, "I've known about it for a couple of days. We've tried to keep a lid on the situation, but tonight, somehow, the Post latched on to the story."

Alarmed by Robin's unconcealed distress, the president made a valiant attempt to throw water on the fire, "We aren't sure. It could be nothing. A false alarm."

"I'm so sorry," Pasha lamented, "I did not wish to be the bearer of bad tidings. I assumed that every person here knew of the situation. It seems the whole world is talking about it."

Aware of her over-reaction to the threat on her lover's life, Robin initiated her own version of damage control.

"It's quite all right, Mr. Ambassador, I was so busy all day, I just hadn't heard the news."

She turned to her husband and forced a question that at least two people in the room knew was uninspired.

"Sidney, could this plot involve you?"

### Somewhere in Tennessee

Tabou, Libyan, Mustafa Al Jaabir, and Syrian, Mohammed Al Sharif, drove north along interstate 26, taking special care to keep their black Chevy van at or below the speed limit.

The highly excitable Jaabir, always a degree from meltdown, repeated an oft asked question.

"Are they with us? Do you see them?"

Tabou glanced at his side mirror. The vehicle trailing behind them was so close to their rear bumper that only one headlight was visible.

"Yes, yes, for the hundredth time yes! Stop worrying, Jaabir! They are right behind us!"

Mohammed Al Sharif was the quietest of the group. His dark broody manner allowed him few friends; by choice he was a seldom spoken to loner.

"I am tired of hearing the same question. Shut your face!"

Jaabir was a quick-tempered fanatic, but he wasn't self-destructive. Without comment, he returned to his makeshift bed, on the floor, between the two front seats. He would have rather slept in the back of the van, but who could rest while lying on fifty-caliber machine guns and RPG-7 Soviet rockets?

## The White House
## President's Living Quarters

After expressing their gratitude for a fine meal, Robin and Sidney bid the president good night. With a Hollywood hug – the type where cheeks barely touch, Robin expressed her gratitude for the fine meal. Sidney added his own thank you before turning to enter the elevator that would take him and his wife to the main floor of the White House.

For the briefest of moments, the president's eyes met those of his lover's. Her anxiety, since hearing Ambassador Pasha's indelicate announcement that a hit squad of assassins could be stalking him, was evident. In that instant, he wanted nothing more than to hold her in his arms. Instead, they would be forced to perpetuate their charade. With little or no fanfare, the door between them swung closed - she was gone.

The president took a moment to gather his thoughts before returning to his quarters where Ambassador Pasha waited, expecting an answer to his country's request for assistance in locating the assembly point of Jabal's four atomic bombs. The two men made themselves comfortable in the study, just off the main living room. The president was the first to address the problem at hand.

"It appears that one individual is responsible for our mutual dilemma. There seems no end in sight."

"You mean, Kabazi?" Pasha asked, eliminating any doubt.

"Yes. How many lives could we save if he were stopped?"

"You mean, including your own?"

The ambassador's remark cut straight to the quick of the president's own self-doubt.

"I can only hope that my judgment is for the greater good," he answered.

"The asking of this question then, is coincidental to the fact that you believe Kabazi has sent men to kill you?" asked Pasha.

The question, so directly put, forced the president to make a rare admission.

"I have agonized over that possibility. I am just a man - like you. Could either of us – under these circumstances, ever know ... for sure?"

Pasha's hesitation conceded the obvious answer. His preoccupation with the purpose of his visit could no longer be concealed.

"Can you help us find the bombs?"

"Yes, I believe I can," the president was concise. "We have a new reconnaissance satellite called LEPERS. It's the most sophisticated instrument of its kind ever built. As luck would have it, it was to be placed in orbit over a different area of the world. With an all-out effort and many millions of dollars, we reassigned its mission. If *Endeavour* goes up on schedule, LEPERS will be placed in geostationary orbit over Jabal in two days."

"You will help us then?" Pasha pressed, searching for a firm commitment.

"Yes. We shall try. But there are no guarantees."

By preserving his integrity and surrendering all hope of bargaining for the death of Kabazi, James Atwater had relieved his conscience. A smiling Pasha brought his hands together in a prayer-like position.

"Thank you. Thank you so much."

In a confiding gesture the Israeli placed his outstretched fingers on the president's sleeve. His voice was quiet and cautious.

"My friend, I am going to inform you of a fact that I have no authority to divulge. I think it concerns something, that in my own humble opinion, you might have anticipated asking me." The elder-statesman moved closer, "Remember, we Israelis always fight with a double-edged sword. It just might be that Kabazi's passing is being planned at this moment. I cannot say. However, it seems reasonable. A man like him makes so many enemies and so few friends."

Relief. Without saying a word, or placing the United States in moral jeopardy, the president had secured his hoped-for result.

"You are most perceptive, Mr. Ambassador. I appreciate your candor."

Pasha patted the president's arm, "If your satellite fulfills its promise, it is my country that will be in your debt. One more thing ..." The old man's mood turned morose, "The candor of this evening's conversation has convinced me that I should inform you of an ugly rumor that has begun to circulate. It seems an intelligence organization has uncovered some information concerning a high official in your government."

"You mean the Mossad?" asked the president.

"The exact source is unclear," Pasha's faint smile confirmed the accuracy of the president's educated guess.

"It seems this person is involved with the wife of another official in your government. I would never mention it but, what a disaster for your administration if – well, I think you know."

The president's blood ran cold. He knew that Pasha was watching him closely. Any reluctance or hesitation in his reply would confirm the Israeli's obvious suspicion.

"I can't imagine who that would be. I've heard nothing. If it were true, and I hope it isn't, that person would either be very foolish or," smiled the president, "very much in love. I'll look into it."

Pasha immediately picked up on the potential for a game of cat and mouse.

"Lust, or did you say love – is a luxury for the young and those willing to risk everything. Most men are reluctant to take another man's wife for fear of the scorn of their neighbors. It would take a brave – or very stupid man to risk the scorn of the entire world. There would be no place for such a man and woman to hide."

# CHAPTER FOUR

## MAY 21
## Washington, D.C.
## The Royal Haven Motel

Before his evening could begin, Pierre Coutre had several tasks to perform. With his jacket tucked under one arm, he strolled to the television, turned it on, and then walked to the night stand next to the double bed nearest the door.

A Teac reel-to-reel tape recorder had been placed on the top of the scarred Formica surface. The audio tape on the recorder's eleven-inch metal supply reel was loaded to the limit, well beyond its normal capacity. Coutre pushed the blue button marked FORWARD.

A single speaker, resting on the floor next to the table, filled the room with heavily accented voices punctuated by varying degrees of raucous laughter. After adjusting the volume to a level calculated to gain attention, but not loud enough to force the hand of motel management, the Frenchman left the room in search of a beer and any woman he could find.

## The White House
## President's Living Quarters

Robin flew into the president's arms the moment he walked through the front door of his second floor residence. He savored the feeling of her hair against his cheek; the softness of her skin; her very essence – she was intoxicating, and he was a willing addict.

This wonderful woman made him feel as he had never felt before. Nothing in his event-filled life had ever given him the euphoric high that he experienced in her presence. His surprise and total delight was unavoidably tempered by a disturbing thought.

"What about the staff?" he asked, holding her at arm's length.

"Sean took care of it – he's a doll."

The president pulled her to him, resuming their embrace. After a storybook kiss, he released her from his grip and stepped back far enough to admire her flawlessly tailored blue dress. The linen fabric, drawn in at the waist and knees, tastefully displayed every curve of her luscious body. He knew the detail of every square inch of gorgeous flesh and the secrets hidden by the dress.

"Wow!" he exclaimed, "you look absolutely fabulous." Robin made an exaggerated model-turn and smiled.

"It's all for you," she said with a seductive inflection that made it clear she was alluding to a lot more than the dress. Again, he reached to take her in his arms – this time she held him at bay.

"We need to talk," she said firmly, "I've been worried sick since dinner last night."

"There's no need to brood over this," he assured her, "I'm well protected. There's always somebody trying to kill the president. This time, we just might have an advantage, we know who they are. How are you? I've never seen you look better!"

"Thank you. But I don't want to be patronized. I want to know more about these assassins."

Hand-in-hand they walked toward his bedroom and a change of clothes.

"They appear to be Arab or at least Arab-sponsored. One of them is French; the rest is guess work. From what I've read, the newspapers seem to know as much as we do at this point."

"What can be done to stop them?" Once inside the bedroom door, he began removing his tie.

"There are a lot of possibilities. They could be detected; they could call it off; it's even possible we've misinterpreted the purpose of their mission."

"What if you haven't?"

He turned and looked directly into her eyes. "Security has been stepped-up. We've got some good people on it. Everything will be fine. Please! Just put it out of your mind." He was determined to change the subject. "How did you get over here tonight?"

"Sean met me with a limo."

Robin sat on the edge of the bed while the president began unbuttoning his shirt.

"He got me past the gate and inside. We used the side entrance. I wore my black jacket with the collar up and dark glasses. We only saw two security guards besides the Secret Service Agents. With the coat there's no way anyone knew who I was," Robin smiled. "Sean said being seen with a mysterious woman was good for his 'overall image'."

The president chuckled then added, "Thank God for tinted glass, and if it weren't for Sean, our relationship would be a lot more difficult, if not impossible."

Wearing only his shorts, he sat down next to Robin on the edge of the bed.

"Sean's big happy face is known and trusted by everyone from the cook to the office staff.

"I just love him," she said. "He's one of the nicest people I know."

"Where is Sidney?" he asked, Darkening the mood of the moment with an important, but untimely, question he knew his inquiry would spoil the tranquility of the evening.

"You'd be more likely to know that than I would," she stated. "He just said he'd be late. We don't chitchat much anymore. If he weren't so caught up in his own political career, I think he would divorce me. He thinks he's going to be the next president."

Her remark amused him, "Sidney, the president? I don't see how. For some reason, he just doesn't wear well."

Talk of his lover's husband had gone on far too long.

"I just love the way you look tonight. You're so beautiful."

"I wanted you to like it. I bought it just for you," she said coyly.

The invitation offered by his outstretched arms was quickly accepted.

"When this is all over, you and I are going to be together," he said

"I want that more than anything," she assured him.

In the wake of another smoldering kiss and long embrace, the president walked to the closet and changed into his most comfortable outfit; blue jeans, T-shirt and tennis shoes. At the same time, the leggy blonde stood, kicked off her high heels and began removing the blue linen dress.

Her spectacular figure emerged to appreciative eyes. Her lover's flagrant visual exploration of her emerging body excited her. She responded by sensually caressing her breasts and tweaking the tips of her nipples with her thumb and forefinger.

This was a game they played often. A well-orchestrated overture that frequently continued until Robin could see the enlarging effect it had on her audience. By the time this occurred, both of them were usually past the point of restraint. Her flesh tingled at the lusty thoughts she knew were racing through his mind. A move to take her in his arms was met with contrived resistance.

"Ah, ah ... Not yet," she cautioned, "we haven't even had dinner."

"You look like the perfect entree to me."

"No, no. Think of me as dessert. An after dinner treat with no calories."

As he reached for her arm, the inside of his wrist brushed against the hard tip of her nipple. In response to the touch, they both paused and looked into each other's eyes. Despite a brief rush of emotion, she continued to resist.

"Not yet, Mr. President," she teased.

With a burst of effort Robin managed to scramble to her feet and run to the president's walk-in closet where she removed his blue terry cloth bathrobe from its expensive wooden hanger. In an effort to deter her lover's amorous pursuit, she wrapped herself in the warmth and protection of the garment's coarse fabric. After tying the belt loosely around her waist, she returned to the foot of the bed and declared her intentions.

"I'm on strike! Food! Food! Food!" she chanted.

The president took her playfulness as a challenge. As for Robin, she'd seen that look in his eyes before. Her frantic dash for the bedroom door was cut short by a waist high tackle that sent them both tumbling to the carpeted floor. The resulting scuffle was a fractional effort punctuated with laughter and mock anger. A sudden twist of Robin's hips loosened the belt on her oversize robe and brought the provocative wrestling match to a screeching halt.

With her arms extended high above her head, she nestled up against his thigh. Robin's movement had loosened her robe, removing all that was blocking her lover's view. Her token resistance was replaced by an earthy lust. Robin's near perfect body stretched before her lover in a tantalizing tribute to the female form. Without saying a word, she had given him permission to take her and do as he pleased.

The look in her green eyes brought him to his feet, where he held out his hand and lifted the most beautiful woman he had ever seen to her knees. She knew what he wanted. Her hands tugged at the top of his jeans. Inch by tantalizing inch she exposed him to her appreciative view.

Each area of newly exposed flesh received loving attention from her rapidly moving tongue. Several minutes passed before his throbbing erection was mercifully freed.

Ever so slowly, she slid the fingertips of her right hand along an erogenous journey calculated to cover his full length. With the palm of her left hand she traced a series of ever widening circles through the short dark hair covering his stomach. By repeating the movement over and over, she was able to stimulate him to his full potential, just short of orgasm. Each heartbeat intensified the fervor of his unrestrained response.

A few knowing strokes of her loving hand produced a drop of lubricant. She placed him inside her hungry mouth; the sudden warmth induced a sigh, accompanied by a forward thrust of his powerful hips. He began to move in perfect time to the motion of her soft wet mouth. The sight of him, tense, inflamed and in her control, pushed Robin to a level of arousal approaching that of her lover's.

Never missing a stroke, she assumed a squatting position that allowed her unrestricted access to the area between her outstretched legs. With eager fingers she attempted to satisfy a crucial need. Her wetness, coupled with the down pressure created by her position, made her seem large and extremely sensitive. Robin's moist fingers moved rapidly across her puffy lips and up under, then over, her protruding clitoris.

By placing his outstretched hands on either side of her beautiful face, he urged her to a faster stroke. With his head tipped back and his eyes closed, he prepared to ejaculate. Robin could feel the welcome onslaught of her own release. His controlled rhythmic thrusts were replaced by jerky less disciplined movements. A paralyzing numbness quickly spread across her face and upper body, signaling the onset of the climax she needed so desperately.

Her self-probing fingers and slippery mouth made their final tearing thrusts. His pounding discharge, coupled with the onset of her own orgasm, was welcomed with a sudden gush of emotion. Cuming, she fell back on the floor with her knees held high and wide apart. Her trembling fingers parted the folds of wet flesh that covered her most secret place. Only here, in this exact spot, did she want him to deposit the liquid that had already begun to flow.

Her invitation was immediately accepted. Dropping to his knees, he penetrated her as far as his length would allow with a single push. They finished their orgasm together, as one; locked inside each other, kissing, touching and loving a forbidden love.

## Washington, D.C.
## Martin Luther King Avenue

Pierre Coutre pulled his late-model Pontiac Firebird to the curb where Tracy Parks, a cocaine-addicted prostitute, stood ready to ply her trade. Even in the heavily shadowed street light it was easy to see that the attractive brunette was little more than a teenager. The Frenchman leaned across the front seat of his car and looked through the open passenger side window.

"Hey Baby! You looking for some fun?" he asked in a monotone that indicated she probably wouldn't be having any.

"Sure," she replied with effort, "anytime with a stud like you."

"How much?" he asked.

The teenager crossed the sidewalk and approached his car. She leaned forward far enough to see his face, but not close enough for him to grab her.

"Are you a cop ... or some kind of a law enforcement officer?" she asked.

"I hate cops, baby!"

"You sound different. Where you from?"

"France," he said impatiently. "Let's cut the bullshit. I need a price."

"What do you want?"

"I want it all, baby."

His reply sounded more like a boast than an answer to her question.

"Everybody wants it all. The question is can you afford it all? With me, all is a lot," she smiled. "How's your heart?"

Coutre was visibly unimpressed.

"Look baby, don't shit me. Come on. How much?"

His impatience and lack of humor removed the impish smile from the young girl's painted face. "Three hundred bucks," she said with a take-it or leave-it tone in her voice.

"Get in!" He ordered.

Tracy was rarely attracted to the men with whom she had sex; this john would be no exception.

Grateful to avoid the usual price haggle and resigned to her lot, the young woman opened the car door and plopped down on the fabric upholstered bucket seat. A neck-snapping stomp on the Firebird's accelerator launched the sleek automobile into the main stream of traffic.

"In a hurry, huh?" she asked.

"Always, baby. I got places to go, things to do. Where are we going?"

"Go down to the next stoplight and take a left. Whatcha doin' here in Washington?" she asked, not caring if she heard an answer.

"You'd never guess, baby. Never!"

## Washington, D.C.

A need for alcohol and the promise of a good steak lured Henry Saperstein and Constance Freeman to the friendly confines of the Sunshine Factory Bar and Grill, a popular D.C. watering hole.

Foot weary and discouraged, they occupied a small table situated in a corner of the restaurant's noisy bar. Gin and tonics were disappearing at a pace that would soon demand adjustment or unconsciousness.

Connie, happily married herself, questioned the alleged "truth" of their investigation.

"Hank, how could they keep a secret like this? For so long?"

"Power of the presidency? Lucky?"

A waiter approached their table with a plate of assorted appetizers which he preceded to place between them.

"I'm getting nowhere," she said, skewering the largest of the stuffed mushrooms with her fork. "People think I'm crazy."

"I talked to Wingate. He thinks we should give it another couple of days. I personally think there's something going on. Christ! Don't you get a feeling?" he asked.

"Honestly? No. I've interviewed her on several occasions. She seems to be a genuine person. A really nice woman. Her friends, her family, God, I feel like a grave robber when I mention the subject of infidelity – and with the President of the United States! I don't even like me when I ask questions like that."

"I hate to break it to you kid, but 'nice girls' have affairs too. Remember, she's married to a horse's ass."

"Well so am I," she chuckled, "and we've been married almost twenty-eight years."

## Washington, D.C.
## Stardust Hotel

Tracy Parks flipped on the light switch, just inside the door of her hundred dollar a week love nest. Coutre, casting a chary eye, skulked into the room behind her. The meager furnishings in the rundown flea-trap had "garage sale" written all over them.

"The Light," the name Tracy's pimp insisted on being called, took eighty percent of the young woman's earnings. Tonight's 'trick,' who wanted everything, would net her a grand total of sixty dollars.

In contrast to her occupation, stuffed animals, rock posters, and juvenile knickknacks cluttered most of the available area in the single room apartment. They were a sad reminder of the occupant's tender age.

After closing the door, the Frenchman removed his jacket and tossed it in the general direction of the dilapidated dresser situated opposite the bed. Several stuffed rabbits tumbled to the bare wooden floor. Tracy moved quickly to pick them up, returning each of the fuzzy creatures to their original positions with the concern teenagers reserve for very special objects.

Coutre, aggravated by her preoccupation, broke the silence. "What's your name?"

"Tracy," she replied. "What's yours?"

"Pierre."

"I always get paid first, Pierre, nothin' personal."

Coutre peeled off four one hundred dollar bills. "The extra hundred is for the really good time I know I'm going to have."

Out of habit, Tracy turned her back to the Frenchman while depositing his money in an inside compartment of her small shoulder bag. The added tip, which she would most certainly avoid mentioning to her pimp, would more than double her share of the take.

"Ya' sure know how to excite a girl," she said, in a delivery reminiscent of Mae West.

Coutre dragged the only chair in the room to the side of the bed. The fabric on the seat and arms was badly soiled, nearly obscuring its flowered design.

"Show me what you've got," he ordered.

"I like that," she giggled. "Too many guys are hung up on foreplay."

The Frenchman sunk into the chair's misshapen foam cushion and made himself comfortable by placing his right leg over the thickly padded arm.

Tracy walked to the foot of the bed, only a few feet from her 'john' and smiled sweetly, as if pleasing him were important. The red fabric yielded her young body at a deliberate pace.

Coutre watched intently as first the dress, then the bra and panties slipped enticingly to the floor. The girl's natural beauty was indisputable. Beneath all of her makeup, there was a lovely young girl.

Tracy's body hadn't paid the price for her drug habit; not yet, anyway. With her clothing removed, the naked teenager assumed a shy, almost childlike posture. She spoke softly. "I'll do anything for you. Just ask me."

Coutre looked at her with a blank stare.

"Do you want a blow-job?" she asked.

He slowly shook his head. "I want you to lie down."

Tracy complied with his demand by stretching her nude body seductively across the bedspread. Several minutes passed with no sign of approval or encouragement from her client. Certain that he didn't like her and would want his money returned, she played her trump card by revealing her only remaining secret.

With a foot on each arm of his chair she continued to seek approval.

"Like me?" she asked in a seductive voice that begged to be answered.

The Frenchman cracked the faintest of smiles, but still he did not reply. At least, Tracy thought to herself, he didn't ask her to stop. Maybe he just wanted to watch – some guys were that way.

She began to explore her own body in an effort to elicit a reaction from her seemingly passive customer. First her nipples, then between her legs. Her own hands initiated the arousal process. Once again, she prodded Coutre for a response.

"Does this turn ya on? Do you like watchin' me?"

The Frenchman's silence was unnerving. Tracy wanted some assurance that she was earning her fee. Any response at all would help. Another query fell on deaf ears.

"How do' ya' want me? I'll do anything."

Despite her customer's apparent indifference, the young girl made a decision to continue. If he wanted her to do something else, he would have to ask for it.

As her feelings intensified, she closed her eyes and allowed her thoughts to return to home and a boy she knew a long, long time ago. A nice boy. She had conjured up the fantasy many times in an effort to forget the fat ugly men with whom she was often forced to have sex.

By consciously increasing the pace of her own breathing she hoped to attract the attention of the man that had paid her. Concerns over her client's apparent lack of involvement would keep her from having anything approaching an orgasm. Her only alternative was to hope she could turn him on by simulating her own excitement. It had worked before. She turned her head slightly to the side when – the beast was let loose.

The black demon that lived deep inside Pierre Coutre possessed him. In a single fluid motion, he removed a six-inch dagger from his pocket and plunged it deep into Tracy's pumping heart. She had only enough time to make one frantic grab at the black handle protruding from her chest. Her effort to scream was halted by the sudden loss of blood to her brain.

The sixteen year old lying on the bed would never have the chance to find the boy in her fantasy. She would never be the grown up that she had pretended to be – it was over.

A long expulsion of breath emptied her lungs forever. Far from home and family, she died.

Tracy's blood-drenched body was lying limp. The man that everyone had warned her of, had finally appeared - the man who would look like most other men; who would show no sign; offer no second chance to his victim.

Pierre Coutre removed every article of his own clothing, exposing his erection. A few short steps placed him at the side of the bed, where he leaned forward and withdrew the knife from his young victim's chest. Her soft flesh quickly yielded the chrome-plated blade.

After tossing the weapon on the chair, he returned his focus to Tracy's lifeless eyes. They stared up at him, her killer, with a mixture of surprise and bewilderment. Without bothering to close them, he eased himself down on her blood-drenched body. Words flowed from his mouth in a haunting whisper that could no longer frighten his young victim.

"I want you dead, that's how I want you."

Covered with blood and breathing heavily, he lifted himself from Tracy's slender body, and then walked to the shower. Drops of blood and semen marked his grizzly trail. It had taken Coutre less than a minute to commit his second unspeakable crime.

## The White House
## President's Living Quarters

An hour had passed since the president escorted Robin to the limousine that would return her to her husband. He was now seated at the small desk in his private study, critiquing a newly drafted speech calculated to nudge obstinate members of his own party into supporting a crime bill which, at the moment, seemed doomed.

His attention was abruptly diverted by the pulsing tone of his private phone. Irked by the interruption, he grabbed the handset and with a push of his finger, began the conversation, "Yes, what is it?

"It's your brother Michael, Mr. President. He called on your private line."

"Thanks Ruthie, I've got it."

The president pushed the flashing light to the left of the keypad. "Mike! I can't believe it's really you. How are you?"

"I'm fine Jim," he said with detectable reluctance. "It's been a while."

"It sure has. I've missed you."

"That's what I called about. Do you think we could get together ... soon?"

"Sure," replied the president, concerned over the possible motivation of his brother's request, "is everything all right, Mike? Are you okay?"

"I think we just need to talk."

"When do you want to get together?" asked the president.

Mike's voice lightened up, "You're the guy that probably has the tougher schedule. You tell me."

The president rummaged through a stack of papers and retrieved his weekly schedule. By necessity, the four-page single spaced document was updated no less than once a day by Appointments Secretary Bainbridge. Foreseeable appointments and appearances left little time for personal concerns. "How about ... Well first, how long can you stay? At least a couple of days I hope."

"Just one, I think. Parish priests don't have much time to travel. Not on short notice anyway."

"How about next Monday or Tuesday, here at the White House?"

There were no gaps in his immediate itinerary. Whichever day his brother chose would have to be cleared.

"Tuesday would be fine. No big plans, okay? Just you and me."

"Sure, Mike," the president assured his brother. "Are you certain that everything's okay?

"It'll be good to see you, Jim. This may sound silly, but how do I get in?"

"With your brother in the White House for over six years, you shouldn't have to ask – just tell them who you are at the front gate. Oh! And be sure to have some identification along. The security people around here have been pretty wound up lately."

## Washington, D.C.
## The Stardust Hotel

Following a long hot shower, Coutre dressed himself, then moved to the end of the bed where Tracy Parks' naked body remained on gruesome exhibit. Her blood-smeared legs were spread open, the way he had left them.

The Frenchman leaned forward and placed the middle finger of his right hand in her pubic hair where he retrieved a small sample of the clear fluid that had seeped from her vagina. After rubbing the slippery substance between his

94

fingers, he sniffed it, then smeared the useless liquid across the cooling flesh of Tracy's left ankle.

A quick search of the bureau produced a yellow half-used pad of paper upon which Coutre wrote a telephone number. As soon as he was finished, he ripped off the page with the number and proceeded to place it in his pocket. He then placed the remainder of the unused pad back in the bureau under a bright red satin blouse.

Before he left the room, he picked up Tracy's purse and dumped its contents on the bed next to her body. His three hundred dollars and sixty that belonged to her was now his.

## MAY 22
### The White House
### President's Living Quarters

"T-minus ten seconds and counting ... seven ... six ... We have a go for main engine start ... two ... one ... We have SRB ignition ... Lift off. We have lift off!"

The range control officer at the Kennedy Space Center detailed the liftoff of *Endeavour* to an eager, but small audience. SPACENET 2 was beaming the event over Transponder 9, NASA's regular satellite feed channel, to the White House and any network, organization, or individuals who cared enough to watch.

The president, captivated by the spectacular launch of the 4.4-million-pound spacecraft, was resting comfortably in his favorite chair. The crackling thunder of the solid rocket boosters filled his residence and his heart with hope.

Only a select few knew the true purpose of *Endeavour's* mission. By the end of the day, he would know whether LEPERS was operational. He would know whether they had a chance to prevent the delivery and possible use of four nuclear weapons.

## Washington, D.C.
## Fox Hall Road

"Wealth has its privileges," Henry Saperstein thought to himself as he eased his car next to the curb in one of D.C.'s plusher residential areas known as Fox Hall.

The lavish structure sprawled before him was a tribute to good taste and the success of Jonathan Brock's chain of nearly three hundred furniture stores.

Before Henry could remove his finger from the doorbell, Patricia Brock, unaccustomed to media attention that didn't relate to her husband or his businesses, opened the door, excited over the prospect of an upbeat interview regarding her longtime friendship with Robin Holdridge. She wore a white sun dress and a perpetual smile.

Except for an extra twenty pounds, the thirty-six-year-old woman reminded Henry of Hollywood screen legend, Natalie Wood. Ten of those pounds, he mused, appeared to be chest. Warm greetings, coffee in china cups, and cordial banter fulfilled all of Henry's social obligations.

His reputation for cajoling salient facts from individuals, who had no intention of divulging them, was well deserved. He usually began by lulling his subject into unguarded complacency with inconsequential chitchat. Today's probe would be no exception.

For thirty minutes, his conversation with Patricia Brock couldn't have been more pleasant or further from the purpose of his visit. When she finally said, "Henry, please, just call me Patty," he knew it was time.

"Patty," he began, "when did you first learn that Robin was having an affair?"

The question, so out of step with the tone and supposed intent of the interview visibly flustered the unsuspecting woman. The smile that she had sported for the past half hour dissolved for the first time.

"What affair?"

Her acting job was so pitiful that she attempted to re-answer the question without further prompting from her inquisitor.

"I myself know of no affair," she bristled.

Henry waited a long moment before speaking. He wanted Patty's own miserable performance to convince her that the fabrication would never fly.

"Come on Patty, her affair is about to become public knowledge. Everyone in town knows about it. I'm just trying to defend Robin. I want her side." Henry continued his subterfuge. "It's not going to look good for her unless people understand her ... understand why?"

"I only know that she's been unhappy ... for a long time."

"Unhappy in her marriage?" asked Henry.

Patty assumed the demeanor of a small girl caught cheating by her teacher.

"Yes."

He tried again. "How long has the affair gone on?"

Seconds passed with no answer. Finally, with reluctance, she replied, "A while, I guess. I really can't say."

Patty Brock had already said enough. She had confirmed one all-important fact; Robin Holdridge was having an extramarital affair.

"Does her husband know?" asked Henry.

"I don't know. I don't think so."

He reached for the coveted brass ring. "How long has she been seeing James Atwater?"

To Henry's disappointment, Patty appeared to be truly shocked.

"The president," she stammered, "I don't know anything about that. She's been seeing someone, but I don't think ..."

He could see the light bulb over Patricia Brock's head. In a microsecond, the implications of this interview and the role into which she had suddenly been thrust, dawned on her. She found herself in unfamiliar territory approaching imminent catastrophe.

Suddenly, she was a victim. A single thought flashed through her mind – "Shut up!"

"I don't want to talk to you anymore," she stood. "Mr. Saperstein, please leave ... and this interview never took place. I'll deny it."

"What happened to Henry?" he asked, unable to conceal his delight. It was of no consequence that she was kicking him out of the house, but he did resent the woman's threat to recant her confirmation of the affair. "I'll leave, Mrs. Brock, but don't kid yourself about this interview."

He picked up the small recorder that he had informed her of at the outset of the interview and tapped it with his index finger. A cold shiver ignored the summer day and raced down Patty Brock's spine. Henry Saperstein had added an important piece to a scandalous puzzle.

## Washington, D.C.
## Stardust Hotel

Detective Willie Russell, nicknamed 'Slick' by his fellow officers, was leaning against the wall of Tracy Parks' small apartment, trying to imagine what circumstances led to the young woman's bloody death. He and Detective Ted Osborne were working out of D.C. police headquarters on Indiana Avenue where all the homicides committed in the city's eight districts were assigned.

The Stardust Motel was situated within the seamy boundaries of district seven, infamous for prostitution, drugs, and gang activity. Forensic specialists, photographers, and a waiting coroner had all gawked at the blood-crusted body stretched crudely across the room's only bed.

Willie watched in disgust while several of the onlookers made sick remarks that revealed a surprising lack of compassion, and to a lesser degree, seemed to place them in the same category as the perpetrator. There was no doubt in his mind that many of the cops he worked with had mutated into the very thing they were chasing.

The first uniformed officer on the scene, Sergeant Mazlowski approached the twenty-year veteran.

"It's the shits when they're so young, huh, Slick?"

"Murder's always the shits," Willie said in a flat monotone.

"What do you think?" asked Mazlowski.

"I can think of about a thousand crazy assholes out there who would think this was a lot of fun."

Daniel Braemer, a brash young assistant from the coroner's office, approached Detective Russell. "Can we package the broad and get outta here?"

Braemer's attitude pissed Willie off. "I'll tell you when it's time. Just stand over there with your thumb up your ass and try not to get in the way," he snapped.

"I hope I get to pick you up some day, ya' dork!" exclaimed Braemer.

The other detective in the room, Ted Osborne, had heard enough of what was said to know that he'd better step between Willie and the young squirt with the big mouth. "Back off, buddy! We'll unleash you when it's time, okay?"

Braemer, muttering a string of obscenities, shuffled to the side of the room while Osborne paused to look at the body sprawled across the bed.

"Her name's Tracy Parks. She's sixteen, a runaway; been on the streets less than a year. No steady boyfriend. I cornered her pimp downstairs – a guy named 'The Light' – unfucking believable, huh! He's the one that found her and phoned the station."

"Has he got an alibi?" asked Willie.

"The best – he was in our custody until about two hours ago."

"Fuck!" exclaimed Willie. "Why couldn't this one be easy?"

"Parsons just spoke with one of the girls that works the same area as the victim, claims she saw her climb into a late-model Firebird, she thinks it was red, about 10:30 last night. Of course, she didn't see the driver."

"Of course," said Willie.

"There's evidence of drug use – shit, Slick, looks like the same old two and two. She musta picked up some kinda creep."

Willie, ignoring his fellow detective's oversimplified conclusion, walked closer to the foot of the bed and stared at the girl's dead body. Osborne followed and stood a half-step behind him.

"Doc White says the guy probably laid on her stomach, in the blood, and fucked her after he killed her. That's not your guy next door," said Osborne.

"Let's just hope this isn't the beginning of some serial killer bullshit!" said Willie.

"What's the difference!" Osborne shrugged, "we gotta do somethin'."

Willie Russell walked away.

## Washington, D.C.
## Royal Haven Motel

All of Pierre Coutre's personal belongings, including the Teac tape player, were packed in the trunk of the Pontiac Firebird. Only one chore remained. He walked to the passenger side of his car, opened the door, and retrieved a small canvas traveling bag.

Upon entering his room, the Frenchman opened the zippered bag and withdrew a half-dozen beer and soft drink cans. Each container was painstakingly wrapped in Saran Wrap. With care, he removed the clear coverings, making certain he returned each piece of crumpled plastic to the canvas grip. He then distributed the beverage containers in a random fashion throughout the already trashed interior of the room.

From the bottom of the bag he recovered several torn pieces of paper which he placed in the wastebasket next to the sink in the bathroom. From one of the bags' outer pockets, he removed tattered copies of Penthouse and Playboy magazines. With no particular finesse, he pitched them on the floor next to the bed.

A quick survey of the room satisfied him that everything was in place. As he stepped into the damp night air, he paused, reached around to the inside of the door, and retrieved a DO NOT DISTURB sign which he then hung on the outer door knob. Smiling at his own cleverness, he slipped behind the wheel of his car and proceeded to melt into a seamless flow of inner-city traffic.

## Vice President's Residence

Robin had just stepped out of the shower when the phone next to her bed rang. The call was coming in on line two, her private number. She recognized the caller's voice immediately.

"Jimmy, it's good to hear from you," Robin said cheerfully.

"Hi, Rob," Jimmy said, "I'm sorry to bother you ..."

Robin interrupted. "I only wish my little brother would bother me more often."

"I got a call from a woman named, Paula. She said that she had information that would be important to you and your future. I didn't know what to say. She wanted your number, but I wouldn't give it to her."

"Good. Is that all she said?"

"Well," Jimmy stammered, "the last thing she said was 'Sex scandals never go away. Remind her of that.' That sex thing is what made me call. I didn't mention this to mom and dad. Do you know what she's talking about?"

Robin shuddered at the possibilities. "No. There are a lot of kooks out there. I don't know what she could be raving about. Did she leave a number where she could be reached? I'll turn it over to the Secret Service."

"Yeah. She said she'd be there all day tomorrow."

## The Washington Post
## Editor's Office

The take-up reel on the small audio recorder in Henry Saperstein's hand snapped to a halt. It took James Wingate, leaning back in his leather chair, a few seconds to absorb what he had just heard. Elizabeth Freeman, hearing the recording for the first time, couldn't conceal her shock.

"It's true. We need confirmation, but it's true."

Wingate removed a butane lighter encased in a gold-colored case bearing his initials from his pocket and lit the huge black cigar that was clenched firmly between his teeth

"What do we have for sure?" he asked.

"We have an admission by Patty Brock that her friend, Robin Holdridge, is having an affair and we've got a pretty good idea who she's banging," answered Henry."

"Nothing but smoke," observed Beth, "large billowing clouds of black smoke."

"That smoke," Wingate savored the thought as he expelled a large puff of smoke from his own cigar, "is all coming from the president's ass." He placed the leafy black cylinder on the edge of an ashtray and leaned forward.

"Don't leak a word of this. Don't even discuss it 'in house.' I don't want some half-assed gossip columnist piecemealing this story into something palatable. I want all the facts and I want to create a wave so goddamn big that it swamps this whole fucking town!"

## Minnesota
## Interstate-35

Tabou and his men had spent the night in the parking lot of a state-operated rest area located on I-35 six miles south of Rush City, Minnesota. It was Parker who had drawn up their trip plan and suggested that Tabou sequester his restless cohorts in their vehicles until such time as they reached their destination. He feared that public exposure to heavy accents and Mideast dispositions could precipitate an incident that might alert authorities to the presence of a foreign entity; this would negate a crucial advantage – surprise.

Tabou's decision to follow Parker's recommendation, though practical, was far from popular. Vans crammed full of weapons and gear forced human cargo to seek rest in an imaginative assortment of contorted positions.

If it were not for a series of nasty thunderstorms, they would have arrived at their destination the previous night. In the end, fatigue dictated the layover. The last thing they needed was an accident. Machine guns and rockets, strewn across a Midwestern interstate, would unquestionably attract a mission-ending degree of attention.

It was 6:30 a.m. when Bonilla, the first of his group to awaken, slid open the side door of his Chevy van and stepped into the cool morning air- it was only 48 degrees. His decision to wear a T-shirt, rather than the long sleeve flannels chosen by his comrades, was a mistake that he immediately understood.

Except for the diesel rumble of two idling semitrailer trucks parked at opposite ends of an area specifically designated for the commercial behemoths, and a small compact car with no driver, the vicinity appeared void of travelers. By the time the warm-blooded Cuban cut across the well-manicured picnic area and reached the visitors building, he was chilled to the bone.

Just inside the door, he shook like a wet dog. The cold, he quickly discovered, was not so easily shed. An instant attraction to a row of vending machines was cut short by the demands of nature. He reached the first of a half dozen urinals just in time; his much-needed release almost occurred before he freed himself.

As he stood, a mysterious feeling stirred his lifelong penchant for paranoia. He didn't know why, but he was almost certain that he was being watched. A quick glance over each shoulder failed to confirm his fear.

With his business finished, he walked to a nearby sink and began washing his hands. The water felt good, so he lingered a few extra seconds, savoring its warmth. When he raised his head to look in the mirror, he saw the reflection of another man, standing just behind him.

"What do you want?" Bonilla asked gruffly.

The man, no more than seventeen or eighteen years of age, appeared hurt by the Cuban's brusque manner.

"My name's Paul. I could be your friend," he said meekly. "Do you like me?"

Bonilla, still half asleep, didn't catch on – he smiled.

"Yeah kid," he said, looking down at the water cascading over his hands, "just go away."

The young man persisted, placing his hand on Bonilla's back. "I love your accent. May I touch you? Or, would you like to touch me?"

It hit Bonilla all at once. He turned off the faucet and spun around to face his much taller admirer.

"Are you a fucking fag?" he growled.

The boy removed his hand and made a quick side-to-side check, assuring himself that he had a clear avenue of escape.

"Don't hurt me," he said, still clinging to the possibility that the Cuban would succumb to his advances. "I could make you very happy."

In a single catlike motion, Bonilla thrust his wet hand into the young man's long blond hair and with all of his force, pulled the boy's delicately featured face forward against the sink's chromed faucet. Blood spewed from the lad's broken nose, splattering both the sink and surrounding counter. The Cuban held his stunned victim at arm's length, preventing the blood that was streaming off of the boy's chin from soaking his clothing. Again, he rammed the young man's face down on the metal spigot, crushing the bone on the right side of his face and opening up a wicked gash.

"Stop it!" yelled Tabou.

Before Bonilla could release his helpless prey, Tabou seized the impetuous Cuban by the arm.

"You fool," he snarled, "we have done everything to avoid discovery. Have you no brain?"

"He's a fag," yelled Bonilla.

"No one cares what he is – use your head."

Barely conscious, Paul looked up at his attacker and the man who had stopped the senseless assault. "Thank you," he whispered, "I meant no harm."

Exhibiting the precision of a well-trained physician, Tabou reached for the boy and with a single twist, broke his neck. The young man's head, no longer attached to his spine, dangled forward against his chest while the upper half of his body fell backward to the tile floor.

"He could identify you ... and me. Watch the door," he ordered, pushing Bonilla like an errant child toward the front of the building, "see that no one enters."

The boy's angular body was still convulsing when the Jabali reached down and tore away his bloody shirt, then dragged him by the hair into the outer lobby.

"Where are you taking him?" asked Bonilla.

"We will need time. Do you see anyone?"

"No. Wait! Yes, a car is coming."

"Fuck!" Tabou screamed.

"What can we do? asked Bonilla

"Shut up and do as you are told."

Just outside the entrance to the men's lavatory, there was a windowless door identified by a small rectangular sign which read: NO ADMITTANCE. Grateful that the door swung inward, the Jabali gave it a ferocious kick – it opened.

"The woman in the car is coming this way. Should I kill her?" asked Bonilla

"No, Fool! Go back and begin to clean up the blood."

Tabou lifted the boy's body by the belt and flung him through the doorway into the room's closet-size interior. The sound of falling buckets and mops reverberated throughout the building as the lifeless corpse found its place among the many cleaning products stored there by the maintenance crew responsible for the facility's upkeep.

After tossing the blood-soaked shirt into the darkness, the Jabali pulled the door closed. He then removed his own shirt and, walking backward, mopped up the blood trail that led to the men's lavatory. He disappeared from sight just as the woman entered the front door.

"She must not see us," Tabou whispered to the Cuban.

"Why not kill her?"

"Is that all you know? Save your killing for those who need it. It is you who should die, Cuban. Your mindless stupidity has increased our risk of discovery. Finish cleaning up this mess so we can leave. Don't forget to wipe off everything you have touched."

"How long will it be before they discover the body?"

From the contemptuous expression on the Jabali's face, Bonilla knew that he had asked a stupid question. A question to which there could be no certain answer.

With their grisly chores complete, both men stepped into the entry and watched as the young woman sauntered back to her car. She would never know how lucky she had been; had she walked into the visitors building a few seconds earlier, her trip and her life would have ended in a terrifying moment of violence.

After a muscle loosening stretch, she climbed into her automobile and pulled slowly away from the curb.

"Let's go." Tabou commanded.

Together they sprinted for their respective vans. "Tell Arbash we must leave now," yelled the Jabali as he ran.

Bonilla entered the van through the front passenger side door. In order to stretch out in the vehicle's bucket seat, the slumbering Arbash had twisted his body into a shape that challenged the limits of human mechanics.

"We must go!" yelled the excited Cuban. "We must leave now!

"Fuck. What's wrong?" muttered the Palestinian, clearly irritated by the Cuban's screeching.

"Tabou killed a guy inside."

The other van had already backed up and pulled away from the curb by the time Arbash gathered his senses enough to turn the ignition key. "Why would he do something so stupid?" he asked groggily.

Bonilla remained silent, unwilling to divulge his responsibility in the fiasco. The Palestinian continued. "He knows that our presence must not be known."

# CHAPTER FIVE

## MAY 23
## Washington, D.C.
## Police Headquarters

Detective Willie Russell was poring over the coroner's autopsy report on Tracy Parks. Several readings of the wordy document had not produced any information that hadn't been uncovered at the scene.

The sperm and hair samples were useless until they had a suspect. Everything so far pointed toward a random encounter. Perhaps the perpetrator was a transient just passing through town. A man on vacation who wanted to visit the Lincoln Memorial, see the Capitol, and brutally murder a sixteen-year-old girl. "What a fucking world," Willie exclaimed to no one but himself.

Pissed at life in general, he shoved the five-page analysis in the case file and dropped the folder into the bottom right hand drawer of his desk. Edward Gray, who did most of the departments fingerprint work, knocked once on the door. Without waiting for an invitation, he entered.

"I think we've got somethin' here, Slick."

"You forensic pricks haven't come up with anything useful in months. They might as well board up that cave you live in downstairs."

"Yeah! Well outside 'a you holdin' down that desk with your feet, I haven't seen a lot of activity in this office," Gray countered.

"What is it this time? You couldn't lift the prints, find the prints, read the prints, match the prints. Just tell me so I can give up all fucking hope of any contribution from your so-called department."

Gray collapsed into one of the two relics that passed for chairs in front of Russell's desk.

"Fuck you, Slick! On the Parks' case, other than the victims, we lifted fifteen different prints from the room. Eight of them are unknowns, six sets belong to a variety of locals, including a guy named Terrance Chapfield. He was picked up a year ago for showin' his dick to a 17-year-old shopper. Another print belongs to a congressional aide who whores around town regularly.

The third print is the interesting one. We found it in the shower. We ran it through a dozen files before Interpol, of all organizations, gave us a make. It belongs to a Frenchman named Pierre Patrice Coutre – at least that's the name he was born with. They list twenty or so known aliases. And get this! The guy is one of the world's most infamous criminals. The son-of-a-bitch has a blood trail as long as an elephant's dick. The fucker makes Jack the Ripper look like Barney Rubble."

Willie clasped his hands behind his head and tipped further back in his chair.

"Great! A new homicidal maniac in town."

"We've requested more information. If this guy's the perp. we could have a major hitter on our hands."

Detective Osborne strolled unceremoniously through Russell's open office door, "We got somethin', he said in a tone totally lacking in excitement."

Astounded by their timing, Willie threw his hands high in the air.

"Shit! I go weeks on end with nothing. Then you two clowns show up at the same time. What happened? Did the department start paying commissions?"

Osborne paid no attention to Willie's raving, "We found about a dozen phone numbers written on everything from matchbooks to napkins. A girl like that makes a lot of friends I guess. Anyway, we checked them all out, including a number we lifted from a scratch pad that showed an indentation from a page that was apparently torn off. Guess what? We got a bingo! I just got off the phone with a gal that says the room number on the pad is one of two rooms registered to a Philip Moran. Here's the kicker. The guy drives a Pontiac Firebird. A red Pontiac Firebird."

Willie dropped his feet to the floor and moved forward in his chair. "Is he still registered there?"

"Yeah, he's paid up through tomorrow."

Willie rose to his feet.

"Hi-ho silver!" he exclaimed, retrieving his jacket from the clothes tree to the right of his desk.

Gray, hands raised, backed off, "Yeah, well I'm no Tonto! I don't do any of that hero shit! If this guy's Coutre, you'd better take along nuclear weapons. He's one bad fuck!

## The Vice President's Residence

The telephone number given to Robin by her brother required further investigation. Under normal circumstances she would turn the caller over to the Secret Service. But

112

when you're embroiled in an affair with the president, vulnerability is an inescapable consequence. Alone in her bedroom, she dialed the seven-digit number. It was a local call.

After two rings, a woman's voice answered the phone. "Yes,"

"You contacted my brother. What do you want?" There was a long pause.

"I want to talk. I have information that is vital to your future."

"What kind of information?"

"I don't want to get into it over the phone. Meet me at 3 p.m. tomorrow at the Sheridan Hotel, downtown, room 323."

"I don't meet strangers in hotels."

"Your husband has a birthmark on the inside of his upper thigh about two inches below his testicles. He's also got a small black mole on his lower abdomen, just above his pubic hair. Don't be late."

### Royal Haven Motel

In the wake of a twenty-four-hour vigil, common sense forced Willie Russell and a small army of undercover officers to abandon any hope that Coutre or his party would return to their rooms.

The young night clerk at the Royal Haven Motel, Tim Pasonivich, freed the lock and watched from a safe distance as two uniformed officers stepped through the door into one of the rooms registered under Coutre's alias, Philip Moran. A brief search confirmed what a tiny television camera slid under the door had shown them. The room was empty. Pasonivich, entered the room.

"How many people did you see in this room?" Russell asked the wide-eyed twenty-year-old.

"One, I believe."

"Are you sure?" asked Russell.

"Yeah, I just saw the one guy. But like I told you before; I could hear a bunch of guys in here, they were kind of loud."

"Loud?" asked Willie.

"Yeah, their voices were loud, and the TV was really cranked up. Monica works from three to eleven, you should talk to her. She checked 'em in. In fact, one of 'em tried to hit on her. When she didn't go along with it, the guy turned psycho or something."

Osborne, holding a pencil with a beer can impaled on the end of it, chimed in. "What do you mean by psycho?"

"I mean he started swearin' and callin' her names. You know, a real masher."

Osborne turned to Russell. "I suppose we should talk to her, huh?"

"No shit!" exclaimed Willie.

## Elbow Lake
## Northern Minnesota

The cold waters of Elbow Lake meandered in an unpredictable fashion across seven thousand acres of an area known as The Great North Woods. Large pines and thick brush surrounded its rock-strewn shores. Only visitors seeking solace in an unspoiled wilderness and willing to forsake an assortment of creature comforts were attracted to the areas numerous lakes and vast acreage of virgin forests.

A two-lane blacktop highway, that encircled all but the north end of the lake, provided the only surfaced access to the area. The narrow gravel road maintained a half to quarter of-a mile distance from the shore itself. Despite its proximity to the lake, there were only one or two places along the narrow winding road where you could see through the brush and trees to the water's surface.

Nestled into the northwest corner of the lake, amidst a thick stand of mature Jack pine, stood a modest two-bedroom cabin. From the slump of the poorly braced roof, it was easy to identify the vintage structure as a hastily constructed pre-code building of the late forties. The small two bedroom hideaway, probably erected by a weekend carpenter on a limited budget, rested fewer than thirty yards from water's edge. A coat of chocolate brown paint helped the primitive summer retreat melt unobtrusively into the sheltered protection of the surrounding forest.

In vivid contrast to the modest living accommodations, a pair of Mariah Z-275 Davanti speed boats, each powered by a 415 horse V-8 inboard engine, were tied on either side of the badly weathered dock built to service the cabin's occupants. The rickety four-foot-wide platform extended nearly sixty feet from shore into the lake's unsullied water

Two muddy wheel ruts connected the gravel perimeter road with the rear of the cabin. Parked on the east side of the building were two late model vans bearing Virginia plates. On the small screen porch, built around the front entry, five of the world's most wanted criminals enjoyed the beauty and serenity of Minnesota, the "Land of 10,000 Lakes."

## MAY 24
## The White House
## Oval Office

CIA Director Matthew Handelman, Sean, and the president, were seated on two couches adjacent to the Oval Office fireplace. Their attention was directed toward eight large photographs spread haphazardly across the antique surface of the walnut coffee table positioned between them.

With great interest, the trio examined the pictures as Handelman explained, "Even with LEPERS it wasn't easy to spot. The Maradah Mountains are as remote and hidden as any location in Jabal. It's no wonder the Israelis have had trouble."

The president examined the highly magnified photographs. "How sure?" he asked.

"These photographs have been analyzed by our National Photographic Interpretation Center and DEFSMAC, the Defense Special Missile and Astronautics Center. Every opinion has been in the affirmative. This is it."

"Any consensus on a completion date?"

"Just about impossible. The NSC has recorded some radio traffic that might indicate six or seven days. They're still sifting through thousands of potentially pertinent transmissions. We do know that there are no vehicles, in our estimation, large enough to haul a completed bomb out of those mountains. So, it's reasonable to assume that they aren't going to move them in the next couple of days."

"Do we have any operatives in the area?" asked the president.

"No sir. In fact, we have only a handful of 'friendlies' in the whole country. It seems they'll take our money for anything except spying on a fellow Jabali. I think it has more to do with fear, than with loyalty."

"If Kabazi loses his bombs in an Israeli raid, what will he do? Can we keep our part in the Israeli air attack a secret?" asked the president.

"My guess is, there won't be an American anywhere in the world that will be safe from terrorist bombings. The Israelis are going to need a comprehensive briefing on the assembly sight, complete with photographs. That means that all the personnel involved, even the pilots, are going to know the source of their reconnaissance. Somehow, someway, this type of high profile intelligence always finds the wrong ears. Kabazi is paranoid as hell anyway, he'll know, or at least suspect, who put the finger on him."

"What if we hold back the detail and provide the Israelis with a location only?" asked the president. Handelman began gathering his photographs.

"They're going to get one chance. No more. I don't think the success of their mission can be guaranteed with a simple geographic fix on the target. The area is well defended and nestles into the side of a mountain. Their pilots will need to see these photographs. I wouldn't recommend that we short change them like that, Mr. President."

The president stood.

"You're right. Let's give them the whole nine yards. I'll send Herb Wells, Assistant Secretary of State, to Israel as soon as the arrangements can be made. He'll set up a briefing with you and deliver the information to Prime Minister Davidtz, personally. Give Wells everything you've got, right up to the moment he leaves."

While gathering his photographs, Handelman assured the president that his instructions would be carried out to the letter. As they walked to the door, the chief executive placed his hand on the Director's shoulder, "You guys have done a hell of job on this, Matt."

## Sheraton Hotel
## Washington, D.C.

Accompanied by Agent Daniel Warren, Robin Holdridge approached the third floor room of the mysterious woman who had contacted her brother, demanding a meeting.

"I haven't seen Marie for years," Robin gushed, paranoid that her exuberance, designed to hide her deception, sounded as phony to the agent as it did to herself.

"Would you like me to go in with you?" he asked.

"No. That's not necessary. I promised her this would be private."

When they arrived at room 323, the agent stepped to one side while Robin tapped gently on the door. Within a few seconds, an attractive brunette appeared – she couldn't have been more than twenty five years old. The woman's face was sullen and intractable; not the demeanor one would expect from an old high school chum.

Robin acted quickly, wrapping the surprised woman in her arms.

"Marie! It's been so long." Momentum, and a little extra push, forced both women into the room, allowing the heavy oak door to close.

Inside, Robin quickly released her grip, stepping backward away from the stranger who had demanded this bizarre meeting. Her enthusiasm, along with her smile, disappeared.

"What's the 'Marie' bullshit all about?" the young woman asked.

"The man with me is a Secret Service Agent. I told him I was going to see an old friend."

"I'm no friend, lady. Are you wearing a wire?"

"No," Robin replied.

"That's not good enough."

The woman stepped forward and initiated a pat search of Robin's body."

"Are you kidding?" Robin cried out indignantly, recoiling from the woman's touch."

"I'm not kidding, and you'd better not be fucking with me. One word from me, and you and your kinky old man will find out what it's like to work for a living."

Robin was seething at the indignity the woman was forcing her to endure. "Who are you?" she asked, as the woman ran both of her hands along the inside of her thighs.

"You can call me Paula."

Paula finished her search then walked from the hall into the hotel room's unimaginative living area furnished with the usual double-bed, credenza, and small round table flanked by two uncomfortable looking wooden chairs.

"Sit down," Paula said, gesturing to one of the two chairs.

Robin stopped just inside the room and continued to stand. "I'm not here to make friends. How do you know so much about my husband? What's this all about?"

"Okay, if that's the way you want it. I fucked him. Of course, you must have figured that out by now."

Even though common sense had prepared her for the moment, the caustic beauty's brazen admission was infuriating. For years Robin had suspected that Sidney was unfaithful, but she could never prove it; not until now.

The woman continued, "From what I hear it's not an exclusive club, but I am a card-carrying member."

"Okay," Robin said coldly, "so you slept with my husband. I'm sure that's not your first experience."

"Well from what your husband said, I don't think matters of sex are really your strong point."

Robin had heard enough. She whirled toward the door.

"I'm pregnant," Paula shouted.

Eyes ablaze, Robin turned to face her nemesis. "How would someone like you know whose baby you are carrying?"

"I know," Paula growled.

Robin wanted more confirmation, "I don't believe you!"

"Do you want to bet your future on it, rich bitch?"

"Do you?" asked Robin.

"This IS my future, and I'm going to grab it."

"Prove it."

"I have a witness. A very interesting witness."

"You mean there were three of you?" Robin asked.

"Yeah, my husband was there."

"He watched?"

"That's right. You don't know, do you?"

"Know what?"

"Your old man is 'bi.' He swings from either side of the plate. It was Clifford he was after. I was just along for variety. It's not every day you can fuck a vice president. We made it kind of a family thing."

Irregular pieces from a thousand puzzles fell into place with a horrible thud. Why hadn't she thought of it before? Unresolved images raced through her mind; knowing smiles, unforeseen meetings, the feminine young men who fussed over her husband's every move – it was all agonizingly clear.

The pain in Robin's face was clear and unmistakable. Paula knew that she had dealt her adversary a heart-rending blow. The 'media creation' that she was so eager to crush, suddenly became a person. Her voice softened. "You really didn't know, did you?"

"It doesn't matter what I knew. What do you want?"

The defiance in Robin's voice nudged Paula out of her empathetic lull. "Money, pure and simple."

"If this is about money, why didn't you talk to my husband?"

"Neither you or your husband could be reached; we tried for two weeks. I was the one that thought of contacting your brother. I got his name from an article in *People* that I found at the library."

"Where's your husband?"

"Cliff really hasn't got the balls for this."

A startling metal-on-metal click compelled Robin to turn around. A dark-skinned young man opened the bathroom door and stepped into the hall. He was short, young, and possibly Italian. His black curly hair could be attributed to any one of a dozen nationalities.

"My wife frequently underestimates me," he said, thrusting his open hand toward Robin. "I'm Clifford."

She ignored it. "I couldn't give you a number, but I'll bet blackmail carries a pretty stiff sentence in the District of Columbia."

"Worst case for us; we'll all be famous," Paula said, allowing a smile to warm her pretty face. "I'll write a book, tell Oprah my naughty tale of seduction and become a Jennifer Flowers-type celebrity. On the flip-side, middle-aged politicians who seduce newlyweds and leave them with a child find themselves disgraced and out of work. You two will be lucky to catch on with the post office. Sure, we might get slapped on the wrist, but who could blame two young parents charged with raising a tiny child for seeking financial help?"

"How much help?" Robin asked.

"For two hundred and fifty thousand dollars, I'll get an abortion and we'll disappear ... forever."

## The White House
## Main Building

A White House security guard was escorting Mike Atwater toward the elevator that would transport him to his brother's private residence. Though he was slighter of build and two inches shorter, his resemblance to the president was striking. The sight of him a half building away stepped up Sean MacDougal's brisk walk to a near trot. Until Jim moved to Washington, Sean and Mike were close and always maintained a sporadic yet continual line of communication.

It had been ten years since the pair had swapped fish stories at the family summer residence on Lake Vermillion, in the Atwater's home state of Minnesota. Even though he had known him since he was a teenager, the old Irishman addressed his friend with a salutation befitting his position. Enthusiastic smiles warmed both of their faces.

"Welcome, Father!" Sean gave him an enthusiastic hug. "It's been a long time."

Mike returned the embrace with equal fervor, "Sean, I've thought of you so many times."

The Irishman held him at arm's length. "Where have you been, Mike? Your brother and I have missed you."

"Finding my way, Sean. I was lost."

"Well thank God you're here with us now. Jim's been held up with an emergency meeting of the National Security Council. He said to make yourself at home and that he'd be here as soon as he can. He's excited to see you."

## Washington, D.C.
## Woodley Park

Henry Saperstein and Beth Freeman had talked their way into the fourth floor apartment of former Holdridge campaign advisor, Clinton Walsh. The thirty-eight-year-old attorney, dressed in a black sweat suit and wearing running shoes, ushered the two reporters into the elegant confines of his spacious den. It didn't take a Rhodes Scholar to figure out that Mr. Walsh was a wealthy man.

"So, you guys are doing a feature on old Sidney," he began.

"Yes," answered Henry, confirming the deception he had perpetrated in dozens of interviews.

"Well, like I told you on the phone, you've come to the wrong guy. I wouldn't piss on him if he were on fire. Does that surprise you?" asked Walsh.

Clinton Walsh's undisguised contempt for his former client caught his inquisitor off-guard. With just a few words, he had rendered Henry's plan of attack useless.

"Maybe," Beth cut in, "you're just the person we're looking for. In conjunction with our feature, we are investigating allegations that the vice president's wife is having an affair with another high-profile Washington resident."

"Again, I think you're talking to the wrong man. I don't have any dirt on Robin Holdridge. I only met her a couple of times. She seemed okay, but from what I saw, her taste in men left something to be desired."

"Did they seem like a happy couple?" asked Beth.

"Who knows? I hardly ever saw them together. You know it's been over two years since the election."

Henry's decision to stand signaled an end to the interview, prompting Beth to retrieve the microcassette recorder that she had placed on the corner of the desk. Walsh remained seated.

"Put that thing away, and I'll give you a little dirt, off the record," offered Walsh.

Beth dropped the recorder into her purse and closed the leather flap. "Off the record – you've got it,"

"Sidney Holdridge is a bisexual who leans pretty heavy toward the gay side. Consequently, I don't think he spends too much time drooling over the abundant assets of his pert little wife."

"How do you know?" asked Henry.

"I was his lover," Walsh declared with an 'in your face' delivery. "I came out of the closet over a year ago. So, I really don't mind telling you. Maybe it'll get the sleazy little bastard in trouble. Remember, no source on this! That was the deal."

"What happened between you two? Off the record," asked Beth, not expecting an answer.

Walsh grinned, "Probably the same reason his wife is in someone else's bed. He was a cheat. You couldn't trust him. The little worm slept around and around and around. I violated my own rule – you can't fuck a politician – they're already fucked."

## Washington, D.C.

Post-rush hour traffic on I-395 had slowed Henry Saperstein's new Chevy Nova to a maddening crawl. Both he and his passenger, Constance Freeman, were eager to reach their offices at the Washington Post. This delay would normally set a match to Henry's Type A personality, but not tonight. He was not going to allow anything so trivial to overshadow their recent coup.

For a second time, Beth replayed the interview with Clinton Walsh on her small audio recorder. At the conclusion of the tape, she tucked the small unit back in her purse.

"Well, we know Holdridge is gay and his wife has a lover. Either one of those facts, in print, would light one hell of a bonfire," mused Beth.

"We don't want fires. We want explosions," Henry exclaimed with undisguised glee.

"We still haven't put her in Atwater's bed," Beth reminded him.

"We're a lot closer," Henry grinned, "we've got her standing in the bedroom reaching for his dick."

## The White House
## President's Living Quarters

The president flew through the door of his residence, past his valet and into the main living room. Mike barely had time to stand before his brother's long-awaited embrace engulfed him. Both men were overwhelmed with profound feelings generated by the long-anticipated reunion.

Tears welled in the president's eyes, "Mike! I've missed you so much! My God." Again, they embraced. "I've got so many questions."

"It's been a long time, Jim."

Minutes turned into hours as the two brothers rekindled their relationship. Childhood memories, particularly those involving their parents, peppered their conversation with warm remembrances.

"Why?" the president asked, "Why so long?"

"Escape," answered his brother.

"The press couldn't have hounded you that much."

"It wasn't the press. I needed the church more than the church needed me."

"Why didn't you stay in touch? We've only spoken twice since I came to Washington. You wouldn't take my calls. You wouldn't return my calls. What did I say or do?"

"I just couldn't face you."

"What do you mean by that?"

The president stood, then walked toward the fireplace while his brother, head bowed, remained seated on the couch.

A long moment of silence was finally broken by Mike's whispered voice, "There is a lot you don't know."

"Like what?" asked the president.

"Twelve years and I still don't know how to tell you."

"Try."

"I'm so sorry," Mike placed his hands to his forehead and moved forward on the couch.

"Sorry about what?" Come on, what's this all about?" asked the president.

"Megan was on her way to see me when she was killed."

"To you?"

"Yes!" Mike said. "We were having an affair! She was late and hurrying to meet me."

"Bullshit! She wouldn't ..."

"Yes!" Mike's voice began to crack. "She would!"

"No!" shouted the president, "I loved her ... she loved me."

127

He crossed the room and attempted to grab his brother by the arm. Before he could secure his grip, Mike wrenched himself free and stood.

"You may have loved her, but you were never there! Never! You were busy running for the Senate. You were always running for something and away from her. Think about it! You were gone so much we didn't even have to sneak around to see each other."

"You son-of-a-bitch!" the president growled. "My own brother, sleeping with my wife."

"She was lonely. Christie was gone, and she couldn't have any more kids. She was alone ... and I loved her."

"Well fuck you and your love – you sanctimonious bastard," he exclaimed. "Why did you come here? Why now? Just to rip me apart?"

"No," Mike said softly, "I've lived with this for a long time. I didn't want to die and not have the opportunity to ask for your forgiveness."

"Forgiveness?" asked the president. "You've got some Cro-Magnon balls, little brother. Forgiveness just isn't the first thought that jumps to mind. I'm going to need some time. What did you expect? Did you think I'd just slap you on the back and say, 'Gee, that's okay'?"

"I don't have any time," Mike said.

"What does that mean?"

"I'm dying, Jim ... cancer ... prostate cancer."

With his brother's words ringing in his ears, the president walked to the couch and sat down.

His anger, so homogeneous only seconds before, was defused by compassion. In the wake of a quiet moment of decision, he spoke. "Are you positive ... about the cancer?"

"Yes, it's not the kind you walk away from."

"I can put you in contact with the finest doctors in the world. Why don't I make an appoin ...""?

"It won't help. We've got some pretty good doctors in Minnesota too. Remember the Mayo Clinic?"

"I don't know what to say," said the president.

"Say you forgive me."

Mike placed his hand on his brother's arm. "About Megan, we both fought it. We started out as friends. She was someone I could talk to. We ...""

"I don't want to hear it. Nothing either of us can say will change anything. You are right about one thing. I wasn't there for her those last four years. That's why you didn't attend the funeral, isn't it?"

"Yes, I considered killing myself. That's when I rediscovered Jesus Christ. That, and a few memories, are the only good things that came out of the whole mess."

"So, the only reason you're here now is to ask for my forgiveness?"

"I'd like that, but, I've lived a long time without it. I want you back in the church. You haven't been to Mass since Megan died, have you?"

"No,"

"Thirty years, Jim. You were a Catholic for over thirty years. You attended Catholic school; you were married in the Catholic Church. Your family was Catholic. Megan was Catholic. What would they say? What do you say?"

"I lost my faith, and I've have seen little in the world that would restore it."

"I need your strength, Jim," Mike implored. "The church needs you. One thing I know; Megan and Christie are in heaven. Their death wasn't God's fault. Death isn't bad. It's as much a part of living as birth. It's a beginning, not an end. Was mom and dad's life for nothing? Are we going to see them again? I know I am. Soon, I'll have a chance to put my arms around them for both of us."

Memories of a time long past forced the middle-aged president to smile. "You miss them too, don't you, Mike?"

"Yes. They're never far from my thoughts. Come back. That's what I want, Jim. Come back – find what you've lost."

Mike retrieved a rosary from the inner breast pocket of his black coat. With care, he placed it in his brother's hand. "Remember how Sister Mary Clemens used to lead the eighth graders in saying the rosary? It still works. The comfort, the peace – it's still there. Look what it brought me through."

## The Vice President's Residence

It was late. Robin had waited nearly two hours for Sidney to walk through the front door. During that time, she had worked herself into a fever pitch. For ten long years she had privately shouldered most of the blame for their miserable marriage.

Throughout their abbreviated engagement, Sidney had eagerly fulfilled the role of an attentive lover. He appeared mesmerized by her sexuality. To a girl from a loving family who had been raised on a rural Illinois farm, he was a dream come true – a man of the world, successful, ambitious. She was dazzled.

To her dismay, her husband's interest withered like a prom-worn corsage. Within weeks of their Jamaican honeymoon, she realized that their storybook marriage might not have a happy ending. The time he was spending in her company, away from public view was suddenly nil. Silence replaced the near-constant flow of communication that once characterized their earlier courtship.

Her repeated attempts to breathe life into their relationship proved futile. Suggestive lingerie, one-on-one candlelight dinners and intimate spur of the moment getaways proved ineffectual. Every rebuff left her more vulnerable. As the years passed, her husband's undisguised rejection took a painful toll. While Sidney's career flourished, her own confidence dwindled. She never told anyone, not even her closest friends, how unhappy her life had become.

On a snowy Washington night, shortly after Sidney's election to a second term as vice president, she innocently suggested that they seek professional counseling for their troubled marriage. Her proposal would prove to be a benchmark in their relationship. The thought of confiding intimate marital details to a third party roused Sidney to a traumatic exhibition of violence. For the next two hours, he threatened and terrorized her. The bruises and cuts that resulted from her beating, particularly a nasty abrasion beneath her left eye, kept her sequestered in her own home for an extended period of time.

Confirmation that their hapless marriage was beyond salvation, amplified by her self-induced isolation, thrust her into a dark foreboding period.

At the depth of her despair, she even considered taking her own life. It was in the wake of this awful depression, that her intimate liaison with James Atwater began – a union that would change her life.

Sidney walked through the front door and entered the living room where Robin was seated on the couch. True to his nature, he did not greet her with the warmth or simple courtesy that he would have extended to a stranger.

"Why are you sitting there like that?" he asked.

"I've been waiting for you," she answered.

"You're lucky. I didn't think I'd be home at all tonight."

"I don't feel very lucky," she said bitterly.

"You should. You've got the best job in town."

"Being your wife?"

"Yeah. No work, a handbag full of credit cards, and a title. What more could a farm girl from Illinois want?"

"I spoke to Paula Rued today," she said.

"Who the fuck is that?" he screamed with suspicious sarcasm.

"You should keep better track of your lovers, Sidney."

He responded angrily by repeating her description. "Lover?"

Robin obviously cherished what she was about to say, "Did you know she's carrying your child? At least she thinks so. It's a good thing men don't get pregnant or you might have knocked her husband up at the same time. Do you remember Clifford Rued?"

Sidney walked to his wet bar in the den and promptly poured himself a scotch and water. Robin followed.

"I'm tired of bullshitting you along," he said. "We might as well settle some things – right here and now."

"Did I mention that the Rueds want $250,000, or they're going public with your little threesome," she said.

Sidney smiled and chugged his drink. "That won't happen."

"Why?" she asked.

"So, the charade is over." Sidney took a deep breath and smiled. "I'm glad. I was getting bored with it anyway."

"You might have mentioned, sometime over the past ten years, that you were bisexual."

"I live my life on a need-to-know basis. You didn't need to know."

"You son-of-a-bitch. How many men have you slept with?"

"Who counts?" he said smugly.

"And the women?" she asked, fearing the answer.

"Not so many of them, he sneered, "they reminded me of you, and nothing turns me off quicker."

Robin had to ask. "You've never loved me, have you?"

Sidney laughed and poured himself another drink. "Love? I needed a wife to distract from my more unconventional appetites. I figured a big-titted blonde would fill the bill – and it did."

"I don't know why I didn't see you for the worm you were," exclaimed Robin.

"I always wondered why you never figured it out. I must have fucked half of the people you know. Remember when your younger brother, Wayne, visited last summer?"

"Yes. Why?" Robin asked suspiciously.

"I love virgins," he smirked.

"Wayne isn't gay."

"He sucked my cock like he'd been doing it all of his life."

"You're scum," she screamed.

"What about you? How long have you been fucking Atwater?"

"What?" Robin asked, even though she understood perfectly.

"You aren't really going to deny it are you?"

"No. I'm really not," she said defiantly. "How long have you known?"

"Long enough."

"Why didn't you say something?"

"Why him? Why Atwater?"

When it became obvious that she wasn't going to reveal anything about her relationship with the president, Sidney pounded his empty glass against the bar and charged toward her. "Why him?" he screamed.

With her husband's history of violence indelibly etched in her mind, Robin took several precautionary steps backward. Her retreat ended when Sidney thrust out his left hand and grabbed a handful of blonde hair.

"You bitch! You've been fucking that arrogant prick," Sidney bellowed, slapping Robin's face with a repetitive back-and-forth motion of his free hand.

"Stop hitting me!" she screamed. "Stop!" Her cries had no effect.

Absorbed by anger and unaccustomed to resistance, Sidney left himself unprotected. Robin responded by sinking her knee into his groin. His groan turned into a wretched scream. In helpless surrender, he writhed into a blubbering heap. Robin bent over and screamed in his ear, "Don't ever touch me again! Never!"

The doorbell announced the presence of an unknown visitor.

"Oh no! Not now," she groaned

One-by-one, she raced through the possibilities. Pinder, the Secret Service agent. Of course, he must have heard the commotion.

With tears streaking down his face, Sidney grabbed her wrist and squeezed, "Get rid of them."

Again, the doorbell chimed.

Robin hurried from the den and through the living room toward the front entry. She was only a few feet from the massive wooden door when it burst open. Agent Pinder had used his own key to gain entrance.

Gun in hand, he advanced through the doorway and entered the main room. His eyes darted about the room, seeking anything out of the ordinary. "What is it, Mrs. Holdridge? What's wrong?"

What could she say? How could their screams be explained? Her hesitation was only making matters worse.

"It's okay," she blurted out, "we were just having a squabble."

Feigning shyness, she continued the deception. "Even vice presidents and their wives argue once in a while."

The agent paused. It seemed possible but ...

" I've got to see the vice president, Mrs. Holdridge. I've got to see that he's all right. It's my job."

Robin led the anxious agent, gun still drawn, toward the den. She knew that no amount of talking would persuade him to back off until he had personally verified the vice president's well-being. She could only pray that her husband's condition had improved.

Before they reached the doorway, Pinder excused himself and stepped in front of her, avoiding the possibility of entering the room behind a woman.

She could hear him ask, "Are you all right, Mr. Vice President?"

Over the agent's shoulder she could see that Sidney had managed to move from the floor to the couch. His hair was uncombed, and he looked generally unkempt, but at least, he had pulled himself together in time to rid them of the pesky agent.

Sidney looked up and gave Pinder a despondent nod. "Yeah, I'm all right. Get the fuck out of here!"

Confirmation of the vice president's well-being provoked an immediate downshift in Pinder's commanding personality. He found himself an unwelcome intruder unwittingly embroiled in a domestic squabble.

He holstered his weapon and turned to Robin, "I'm sorry, Mrs. Holdridge. I hate to involve myself in private matters but ... you know ... I'm responsible for your safety and ..."

Robin sympathized with the awkwardness of the agent's position, but all she wanted at the moment was privacy. As they walked to the front door, she expressed her appreciation for his concern. A few more words of apology and finally, he was gone.

# The White House
## President's Living Quarters

It was nearly two a.m.. The president and his brother had spent the past three hours trying to piece together their fragmented relationship. Mike's shocking admission was so fresh and painful that it inhibited the closeness and commitment that James Atwater had anticipated at the outset of their reunion.

Given the opportunity, the press would have placed a photograph documenting their rekindled relationship in every morning newspaper in the Western World. At Mike's request, with the full support of his brother, their limited time together would preclude media participation.

Even under the circumstances, it was good to have family to talk to again. Neither man had fully realized, until now, how much he had missed the other. It had been a long time since the president sat with another man dressed in blue jeans and a T-shirt. An opportunity to talk with someone from his childhood who wasn't trying to kiss his ass or awed by his presence was welcome.

Submarine sandwiches seemed appropriate to the occasion. After his last bite of a turkey and ham on whole wheat, Mike pressed for an answer to his earlier plea. "How about it, brother? Will you come back to the church?"

Even though the president had not made a decision, he knew that when push came to shove, he would not deny what amounted to his brothers dying wish.

"That's what you want, isn't it? You know, right in this building, I've given people highways, nuclear weapons, billions of dollars in aid, but I've never given anyone something this important. At least not personally so important."

"It's the way you were brought up. It's the way we've always lived. I know, inside, it's what you want."

The president placed his empty plate on the small end-table next to his chair.

"I'd be a liar if I said that I hadn't thought about it over the years. Let's go to church tomorrow morning, together. I'm sure there's an early morning mass at St. Patrick's. It's located just across Lafayette Square."

The spontaneity of the suggestion surprised the president as much as it pleased his brother.

"The Secret Service is going to love this," he said with a wry grin.

## MAY 25
## Cathedral of Saint Matthew The Apostle

The media circus, that the president and his brother had agreed to avoid, was in full swing. A forty-minute church service provided the White House press corps with ample time to assemble and prepare for the exit from church. J

James Atwater and his seldom-seen brother. Mike, dressed in traditional black with a priest's Roman collar, was experiencing a few chaotic minutes of the rapacious media attention that his brother lived with each day of his life.

Still photographs and a wealth of video footage would document this extraordinary moment for millions of Americans who had never seen their chief executive leave a church service that wasn't spawned by crisis. To the delight of the press corps, both men posed proudly with Father O'Leary on the steps leading from the massive doors of the Monsignor's well-known church.

Side-by-side, the Atwaters walked through a narrow corridor created by police and a frenetic contingent of Secret Service Agents toward a black limousine that was waiting to return them to the White House.

A blinding wash of flashbulbs along with the shouted questions from competing reporters helped create a chaotic atmosphere that bewildered the fifty or so unsuspecting, mostly elderly, worshipers that had attended the early 6:30 a.m. service.

Mike scooted across the back seat of the black limousine only seconds before his brother settled into the luxury of the rich leather upholstery.

"Man! I've seen it, but it's hard to imagine how wild it is."

"It goes with the office. I used to dream about the fame. Now, I dream about anonymity. I guess the grass is always greener."

"It is kind of fun," Mike said with a sheepish grin.

"Are you sure you can't stay until tomorrow?" asked the president. "We've got a lot left to talk about."

"Can't. But soon – I can't wait twelve more years."

"Come up to the lake with me next week. I'll be in your backyard. You know the lake property belongs to both of us. I'd love to have you come up."

"I'd like that too," Mike answered.

# Elbow Lake

In a matter of minutes, the new morning sky was sheathed in a scabbard of onrushing clouds. The gathering storm threatened to abort the planned fishing expedition of Mustafa Al Jaabir and Muftah Al Arbash.

A flash of lightning, followed by the unsettling rumble of distant thunder, decided the question once and for all. Less than a mile from shore, the two men reversed their course and headed for the safety of their cabin. In a manner consistent with his peevish nature, Jaabir reacted to his disappointment. "I curse this land."

"It is the sky that threatens us. America is a beautiful land," said Arbash.

"Perhaps," Jaabir smiled, "if it were not full of Americans."

When they reached shore, Jaabir continued to grouse over the weather while Arbash secured the sleek Z-275 Davanti to the doubtful support of the rickety dock. "Rain and more rain! It is too much! I wish we were home," he complained.

Arbash, the calmest of Tabou's assassins, exhibited more patience. "When we are home, think of how often we wish for a cool rain."

"Never again! I'll remember," pledged Jaabir.

"Let us hope that the thing we remember about this mission is not the weather," reminded Arbash.

"I am going crazy, waiting. I want to do it.? When? When will the waiting end?" Jaabir asked, knowing that a precise answer was impossible. With their boat secured, they walked toward the cabin.

"We must be patient. It will happen," assured Arbash.

Jaabir was not so certain. "I say we go back to Washington and end it there."

"Here is better ... easier," said Arbash.

"Easy is for women. Hard ..." laughed Jaabir, "is for men!"

The Cuban, Miguel Bonilla, brandishing a Finnish-made M82 submachine gun, intercepted the returning fishermen ten yards short of the cabin. His weapon gave him the courage to smart off to his old antagonist, Jaabir. "So, you had to come back. Aahh! What's the difference? You never catch shit anyway!"

Bonilla wasn't the only one that was still smarting over the incident at the motel.

"We just need better bait," Jaabir informed Arbash with a devilish smile. "Maybe if we cut up some Cuban asshole and put him on our hook, we might catch a shit eating fish."

From the beginning of their association, the volatile Cuban had discovered that baiting his zealous Arab companions was an easy if not irresistible pursuit.

"You ... cut up somebody? You're fucking losers! How long has it been since you desert fucks won a war? Everybody in the world, including the Jews, have kicked your butts. Arbash, weren't you involved in the war with tiny little Chad? Those shop-keepers smoked your sandy asses all the way back to Mozab. You fight like old women!"

Arbash's temper was less capricious and much more difficult to ignite than that of his companion. Jaabir made a predictable lunge for the Cuban who had anticipated the Libyan's poorly executed attack. A wel-timed sidestep caused his impetuous adversary to tumble awkwardly to the ground. Bonilla waved his gun back and forth between the two Arabs.

"See!" he shouted. "You are clumsy, like those camels you sleep with."

"Stop this foolishness," Arbash commanded. "You already endangered our mission with the stupid murder of the young boy you met on our trip here."

Jaabir pulled himself to his feet, making a firm declaration. "You are a dead Cuban! Write your mother, if you know her name, and tell her you are dead!"

Bonilla shifted the barrel of his machine gun from the center of Jaabir's chest to point only inches from the Libyan's right shoulder.

In a thunderous three second burst, he unleashed thirty rounds of ammunition. Twenty yards away, near the shore, a white seagull exploded like a pillow, filling the air with dirt, water and white feathers. Blue smoke curled from the barrel of Bonilla's gun as he returned his aim to the middle of Jaabir's stomach.

Jean and Martin Balfour had been hiking through the trees and along the shore of Elbow Lake since daybreak. The approaching storm was forcing them to abandon their early morning adventure and scurry in the direction of the road where their car was parked.

The sound of Bonilla's machine gun halted Martin in his tracks. His wife looked at him curiously. "What's that?" she asked.

By placing his index finger a few inches from his lips, Martin called for silence. "Ssshhh! It's some type of automatic weapon. God! I haven't heard one of those since I was in basic."

He made a follow-me gesture with his outstretched hand.

"Martin, I don't think we should interfere," she warned.

"I want to know what's going on. Let's just look."

"Please, Martin. Let's go back to the ..."

"Come on!" he urged.

Cocky and pleased with himself, Miguel Bonilla continued to wield the machine gun back and forth between Jaabir and his bewildered companion.

"Nobody fucks with me!" he crowed.

The words had barely trickled from his mouth when a bullet from a Makarov pistol slammed through the back of Bonilla's skull and exited his cheek under the left eye.

The impact drove the Cuban's body forward, forcing Jaabir to step aside. He landed in a faceless heap at Arbash's feet. The gaping hole in his young face left little doubt about his condition.

Musa Abu Tabou, standing ten yards away, lowered the Russian pistol to his side.

The sound of a single gunshot stopped Martin Balfour just long enough for him to recalculate his course and forge ahead. Jean, reluctant from the beginning, trailed her husband by several yards.

Mohammed Al Sharif ran from the house to join his comrades. They all stared at Bonilla's dead body in silence.

Tabou, still holding the pistol, shook his head. "He was crazy. He would not listen!"

The Jabali turned his attention to Jaabir and Arbash.

"You have put us in danger! They do not allow automatic weapons in this country." He swept his hand across the surrounding landscape, "What person might have heard this fool's shots?"

Jaabir, pleased by the result, ignored the Jabali's question and spit on Bonilla's corpse. "The Cuban scum found what he was looking for."

Fifty yards away, the Balfours peered through thick vegetation at the four men standing over Bonilla's lifeless body. Jean wanted no part of what she saw.

"Let's go! Now!" she pleaded while tugging at the arm of her husband.

"They killed that guy!" he exclaimed.

Jean couldn't stand it any longer; she had seen enough. Abandoning all caution, the frightened young woman bolted from the horror of what had just happened and began to run. Her unbridled flight, through the surrounding brush, left Martin with no choice, he had to follow.

All four Arabs wheeled in the direction of the Balfour's noisy retreat. Tabou aimed his pistol at the middle of Jaabir's chest as if he were going to shoot him.

"See what you've done. Stop them!" he roared.

Sharif stooped to retrieve the submachine gun dropped by Bonilla. Only he and Tabou had weapons.

Arbash, the swiftest of the group, was the first to reach the spot where the Balfours were first seen. A distant flash of Jean's red sweatshirt gave him direction.

With the future of their mission in question, they charged through the woods in ferocious pursuit of two people who could determine their destiny. They cursed as they ran, hurdling fallen limbs and bulldozing through brushy patches of thorny undercover with wild-eyed abandon.

At the edge of a clearing, they paused to listen. The approaching storm brought with it an almost continuous roll of thunder. Angry gray clouds that once darkened the western sky were now churning directly overhead. The forest was dark and foreboding. Even the rhythmic chatter of small creatures was stifled by the sudden intrusion.

Tabou and Sharif continued to listen as Jaabir and Arbash moved several steps forward. There was still no sound. They continued their advance with caution, listening for any noise, however slight, that might betray their quarry.

Again, they stopped. No footsteps, no rustle of leaves, no movement – nothing. Tabou waved Jaabir and Arbash to the north where the trees thickened.

Conscious of every movement, they stalked through the pine forest like the hunters they were, widening their sweep with each step. The distance between Tabou and his men had increased to thirty yards, making visual contact sporadic at best.

Jaabir vaulted over a downed log then stopped. Inexplicably, the Balfours had disappeared. The Libyan resumed his watchful pace.

Sharif, advancing to his left, encountered an area of exceptionally thick brush. The Syrian circled the tangle of scrub oak and weeds, pausing long enough to visually explore every conceivable hiding place. His sweaty fingers were locked tightly around the stock of Bonilla's machine gun. He was ready. Still … nothing!

A few widely spaced drops of rain added another degree of urgency to the hunt; had they gotten away? Tabou was angry at himself and their circumstance; his patience was exhausted. He wanted to shoot them all. His deep growl overcame the thunder.

"Faster! Move faster! They must not escape!"

With a downpour only seconds away, Jaabir turned from the direction of Tabou's voice into the blinding path of a metal camping shovel.

Martin Balfour's baseball swing struck the Libyan square in the face. The force of the unexpected blow threw him backward against the trunk of a large pine tree.

Martin paused a fraction of a second to glimpse the damage he'd inflicted.

His hesitation was costly. A 9mm bullet splintered his collarbone, hurling him to the ground. Screams of agony forced Jean to break from the cover of a nearby tree. By the time she reached her husband's side, the heavens opened up, and it began pouring rain.

"Oh Jesus, Martin! What have they done?"

In a panic, she struggled to lift her bloodied partner and friend to his feet. He was still in shock and unable to gather his senses when Tabou arrived.

Rain had flattened the Jabali's unwashed hair into thick black strings that clung to his forehead and face. The rage in his expression left no doubt about his intentions. Jean tried desperately to place her own body between Martin and his attacker. "No! No!" she pleaded, "don't hurt him anymore!"

A savage kick from Tabou's heavy boot sent her sprawling. Before she could recover, the angry Jabali pressed the dull black barrel of his pistol against Martin's forehead and pulled the trigger. Jean screamed. The deafening roar splattered gray pulp, mixed with blood and bone, across her rain-soaked face, shirt, and the nearby foliage.

In a fit of temper, Tabou moved the pistol to the other side of what remained of Martin's head and again pulled the trigger. For a second time, Jean found herself caught in the horrific spray of her husband's splintered skull.

Shocked into silence, she crawled along the wet ground in a mindless effort to escape the terror. Her short flight was halted by Sharif, the coldest of them all. He grabbed her by her hair, pulling her blood-spattered face to within inches of his ugly, bearded mouth. Rain dripped from his face to hers. The Syrian's yellow rotted teeth, coupled with the odor of his foul breath, caused the already nauseous woman to vomit. Bubbly yellow liquid spewed from between her lips. Revulsion fueled by desperation forced a hopeless attempt to escape. Her pitiful effort proved futile.

"No more!" bellowed Sharif, forcing the barrel of his gun into the puke, then pushing the cold metal down her throat. The Syrian watched, fascinated by his own cruelty, while Jean continued to choke and gag. He wanted to pull the trigger.

Tabou yelled. "No! Let her live! It would be foolish to kill her now."

Sharif had roused his own sadistic appetite to a point of frenzy. His addiction craved satisfaction. He needed blood; he wanted to watch the expression on her face when the gun discharged in her mouth.

"Why! Why spare her life?" he demanded to know.

Tabou's rage matched that of his companion, "Because I said so!" he screamed. "Americans value life, even a woman's. If something happens, we can use her to obtain our freedom!"

The fun was over. Sharif shot an angry glance at Tabou, then jerked the barrel of the gun from between the woman's bloody lips.

"We have many things to put in your mouth, bitch."

With his open hand, Sharif delivered a jarring blow to the side of the thirty-one-year-old woman's face, driving her to the ground. Jean Balfour, a portrait photographer, had no idea what was happening. Shocked and in pain, she watched her brutal tormentors in absolute total terror.

# CHAPTER SIX

## Hibbing, Minnesota
## Hibbing Airport

Musa Abu Tabou stared intently as Pierre Coutre emerged from a bedraggled line of travelers who were deplaning the small Shorts 330 that had flown them two hundred miles from Minneapolis to the northern Minnesota community of Hibbing.

Dressed in a brown leather jacket over a plain black T-shirt, the Frenchman entered the passenger reception area of the small single-level terminal.

Tabou's terse greeting placed little emphasis on fellowship; there was only one thing he wanted to hear from Coutre.

"Is it done?" Tabou asked.

"Yes. Now we can only hope that the American police aren't too stupid to figure it out."

"Bonilla is dead," declared Tabou.

"How? What went wrong?" asked the Frenchman.

"He could not be controlled. Too young, too crazy, too hot tempered. I don't know. His presence was a serious miscalculation. He was a danger to us all."

"What are you going to do about it?" Coutre asked with emphasis on the word *you*, removing any thought that *he* might be expected to help solve the problem.

"It has already been done. Another is coming," assured the Jabali.

"Who?"

"One who can do the job," Tabou said with a hint of mystery and self-satisfaction.

The pair walked through the spartan corridors of the Hibbing Airport unnoticed. The Jabali's dark complexion did little to distinguish him from the substantial Native American population that peppered the northern half of the state. The few locals who passed these casually dressed interlopers could hardly have guessed that their conversation centered on a plot to kill the president of the United States.

In the luggage claim area, they found the Frenchman's two suitcases easy to spot among the half dozen bags removed from the plane. Within five minutes of the time he landed, they were on the road to Elbow Lake nearly sixty miles away.

## The White House

Sean MacDougal and the president were having lunch in a small alcove adjacent to the Oval Office. Many former presidents used the cubicle as a private get-away; a secluded office within an office.

James Atwater had the desk and shelving installed by the previous administration, replaced with a small two-leaf table and four chairs. Sean, who worried about the president more than the president worried about himself, voiced his concern over the pending Israeli air attack on Jabal.

"What if it fails?"

"We'll have to go in. I've put the *Carl Vinson* on alert. The plans are set. God willing, we won't need them."

The president poured himself and his friend a cup of coffee from the percolator left by the steward.

"You take too many chances. You're turning into a political sky diver," Sean said with a grin.

The old Irishman placed his fork on the edge of the plate and leaned back in his chair. "Can I talk to you about something?" he asked with a ponderous intonation that the president immediately recognized as important.

"What do you think?" asked the president with an impish smile.

Uncertain of how he should proceed, Sean struggled for the appropriate wording. "What you do is your business, but Christ, Jim, I'm worried about this thing with Robin Holdridge. Don't get me wrong, I like the girl, I like her a lot, but think of how many people must know about you two by now.

"We're on the final leg of an eight-year run. Maybe we can ..."

"Come on, Jim. The press isn't going to kid-glove you like they did Kennedy. He was one of the 'good old boys.' Times have changed. No one's going to smile and look the other way. You two just might bring back public stoning. In fact, I'm not so damned sure they wouldn't impeach you for a thing like this. At the least, your leadership would be compromised. You'd be ineffective; you'd be forced to resign."

Lunch was over. The president placed his plate on the serving cart and swept away a few of the crumbs that were soiling the white linen table cloth.

After neatly refolding his napkin and placing it next to his plate, he acknowledged Sean's concern. "I love her,

Sean. When Megan died, I thought I'd never find anyone again, but I was wrong ...."

Sean cut in, "Impeachment would make a man pretty god damn lonely. Nixon could probably fill you in on a few of the more salient aspects of presidential misconduct."

"Fuck Richard Nixon. When did he become our role model?"

"Exactly! Is that how you want to be remembered ... for a lapse of judgment? Jim, you can have any single woman in America," Sean pleaded. "For Christ's sake, our secretaries are having orgasms just reading your mail. Why her?"

"I didn't plan it this way, it just happened. Does anyone plan who they're going to fall in love with?"

"You're the president. You're expected to plan. You live under a fucking microscope. Nobody knows that better than you."

"I'm not leaving her."

"Then don't listen. Remember the old joke about the guy they called 'Joe, the butcher.' He had spent his whole life working as a butcher, then he sucked just one cock, and when people found out, they never called him 'Joe the butcher' again. The same thing that happened to 'Joe the cocksucker' can happen to you."

"Stay out of it," shouted the president.

"Someone has to tell you that you're making a damn fool out of yourself. I'm not a presidential 'yes man.' If you can't accept that, you should replace me with one of those milquetoast piss-ants that buzz around you night and day anticipating a small stipend from the king of the civilized world. It isn't always easy to be the king, kid."

Sean's assessment stung. The fact that he was correct only magnified the president's dismay. Without uttering a word, he brushed past the Irishman and left the room.

## Elbow Lake

Tabou, accompanied by Coutre and Jaabir, had just finished anchoring their boat in the middle of Niles Bay when an amphibious aircraft, flying a scant thirty feet above the lake's rippled surface, roared across their bow. The plane, a Cessna 207, acknowledged a wave of the Jabali's outstretched arms with a dip of its wings.

In a few short minutes, the awkward-looking craft touched down amidst a torrent of noise and frothy spray. Fifty feet from the Davanti's starboard side, the plane's three hundred horse engine was silenced.

To prevent his plane from drifting away, the lanky pilot exited the aircraft carrying a rope, one end of which he tossed in the general direction of Tabou's boat. Aided by a long gaff hook, Jaabir retrieved the bright yellow tether, and with Tabou's assistance, pulled the plane and boat close enough together to allow the stranger to jump aboard.

Coutre, in step with his minimalist mercenary philosophy, was careful to avoid participation. With the pilot's feet planted firmly on the deck, Jaabir tied off the rope, guaranteeing the Cessna's retrieval.

Dooley Johnston made his living ferrying well-healed clients into areas so remote that more traditional means of entry were impossible. Like many of his fellow "bush pilots," Johnston was short on education and long on horse sense. He earned his reputation as a 'cowboy' by taking chances. Money was the crank that turned Dooley's engine. If there was a dollar at stake, he would do what was required, legal or not, to obtain it.

His compulsory uniform consisted of an old leather jacket, dirty Levi's, and a T-shirt, which was frequently embellished with a symbol or message calculated to stir up controversy. Today's words of wisdom, spelled out in block letters that dripped blood, were  FEAR ME.

"Name is Dooley, eh." he said with a steeped Canadian lilt, typical of border country. No one reached for the tall Swede's outstretched hand.

"Do you understand what is required of you?" asked Tabou.

"I guess, but the guy who hired me didn't tell me shit."

"Shit," Coutre injected.

Dooley, clearly out of his league, hesitated then managed a nervous snicker.

"You boys are offerin' me a lot of money for this. But it don't matter how much you pay if I ain't alive to spend it, eh."

"You were given a time, a place, and a lot of money – be there. There's nothing else you need to know."
"What would you be doin' on Wolf Island in the wee hours of the morning? You don't look like the type the president would be havin' supper with, eh."

"You blonde fuck!" the Frenchman snarled, turning to Tabou. "Let's kill this asshole and get somebody else.?"

"Whoa there!" Dooley said, "I didn't say I wouldn't do it."

"You were hired and paid," said the Jabali, "you don't want to know any more."

"When Atwater's there, the air space around Wolf Island is restricted. I could lose my license."

Tabou got right in the Swede's face.

"You know fucking well what this is about. You aren't being paid a half million dollars to take us fishing."

"What if I don't want to be a part of something like that, eh?"

The Jabali grabbed Johnston by his "Fear Me" shirt.

"You made that decision when you took the first hundred thousand dollars. If you back out or don't show, you and everyone you know will be dead. There are many of us. There will be no rock on earth big enough to hide you."

## The White House
## Oval Office

The president was seated at his desk reading the Wall Street Journal when Sean entered the room. They had not spoken to each other since their post-lunch run-in.

Still chaffing over his advisor's caustic remarks, James Atwater was determined that he would not be the one to initiate a conversation. Sean robbed the moment of drama by immediately breaking the ice.

"Still pissed?" he asked.

The president lifted his head slowly until he could see his friend of thirty years over the top of the newspaper. He couldn't help but crack the faintest of smiles.

"MacDougal, You're one cold-old-bold-fuck."

Sean beamed. "I'm glad you have a firm grasp on the situation ... before your little tantrum ended our earlier 'meeting,' I was going to tell you that a reporter from the Post has been snooping around town. He's trying to find out if you're 'dating' ... and who. It sounds as if the bastard's already got some of the answers and all of a sudden, I'm getting a lot of concerned calls from our own people. They want to know what's up."

"Has anyone mentioned her by name?" the president asked.

"They haven't had the balls to do that yet, but it's coming."

"I'll risk the consequences. I'm not going to live without her."

Sean's smile suggested a more philosophic approach.

"Well, as my old pappy used to tell me, 'Love is like a mushroom: you can never tell if it's the real thing until it's too late.' In your case Jimmy, whether she loves you or not, I'm afraid it's going to be too late."

The chief executive returned his attention to the Journal, stubbornly refusing to lend credence to his friend's pessimism.

"And by the way," Sean added, "Press Secretary Kincaid was also contacted yesterday. He's laughing over the whole thing. I guess he has no idea."

"Good. Keep it that way," the president exclaimed, "Let's hope the Post is on a fishing expedition."

"Speaking of catching big fish, are we going to carry through with the Minnesota trip?"

"Yes," the president's spirits suddenly brightened. "We've had the trip scheduled for months. We'll be going up Sunday, the day after the Israeli's go after Jabal's nuclear facility. I'm looking forward to it. We'll either be celebrating or lamenting."

Sean warmed to the idea, "It would be nice to get out of town for a few days."

"Wolf Island is the one place on earth that I love more than any other," affirmed the president.

"What about Sidney and his wife?" asked Sean.

"I'm not going to cancel an invitation that was extended nearly a year ago, not under the circumstances."

"You must love excitement," exclaimed Sean. "And what about those Secret Service boys? I'll bet they're anxious to keep you on a short leash, especially since that death squad thing a week ago."

The president's voice was firm. "The tail isn't going to wag the dog. They go where I go."

"Hell," Sean laughed, "you should take up splat ball. You spend your life surrounded by little boys who like to play with guns ... and that's excitement you could handle."

"Get out of here you old fart," the president said with a broad grin.

### Elbow Lake

In one of the cabin's two bedrooms, Jean Balfour was tied spread-eagle to a standard size single bed. Just outside her door, Tabou and his men sat crowded around the small rectangular table that stood between the living room and the kitchen.

Jean's face and clothing were crusted with blotches of her husband's dried blood. A wide band of gray adhesive tape covered her mouth. Helpless, alone, and in total darkness, she lived with the certain knowledge that her captors were going to kill her. If their intentions were to let her live, she reasoned, they would take more care to conceal their plans. In disbelief, she listened as Tabou and his comrades plotted the assassination of the president.

Hours passed before the movement of chairs and noise from the television signaled the end of their nefarious discussion. She had wondered what this moment might bring.

The approach of footsteps, followed by the sound of a hand grasping the doorknob, numbed her with fear. The emerging silhouette of Pierre Coutre against the soft light of the outer room compelled the defenseless young woman to close her eyes and pray to God. "Would he be the one?" she asked herself.

The Frenchman moved the only chair in the room to the side of the bed and sat, then he leaned forward, placing his elbows on his knees, and stared.

Jean had not seen this man's face among those who captured her and killed her husband. "My God!" she thought, "how many assassins were there?" No fewer than five, she concluded, perhaps more.

Coutre continued to study her with an intensity that she couldn't explain. What dark thoughts were churning behind his lifeless eyes? "Why doesn't he get it over with?" she wondered. It didn't matter whether he pulled out a gun or his cock; she was resigned to suffering and the probability of death.

A full minute passed before he extended his hand toward her face and with a quick painful jerk, ripped the sticky tape away from her mouth.

"What's your name, baby?"

His soft voice and thick French accent, coupled with the fact that she had not seen him involved in the horror of the day's earlier events, provided her with a faint ray of hope.

"Jean ... Jean Balfour," her voice trembled.

"Where are you from, Jean Balfour?"

"Iowa."

"I have never heard of, Iowa. Is it near?"

"Four hundred miles," she said, studying him more than answering his question.

The Frenchman began to twirl a lock of Jean's long dark hair around the forefinger of his left hand.

"Was that your husband they shot, or your lover?"

Her attempt to evade Coutre's attention proved futile. No matter how hard she twisted and turned, she found it impossible to escape his unwanted touch.

"You're a very good looking woman, Jean."

Any hope that this man would be her savior, was gone. He was no friend. He was only interested in what she wanted to do least.

In the face of a hopeless situation, she made a decision to go down as a lion rather than a lamb. With any luck, he would just kill her. She screamed as loud as she could. "Get away! Leave me alone!"

Angered by her outburst, the Frenchman pinched her chin with his fingers, forcing her mouth shut and twisting her head to face him.

"Why would you shout like that ... Jean?" His black-handled dagger suddenly appeared.

"I've known women like you," he muttered, pressing the sharp tip of his knife against her upper lip. "Do you fuck much, baby?"

"Go ahead!" she screamed, "Do it!"

A quick death was far preferable to the fate Jean feared her tormentor had in mind. She watched as Coutre moved the knife across her breasts and down to her waist. He then slid the cold metal under the ribbed bottom of her red sweatshirt and, with the flat side of the razor-sharp blade, stretched the fabric high enough to expose her bra.

"Nice tits," he leered.

By squirming and turning, she attempted to obstruct his view, but it was useless. She found herself at his mercy.

"Leave me alone! Don't touch me!" she shrieked.

The dispassionate cruelty in the Frenchman's voice was terrifying.

"You should have stayed home, bitch! You picked a bad fucking day for a walk in the woods."

Coutre's fingers were clasped around the handle of the knife with such ferocity that his knuckles were bleached white. The lethal tip of the dagger was pointed directly at Jean's pounding heart.

"I don't want to touch you, baby. I want to kill you."

Tabou appeared in the doorway.

"Stop it, Frenchman!" he snarled.

Two lumbering steps placed the Jabali at Coutre's side where he leaned forward placing his mouth only inches from the Frenchman's ear.

"Sink that knife in her chest and the Cuban will have a companion." Tabou's raspy growl was as deep as any voice Jean Balfour had ever heard.

Coutre removed the knife and smiled as if the Jabali had merely interrupted a game.

"Just kidding, you know." He playfully tapped the tip of the knife on Jean's bare stomach while Tabou continued to admonish his behavior.

"No killing! Let her be! She is a tool that we may need later."

The Frenchman stood. "Stick around, baby – I'll be back."

## The Vice President's Residence

The alarm clock, resting on the nightstand next to Robin's bed, had taunted her for three long hours. It was exactly 2:58 a.m. The more she thought of the late hour, the harder it was for her to fall asleep. "Whatever happened to clocks with hands," she thought, as if it would make any difference.

For the past forty-eight hours, she had dredged through her life in agonizing detail. Every value and decision were brought into question and often found wanting. What had happened?

## MAY 26
## The White House

It was 5 a.m. when the jangle of the telephone next to the president's bed shattered what remained of an uneasy slumber. He hated these off-hour calls, which, over the course of his administration, had become commonplace.

Events in a tumultuous world proceeded with little regard for scheduling. One thing was certain; middle of the night calls were never made to announce good news. The only question posed was: How bad will it be? From a sitting position he turned on the light, then reached for the phone. "This is the president."

"Mr. President, I have a priority call from Secretary of State Thomas Bertrand."

"Go ahead, put it through."

"Mr. President, I'm sorry to wake you, but we've got a problem. I received a DEFSMAC critical intelligence communication about five minutes ago. We need to talk. Now."

"Explain?"

"I just spoke to Handelman. It appears, from the latest satellite pictures, that the Jabalis are prepared to move one or perhaps all of the atomic bombs. They must have completed the assembly."

Bertrand's alarming news brought the president to his feet.

"Goddamn it! What sort of time frame are we talking about?"

"They apparently brought the equipment in overnight. It's 9 a.m. in Jabal. They could take-off anytime."

"The Israeli attack isn't scheduled until later today. I'll inform the ambassador, so they can get those planes in the air. Thanks for the call."

# Elbow Lake

Cries of a distant loon pierced the early morning quiet. The influence of the yet to be seen sun on the eastern sky was breathtaking. Warm red waves, streaked with purple valleys and yellow crests, were colorfully reflected in the smooth surface of the lakes black water.

An aging Volvo with illuminated headlights no longer necessary in the morning light turned from the narrow gravel access road toward Tabou's cabin hideout. The faded blue automobile, distinguished by a dozen irregular patches of primer paint, moved at a snail's pace along the bumpy driveway leading to the rear of the rustic building. Coughing in post ignition protest, the battered vehicle pulled to a stutter stop next to the two vans.

Inside the cabin, the thud of a closing car door awakened the slumbering Sharif, prompting him to throw back his wool blanket and stand. A terse Arabic warning alerted his sleeping comrades to the presence of a stranger. Nearby weapons were suddenly more important than clothes. By the time a knock on the screen door reverberated through the cabin, the five occupants stood armed, ready and nearly naked.

Sharif and Arbash were wearing only boxer shorts while Jaabir, face swollen and bruised, was wearing nothing. Coutre's calf-high white athletic socks and red bikini briefs did little to protect his tough guy image. Only Tabou, who walked to the door carrying a pistol in his right hand, had taken the time to throw on a pair of trousers and a still unbuttoned shirt.

The Jabali opened the door just far enough to identify their unannounced visitor. Without comment, he looked back at his band of armed half-dressed confederates. The sight of his Beagle Boy assemblage afforded him an uncharacteristic belly laugh.

With unexplained glee, he left the door open and retreated to the kitchen table. "Come in!" he called out.

In walked Sukayna Ayesha, a twenty-two-year-old Iranian beauty who had only one thing in common with the cabin's occupants; she wanted to kill the president of the United States.

When it became apparent that their caller was a young woman, Jaabir scrambled for the bedroom and clothing. Sharif, confused and embarrassed, scowled at Tabou. "Who is this ... woman?"

Tabou, still snickering, relished the impact of his next statement.

"She will replace Bonilla in our plan. Her name is Sukayna Ayesha. She is a student at the university in this state. I know her father."

Sharif made no pretense at hiding his displeasure. He was outraged that a woman would be considered for a mission of such importance.

Oblivious to the commotion she was causing, the five feet four inch woman approached the Jabali leader.

"You must be Musa Abu Tabou. Your deeds precede you. I bring my father's regards. It is a pleasure to meet you. I am honored that you have included me."

Tabou, a rare practitioner of social amenities, shook the dainty hand that had been thrust in front of him. His comment was typical of an Arab world where most women were considered little more than chattel.

"You are small. I hope you can do your job."

Ayesha held her head high. "I can handle any job you give me. Do not make the mistake of underestimating me."

"You are a woman!" barked Sharif. "And a puny one at that. This is man's work!"

Ayesha moved to confront her antagonist.

"It is strange for a man like yourself to have missed a revolution. In the last thirty years, the women of the world have fought and won against such old and stupid notions."

Sharif peered down at the diminutive figure standing before him. She stood as tall and defiant as her petite frame would allow. The Syrian's deep voice dripped with sarcasm.

"Have you ever killed a man?"

"Yes," she replied, displaying her belligerence as if it were a badge. "A big fat ugly fucker, like you!"

The personal nature of her spiteful attack caught Sharif off guard. He responded the way he had always responded to adversity. With a single hand, he grabbed his combative adversary by the throat and walked her to the side of the room where he pinned her hard against the wall.

"No one speaks to me as you have done! You are ..."

Much to his humiliation, the Syrian's words were halted by the sudden appearance of snub nose .38 caliber Smith & Wesson pistol.

Ayesha pressed the weapon's short barrel hard against Sharif's temple. Despite his predicament, the Syrian refused to be intimidated. His bitter admonishment continued unabated.

"You are a disrespectful bitch. I will never fight at the side of a woman."

Ayesha tightened her grip on the trigger. As the hammer rose to strike the firing pin, Tabou dove toward the weapon. His hand struck the barrel at the moment of discharge.

Everyone in the room froze, waiting to see whether Sharif would fall. He did not. The bullet was embedded in the wall, missing the Syrian's head by only a fraction of an inch.

Coutre and Arbash grabbed Sharif's hulking frame, forcing the release of the girl. It took their combined strength to hold their comrade back. Tabou, no longer amused by the addition of the young woman to his group, was forced to disarm and restrain the female spitfire that had suddenly complicated his life. He growled at the combatants.

"Stop this foolishness! Again, you endanger our entire mission." His words fell on deaf ears.

"I will never forget this! No woman has ever spoken to me in this way – and lived!" Sharif shouted while his rival continued to match his rage, Insult for insult.

"Fuck you!" she screamed. "You are no better than I am!"

Tabou wedged himself between them.

"No more!" he shouted. "Bonilla is dead because he could not control his temper. I will not hesitate to kill any one of you for the same reason. We have a job that is more important than any or all of us. We must do nothing that distracts us from our goal."

Jaabir made a well-intentioned, but misguided stab at finding a positive side to the girl's presence.

"It will be good to have a woman here. We need someone to prepare food and wash clothes."

"I am no one's cook!" bristled the black-haired Iranian, "I will take my turn, like the rest of you. But I will not do more. Also, I will not clean your clothes. I am the equal of any one of you ... and I expect to be treated with respect."

For the first time since the young woman arrived, everyone was silent. In the wake of Sukayna Ayesha's incendiary introduction, Tabou could not help but wonder if he had not made a mistake in exchanging the volatile Cuban, Bonilla, for an equally hot-headed and even more abrasive Iranian woman. At least, he thought to himself, she appeared more intelligent than the man she was replacing.

# CHAPTER SEVEN

## Washington, D.C.
## Police Headquarters

The oversize cork message board on Detective Willie Russell's office wall dominated the room and the forty-three-year-old investigator's complete attention.

A grisly series of photos, taken at the Royal Haven Motel murder scene compelled Willie to gesture toward a particularly disturbing 8 x 10 photo of Tracy Parks. Her nude body was soaked in blood. Even in death, her contorted body couldn't disguise her youthful beauty.

The Detective turned his attention to Forensic Specialist Ed Gray who was standing at his elbow.

"Who could do something like that to a young girl?" pondered Russell.

Gray let the question pass without comment. He was still excited over the results of his own findings.

"Killing the girl was just practice for these guys. They do this shit for a living," he said, enjoying himself a little too much.

With folded arms, Willie shook his head.

"Unfucking believable! According to Interpol, I've got half the top ten assholes in the world in my city!"

"No, we've got 'em all ... but I guess the other five were elected," Gray snickered, "you going to try and bring 'em in?"

"Bring 'em in?" Willie sneered, "I'm going to issue an alert to warn the entire department. We aren't equipped for international heavies like this. I've already contacted the FBI."

"Ever find out anything about the girl?" asked Gray.

"Tracy Parks? Yeah, she's from Salmon, Idaho, population 3,308. She's been missing for nineteen months. The pussy squad is familiar with her work. She's been picked up a half dozen times."

"Not anymore!" Gray countered.

## The White House
## Cabinet Room

The president's weekly cabinet meeting, delayed two days by the Israeli crisis, had just adjourned. Vice President Holdridge was standing in front of his chair, gathering his notes when the president approached. He and his boss were the only two people left in the room.

"Sidney, you didn't seem yourself. Any apprehensions?" asked the president.

Sidney ignored the question and continued to sort his paperwork. When he decided it was time, he took the conversation in a different direction.

"I'm looking forward to visiting your island in Minnesota. We've got a lot to talk about?" The chill in Sidney's voice was unmistakable.

"So am I. We've had this trip planned for a long time."

His vice president's failure to follow up on his comment prompted further inquiry.

"Is there something you'd like to discuss, now?" asked the president.

"No, I don't think so."

Something in Sidney's voice warned the president not to proceed.

"Well, until the weekend then. We should all have a good time."

Sidney spun the four-digit security tumbler next to the latch on his briefcase then looked up at the president.

"I know Robin's looking forward to it," he said, staring directly into the president's eyes. The ensuing awkwardness left no doubt in the president's mind; Sidney knew.

## Vice President's Residence

Robin's scheduled appearance, before a symposium on 'sexual harassment in the workplace was only an hour and a half away. Absent nylons and a dress, she laid on her king-size bed reviewing the speech that she and co-author Tanya Pelgram, a White House speech writer, had prepared for the occasion. She felt this conference sponsored by the National Organization for Women was important enough to merit this extra measure of attention.

Satisfied with her knowledge of the material, she closed her eyes and rolled over on her back, attempting to calm the jitters that always preceded a media event of this magnitude. She had never told anyone, not even her lover, how uncomfortable she was with her newfound celebrity.

Despite her confident demeanor, the frenzied atmosphere and suffocating attention that drew many men and women to public life, this was the most disturbing aspect of her many duties as wife of the vice president. This contradiction meshed perfectly with her image as a happily married woman. Her whole life was mired in a ballooning jumble of lies. It seemed the harder she fought to free herself, the more entangled she became.

When she finally opened her eyes, an image on the fifty-two-inch flat screen high definition television that dominated the wall opposite the bed took her breath away.

"No," she muttered, bounding to her feet. Before she could find the remote control that would enable her to cancel the mute mode on the television, the face of a popular Washington newscaster appeared. The story that would explain the photograph of Paula and Clifford Rued was over.

## The White House
## Oval Office

The president's telephone doodling degenerated into frustrated scribbling as he waited for the call from Israeli Ambassador Zalman Pasha to be patched through to his office. An irritating switchboard screw-up on the Israeli end was responsible for the delay. Finally, he heard Pasha's voice.

"Hello. Hello," the Israeli repeated.

"Mr. Ambassador," the president said, "thank you for calling."

"I am so sorry for the delay. We have a new secured phone system that was, I fear, designed for us by our Arab friends."

"Well I can hear you fine now. What has happened," asked the president.

"I am pleased to report that our mission was a success. Our aircraft intercepted and destroyed a four-truck convoy approximately a mile from the assembly point. We were very fortunate. Another few minutes and it might have been too late."

"And the assembly point itself?" asked the president.

"With their ordnance depleted by their attack on the convoy, our first strike met with only partial success. A second strike was required to eliminate the threat."

"Did you suffer any losses?" asked the president.

"Our losses were grave. Seven of the eight planes involved did not return. As we speak, other men are risking their lives in a desperate search for the pilots of those missing planes. I would ask that you please say a prayer on their behalf."

"Believe me, I will. Congratulations on your success. May God be with your pilots and their families."

"Thank you, Mr. President."

## Vice President's Residence

The photograph of Paula and Clifford Rued that appeared on the television screen in Robin's bedroom set off a frantic search.

Her hands shook as she scanned the newspaper that she had only skimmed through earlier in the day. Page three, there it was. The picture of the Rueds in the *Post* was different than the one she had seen on television – much harder to recognize.

Upon finishing the article, she flung the paper across the kitchen causing several of the pages to unfold and float to the floor.

The Rueds were found shot to death in their Washington home. According to the newspaper report, robbery was dismissed as a likely motive since it appeared that nothing, including Clifford Rued's wallet, was taken from their residence.

For the first time in her life, Robin was truly scared. She had no doubt that it was her husband who pulled the trigger; not personally, of course, but he was undoubtedly responsible for their deaths.

Coincidence could never explain the slaughter of both Rueds within forty-eight hours of the time Sidney had learned of their career-threatening treachery. The man with the secretive past, the man she had married, was apparently capable of almost anything – including murder. One question haunted her – how far would he go?

Consumed by her nightmarish circumstance, Robin did not hear her husband enter the front door. Startled by the sight of him standing in the doorway of the kitchen, she let out an involuntary yelp.

The pages of newspaper that she had impetuously scattered across the kitchen floor appeared to dominate Sidney's immediate attention. "Was *Dear Abby* disappointing?" he asked dryly.

"You killed them, didn't you? You son-of-a-bitch!" Robin charged in a slow seething tone.

"Killed who?"

"The Rueds. I know you killed them."

"So, the Rueds are no longer with us. How fortuitous. A car accident?"

"They were shot to death; gangland style, the paper said."

"And you think I did it? I had meetings all day yesterday. The Secret Service can vouch for my whereabouts. Vice presidents don't have many opportunities to murder people."

"You had it done, and we both know it."

"Blackmailers take risks. The Rueds must have fucked with the wrong guy."

"This was no coincidence, was it?"

Sidney approached his wife, then leaning forward, placed one hand on the kitchen table and the other on the back of her chair. His face was only inches from hers.

"Forget this and keep your fucking mouth shut. Anything you say to the police or the press will come back to haunt us. There's no one out there who can help you. I'm no fool. If I did have anything to do with this, I would position myself many layers from the event."

"There are people who can't be intimidated in this town," she warned.

"You don't want to go there. That's one can of worms you definitely don't want to open. Your boyfriend is the one with his balls on the line here. He's the one who's vulnerable. Tell him about this and you'll force 'Saint Atwater' to respond. In the end he'll be impeached, and I'll be the wounded spouse left in the lurch, betrayed by a cheating wife."

A wicked grin fouled Sidney's expression. "Maybe you should tell him. This could be a win-win situation for me."

# MAY 27
## Elbow Lake

Pierre Coutre returned from Cook, Minnesota with assorted supplies and a copy of the *Duluth Sentinel,* the only daily newspaper published in that part of the state. A few steps inside the cabin door, he tossed the bold headlines, BOMBS DESTROYED, on the table under the nose of Musa Abu Tabou.

The Jabali rose almost immediately, tipping the chair he had been sitting on to the floor. His eyes darted across the paper, searching for details.

"The bastard Jew pigs!" He bellowed.

His voice summoned the group to their feet. They waited for news while Tabou continued his search for information.

When he was finished, he turned the paper so that his cohorts could read the headlines.

"This is why we are here!" he shouted.

Everyone gasped. The paper was quickly passed around the room amid curses and denouncements. Jabal's embarrassing failure had suddenly become their personal defeat.

Sharif, the last man to wade through the lengthy article, threw the paper back to Coutre. The Syrian's anger, as always, stemmed from his heart and not his head. He wanted blood.

"I am finished waiting! I will go to Washington and kill the scum myself!"

The Palestinian, Muftah al Arbash, was upset for other reasons.

175

"How could the Jews reach into the heart of Jabal? How could such a thing happen?"

Tabou once again attempted to redirect the unbridled anger of his group into a reaffirmation of their mission.

"The world is laughing at us! The Jews, the Americans, they spit on us! They have no respect! They will only respect this!"

He jerked the Beretta from his belt and shook it as if it were an extension of his fist.

"Kill the American president and we will regain our honor!" he shouted.

An impatient Sharif stood tall and ugly before Tabou, "We waste away here!"

Coutre, always the mercenary, sat calmly amidst the chaotic atmosphere created by his enraged companions. The argument over lost pride and respect was of no particular concern to him. Oblivious to the turmoil, he thumbed through the remaining portions of the newspaper until a small Associated Press release at the bottom of page six, caught his eye. He began to read aloud despite the anguished cries of his nearby associates.

"At a morning White House briefing, Press Secretary Kincaid confirmed that President Atwater will spend six days beginning May 28th at his summer White House residence. His annual summer visit, to the northern Minnesota retreat, will be the chief executive's first vacation since November 12th of last year. No further details of the trip were made available."

The impassioned pronouncements of Tabou and his countrymen covered the Frenchman's soft voice.

Only Sharif happened to catch his last few words. "What! What did you say?" he asked Coutre. "Listen! Listen to Coutre," he shouted at the others. "Go ahead, Coutre. Read!"

Coutre didn't read things twice – not for anyone. He folded the paper and flipped it to Sharif. In one short sentence, the Frenchman summed up the only item of real significance, "The American president will be here tomorrow."

Cheers and praise to an Arab God replaced the outrage over Jewish victories with a sudden mood of optimism and a terrible resolve.

## The White House

The Oval Office was cluttered with the men and equipment required to broadcast the details of America's contribution to the successful Israeli attack. President Atwater had just finished his address when staff personnel, and even a few members from the press pool allowed to attend, rushed to congratulate him on the success of the attack

A last-minute meeting with Supervisor of the White House Secret Service Detail John Solis was set to take place in the small dining area adjacent to the Oval Office.

Seated at the kitchen-sized table, the two men discussed the president's upcoming vacation. Solis pled his case with passionate concern.

"I must suggest, in the strongest of terms that you remain in Washington, Mr. President. Our protective ring is so much stronger here ..."

"John," interrupted the president, "it's been over a week since we've heard anything about these so-called assassins. I can't stay penned up for the remainder of my term like this. I need the rest."

Solis was prepared for the president 's reply.

"That's why I asked for this meeting. Late this afternoon, the FBI was advised by local authorities of the presence of six internationally known criminals. Their names confirm our worst fears. We are 99% sure that these are the men who fired on our Coast Guard Cutter. These are the men that want to assassinate you. It seems one of them, a Frenchman named Coutre, is a suspect in the knifing of a prostitute right here in town several days ago."

"Was he apprehended?"

"No! But in the course of the investigation, they found the fingerprints of five other men, the men we've earmarked as assassins, in a Washington motel room occupied by the suspect. The NSA, FBI, and the CIA. are all assisting in the investigation."

"John, it would seem this reinforces my case. If they're in the Washington area, why should I worry about traveling to Minnesota? Everything seems to indicate that these men are prepared to try something here … in this town. What are the chances of them traveling twelve hundred miles to the interior of our country to kill me? It's doubtful that they could find Minnesota on a map."

"No disrespect, Mr. President. But we don't know that."

The president remained adamant, "I must insist, John. I'm not going to live a prisoner of maybes and mights. But, I do appreciate your concern."

## President's Quarters

The president stepped into the elevator that would take him to his second floor residence with the exuberance and excitement of a teenager. From an earlier message, conveyed by Sean, he knew Robin would be there to greet him.

Upon entering the door, he searched for the woman that had captured his heart along with his imagination. Much to his disappointment, her customary fly-in to-his-arms reception wasn't there.

A pleasant recollection of their most recent tryst, a little more than a week ago, prompted a suspicion that she might be waiting for him in the expansive comfort of his own bed. Memories of that night produced a shameless mental snapshot that immediately enlivened the presidential pace. A quick check of the bedroom only added to his frustration.

After backtracking through the hall, he passed by the kitchen, then walked through the dining room to his den. It was here that he spent the bulk of his leisure time.

Relief. Robin was seated on the larger of two couches situated in the center of the room. Her straight-back posture along with the inordinate time it took her to acknowledge his presence signaled trouble. He knew something was wrong.

"Hey! What is it? What's the matter?"

She stood and placed her arms around his waist. Her continued silence was disarming.

"I love you so much, Jim," she whispered

He returned the endearment while encouraging her to nestle into the security of his strong embrace. In deference to her apparent distress, he declined to ask the natural question. She would tell him when the time was right.

In a calm and reassuring voice, he attempted to ease whatever pain she was feeling.

"I was so happy when Sean told me that you would be here," he said, moving his head to kiss her.

Before she could turn away, her eyes, red from crying and lack of sleep, met his for the first time.

"We've got to talk," she cried.

She ushered him to the couch where they both assumed a quartering position that would enable them to face each other.

With his hand locked firmly in her own, she began, "Have you spoken to Sidney?"

"Briefly. I think he knows about us."

"Yes, he does." Robin paused, took a deep breath, stiffened her posture and began to explain. "I can't believe it myself. It just seems impossible."

"We knew there was always a chance that ..."

"No," she cautioned, "that's not what I'm talking about."

"Okay, I'll just shut up and listen."

"Sidney is gay or at least bisexual," she blurted out.

"I never knew."

"There's more," she said with a faltering inflection that warned him the worst was yet to come. "A husband and wife that he had sex with were blackmailing him. The woman claimed she was pregnant."

"You said *was*. Does that mean they've been paid off?"

"They weren't paid off. They're both dead."

"You're not inferring ..."

"Yes. He did it ... I know he did it – not himself, but he had it done."

"Come on," he pleaded. Sidney Holdridge can't be a murderer."

"He all but admitted it."

"Why would he concede a thing like that?"

"He feels safe. He says that we're the ones who are vulnerable."

"The bastard's right."

"What are we going to do?" she asked.

"I don't know. The fallout would probably kill us."

"Meaning?"

"I'm not going to make any decisions until we talk. We all need to sit down and make some hard decisions."

"He's not the man you thought he was. He's consumed with hate."

"You've been through hell, haven't you?"

The concern in his voice touched her. Emotions that had been suppressed over the past two days, began to surface.

"I'm so scared. I think he's capable of almost anything."

All of James Atwater's protective instincts were called to serve. With the fingertips of his right hand pressed lightly against her cheek, he looked into her beautiful green eyes.

"We'll get through this," he assured her.

The little girl in Robin surfaced as she snuggled forward like a wounded fawn into the sanctuary of his nurturing embrace. Determined to improve her outlook, she pushed reality to the farthest reaches of her conscious mind.

With her head tucked between his cheek and shoulder, she closed her eyes. A quiet minute passed before she moved to face him. Their lips touched and for a long intimate moment they were one. At the conclusion of their kiss he inconspicuously slipped his hand around her slender wrist.

"Come with me," he ordered.

In meek compliance, she followed his lead.

"I want to see you," he whispered.

In a single swift movement, he swept her from her feet into the support of his powerful arms. He had never held her like this before. Along their walk to his bedroom, they kissed as if they had never kissed before. When they reached the platform, upon which so many fantasies had been fulfilled, he placed her on the bedspread and smiled.

"I'm going to call the kitchen and have two fantastic dinners sent up. You and I are going to eat, watch a movie, talk, and just be together. I think we need each other. I know I need you."

Anxious to proceed, he opened the closet and removed a bathrobe for each of them.

"Get comfortable," he said, tossing the smaller of the fluffy robes into her waiting arms.

Each of them undressed to the always appreciative eyes of the other. Once their clothes had been discarded, they peeled down the covers of the king size bed and wrapped themselves in the warmth of the sheet and comforter. Their tender touches were sexual and loving. As always, it felt wonderful to be together.

Due to the nature of their two year love affair, time was always in short supply. More than anything, they missed the hours of small talk and playful banter that most couples

took for granted. The consequence of their circumstance was expressed in a greater than ordinary emphasis on sex. The spark that ignited their initial relationship remained hot and inexhaustible. Every moment they spent together was edged with a physical tension that
begged for constant attention.

The thirsty lovers drank of each other's presence with unbridled enthusiasm. The sight of Robin's body had an always predictable effect. She could feel his hardness pressing against her thigh; he was anxious and ready. A kick of the covers exposed his throbbing erection and muscular body to full view.

"I want to make you cum," she whispered seductively.

"It's okay with me," he said with a wink, "how do you want me?"

"Over easy," she cooed. "Just lie there. I'll take care of the rest."

She rose to her feet and walked to the bathroom. After a few short moments, she returned with a mischievous grin and a small jar of Vaseline.

"Way too bright," she whispered.

He watched in rapt anticipation as Robin retrieved a half dozen votive candles from a nearby bureau drawer, lit each wick and dispersed the small glass holders evenly about the room. Bathed in a golden flicker of light, she stretched enticingly across the bed on her stomach. Her gorgeous green eyes were captivated by his pulsing erection.

Without shifting her focus, she opened the container of petroleum jelly, removed a scoop of the grease like substance, and smeared it across the inside of her right palm. With one long stroke, she covered his entire length. Her loving application summoned an appreciative groan that sparked an expected flash of excitement through her own body.

Her slippery fingers closed softly around him and began to pump. Slowly, deliberately, she massaged and rubbed him. Again, and again, her warm knowing strokes summoned him to the edge of release. As the minutes past, she could feel the persistent pull of his hand, trying to coax her to move closer.

Aroused by the potential of such a move, she complied. Without missing a stroke, she scooted the lower portion of her body up against his left hip. This new position afforded her impassioned lover with a tantalizing view between her now open legs.

At that moment, he wanted nothing more than to touch the alluring folds of wet flesh that were moving so feverishly against the blue silk sheet. His eager fingers probed gently between her already open lips. She accepted his penetration with ease.

Her hungry hips rose and fell in a frantic attempt to make clitoral contact with anything that might offer resistance. Her lover's three middle fingers provided the much-needed contact.

With her hips moving in a precise rhythm, she brought herself to the threshold of orgasm. She slowed her pending climax, by changing her position. On her knees and elbows, she was poised to cum. The sight of her, spread open before him and wild with excitement, brought her lover to a violent climax. Thick white liquid spurted into the air, precipitating Robin's own release. Neither of them stopped until they had milked the last few drops from each other's body. For a few glorious moments they had no problems; no thoughts; just each other.

Still gasping for breath, they embraced. Their love play had left Robin more optimistic. For the first time, in what seemed like a long time, she asked a question that assumed there might be a future.

"If we got married ... would you want a baby?"

"Yes, WHEN we get married, I want a baby. I want a little girl, and I want to spoil her."

Robin was pleased by the sincerity in her lover's reply. Inspired by his alacrity, she curled up next to him and allowed herself to fantasize.

"Wouldn't it be wonderful to have a family – to just live like normal people. To cook a meal, burn the toast, sleep late, play with the baby, go to the movies, just walk down the street without a guard? I want that so much, Jim." Robin's idyllic vision took a dark turn. "Even if the worst happens, please promise me we'll be together."

"No matter what happens, I'll always be there," he assured her. At least for the moment, he was able to place Robin at peace.

She whispered softly in his ear. "I love you so much. We'll live a dream life."

He pulled her to him, cradling her in his arms. His mind skipped through the possibilities. If she could look into his eyes, he knew she would easily detect his apprehension. The thought of what might lay ahead was troubling. Somehow, they had to come through it – together.

# MAY 28
## Elbow Lake

A St. Louis County Sheriff's vehicle picked its way along the narrow gravel road that encircled Elbow Lake. Every area cabin, abandoned or not, was being checked for any sign of Martin and Jean Balfour. The small two bedroom bungalow occupied by Tabou and his people was one of only two residences yet to be checked.

Sheriff's Deputies Royal Smith and Rudy Flaskerud, favored for such menial tasks, had combed the northern Minnesota woods for any sign of the Balfours since an inquiry into their whereabouts was filed two days ago by Jean Balfour's father. Following the discovery of a Jeep vehicle belonging to Martin Balfour, the search was narrowed to the vast wilderness north and west of Elbow Lake.

Two muddy ruts leading to the cabin kept the black and white patrol car at bay. Deputies Smith and Flaskerud shared little interest in the ribbing that would result from a call for a tow truck. Besides, a seventy-four-degree temperature and bright sunshine made a short walk through fragrant pines an inviting excursion.

From their window, Tabou and Coutre watched the two deputies walk away from their car and saunter toward the cabin. They had no idea why these two lone figures would choose them for an unannounced visit. Regardless of the reason, they were confident in their ability to handle anything a rural county sheriff's department could throw at them.

Even though the two officers appeared to pose a minimal threat, it had been decided that suspicious behavior, on the part of either deputy, would result in a lethal response. If the mission hadn't required that they remain undetected, the hapless deputies would have been eliminated without a second thought.

Sharif, Arbash, and Jaabir stood in the bedroom where Jean Balfour was bound and gagged. Each of them held a Finnish M-82 submachine gun. Tabou knew that the tiny bedroom would not contain the volatile trio for long.

Along his walk to the cabin, Royal Smith couldn't help noticing the Virginia license plates on the vans parked to the rear of the building. Most of the tourist traffic in this area was generated from the southern part of Minnesota or a surrounding Midwestern state.

Smith rapped the knuckle of his right hand against the weathered entry. Coutre, the fairest skinned of the group, opened the door and peered at the deputies through the rusty screen.

"What can I do for you?" he asked.

The Frenchman's accent momentarily disarmed Smith, causing him to pause awkwardly before answering.

"Aaah ... we're lookin' for a man and a woman that might'a gotten lost in this area."

"We have seen no one," Coutre replied.

"Well now, ya' must've seen somebody. The second week of fishin' season brings a lot of people to the lakes around here. That must be why you're up here ain't it?"

Coutre fingered the dagger in his pocket. An impulse to scream *fuck you* ran through his head. Common sense forced a more tactful reply.

"Yes, the fishing is good. I meant that we saw no one who appeared lost or troubled. You understand."

Smith peered at the Frenchman suspiciously.

"Let me show you what these people look like so if you see 'em you'll know who you're lookin" at. Are the rest of your bunch inside? I might as well step in an' show ya' all at the same time."

As both deputies advanced, Coutre's grip tightened around the handle of his dagger. A restraining touch of Tabou's hand on the Frenchman's arm postponed the confrontation. Together, they stepped aside. The Jabali was as cordial as his manner would allow.

"Yes, come in. Let us know what these people look like so that we may watch for them."

Tabou's thick Arab accent caused Flaskerud, on the county payroll by virtue of nepotistic appointment, to blurt out an insensitive redneck question.

"Are you one of those A-rabs ... From the Middle East?" Before Tabou could answer, the deputy laughed at his own remark and continued, "If you are, I ought to thank you for lowerin' those goddamn high gas prices we were payin' up here last winter. I like ta' shit when it hit three bucks.

Tabou disregarded the deputy's inquiry along with the fatuous statement that followed. From his nervous fidgeting, any thinking man would have recognized the Jabali's growing impatience. Smith and Flaskerud remained blissfully ignorant.

"Let us see the pictures," ordered Tabou.

Both deputies took obvious notice of Ayesha, standing next to the kitchen table. Deputy Flaskerud acknowledged her presence with a folksy Midwest salutation. "Howdy! Ma'am."

The Iranian responded with a silent nod. Meanwhile, Smith continued his unwitting effort to tighten the noose around his own neck. "There's only three of you and you drove two big ol' vans from Virginia to Minnesota? Most folks would have found a way to ride together."

Tabou and Coutre exchanged quick glances. The deputies had just about reached the agreed upon point of no return.

Flaskerud's big mouth broke the tension and temporarily staved off certain death.

"Shit, Royal! A-rabs don't need to worry about buyin' gas."

The two deputies laughed while Tabou managed a forced half smile. The only thing preventing Coutre from killing the half-wit deputies on the spot was the presence of his Jabali comrade. To Ayesha, these Americans had two strikes against them; they were rude, and they were men.

"The pictures," Tabou demanded. Smith removed a small wedding picture of Martin and Jean Balfour from his inside jacket pocket. He then handed it to Tabou who feigned interest as he examined the 5 x 7 photograph before passing it to Coutre and Ayesha.

Flaskerud, meanwhile, began strolling across the room. His mindless journey was taking him in the general direction of the bedroom. He couldn't know that on the other side of the door, two machine guns were poised to greet him. The third gun was pointed at the head of a wide-eyed Jean Balfour. If the knob turned, two of St. Louis

County's so-called deputies would never hear the shots that killed them.

Dumb luck, the only kind Flaskerud could have, stopped him several feet short of the bedroom door, temporarily preserving both he and his partner's life. Oblivious to his good fortune, he wandered in the direction of the window overlooking the lake.

After returning the Balfour picture to Smith, Tabou attempted to Pied Piper the deputies outside of the cabin. He spoke as he sauntered toward the door.

"We will look for any sign of these two. If they should appear, we will inform them that the authorities are looking for them."

Smith, following a few steps behind the Jabali, laughed.

"Better not put it that way. You'll scare the piss out of 'em."

The deputies, like sheep in so many ways, followed Tabou through the door and out of the cabin. Once outside, Smith debunked a favorite theory of the less informed members of the community.

"Some folks wonder if bears didn't get 'em. Hell! No bear's gonna eat two full grown people. They just ain't flesh eaters."

Flaskerud threw in his two cents.

"They'll show up. They're probably campin' and havin' a high ol' time. It's only been three or four days."

A few steps from the cabin, Smith turned to Tabou.

"Been catchin" any fish?"

The Jabali, who hadn't fished at all, groped for a reply.

"Yes, the fishing has been good."

"Whatcha been catchin' 'em on?"

Tabou had no idea what bait was appropriate to the area. He remembered a frog lure that he had seen in one of the nearby service station bait stores.

"Aaaah ... frogs."

The statement sent Flaskerud, a lifelong fisherman, into a tizzy.

"Frogs! There ain't no bass in this lake. What the hell bites on frogs?"

Tabou stuck by his statement, "I catch many fish on frogs."

Tired of the banter, Smith urged his hapless partner to head for the car, "Come on Rudy! Let's get goin'. We've still got to hit the Hejda place."

"I'm comin'."

Tabou and his people listened as the two deputies strolled back to their patrol car. In the still morning air, their voices were plainly audible.

"Hey Royal! You believe that ... frogs! No wonder. What the hell would an A-rab know about fishin'. They buy water like we buy fuckin' gasoline."

Tabou entered the cabin. Everyone inside was laughing and joking over the bimbo cops who had unwittingly come within inches of losing their lives. The visit was reassuring. If the level of resistance encountered by the group since arriving in America was typical of all law enforcement, their mission could be accomplished with relative ease. They might even live through it. A possibility that all but Coutre, had never seriously considered.

## The White House
## President's Living Quarters

This was the day, the time, and the place. In a few minutes, James Atwater would confront his vice president.

To insure privacy, the domestic staff had been dismissed for the remainder of the day. No matter how well the involved parties handled their little tête-à-tête, the president knew that it wasn't going to be pretty. For no particular reason, the den was chosen as the site for their meeting. Anxiously, the president and Robin waited.

"Does he know what this meeting is all about?" asked Robin.

"Yes. I told him that we had some problems to iron out. He knew what I was talking about."

"Did you find out any more about the murders?"

"Enough to know that the police don't have a clue."

"Are you going to initiate an investigation?"

"I haven't decided."

Robin watched as the president did something she had never seen him do before. He filled a shot glass with tequila and downed the contents with a single gulp.

### Elbow Lake

When Ayesha saw that Tabou was standing alone, near water's edge, she took advantage of the opportunity and approached him.

The breeze coming off of the lake was sufficient to make her appreciate the balmy afternoon sun. For several minutes they stood shoulder-to-shoulder, mesmerized by the expanse of restless blue water that stretched before them as far as the eye could see. Comfortable with the moment, the beautiful young Iranian spoke. Her usual pugnacity was replaced with a contradicting air of tractability.

"We have never spoken ... just you and me," she said softly.

The Jabali did not answer.

"First, understand that I will do as I am told. I only ask that you please answer my questions. I need to understand."

"Understand what?" Tabou asked in a voice that proved he wasn't always angry.

"Who is this 'Parker' you speak of?

"He is our American contact. He's the one who made this possible. It was he who bought the cars and boats. He also rented this cabin and arranged for the plane."

"Does he hate Atwater, as we do?"

"No," Tabou said, managing a partial smile. "He is a true American. He was bought and paid for."

"Tell me why we are killing Atwater in this way? It would be so easy to kill him as other American presidents have been killed?"

"It's more than the killing. Sirhan, Sirhan killed a man destined to be the president. Did it bring him or our people honor? Did Kennedy's assassins bring honor on themselves?"

"No," she answered, "that is because they were cowardly acts. For forty years, the Arab world has done nothing but retreat in the face of Zionist aggression. The deserts of our homeland are littered with the unused tanks and guns of our armies. Our people have been branded as ignorant nomads by a world taught to respect only one thing: power. Even our leaders have lost faith in their own people, bargaining away our birthright to the Jews and receiving nothing in return. Generations of Arab children have had no heroes. They only know of battles lost."

"Can we change that?" Ayesha asked.

"I believe, yes., answered Tabou, "this will be no cowardly attack from afar. No rifles poking through bushes or out of windows. We will kill the American president in his lair, surrounded by their best, their sharpest. The six of us against many of them. No one has ever done such a thing. Kabazi will use our victory as a rallying point. Muslims from every quarter will look at themselves in a new way. They will put aside their differences and come together to fight as one. The world will feel our thunder. They will never forget what we have done, or what they did to our people to bring about this revenge."

## The White House
## President's Living Quarters

"I didn't know you were going to be present, my dear," Sidney said, as he strolled into the den where the president and Robin were seated. "That brings up an interesting question: How have you snuck in and out of here so often without anyone noticing?"

"I don't think it ...," Robin began before Sidney interrupted.

"Aahh yes, those nasty little Secret Service boys. They never talk, do they?

"You should know," Robin said bitterly.

"Yes," Sidney answered with a mischievous grin, "I do."

"Okay," said the president, "that's about enough of that. We all know that we all know. Now, what are we going to do about it?"

"You could start by keeping your hands and anything else that's hanging out, off of my wife. Don't get me wrong, I wouldn't fuck her if she *was* a good lay. I just won't allow you to have her."

The president stood, "You don't love her. Why do you care?"

"I'm not on trial here. Suffice it to say, I do care."

"What about this blackmail thing. Sidney, did you have a hand in murdering the Rueds?"

"Ridiculous. The whole thing was a fabrication. Their unfortunate demise was a coincidence. From what I've read in the newspaper, the Rueds led a rather precarious life style."

"I think we've got one hell of a coincidence here," said the president.

"You've been listening to my wife. She wouldn't know the truth if it bit her in the ass. I had nothing to do with their deaths and you can't prove otherwise."

"With what I know, I'm duty bound to launch an investigation."

"Just how are you going to do that? Are you going to tell the FBI that you were fucking my wife and she just happened to mention that I had two people killed? An investigation will bury you in shit up to your eyebrows. I always thought you were brighter than that."

"Neither one of us is above the law."

"The difference here is – I didn't kill anyone, but you did fuck my wife.

"Then you wouldn't mind an investigation into the matter?"

"I could survive. Could you? What about all the men you've already had contact with? cautioned the president.

"Are they going to maintain their silence?"

"They have for the past ten years," Sidney said, pausing long enough to enjoy the pain in his wife's expression. "What about all of the wags who must know you're banging my wife? Or, doesn't that count? Does adultery get higher marks today than homosexuality?"

"Don't draw an analogy between your years of cheating and my relationship with Robin. There isn't one. Our affair is the result of your inattention, not the cause of it."

"Is that how you've rationalized your licentious behavior? Interesting … bullshit!"

"And how do you rationalize your indiscriminate pursuits, Sidney? asked the president.

"I don't," answered Sidney, " I am who I am, and I accept it."

"I can't stand by and ignore the fact that you may have ordered the Rueds killed," warned the president.

"You expose me to ridicule with some phony investigation, and I'll make sure the world knows every lurid detail of your sordid little affair with my wife. History will remember you as the president who fucked the vice president's wife. You'll be the butt of every joke, in every bar, on the whole fucking planet. Richard Nixon will look like Mother Theresa next to you. Deal with it, Jimmy,"

Sidney snarled, "It's a Mexican standoff."

It was pay day. Time to pay for all those wonderful evenings with another man's wife. For all the power of the presidency, James Atwater was helpless.

"You don't give one damn about this country, do you?"

"And what about you, you pompous prick? What national crisis did you expect to resolve when you slipped your dick into my wife?"

"You think you're going to be the next president, don't you?"

"Who told you that? Who said I was running?" Sidney's face flushed with anger.

To avoid implicating Robin, the president sidestepped the question.

"What matters is the American ...."

"I told him," Robin injected, anxious to take the blame. "It's the truth. You told me you were going to be the next president, and I might add, you said nothing that would indicate your decision was some deep dark secret."

"My future and my plans are my own. As my wife, and I use the word loosely, I expect you to keep your mouth shut."

"Look," said the president, "as far as your run at the presidency goes, forget it. It isn't going to happen," Sidney's anger surfaced again.

"That's not for you to decide," snarled Sidney.

"You aren't electable," the president continued, "you need a reality check. I carried you on my back through the last election. All of my advisors recommended that I dump you. I said, no. I believed in loyalty. Did you ever read the newspapers? Did you look at the polls? Did you notice that when they paired me with anyone else in the country, the ticket was stronger? Christ, Sidney, I could have run with O.J. Simpson at my side and pulled as many votes. The perceptions of the American public were apparently far more reliable than my own."

The president moved closer, "Face it Sidney, you just aren't a viable candidate. And there's another thorn in this little bouquet of yours. As a presidential candidate, you'd be subject to intense scrutiny. Your aberrant life style could never withstand that kind of probing."

The president's forthright appraisal of Sidney's political outlook exposed a raw nerve.

"Who do you think you are, Atwater? God almighty?" Sidney said.

"I'm the president, Sidney. Something you'll never be."

Exhibiting his penchant for sudden changes of mood, Sidney smiled.

"A single bullet fired by a mad man could change everything."

"Sidney!" Robin screamed, "how could you even suggest such a thing?"

Sidney shook his head.

"I'll just let the people decide. That's the American way, right, Jimmy?"

"What about us? I want a divorce," Robin injected.

"I don't think so," said Sidney, glaring at his wife. "Your little deception has been quite helpful. Presidents need wives. Think of the status bump; whore to first lady."

Sidney smirked at his wife, "Now, they might even allow you to use the front door of the White House."

"Okay," said the president, "everyone's cards are on the table. We need ..."

Sidney interrupted, "And I've got the royal flush,"

"I can determine the fate of everyone in this room," the president's voice was stern yet controlled. "Ride out your term quietly and don't run for public office – ever again. That's my offer, Sidney."

"Or?" Sidney asked.

"We all fall," warned Sidney's boss, "I launch an investigation, and everyone, including the American public, loses. We all get dirty."

Sidney was stone-faced.

The president continued, "You don't have to tell me now. I want you to think it over. Give me your answer at the lake."

"Okay, but you should consider the ramifications. I can't be connected to those murders. All you'll be doing is wrecking both of our careers and throwing away everything you've done for the past six years. Who wins?"

# CHAPTER EIGHT

## Aboard Air Force One

Today's two-hour flight to Duluth, Minnesota, the nearest airport to the summer White House with runways long enough to accommodate a 747, was not the carefree trip that the president had anticipated. The sunny prospect of visiting Wolf Island was suddenly overshadowed by Sidney Holdridge and his possible involvement in a double murder.

The investigation, that the president felt morally bound to conduct, would severely erode what little remained of America's faith in its political system. Personally, it would open his administration to microscopic scrutiny. Exposing his indefensible relationship with the vice president's wife.

In a matter of weeks, their torrid affair could be a matter of public record. He knew that the nation would judge them harshly. His days as the free-world's most powerful political leader would be over. Impeachment wasn't likely, but there was no doubt that he would be forced to resign.

Since his "vacation" had a high potential for conflict, the guest list for the six-day visit was trimmed to a bare minimum. Passengers on today's flight included: Sean MacDougal, twelve Secret Service agents, five flight attendants, a communications officer, military attaché, the president's personal physician, Press Secretary Donald Kincaid, and a representative group from the White House Press Corps. The chief executive's brother, Michael, who was invited when the trip was still thought of as a "vacation," lived in Minnesota and would drive to Boulder Lake joining the presidential party later in the day.

Seated alone in two facing recliners, Sean and the president were rehashing the highlights of a previous trip. Prior to their arrival, the president wanted to discuss a far more serious topic.

"Sean, we're going to be confronted with a situation this weekend. I'd appreciate your advice."

"Fire away."

James Atwater didn't mince around. He knew the information he was about to divulge would be a shocker.

"Holdridge is gay, or more probably bisexual," he blurted.

"Christ, Jim! I hope you mean he's real happy."

"Nobody is happy in this scenario," said the president.

"Sidney Holdridge? Come on, how do you know?"

"Robin. Apparently, he impregnated the wife of one of his sexual partners and they tried to blackmail him."

"Tried?" asked Sean.

"Yes. They were found dead in their home forty-eight hours after Holdridge was told of their threat."

"You're not going where I think you are with this, are you?"

"Robin says he all but admitted it."

"My God! Is he crazy?"

"I don't know. She's really upset."

"And I thought in sixty-three years, I'd heard everything. Sidney Holdridge ... a bisexual murderer! I need a drink after that one."

"I'll join you," said the president.

The president pressed a small red button, built into the right arm of his chair. Within seconds, a white-jacketed flight attendant was standing at his side. Both men ordered gin and tonics then waited patiently while the young Navy steward exited the cabin.

"What are you going to do?" Sean asked.

"That's what I wanted to ask you. I believe that I'm bound by oath and morality to investigate her suspicions."

Sean was incredulous.

"You know he didn't pull the trigger. It's unlikely that his kind of involvement, if it exists, could ever be proved. Old Sidney must have made some very powerful, very bad friends."

"Does that mean we should forget it?" asked the president.

"We'd all fry. What's the point?"

"I just want this mess to go away," droned the president in his most sincere tone.

The Irishman shook his head, indicating his own take on the subject. Then he spoke.

"People in hell want ice water. In order to investigate, you've got to ask people questions. This is too volatile and too hot. The story is worth too much money. We'd end up checking the *Post* for the scoop on our own investigation."

The conversation ground to a halt while the attendant distributed drinks. The moment he left the room, their talk resumed.

"So, your recommendation is to drop it?" asked the president."

"Absolutely. You're wearing a white shirt in a shit storm, and you've forgotten your umbrella. You'll never escape this mess without career-ending collateral damage."

"I've never put my own needs above those of the country," countered the president.

"If that were true, you wouldn't be in this mess."

"You're probably right. And what about Sidney?" asked the president. "If our suspicions are unfounded, we'll have done irreparable damage to his reputation. An inquiry of any kind, regardless of the outcome, will ruin him. No matter what facts emerge, the American public draws its own conclusions."

A rare flash of anger soured Sean's expression.

"If you were all that worried about Sidney, you wouldn't have fucked his wife, huh Jimmy?"

The bluntness of Sean's reply stung.

"You shouldn't drink and fly, Sean. It turns you into a real son-of-a-bitch."

"You're shooting the messenger again, kid. Never bullshit yourself, save it for the fawning masses."

As much as he hated it, the president knew that Sean was right. He didn't give one fuck about Sidney Holdridge. Noble platitudes and mock concern were bullshit. If he failed to instigate an investigation it would be to protect himself and the country – in that order.

"It's even more complicated. Sidney knows about Robin and me."

"Holy fuck, what next? Have the Chinese invaded Taiwan?"

"I know. It just seems to get worse. The three of us have already discussed the situation. He's had a total change in personality. He acts like he's got me by the short-hair, instead of the other way around."

"Back off and let things cool down. You've only got eighteen months to ride this mess out. Leave a winner."

"It should be quite a weekend," lamented the president.

"Why the hell did you invite him up here with all of this going on?"

"I'm worried about Robin. When you misjudge someone as badly as I misjudged Sidney, you aren't sure how far they'll go."

"You don't think ..."

"I don't know," said the president, "his behavior is so irrational."

"How rational can old Sidney be, Jim?" asked Sean, "you suggest investigating him for murder while his wife is being popped by another man. No, not another man, the president! I don't know about you, but that would really piss me off."

A sardonic grin broke across the president's face.

"Don't sugar coat it like that. God, you're feeling feisty today."

"There's enough material here to keep the *National Enquirer* in headlines for the next three years. Maybe I'm overreacting or maybe I'm just crazy, but I think we're in some deep shit!"

### Elbow Lake

Tabou, Sharif, and Ayesha were lakeside preparing their two Z-275 Davanti boats for the upcoming attack. Jaabir and Arbash had been sent to town for a few last-minute supplies; only Coutre remained in the cabin. The Frenchman had waited diligently for an opportunity to be alone with Jean Balfour – his chance had finally come.

Through the cabin's large front window, he made a reaffirming check on the whereabouts of his confederates. Satisfied that they were some distance away and preoccupied with their chores, he entered the small bedroom where Jean was bound to an upright chair located in the far corner of the room. She was still wearing the same clothing in which she was captured.

Her blue eyes widened as the Frenchman entered her room, closing the door behind him. He had harassed her with obscene gestures and knowing looks a dozen times over the past two days, but this time it appeared he meant business.

By the time she made her determination, it was too late. Coutre had slapped another strip of duct tape across her already tender mouth. His intensity and speed of movement left little doubt about his intentions. She knew she was in real trouble.

The Frenchman's ever-present dagger made another appearance. Two deft strokes of the razor-sharp blade quickly severed the ropes that were binding her ankles. Her initial impulse, to kick him, was dampened by the sharp point of the dagger pressed against her right thigh.

"Kick me, bitch, and I'll cut your throat right here, right fucking now!"

After tossing his knife on the bed, he began to pull Jean's pants and panties down over her hips. The ensuing struggle resulted in a mind-rattling blow to the side of her head.

Before she could regain her senses, the Frenchman managed to remove her blue jeans and black silk panties. The chair had served its purpose and now only hindered his intentions.

He grabbed the dagger from the bed and quickly cut the rope that secured her upper body to the chair. The binding around her wrists was left intact.

Before she could gain her balance, a quick shove hurled her half-naked body to the dirty gray sheets atop the small bed in the corner of the room.

With the point of his dagger, he prodded the inside of her bare thighs, forcing her to spread her legs so far apart that they hung over either side of the bed.

Helpless, she lay fully exposed to his hungry gaze. The sight of her prompted him to kneel on the bed between her outstretched legs.

With his free hand, he reached down and fluffed her matted pubic hair. In light of his many sexual conquests, the Frenchman exhibited little or no technique. His clumsy attempt to stroke her partially exposed clitoris only intensified her humiliation. By turning her head to one side and closing her eyes, she sought to escape the reality of his disgusting effort.

Having excited only himself, Coutre allowed his pants to fall to his knees. With his right hand, he reached between her legs and probed her flesh for an opening. With all the finesse of an inept teenager, he eventually discovered the object of his ungainly search.

The repugnance she felt for the man who was forcing himself on her, and the abruptness of the act had left her dry. He addressed the problem by spitting on his fingers, then massaging the slippery liquid into her skin.

As the weight of Coutre's body began to press her into the mattress and his stringy black hair fell forward against her neck and face, she found herself engulfed in a wave of nausea. If she had just one bullet, she thought, she would use it on herself, not on him.

An ominous metal on metal click halted the Frenchman's assault just short of penetration. Jean opened her eyes and searched for the source of the strange noise. Past the greasy glob of hair that was mashed against the left side of her face, she could see the barrel of a snub-nose pistol pointed at her attacker's brain. It was held by the girl, Sukayna Ayesha.

"Get off her!" she ordered.

The Iranian's run-in with Sharif was a grim reminder. Coutre knew that she would not hesitate to pull the trigger.

"What's it to you?" he asked.

"I hate to see slime like you force themselves on women. What's the matter with you? Couldn't you get a date as a kid?"

Ayesha's forced laugh concluded the deflation of the Frenchman's limp penis. In a push-up like movement, he slowly lifted himself from Jean's body.

"You're next, Butch." he scoffed, "you can have the bitch – I'll fuck her later."

"Put that little thing away and don't make promises you can't keep," she said, continuing to hold the gun on him while he stood and pulled up his pants.

Coutre turned toward Jean Balfour.

"I have already talked to the others. I'll be the last person you ever see ... and don't feel as if you just missed out – I will fuck you first," he smirked, "or maybe afterwards."

His threat rankled Ayesha.

"You sick fuck," she said, motioning toward the door with her pistol, "get out of here!"

Coutre glared at his Iranian nemesis.

"And you, cunt!" he said, walking away. "You're making a lot of enemies around here."

"Go out in the woods with the other squirrels," she yelled, "and jerk-off, you fucking pervert."

With the Frenchman outside the room, Ayesha kicked the door closed and returned her pistol to the belt underneath her blouse. For several seconds, she examined the well-proportioned body that was spread across the breadth of the bed. By simply watching the young woman's eyes, Jean knew what she was thinking. She knew that a decision was being made.

A long awkward silence was broken when the attractive Iranian sat on the edge of the bed. With surprising tenderness, she began peeling the sticky gray tape from the welted skin around Jean's sore mouth.

"Thank you. I didn't think anyone would help."

"I shouldn't have. I just didn't want that pig on you."

"We were just camping near here. We didn't ..."

"I know. They told me. You were in the wrong place at the wrong time. Things work like that sometimes."

"They're going to kill me, aren't they?"

"Yes. You had to know that. These men ... they solve problems that way. It's all they know."

Ayesha was right. Jean had already guessed the answer; her question was more of a test than a query for information. She wanted to know if the Iranian would tell her the truth. The resulting news was no surprise. Her real fear had now become, Coutre.

"Please! Don't let him do it. I don't want to die like that."

"I'll do what I can. I'm not the Playmate of the Month around here myself," the Iranian declared while untying the rope that secured Jean's wrists. "Get dressed."

Ayesha's conduct contradicted her involvement with the scoundrels who had captured her.

"Why would you take part in this terrible thing they are planning? Why are you here?"

"I am Islam. Your government is my enemy."

"You have your whole life ahead of you."

"My life is pledged. I have no life."

"How can you believe that?" Jean asked.

"You would not understand. It is hopeless for ..."

Tabou exploded through the closed bedroom door. Jean, partially clothed, retreated to the far wall.

"Tie her up!" he bellowed.

Ayesha remained calm.

"I intend to. She was being mauled by that French animal."

The Jabali was unimpressed.

"What does it matter. It will be over in hours."

"It matters!" Ayesha protested. "She is a woman. She deserves, at the least, to be left alone."

"She deserves nothing. I deserve nothing. We get what we can take," he scoffed.

"Musa Abu Tabou, your Jabali heart is cold."
"I have no heart! Remember that!"

## Duluth, Minnesota
## Duluth International Airport

The president's aircraft was only five minutes away. As always this signaled the president's security contingent to lock - down the facility.

Minnesota was home to the president, and though he had been schooled in Minneapolis, his fondest memories stemmed from the northern part of the state. The Hibbing-Virginia area, known as the iron range, was beautiful, remote, and unspoiled.

Many of the rugged individuals who sparsely populated the lake spotted terrain were of Native American or Scandinavian descent. They brought a strong sense of determination to an unyielding environment that more fragile men termed hostile. These trusting and honorable people served as role models for James Atwater in his formative years.

No amount of planning could prepare Duluth International Airport for a presidential visit. At the chief executive's insistence, barriers between him and the people were kept to a minimum. The scene was always the same pandemonium.

Air Force One settled to the safety of the Duluth runway with expected precision. Pressed against the fence, seventy-five yards behind the small knot of dignitaries waiting to greet the president, stood a crowd of eager well-wishers, nearly a thousand strong. Most of those gathered, split evenly between area residents and tourists, had been waiting hours for a glimpse of the most famous man in the world.

The huge Boeing, emblazoned with the Presidential Seal, rolled along the taxi way to the concrete apron leading to the terminal where three spotless black limousines were easing into position. A narrow red carpet would usher the president from Air Force One to a cluster of local dignitaries who had gathered to welcome him. As the lumbering jet approached, the whine of its powerful engines intensified to a level bordering on discomfort.

Swarms of uniformed police officers, under the supervision of twenty-three Secret Service agents, engulfed the immediate vicinity, particularly the area between the plane and the fence. The overworked Duluth police department and the Minnesota Highway Patrol were an important supplement to the president's D.C. security contingent, most of whom had arrived in the C141 cargo plane enlisted to deliver the two presidential limos known simply as the "beasts" which arrived the previous day.

While the jet's powerful engines faded from an earsplitting shriek to a more tolerable purr, two blue coveralled airport employees wheeled the stair ramp into place against the fuselage of the plane. A few seconds later, the forward door swung open allowing a vigilant Secret Service agent to step from the plane.

Those with the worst view and the poorest eyesight cheered wildly. Their enthusiasm was cut short by the laughter of those who knew that the young man wearing a trench coat and sunglasses was not the president. Eight of the nine on-board agents then proceeded to jog watchfully down the twelve step ramp. Finally, the chief executive emerged into the warm Minnesota sunlight. This time, the cheers of the crowd were unrestrained and vigorous.

Near the base of the ramp, a throng of national and international reporters had pushed aside the less carnivorous among them for a front row position. As was his custom, the president graciously paused for pictures and a few informally answered questions.

The genuine warmth that he felt for the people was made evident by his determination to reward their patient vigil. He was not running for reelection, yet he risked his life to walk to the fence and shake hands with those who had waited for hours to wish him well.

The president's perilous ad hoc journey signaled a predictable alarm among the several dozen men responsible for his immediate safety. Potential for disaster had increased tenfold. The half dozen agents, who rushed to the chief executive's side, did their best to scan the sea of energetic faces and make split-second judgments as to their intent.

Every man knew that if someone was determined to assassinate the president, under these conditions, it would be difficult, if not impossible to prevent the attack. Their only advantage was the spontaneity with which a public flesh pressing always occurred.

The fact that the president's risky excursions into unchecked crowds were random and seldom planned was a big plus. A potential assassin might find it necessary to wait for months, to be in the right place at the right time. Sadly, history had taught such people do exist.

Fifteen anxious minutes passed before the fretful agents were able to steer the president to the protective confines of the second limousine. The chief executive's disdain for helicopter travel created a security nightmare.

Special vehicles, equipped for bomb detection, had swept the eighty mile route to Boulder Lake continually since 5 a.m. During the same period, a company of Marines, flown in from Fort Bragg, were patrolling the thick ground cover adjacent to the roadway for possible sniper activity.

Over ninety law enforcement officers and their cars were expropriated from a variety of agencies to provide constant highway surveillance. Each of the small towns along the route, large enough to have a police force, made its own contribution. Even in a rural area of his home state, a short presidential jaunt to the summer White House required days of planning and the cooperation from dozens of agencies involving hundreds of people.

With everyone loaded, the spotless black limousines dovetailed into the long procession of local, county, state and federal vehicles that would accompany the presidential caravan. Adorned with small flags atop each fender, the president's vehicle pulled cautiously across Stebner Road and began its picturesque journey to Boulder Lake.

In the parking lot of a lumber company, across from the airport's main entrance, an automobile, cloaked in heavily tinted glass waited. The vehicle's lone occupant watched the president's motorcade advance with uncommon interest. Parker actually liked James Atwater. "It was too bad," he thought to himself, "that it had to end here, in the woods of northern Minnesota."

213

# Boulder Lake

The summer White House was situated on a small thirty-five acre island just off the southern shore of rock strewn, Boulder Lake. Ownership of the island traced back to William Atwater, the president's grandfather, who purchased the property in the late twenties as a family retreat. James had continued the tradition, and in the process, made tiny Wolf Island world famous.

Spread over 46,000 acres, Boulder Lake was large, even by Minnesota standards. Three hundred and fifty-eight islands ranging from mere rock piles to the mammoth two thousand four hundred acre Johnson Island irregularly dotted its surface. The lake's craggy east-west shore protruded and receded sharply, forming numerous bays along its uneven forty-six mile length. From north to south, the water extended only seven miles across at its furthest point.

Boomerang-shaped Wolf Island was positioned in the middle of the lake fewer than a thousand feet off its southern shore. White birch, sprinkled with an occasional pine, formed a thick green blanket over ninety percent of the island's virgin ground. An assortment of wild animals that included Black Bear, white tail deer, timber wolves, and beaver could all claim full or part-time residence.

The structures on Wolf Island had multiplied twofold since the president took office. The four thousand square foot lodge, small fish cleaning house, boat house, and double guest cabin were not adequate for the sizable entourage that often trailed behind the chief executive.

Two months after James Atwater took office, a communications building was erected in the woods one hundred yards behind the main lodge. The single-story structure was built to accommodate a state-of-the-art communications system, costing two and one half million dollars complimented by an elaborate alarm system designed to warn of intruders anywhere on the island. The buildings official designation, among agents, was Communications Control One. On a less formal basis, most of its occupants referred to it simply as Vigil One.

To shelter agents and house additional monitoring equipment, three small guard posts were constructed on strategic sites around the island's perimeter. The twenty by twelve foot buildings, known candidly as *wack shacks*, were designed to accommodate air and surface radar along with an assortment of sophisticated alarm equipment designed to indicate points of intrusion in the area covered by each facility. Each system was electronically tethered to Communications Control One.

Together, the three guard posts were able to monitor a three hundred and sixty degree safe zone around the island's entire perimeter. Guard One, as it was officially referred to, was situated on shore near the main dock. Guard Two, was positioned in the middle of the island, overlooking the water to the west. The furthest building from the lodge, Guard Three, had been constructed on the southeast tip of the island where both the far shore and the main lodge were easily visible. Agents manning these remote outposts were ferried to and from their stations by boat which exchanged the two-man teams every eight hours.

The president was able to access either Vigil One or Guard One by telephone or by hitting any one of a dozen Panic Buttons placed strategically throughout the main lodge.

Over the mild protests of the chief executive, an acre of trees was cleared for a helicopter landing area that, partly out of spite, he seldom, if ever used. The circular pad, exactly one hundred and twelve feet in diameter, was used by the helicopters charged with transporting a variety of government personnel, including agents of the Secret Service to and from their sleeping quarters in nearby Virginia, Minnesota. Between shift changes, the chopper was kept on Wolf Island.

A second guest cabin, half the size of the main lodge, was erected three years ago, enabling the president to entertain heads of state in an informal and often more productive atmosphere than could be found in the more traditional trappings of Washington D.C.

Nonstop barking was an unavoidable consequence of Secret Service agents roaming the grounds during night time hours. The president of Azerbaijan, the first in a string of distinguished visitors to the island, was also the first and last world leader to experience the incongruity of restless golden retrievers and sleep. Thereafter, it was decided that the president's two dogs, Riggs and Murtaugh, would no longer be permitted to spend the night in the main building. Consequently, a small windowless structure was erected fifty yards behind the lodge. Agents were instructed to give the oversize kennel a wide berth, lest they stir up the protective instincts of its furry inhabitants.

The tax payers were tabbed for the building of the four security facilities, the helicopter landing pad, and the installation of electronic communications and surveillance equipment. The six hundred thousand dollars spent in the construction and improvement of the other buildings was paid for by the president himself; a bargain, compared to the five million dollars in advertising that would have been required to explain the purchases if they had been paid for with tax dollars.

The arrival of the presidential caravan created a carnival atmosphere that temporarily sullied the serene ambiance of Boulder Lake. A one acre parcel, situated on the mainland and owned by the president served as a parking lot and launching point for anyone traveling to Wolf Island. The only building on the lakeshore property, a three-car garage, was so crammed with life jackets, canoes, and other paraphernalia associated with island living, that there was no longer room to shelter the automobiles for which it was built.

Since assuming the presidency, the Atwater family had found it necessary to hire a year-round resident to act as caretaker of the small wooded lot. Vandals and souvenir seekers were breaking windows and wreaking general havoc on the grounds, including the four boats parked on either side of the eighty-five foot wooden dock.

Regardless of planning, someone always left the dock minus a life jacket or found themselves without a necessary piece of equipment or clothing. Amidst a torrent of predictable confusion, the three boats, transporting the chief executive and his party, backed cautiously away from the dock. Even at half speed, the trip to Wolf Island would only take a few minutes.

Two of the boats, seventeen-foot Sylvan runabouts, had been in the Atwater family for nearly ten years. A sixty-two foot houseboat and a twenty-eight foot cruiser were added to the modest fleet after James Atwater's election to a second term. Both purchases were a necessity. While he didn't mind it himself, the president found it awkward to transport another country's leader in what was primarily a seventeen-foot fishing boat.

To the relief of everyone, the miniature armada reached the island. As usual the island was officially locked down by the Secret Service five minutes before the president's arrival. No one outside of the presidential party was allowed to leave or set foot on the premises. The sight of the approaching dock and "home" was a happy occasion for the fatigued president. It was time to unwind.

"Isn't that a beautiful sight?" the president observed.

Sean, who had visited the island nearly as often as his boss, concurred.

"I love this island, Jim. There's not a place on earth where I feel more at home."

### Elbow Lake

As their rendezvous with history neared, an uneasy tension settled over Tabou and his comrades. There was nothing more to discuss; plans for the mission were complete, and everyone, including their quarry, was in position. Only time separated them from their goal. An inability to form friendships and an intrinsic paranoia, previously satiated by endless rehearsals and hours of observation, became increasingly apparent.

Inside their cabin, the would-be assassins focused their nervous energy on the tools of their violent trade. Six Finnish M-82 submachine guns rested in a neat row against the wall next to the living room couch. Tabou and Sharif, seated at the kitchen table, preoccupied themselves with the inspection of a shoulder-fired RPG-7 Soviet rocket launcher.

Jaabir and Arbash, sitting on the floor near the open front door, were dividing grenades and ammunition into six separate piles appropriate to each individual's weapons and responsibilities. Seated on the couch, Coutre sharpened his beloved dagger while Sukayna Ayesha, standing at the kitchen counter, puzzled over the reassembly of a Russian Makarov pistol.

As distasteful as the idea seemed, she was forced to ask for assistance.

"Does this spring fit under or over the metal clip?" she asked of anyone who might have an answer.

Tabou's attempt to respond was cut short by Coutre, who was still vexed over his emasculating run-in with the scrappy Iranian. She had stuck her nose where he felt it didn't belong, and he was not about to forget it.

"You don't cook, clean, fuck or know anything about guns. What do you do?" he asked.

"You will see what I do. Worry about yourself, Frenchman."

The Palestinian, Arbash, rose to his feet and walked to the young woman's side,

"I will help you."

Coutre took the gesture as a personal affront, which it was.

"You work well with women, Arbash."

"I work well with many people. You might try and do the same."

To display the razor-sharp edge of his infamous dagger, the Frenchman seized a wrinkled page from a two-day old edition of the *Duluth Sentinel*. He spoke while ribbons of shredded paper floated to the floor.

"Maybe I should eliminate those with whom I do not work well," he warned.

Ayesha ignored the childish exhibition, savoring the opportunity to make a comment of her own.

"Then we'd all be dead," she smirked. "You kill everything around you! You're a fucking psycho!"

The Frenchman sprang to his feet.

"Fuck this job. I've taken enough shit from you."

As he had so many times, Tabou watched his team begin to disintegrate. His words resounded throughout the cabin.

"Shut your mouths! You fight as children! I will have no more of it!"

Unwilling to test an angry Tabou, Coutre sank to the floor and resumed his task while Arbash assisted Ayesha in the reassembly of her pistol. In the back bedroom, Jean Balfour waited and listened. She knew that within hours she would be dead.

# Wolf Island

It was five o'clock when Sean, accompanied by Press Secretary Kincaid, managed to pull away from the main dock in search of the elusive walleye pike. The president would have been the first one in the boat, had he not felt it imperative that he be present for the arrival of Sidney and Robin.

Stretched out on the chaise lounge, at the end of the spacious deck which surrounded the north and east sides of his cabin, James Atwater couldn't help but think of how the presidency had changed his trips to Wolf Island.

Outside of his quarters in the White House, he had no privacy. Even on his own island, in this remote section of America, he was surrounded by Secret Service agents and an unrelenting parade of public gawkers whose curiosity drove them to wait by the hour for a glimpse of him or anyone in the presidential party that they might recognize.

Unlike Camp David, a government-owned retreat enjoyed by many of Atwater's predecessors, Boulder Lake was open to the public. The land surrounding the president's private property belonged to the state of Minnesota and, in the case of nearby Superior National Forest, the Department of the Interior.

In a rare moment of mutual accord, the involved governing factions agreed that public use of Boulder Lake, during a presidential visit, should be partially curtailed. The restricted area stretched five hundred yards in all directions from the Wolf Island shoreline. This "no-man's land" was marked by fluorescent orange buoys spaced at twenty-five yard intervals. A warning sign was affixed to the top of each marker. It read:

# -WARNING!-
## RESTRICTED AREA
### NO ADMITTANCE UNDER
### PENALTY OF FEDERAL LAW
### PATROLLED BY THE
### UNITED STATES COAST GUARD.

The teeth of the warning was furnished by three Coast Guard patrol boats outfitted with M-60 machine guns. Traveling just inside the buoys, they policed their assigned areas in a back and forth endless loop. Their four men crews changed shifts every twelve hours and worked three days one week, then four days the next.

Depending on the president's length of stay, it took between twenty-seven and fifty-one Coast Guardsman, including three seaman on-call, to provide Wolf Island with twenty-four-hour security.

An always curious public garnered a lion's share of the Coast Guard's attention. By order of the president, all contacts were to be courteous with thoughtful explanations extended to any questioning individual. This took extra time and often resulted in unavoidable distractions and delays.

On the island, security was never placed in the hands of fewer than fourteen agents. Two in each of the guard posts; one at the front door or with the president if he was outside of the lodge; two walking the grounds, adjacent to the lodge; one shift commander in the communications building monitoring the FIB, Fire and Intruder Board, and two agents walking the grounds around and near the guest cabins. This number did not include the agents on call in Minneapolis.

In light of the recent terrorist threat, three uniformed officers from the canine unit out of Beltsville, Maryland, were assigned to bolster Wolf Island security. They patrolled, with their dogs in a random pattern around the island perimeter. Also, not included in the twelve agents on the island, were two agents assigned to the checkpoint at the entrance to the only road leading to the south end of the lake. In all, a contingent of fifty-one agents was responsible for the onsite physical well-being of the president and his guests.

The Navy had contributed a dock boy and an experienced seaman to act as crew of the presidential boat. Both men were billeted on the near shore in a cabin purchased for the purpose by the United States Government. A cook and two stewards were selected from Navy ranks to run the island mess. Because of their irregular hours and meager needs, the three were billeted on Wolf Island in the Main Cabin.

Four Navy Communications specialists were assigned to around-the-clock duty in Vigil One. They rotated eight hour shifts with one man always on call.

The communications officer, along with the president's personal military attaché were sequestered with the Secret Service shift commander in the Communications Control Building. The attaché, responsible for the ominous black briefcase containing the secret codes necessary to initiate a nuclear response, referred to as the "nuclear football," was never far from the president's side.

Four Marine helicopter pilots were assigned to handle daily transportation between shore and the island. Excluding the needs of dignitaries and guests, there were at least four daily helicopter flights to and from Virginia, Minnesota. These thirty-minute hops were timed to coincide with shift changes of island security.

Even though the faces changed every eight hours, the duty remained the same, protect the President of the United States. Between the Secret Service, the Coast Guard, and the military, a minimum of ninety-five men were assigned to Wolf Island for the duration of the president's Minnesota vacation. Regional agents cast in a variety of offsite support roles would easily triple that number.

## North of Virginia, Minnesota
## County Road 38

The vice president and his wife Robin, traveling in the same limousine that had transported the president three hours earlier, were only twenty minutes from Boulder Lake. The tension between Sidney and Robin had reached a point of explosive saturation. For the past half hour, neither of them had uttered a single word.

Anxious to avoid a scene at the island, Robin broke the silence. Her voice was calm, offering no challenge to her husband's grim mood.

"Remember. We agreed ... no scenes."

Her words appeared to go unnoticed as Sidney continued his dead-eyed stare at the passing countryside through the limousine's thick bullet proof side-window. They had traveled a mile or more before he decided to reply.

"You mean I shouldn't elaborate on your whoring?"

"It's all been said. What purpose would it serve?" she asked, resisting the urge to defend herself.

He turned to face her, "I might just enjoy the hell out of it."

"When do we discuss all the young boys you've been with over the years?"

"Anytime you've got a few hours," he smirked, "I'll talk fast."

Robin countered viciously, "Fuck you! You're a real bastard."

Sidney sprang to life.

"Don't make me the only villain in this little scenario. Let's not forget who fucked who."

"If you had paid any attention to me, even a little, there wouldn't be a scenario."

"It doesn't matter what I did. You took a vow and broke it," he snapped.

With difficulty, Robin suppressed the level of her response.

"How about your vow to me?"

"I can't help what I am. I've always been this way. It's not my fault you were too stupid to recognize the obvious. God knows I never worked that hard to hide it."

"I still can't understand why you married me?"

"You were a commodity – perfectly suited to my purpose. It must have been a good move. After all, I am the Vice President of the United States."

In a rare lapse of emotional judgment, Robin lowered her guard. "I meant nothing?"

With an impish smile, Sidney went right for the kill.

"You were a good poke once in a while. I'm not one of those guys who can't get it up for a woman. I just think men are usually a better lay. You know what? And you'll appreciate this – I even fucked that girl who used to keep house for us. What was her name? Julie, or something?"

Robin was repelled.

"She was retarded."

"I know," he snickered, "I promised her a raise for her extra effort. Did you ever give her one?"

Sidney's words had cut deep, as he knew they would. Robin turned to the window, determined to fight back the tears that threatened to disclose the depth of her humiliation. His admission struck like a slap across the face. He had been unfaithful from the beginning. While she was trying to make a home and a life, he was sleeping with every man and woman she knew.

What had Sidney's lovers thought of her, she wondered. One by one a card file of faces flipped through her mind. Robin was a proud woman. The imagined laughter of her husband's lovers haunted her. How could she have been so blind for all those years?

"You make me sick," she said. "There's no way that I'm staying with you."

"You'll stay," Sidney countered. "I don't want any waves, not even a ripple."

"I don't give one fuck what you want. I want out."

"We have a fragile balance here. If anyone shifts his weight, we all fall. You'll be the most expensive piece of ass in history. He'll hate you."

"You've got your own skeletons to worry about."

"A divorce would muddy the water. I could go from a front-runner to an also-ran. If we go that route, I might as well play the role of the dutiful vice president who was sent skipping around the world while his boss seduced his unfaithful wife. Your boyfriend's threat of a murder investigation will look like so many sour grapes."

"What about your homosexual affairs? The involvement with the Rueds that you've already admitted to won't earn you many accolades."

"Prove it. You'll sound like the desperate losers that you are. I learned something from J. Edgar Hoover. He was gay, you know. He had something on everybody. I make it a point to secure my relationships with information. The Rueds were a rare exception, and, of course, I paid the price ... or I guess they did."

"My God! You can't kill two people and get away with it. Who do you think you are?"

Sidney scooted across the seat, forced his arm around her shoulder and with his free hand, grabbed her face, forcing her to face him. His voice was low and deadly.

"I'm connected. I'm careful. I'm lethal – that's who I am."


## Boulder Lake


Just beyond the bright orange marker buoys surrounding Wolf Island, a sleek 27-foot boat bobbed lazily in the afternoon breeze. The two "fishermen" seated in the stern of the boat with fishing poles cradled in their arms, were not likely to catch anything. In fact, Tabou and Sharif had not bothered to bait their hooks; they were after much bigger fish.

Both men had traveled the fifty miles to Boulder Lake many times over the past few weeks. Each time they had fished or pretended to fish as near the island as possible. This was the first time they had been able to observe the full security contingent surrounding the president. Through binoculars, Tabou described his observations to Sharif.

"Two on the dock ... in the small building. Two ... no three near the main building. It is as we were told. Our intelligence appears to be excellent. Past the boats, there are only seven men within one hundred meters of Atwater."

Sharif scanned an area away from the main cabin. "A man with a dog ... and he's armed."

"We must advise our comrades," Tabou cautioned. "If he is to the far end of the island, he will be nearly a kilometer away. His presence will not be a factor."

"Atwater is dead," Sharif sneered, "the pig just doesn't know it."

"Look," Tabou pointed to the helicopter ferrying agents to and from the island as it rose above the trees a hundred yards behind the main lodge. "It is exactly on time. It should not return for thirty minutes."

*Patrol Two*, the Coast Guard boat responsible for the water area on the east side of the island, neared Tabou's large, by Minnesota standards, vessel. Second Class Petty Officer Spivey had been observing Tabou's boat for the past thirty seconds. He relayed his observation to Lieutenant J.G. Donnerelli.

"That boat's a beauty. I've seen it around here a couple of times."

"Yeah, more guys with a big boat, a prayer and no fish. If I could afford that boat, I'd buy my fish and do something else with my time."

"You know what's funny though? I remember it because of that thing on the aft deck. It looks like a pole or something bolted to the floor. In fact, it looks like a machine gun mount."

The lieutenant took the binoculars.

"Who knows? Maybe it's some sort of rod holder."

"Think we should check it out?" Spivey asked.

"Are you kidding?" stormed the lieutenant. "Remember our orders? All civilian contact will be courteous and kept to a minimum."

"Hey!" Donnerelli shouted, "see the blonde sunbathing on the houseboat?"

"Does that mean we're not supposed to check out suspicious activity?" Spivey couldn't hide his excitement. "What an ass ... and look! I think she's unhooking her top."

"What about suspicious activity?" Spivey repeated in the hope that he might possibly convince Donnerelli to board the boat.

"Look!" Donnerelli said, lowering his binoculars, "this is a candy ass P.R. job. We make friends and keep the public far enough away so that fat old politicians can go swimming and not be embarrassed. We're part of the official scenery around here."

"I thought we were protecting the president," Spivey declared with wide-eyed innocence.

Donnerelli was incredulous.

"You think somebody's going to attack the president from a boat or submarine ... in Boulder Lake ... in Minnesota, get a life!"

"Presidents have been attacked plenty of times," Spivey replied defensively.

"Get fucking serious! I don't know about you, but this isn't exactly what I had in mind when I joined the Coast Guard. This is high profile horse shit. All I need is a couple of guys complaining to the brass that they were hassled on their fishing trip. Fuck up at sea, and you've made a mistake. Fuck up around here, and you'll be so far down on the list you'll have to look up to see whale shit."

Spivey could not do anything but back off. *Patrol Two* passed within fifty yards of the small craft carrying the two "fishermen."

## Wolf Island

One of the Navy stewards assigned to care for the president approached the chief executive on the outside deck of the main lodge.

"Mr. President."

"Yes. What is it?"

"Vice President Holdridge has arrived on shore. He and his party should be here in the next ..."

The young steward, looking over the president's shoulder could see the boat transporting the vice president emerge from behind the far corner of the island.

"... actually, they're here now, Mr. President."

The president, noting the steward's distraction, turned. The boat carrying Sidney and Robin was less than two hundred yards from the dock. The sight of his lover gave the president a rush, reminding him that six days would be a long time to keep his feelings in check.

The boat, transporting the vice president and his wife cut its engine to an idle, fifty yards from shore. Momentum easily propelled the craft to the side of the well-kept wooden dock.

Before the boat stopped heaving in the waves created by its own backwash, Sidney stepped to the dock leaving his wife to fend for herself. Robin, still wearing high heels, found it difficult to maintain her balance and step out of the boat at the same time. Contrary to standing orders, a Secret Service agent extended his hand to lend welcome support. The gesture drew an appreciative thank you from Robin and a glare from the vice president.

Only the Navy seaman piloting the boat and the vice president's Secret Service agent were left on board. A dock boy, also provided by the Navy, secured the boat long enough to remove the luggage and place it in the new guest cabin where the pair would be spending the night. The agent, who had accompanied the vice president from Duluth, left his charge to the care of island security and returned to shore with the boat.

Halfway down the path between the main lodge and the dock, the President greeted his guests.

"Sidney, Robin. I'm glad you could make it. Welcome to Wolf Island."

"Hello, Jim," Sidney said with surprising enthusiasm.

"Wolf Island is beautiful, Mr. President," Robin said with a big smile, "Thank you for inviting us."

Sidney seemed irascibly amused by his wife's remark.

"Is that really what you call him? Mr. President?"

Embarrassed by her husband's question, Robin made a hushed appeal.

"Sidney, don't."

"Let's have a pleasant weekend," said the president. "Maybe we can iron out some of our mutual problems."

Sidney grinned. "You're the one with problems."

The president refused to be baited into a confrontation. It was the wrong time and the wrong place. Instead, he proceeded to usher the vice president and his wife to their cabin, the farthest habitable structure on the property.

Like the main lodge, the spacious single-story building featured an elevated twelve-foot wide deck that stretched from corner to corner across the front of the rustic retreat. A six-step climb led the trio to a glass door which the president slid open, allowing him and his guests to enter.

The cabin's natural pine interior was gorgeous. Heavy beamed ceilings and extensive use of glass engendered an immediate sense of communion with the surrounding environment. Colorful Native American artifacts furnished the main living area with a distinctive theme. Authentic soapstone carvings, intricate bead work, and oil paintings appropriate to lake country contributed to the backwoods charm of the newly built island hideaway.

A stone fireplace, warmed by a bright three-log fire, dominated the expansive south wall. A bearskin rug, seven feet across, hung on the opposite wall, over a comfortable looking quilted couch.

Robin examined the room's authentic artwork with genuine enthusiasm.

"It's so warm and comfortable, Mr. President. I don't think I've ever been any place quite like this."

The president found it difficult to conceal his satisfaction over her approval.

"I love it here! Someday Wolf Island will be my permanent home."

An uneventful tour of the cabin's spacious accommodations ended in the modest but efficient kitchenette.

"The refrigerator is stocked with beer, wine, cheese and a variety of snacks. I hope you'll both be having your meals with me in the main lodge, but ..."

The cabin's wet-bar attracted Sidney's attention; he selected a bottle of scotch and poured himself a quick drink. Without asking his wife or host if they would care to join him, he slammed down the double shot with a single gulp.

"... If you want or need anything, just pick up the phone and dial six. That will put you in touch with the main kitchen. There's a chef and steward on duty between 6 a.m. and 12 p.m. ... and incidentally, a housekeeper usually tidies up between 10 a.m. and noon. If you don't require her services, just leave word with the kitchen."

"Sounds like paradise," Robin said, visibly distracted by her husband's rudeness.

"Well, I'll let you two relax and freshen up. Dinner is at eight o'clock."

"Thanks for everything," Robin said. "We'll be over at eight."

As soon as the sliding glass door closed behind her host and lover, Robin addressed her husband.

"That was rude."

"Fuck him," Sidney snarled.

"No one wants a week-long fight."

"We could always fuck."

"Who are you kidding, Sidney. You never wanted to fuck all weekend."

"Not with you maybe,"

Robin didn't care what he said. Her feelings had been resolved in the car, on their way to the island. Somehow, someway, she would get away from him.

## On Boulder Lake

A small fishing boat was plodding toward Wolf Island at little more than an idle. An inquisitive fleet of onlookers, held at bay by marker buoys and the ever-present Coast Guard, made the dogleg shaped island stand out like the tourist attraction it had become.

Parker, the man holding the throttle arm of the boat's modest fifteen horse motor, had toured the president's retreat on several occasions. But since his most recent visit was over two years ago, he wanted to take one final look.

# CHAPTER NINE

## Wolf Island

Both Riggs and Murtaugh greeted Sean the moment he burst through the front door of the main lodge. Their unbridled enthusiasm was promptly returned as he wrestled the playful canines to the carpeted floor. They loved to be teased and tossed around as much as the gregarious Irishman loved to do it. With his tail wagging furiously and his front legs flat on the floor, Riggs began to bark. It was time for the high-spirited romp to end. With a gentle hand and an unruffled voice, Sean calmed his too happy playmates.

Seated at a roll-top desk that once belonged to his father, the chief executive continued his work, narrowing a list of Supreme Court candidates from twelve to a more manageable number of three. Most of his afternoon would be spent chipping away at the ceaseless work load that followed and consumed him wherever he went, regardless of the occasion. For James Atwater, a vacation's principal offering was the opportunity to spend the day in an informal atmosphere without the scrutiny of the press and a complete absence of cameras. In an unusual move, even his own White House photographer was left behind for this trip. Sean, anxious to tell his story, entered the cabin.

"By golly Jim, we hauled in some nice ones," Sean proclaimed, as he neared the president.

"How big is nice?" questioned the president, peering over the top of his reading glasses.

"Three and four pounders. Don and I picked up six of them in that twenty-foot drop-off on the east side of Glover Island. I gave them to the cook. How about a couple of fillets for breakfast?" Sean suggested, patting the president on the back, "you and I damn near lived on Boulder Lake fish one summer."

"Damned if we didn't," exclaimed the president." Why don't you cook breakfast, like you use to?"

"I knew it!" Sean exclaimed. "You liked my cooking all along. When I think of all the shit I took."

"You're right. I'm a lot fonder of the memory than I was of the food."

Sean plopped down on the couch, across from the president. "Has Sidney arrived?"

"Yes," moaned the president.

"Sorry you invited him up here?" Sean asked with a twinkle in his eye.

"Not yet, but I can see it coming." replied the president. "The guy's always been a class A prick, and under the circumstances, why should today be any different?" Sean decided to change the subject. "What about tonight?"

"We need to talk about it. Can you take Doc Harper and Don Kincaid out for dinner? Sidney's a loose cannon. God only knows what he's got going for tonight."

"Sure. How about Mike?"

"I want him with me. I'm sure his feelings would be hurt if we didn't have dinner together on his first night here."

"Good thing he's a priest, huh?" Sean winked and added, "he can hear all of your confessions tonight."

The president's face turned sullen.

"About Mike, did you know he was seeing Megan those last few months?"

A lumbering silence preceded Sean's reply.

"I wasn't sure. Remember the time I left the campaign and returned to Minneapolis to fire Ted Baines while you stayed in Utah? Well, I stopped by the house that night to see if Megan wanted anything. As I pulled up, I noticed Mike's car parked several doors away. When I knocked, no one answered, but there were lights on, and I could hear a television set inside. I didn't think much of it until the next day. I asked Mike about it and he said it wasn't his car. I *knew* it was his car, so I guessed something was up."

"Why didn't you tell me?" the president asked.

"I was your friend, Mike's friend, and Megan's friend. I didn't want to light a fire until I was sure I had a match. I was going to do a little more investigating after the election. When Megan was killed a couple of weeks later, I was glad that I hadn't said anything. I didn't want to spoil your memories of her or your relationship with your brother."

"I guess I was the only one left in the dark," the president said, reluctant to accept the truth.

Sean, aware of Jim's pain, tried to supply an answer, "We were gone a lot … weeks at a stretch. After the Mike incident, I got to thinking about it. I remembered how lonely she told me she felt. It may not have been right, but …"

" My own brother?" lamented the president.

Sean responded immediately, "Mike got lost in the shuffle. You received all of the attention ... he was always an emotional kid. Megan must have sensed his pain. In retrospect, it's not difficult to see how it happened."

"No, I guess it's not," the president reluctantly admitted.

Sean stood and walked toward the door.

"I'm not blaming you," assured the president. "Under the circumstances, I think you did the right thing."

Sean stopped and turned, "Thanks. But I'm not sure there was a 'right thing'."

## Elbow Lake

Crowded around their small kitchen table, Tabou and his comrades discussed the details of their pending attack in what could only be described as an old-fashioned pep talk. At every juncture, they stopped to reassure one another of their certain success.

"Surprise is our great weapon," heralded Tabou, "Tomorrow, at night ... we will strike fast. No American president has ever been attacked in such a way. The world will know we are not cowards. They will see that we are soldiers without fear. The coalition will be forced to admit the injustices we suffered in Iraq and Afghanistan."

Jaabir, like many Arabs, was superstitious, "I had a dream last night. In that dream we were successful. The entire Muslim world was heralding our victory We will once again felt proud. Our women were waiting to honor us. It is meant to be."

Coutre flashed a knowing glance at Tabou while Sharif pounded his fist against the table, "Our success was also revealed to me in a dream that I had on the last day of

Ramadan. I could see the face of the dead American president."

The five Muslims seated at the table began to shout religious proclamations and words of praise, affirming the truth of their Palestinian comrade's dark vision.

Coutre, in the meantime, quietly filled a cigarette paper with tobacco and sealed it by running his tongue along the edge of the thin white tissue. When the tide of emotion finally subsided, he lit the cigarette and voiced his own concern.

"I hope that asshole pilot shows up. He doesn't sound very dependable."

"If he does," said Arbash, "we can escape in one of the boats. As you have seen, there is a huge treed area called Superior National Forest on the other side of the lake. It is kept without buildings and cabins. We could escape there."

Tabou laughed, "Have you ever heard of thermal imaging? Their helicopters can see through leaves and trees. It would be as if we were standing in the desert."

Sharif was blunt in his pessimism, "Why bother anyway? Whether the plane arrives or not, we are dead. We all knew that this was a suicide mission. Why do we pretend?"

Regardless of their dedication and commitment, the Palestinian's dark outlook threw a wet blanket over everyone's spirits. The probable result of their mission had seldom been discussed.

"I will live," Coutre said with certainty. "I will collect my money."

"I too, expect to live," Arbash concurred, "we should all expect to live. The plane will be there."

Apprehensive as he was, Tabou realized the value of hope.

"If we follow our plan, we can all walk away from this."

Sharif held no illusions and would not be swayed, "To walk away alive, one should start walking now."

## Shoreline
## Boulder Lake

Henry Saperstein and fellow newspaperman, photographer Corey Kamen, picked their way along the shoreline opposite the south end of Wolf Island. From their vantage point, the president's cabin, on the far side of the property, was not visible. Huge rocks, tall trees, and thick brush formed an impenetrable wall at water's edge. Only one garage-size security building tendered proof of human habitation.

After determining that this would be their best vantage point, Henry suggested Kamen take a few mood shots of the president's island in the heavily shadowed light offered by the disappearing sun.

Kamen dutifully readied the 35mm Nikon around his neck and put his experience to use. They would need many pictures, Henry thought to himself, for the story he was about to break.

# Wolf Island
## Main Lodge

A few minutes after eight o'clock, the president and his guests took their places at one of the round oak tables situated in the center of the spacious dining room. Both the main lodge and the guest cabin featured a natural knotty pine interior. Rays of the setting sun reflected off the yellowish pine immersed the entire room in a warm summer glow.

Robin was seated opposite Mike, while her husband sat nose-to-nose across from the president. Their table's proximity to the floor to ceiling glass windows, that ran the full length of the west wall, afforded the chief executive and his party a gorgeous postcard view of the lake.

In keeping with the informal atmosphere of their wilderness retreat, the president was dressed in a yellow cotton shirt and dark blue khakis. Mike's black trousers and shirt were apropos for a priest, while Sidney, wearing a gray checked sport coat and dark blue tie, chose a more formal look despite the expressed wishes of his host.

As always, the evening went to Robin Holdridge. Her natural beauty had never been more evident. A silk pink sun dress, fitted to the waist with a beaded bodice, perfectly complimented her long, leggy, near flawless figure. A soft luster of reflected light further enhanced her clear complexion and alluring blonde hair. Robin's radiance filled the room. From the moment she entered, the president found it impossible to keep his eyes off the woman he loved.

The few times their eyes actually met resulted in pain. Robin's big green eyes were aglow. When he looked directly into them he felt a short jab in his chest, near the heart.

James Atwater was head-over-heels in love. Dinner conversation was sparse. A few words between the president and his brother underscored by an occasional remark from Robin, did little to enliven the group's collective languor.

Mike found the strained atmosphere that permeated the meal, puzzling. A twinge of guilt induced paranoia prompted him to wonder if his presence wasn't the evening's disruptive catalyst. Perhaps his brother had told the vice president about his affair with Megan. If he had, it was obvious to Mike that Sidney didn't approve of him or his presence on the island.

Sidney covered the Presidential Seal on his plate with a single plop of mashed potatoes. A T-bone steak, corn on the cob, and garlic bread were served in rapid succession. After a few awkward moments, Sidney broke his self-imposed silence.

"Hard to keep your eyes off her, huh Jimmy?"

The statement rankled the president, particularly with his brother present. But he had no choice except to agree. After all, Robin was eye-candy that any man would appreciate. By simply affirming Sidney's sarcasm he hoped that he might return the husband of his lover to a preferable posture of contentious silence.

"She is a beautiful woman, Sidney."

In the wake of an undisguised sneer, directed at his wife, the vice president poured himself another glass of wine which he promptly gulped as if it were an antidote to a recently ingested poison. Added to the liquor he had consumed in his cabin, he was beginning to exhibit conspicuous signs of drunkenness.

"Maybe I should just leave the room and you two can go at it right here on the table."

Mike looked at his brother for a reaction to the vice president's vulgar remark.

"Please," Robin implored, "don't talk like that."

Sidney was amused by his wife's choice of words.

"You mean I should talk with a lisp? Then you should talk like a whore, and Jimmy, what does a man who fucks another man's wife sound like? Pretty cocky, I suppose, no pun intended."

The unconcealed astonishment in Mike's expression captured the vice president's attention.

"Oh Father! Forgive us, for we have sinned," mocked Sidney. "Did you know that your brother has been slipping the presidential pickle to my wife?"

An attempt by Mike to make eye contact with his brother was unsuccessful. From the rueful expression on Jim's face, the young priest knew that the vice president's scurrilous allegations were true.

Whatever was going to be said, the president wanted it said now. He tackled the explosive accusations, as he tackled everything, head-on.

"I love your wife, Sidney. You know that we've had an affair. I think we've already discussed our situation, don't you?"

Sidney's snowballing intoxication was taking charge of his behavior.

"You prick, Jim! I'm sorry... no, no," he mocked, "you prick, Mr. President! I just want you to know that you're through diddling Goldilocks over there. I want it to stop."

Mike turned to his brother, "I think I should leave you three alone ... to iron this thing ..."

"No! No!" Sidney interjected, "these two need a priest. Maybe a little holy water will cool them off."

"Stay, Mike," the president commanded. "Please. You should hear this. I would have told you anyway."

Mike's continued presence served as his reply.

The president redirected his attention to his vice president.

"Sidney, let's not continue to beat ourselves to death."

The chief executive was the first of the group to glimpse the wide-eyed Navy steward who had quietly entered the room from the kitchen. Atwater addressed his vice president in a stern voice.

"The steward is here; let's not embarrass ourselves more than we have."

Sidney ignored the warning, "That's easy for you to say."

The muddled expression plastered across the steward's face as he timorously approached the table revealed to everyone, but Sidney, that the whiskerless twenty-one year old had heard all or most of what had been said over the past few minutes.

The young man waited for Sidney to finish speaking, "... *your* wife isn't in bed with another man."

"Mr. President," the young man said softly, "is everything satisfactory?"

"Yes. I think we're fine, thank you."

"May I bring you or your party anything? A drink perhaps?"

"I could use a fucking drink," Sidney bellowed. "Make it a vodka tonic and make it *fast*."

Even the steward, who was barely old enough to drink himself, knew that the last thing in the world Sidney Holdridge needed was more alcohol.

The young man glanced at the president for a confirming nod or some sign of approval.

"Thank you, we're set for the evening," the president said while shaking his head.

Grateful that he would not be required to make another appearance, the young steward left the table and returned to the kitchen. The moment he disappeared from sight, the president returned his attention to Sidney.

"You know my offer. I expect your answer before we return home."

### Elbow Lake

Ayesha leaned against the side of her Volvo pondering the far-reaching effects of tomorrow's assassination. A light fog had softened the yard light, attached to the side of the cabin, reducing its output to a misty glow.

From inside the building, not more than seventy-five feet away, she could hear the raucous laughter of her five companions. They weren't the type of individuals with whom she would have chosen to spend her last few hours.

The sound of the front screen door opening, then slamming shut, snapped the beautiful Iranian back to reality. Tonight, of all nights, she was not in the mood for a fight. If Coutre appeared, she would avoid him – even if it meant retreat. To her relief, the figure that emerged was that of Arbash, the Palestinian.

"Why do you stand out here – alone?" he asked.

"It's peaceful."

Arbash appeared more relaxed than she was accustomed to seeing him. He stood at her side and together they stared out toward the lake. After a few quiet moments, he spoke.

"Do you think we will die?"

"With my heart – no. With my head – yes."

"Do you have people here?" he asked.

"Yes. My family lives in St. Paul, a town in the southern part of this state. What about you?"

"I have only one younger brother. My mother was killed by the Jews in a raid. My father died avenging her death. My older brother was killed when a bomb he was making exploded.

"Are you afraid of dying?" she asked.

Arbash hesitated, "You will not speak of this to the others?"

"No," She shook her head. "As you've seen, I keep to myself."

"I am afraid we will not succeed," he said. "I fear the laughter of my enemies.

We Palestinians have had our homeland taken from us. Our children are gypsies with no pride, no dignity. We are always visitors, trespassing on someone else's land. As a people we have died."

"You have many reasons to hate."

"The men who killed my father wrote 'nebbish' on our door. In Yiddish, the word means a nobody – a loser. I have never forgotten that word."

## Wolf Island

Robin and Sidney returned to their cabin in the wake of a disastrous evening. The stewards, and possibly the cook, had been exposed to the vice president's unseemly remarks.

Their hushed affair, now inexorably coupled to Sidney's aspirations and vulnerability, was spiraling into a public extravaganza. The vice president's intemperate behavior had further dashed any hope that the president harbored of concealing his relationship with Robin for another two years.

The president and his brother, each carrying an old-fashioned glass filled with ice and a double shot of Southern Comfort, retired to the main room of the lodge.

"I'm sorry you had to see this, Mike. I was going to tell you, but you and I have had our own problems, so ... I just put it ..."

"I don't have much room to talk ... but wow Jim, you've got a real mess here."

Before joining his brother on the couch in front of the fireplace, the president reached under the glass shade of an expensive Handel table lamp that was sitting on a maple work table in the corner of the room and turned off the light. Shadowy tongues of orange fire danced across their faces as both men sat, staring into the flames.

"We didn't plan it this way, Mike. You can't plan to fall in love?"

"There's a certain irony to this whole thing," Mike said, exhibiting a trace of satisfaction.

"The vice president wasn't my brother," the president said coldly.

"That's true, but a nation wasn't looking to me for moral and ethical leadership."

A sip of whisky warmed the president's throat.

"It's easy to forget you're a priest, kid."

"I'm not a priest tonight. Tonight, none of us are who we seem. If you were the president, you wouldn't be arguing with your lover's husband. If Sidney were the vice president, he wouldn't be the crude drunk that I just had dinner with. If Robin was truly the vice president's wife, we wouldn't be having this conversation. And as for me, well, if I was a priest, I'd be upstairs praying for all of us. Instead, I'm sitting here wallowing in self-pity and guilt with everyone else."

## Virginia, Minnesota
## Pumpers Bar

With a country music band, stuck forever on the bottom rung of show business, wailing in the background, Dooley Johnston sat with his chair tipped against the wall of a local Virginia, Minnesota honky-tonk locally referred to as Pumpers Bar and Grill. At the insistence of the Scott County Health Department, the words "and Grill" were dropped three years ago.

Surrounded by a half dozen of his low-life buddies, the Swede took his place as the featured attraction. To the most casual of observers, it was apparent that he reveled in his entrepreneur status among the establishment's blue-collar, mostly unemployed, clientele. The empty PBR bottles that stood before him in empty disarray were legion – even by Pumpers standard.

"I'm getting a new plane boys," Dooley proclaimed loud enough to be heard over a shameless rendition of *Straight Tequila Night.*

"No way, eh! You and that bird of yours are married for life," blubbered one of his stewed friends.

"You got that right, eh. I'm addin' a plane. Not tradin' one in."

"How the fuck you gonna do that?"

"I got a big job comin' up, eh."

"What kind of mother fuckin' job you got," laughed a bearded onlooker. "You smugglin' good-looks' into Canada?"

Dooley laughed along with his friends.

"Shorty," he hollered, "I got a job tomorrow night that's going to put more money in my hands than you guys …"

The Swede's face turned grim. His voice, along with his exuberance, trailed off in mid-sentence. A glimpse of a man standing on the opposite side of the bar jolted his alcohol-soaked brain with a portentous reminder.

The man, who stood tall and motionless among the individuals who were frolicking around him, was staring directly into his eyes. The man's name was Parker. Before he disappeared, he motioned the Swede outside.

"What's a matter, Dooley?" asked the only person at the table who was sober enough to recognize the Swede's somber mood swing.

"Nothin', eh," he replied.

With a beer locked firmly in his grasp, he stood and threaded his way through the rowdy late-night crowd toward the door.

A single bulb pole light expected to illuminate the bar's seedy exterior revealed an unpaved parking lot filled with pick-up trucks and a few aging automobiles that would soon fulfill their destiny as rural lawn ornaments.

A spotless late Model Torino idling next to the curb on the far side of the street stood out like an honest politician. Its headlights blinked twice, confirming the obvious. Despite his condition, Dooley traversed the pot-hole spotted roadway with surprising agility.

As he neared the automobile's drivers' side window, a burst of 12-volt current dropped the heavily tinted glass several inches.

"Get in," Parker's familiar voice ordered.

Dooley didn't question the command. He walked around the front of the car and opened the door.

The interior light that he expected to see remained unlit. He found no comfort in the Torino's plush bucket seat. It reminded him of the witness chair next to a judge's bench. Even in near darkness, he could see the oversize chrome revolver resting in Parker's lap.

"What's that for?" he asked nervously.

Without comment, Parker wrapped his hand around the pistol's white grip and pointed it at the Swede's temple.

"What are you doing, eh?" Dooley asked.

"Did I hear you discuss the job I hired you for with your friends? Yes or no."

"I just said ..."

Parker cocked the pistol.

"Yes or no?" he repeated.

"Yes," Dooley admitted, convinced that a lie would get his head blown off.

"Listen, fuck head. You don't mention your job, me, or the money to anyone. Not now. Not ever. This is your first, last, and only warning. You'll never know where or when we'll be listening. The next time I, or one of my associates, will end your so-called existence with no questions asked. Sorry won't mean shit. Be a smart fly-boy and live through this. Got it, eh?"

## MAY 29
### Wolf Island
### Main Lodge

Breakfast was usually served by the Wolf Island kitchen on demand. As each of the presidential party arose, they were able to saunter into the dining room and choose from a wide variety of traditional morning fare.

It was 7:15 a.m. The president, Sean, Don Kincaid and Dr. Ralph Harper were seated at a window side table enjoying a family style breakfast.

"You were right, Sean," the president said, "these walleyes of yours are delicious."

Sean beamed.

"All in a day's work."

Kincaid, sitting across from the chief executive, paused between bites.

"Where are the vice president and his wife?" he asked, confirming his ignorance of last night's melodrama.

"In bed. Where would you be if you were married to a doll like that?" injected the normally sedate Doc Harper, caught up in his masculine surroundings.

Sean grimaced at what would otherwise be considered an innocent male observation. The president, at odds with his natural inclination, nixed a reproachful comment and continued to eat. After all, he reminded himself, she was beautiful. Why should he take umbrage to an otherwise innocent remark?

Oblivious to his boss's personal involvement, Kincaid continued, "What a body. That woman's built like a brick ..."

A disapproving scowl from the president stopped Kincaid in mid-sentence.

Eager to avert a confrontation between an over-sensitive lover and an insensitive press secretary, Sean plunged into the conversation. His words preceded a caustic admonition from the president by only a fraction of a second.

"Don! We should get out of here and head for the boat. We've only got an hour before they stop biting."

From the urgent undertone of Sean's interruption, Kincaid knew that he was guilty of a major faux pas. As press secretary, he recognized the glare in the president's eyes as a frequent precursor to moments when all hell was about to break loose. He didn't know why the remark had upset his boss, but he did know that he wasn't foolish enough to stick around and find out.

"Yeah Sean, let's go! I'm not that hungry anyway."

With half of his breakfast uneaten, Sean ushered Kincaid away from the table and toward the dock. On the way out the door they passed Robin, dressed in white shorts and an eye-popping halter. The president couldn't help but smile. Kincaid was right.

"Good morning, Mr. President," she said cheerfully.

"Good morning, Robin. I trust you had a good night's rest?"

"Great! It sure cools off up here in the wee hours."

Doctor Harper, who only moments earlier had traversed the perils of a verbal mine field himself, revived a question asked by Don Kincaid.

"Where is the vice president?"

A coded glance at the president preceded Robin's reply, "He's still in bed – enjoying the peace and quiet."

"Too bad. I wanted to take him fishing. He does like to fish, doesn't he?"

"I don't think he's done very much of it. You'll have to ask him when he wakes up."

Robin filled her plate while the president and his doctor continued their breakfast. The conversation remained in the "How's the weather" mode until Doctor Harper excused himself.

"Tell Sidney I'm looking for him."

"I will," assured Robin.

With only Robin and the president left at the table, the conversation made a predictable turn. To reduce the risk of being overheard, they lowered their voices to a near whisper.

"I wanted you so badly last night. I even thought about sneaking over. I must be losing it," she admitted.

"Me, too. It was a long night. I think we're in love. It's a great feeling. We've got everything going for us but timing."

Both of them knew where this conversation would lead if they were alone. A look that only lovers could appreciate initiated a form of mental petting. They savored the moment like the addicts they had become. It took the appearance of the president's brother to break the spell.

"Good morning, Mike," the president said.

"Hi, Jim," he looked at Robin, "and Robin, how are you this morning?"

"Just fine. Did you sleep well?" she asked

"In view of the evening's 'entertainment,' I guess so. I had plenty to think about."

"Sit down and join us," invited the president.

"I will. I'm hungry." Mike pulled out a chair and sat down next to Robin. Before they could resume their conversation, a white-coated steward arrived and took their breakfast order. The president waited for the young man to complete his task and leave the room before speaking.

"Have you talked to Sidney?"

"No. He was still asleep when I left the cabin. What are you going to do?"

"Hope for a commitment from Sidney that he'll slip into private life quietly.

"If he says no?"

"That would be one of those things beyond my influence. One thing I know for sure. I don't need to be president for us to love each other."

"What do you think will happen?" she asked expectantly.

"We need to ride out the storm as discreetly as possible."

Mike excused himself and stood.

"You two have got two minutes to say the things that I know you won't say in front of me," he smiled. "I'll be back."

"You've sure gotten smart since you were a kid," said the president.

"Maybe you just never noticed."

Assaulted by a variety of emotions, the president watched his brother walk away from the table. Robin took advantage of the privacy.

"This can't go on, Jim. I can't live this way. Somehow I've got to separate myself from Sidney."

"Can you?" asked the president.

"I don't think he'll divorce me. But I'm going to propose a separation. It might raise a few eyebrows, but if we do it quietly ..."

"I agree. I think you should try."

Coffee in hand, the steward approached the table. His presence enforced another moment of silence. After filling Robin's cup, he returned to the kitchen.

"First, I'm going to try and persuade Sidney that we should return to Washington. A few more days of 'vacationing,' and we'll all kill each other."

"I'm sorry your first visit to Wolf Island was so unpleasant."

"It's not the island. It's beautiful here. I want to come back when it's just you and I."

Her reach for the cream pitcher was cut short by the president's hand. The moment was electric but contained.

All they could do was savor the contact and stare into each other's eyes. For now, that would have to be enough.

## Elbow Lake

The midday sun had warmed the cool morning air to a near-perfect seventy-three degrees. Tabou and his comrades were embroiled in the final phase of their preparation. By day's end, they would abandon the cabin that had served as their hideout for the past two weeks.

The decision to place fifty miles between themselves and their target had been a wise one. Had they attempted to stage their attack from a closer, more convenient site, they would have dramatically increased their risk of discovery. An incident such as the Balfours disappearance might not have slipped through the cracks as it so obviously had.

Both Z-275 Davanti boats, purchased under phony names and bearing false identification numbers, had been pulled from the water and placed on trailers attached to the rear of their vans. The process of loading the boats with necessary gear and equipment was already under way. To reduce the threat of possible detection, each weapon or shell was concealed by a blanket until it reached the safety of the boat. In twelve hours it would be over, a fact reflected in the hyperactive mood of the six participants.

## Wolf Island

Sidney Holdridge made his first appearance of the day shortly after 2 p.m. The vice president 's relaxed manner and informal dress marked a sharp contrast to his previous day's demeanor and attire.

A short distance from his cabin, he greeted Don Kincaid. Unaware of the vice president's recent behavior, Kincaid took no particular notice of Sidney's over-sized grin and bubbly salutation.

The president, standing near the boathouse with Sean, Doc Harper, and Mike, paused mid-sentence at the sound of Sidney's familiar voice. Waves splashing against the nearby shore coupled with activity around the president, partially obscured the detail of what the vice president 's was saying. One thing was for certain, his voice was loud – that could mean anything.

After excusing himself, the president moved toward the guest cabin in a walk just short of a run. His desire to meet the vice president in an area where the fewest number of curious ears could collect more damaging information was successful.

Halfway down the path, their rendezvous took place. Sidney, still grinning broadly, thrust an outstretched hand toward his heedful adversary.

"Good afternoon, Jim! It's a beautiful day, isn't it?"

"It certainly is," answered the president.

Encouraged by the fact that Sidney appeared sober and in control, he accepted the vice president 's handshake.

"You look as if you're feeling better."

"I am,"

Sidney sounded like an over-enthusiastic used car salesman. It's a beautiful day, and I feel great."

"I hope you and Robin will join me for dinner again tonight."

"Our pleasure, Mr. President. I wouldn't miss it for the world."

"Good," said the president, "we're dining aboard the houseboat. We'll leave the dock at 6 o'clock."

"We'll be there," gushed the vice president.

"I'll look forward to it," the president replied with a hint of sarcasm.

He turned and watched Sidney walk toward the main lodge dining room. His vice president's newly professed zest for life could be interpreted in many ways.

## Elbow Lake

It was 5 p.m., nearly time for Tabou and his people to leave for Boulder Lake. Their plan called for both of their boats to be unloaded and in the water before dark.

The time had come to deal with Jean Balfour. Coutre, finished with his portion of the loading, sauntered toward the cabin. Sukayna Ayesha, who had planned and waited for this moment, intercepted the Frenchman short of the door.

"Where are you going?" she asked.

"To do a job," he replied smugly.

"Are you going to kill the woman?"

A self-satisfied smile covered the Frenchman's face, "Stay out of it."

"No!" Ayesha yelled.

Tabou was standing fewer than a dozen feet away. Desperate for help, the fiery Iranian turned to the man who professed to have no heart and made an impassioned plea.

"Please! Leave her here, tied up. She has done nothing. No one will find her for days, but she would have a chance!"

Dark and foreboding, the always formidable Jabali looked down at his young comrade.

"She has served her purpose. It would only increase our risk! I will do nothing that might endanger the mission!"

His reply came as no surprise. Ayesha, realizing the futility of her position, pursued a different tack.

"Then let me do it. Not that pig who tried to rape her. She deserves that."

Tabou was a ruthless killer and professed zealot, but he had no history of sanctioning needless torture and cruelty. Even his most ghoulish acts, and there were many, had a purpose.

"She deserves nothing ... but ..," with a wave of his hand he set her to the gruesome task, " ... do it! Do it quickly! We are ready to leave."

Coutre was outraged, "No! I will take care of this! I told you earlier."

Ayesha countered, "You will make her suffer. A pig such as yourself should not go near her. She has done nothing to you."

Already on edge and tired of bickering, Tabou drew his pistol and began marching toward the house.

"I will do it myself! She will not suffer," he fumed.

With no real hope of physically preventing him from entering the cabin, Ayesha placed her tiny body between the charging Jabali and the door. Backing up as she spoke, she pled her case.

"Please! Let me! With me she will not even know what is happening!"

Her words were falling on deaf ears.

"Maybe you want to do more than killing," taunted Coutre, who began flicking his outstretched tongue in a rapid up and down motion.

The Frenchman's crude gesture annoyed Tabou, prompting him to stop dead in his tracks. With a flick of his outstretched hand, he granted Ayesha's request. She knew that he wanted to spite the Frenchman more than he cared about accommodating her wishes.

"Go! Now!" he commanded.

While Tabou and Coutre exchanged angry words, Ayesha ran up the stairs and entered the cabin. Inside the tiny bedroom, she found Jean Balfour bound to the familiar straight-back wooden chair. At the first sight of the pistol in the Iranian's right hand, Jean began to gasp for breath. She knew they were preparing to leave. She knew it was time for her to die.

"I have been sent to kill you," Ayesha said.

Faced with a death that she had spent several days preparing for, Jean made a final statement.

"I hope your mission fails. Our country ..."

"Say no more!" Ayesha warned, placing her hand over Jean's mouth.

The raven-haired beauty slowly lowered her head, positioning herself only inches from Jean's face. Ever so tenderly, she kissed her bewildered captive on the lips. For reasons unknown, even to herself, Jean did nothing to discourage her. She even caught herself wishing that the kiss would continue.

Ayesha backed off, placing the fingertips of her left hand on Jean's cheek. The Iranian's dark brown eyes were bottomless. They looked into her soul. Without saying a word, she pointed the pistol's blue metal barrel at Jean's head.

"They will check to make sure that I have killed you. I am going to fire the gun here."

She pointed to a spot at the top of Jean's head.

"I will shoot so that the bullet only grazes you. After the shot, let your head hang forward so that your face covers with blood. They must think I have killed you. Can you do this?"

Jean nodded her head and closed her eyes. The sudden gift of hope brought with it an equal measure of fear. What if the woman wasn't telling the truth? She couldn't help but wonder if the whole thing wasn't a ruse calculated to make her death come easier. Jean covered her ears and braced herself as best she could. Whatever would happen would happen.

With the barrel of the gun carefully positioned against the top of Jean's head, Ayesha pulled the trigger. The explosion, in the tight confines of the bedroom, was shattering.

Blood gushed from the wound, through her hair and down over her forehead. For several dazed seconds, she couldn't be sure whether she was mortally wounded or not.

The Iranian spoke in a whisper, "You must be strong. I will arrange your shirt to help conceal your breathing as best I can. Do not move!"

Through blood-soaked eyes, Jean looked up at her young ally, "Thank you! I owe you my life."

The Iranian took Jean's hand in her own.

"Ssshhh! Say nothing. Your life has not been saved yet. The rest is up to you. If they discover my deceit ... there will be nothing I can do. Be still and live."

Ayesha left the bedroom with her head lowered in supposed regret. Both Tabou and Coutre entered the cabin before she could reach the outer door.

"I have done it. She is dead," Ayesha barked with the bravado of a private surrounded by generals.

Coutre turned in the direction of the closed bedroom door.

"We will see," he groused.

Ayesha moved to block his path, "You only wish to violate her! You feed off death like a maggot!"

The Iranian's harsh denouncement provoked a sudden attack. Coutre's open hand smacked hard against the left side of her face, dropping her to her knees.

Already angered by the Frenchman's preoccupation with killing their hapless captive, Tabou shouted.

"Leave her alone. I will see for myself!" he proclaimed

A push from the Jabali's dark hand opened the bedroom door. Unmoved by the sight of his hostage's bloody body, he made a quick survey of the gory scene. Two thundering steps placed him only inches from Jean's right leg.

With her heart pounding like a jackhammer, she was certain that he could detect movement. Every instinct she possessed urged her to open her eyes. Was he going to put a bullet in her head she wondered?

As an extra precaution, Tabou gave Jean's left leg a stout kick. The jolting pain that flashed through her body was excruciating. Worse yet, she feared that she had reacted in an involuntary response to the severe impact of the Jabali's unexpected blow.

It took every ounce of her willpower to keep from looking for the bullet that would kill her. The wait was interminable. Seconds seemed like minutes. Finally, the Jabali turned and faced Coutre in the doorway. The Frenchman's knife was clutched firmly in his right hand.

"I will make sure," Coutre declared, eager to salvage what was left of his pride.

Ayesha screamed from over his shoulder, "Leave her dead body alone!"

Tabou motioned the Frenchman away, "Go! It is over! Let us be on our way."

Coutre's disappointment was overwhelming his judgment.

"It isn't over until I say it's over!" he shouted.

This was the first time that Tabou's authority had been openly questioned. The Jabali couldn't let it pass. Coutre had challenged his leadership at a point in the mission where his control must be regarded as absolute.
In a well-executed move, Tabou grabbed Coutre's arm and smashed it down against his knee. Then, as the dagger fell to the floor, the Jabali's thick-fingered hand quickly wrapped around his adversary's pencil-thin throat. E

Exhibiting an unusual degree of strength, he lifted the Frenchman to eye level, pinning him against the nearest wall. When the air trapped in his lungs was drained of all oxygen, Coutre was rendered helpless. Kicking and choking for air, he dangled at Tabou's mercy.

In any other place, at any other time, the Jabali would have simply killed him. As it was, Coutre was an irreplaceable cog in a well-oiled machine designed to crush an American president.

"You are not in charge! I say it is over! Let it be or join her!"

Even if he could have spoken, Coutre would have said nothing. Tabou released his grip allowing the Frenchman's slender frame to collapse awkwardly to the cabin's wooden floor. Humiliation forced him to retaliate with words, the only weapons he had left.

"Musa Abu Tabou!" he wheezed between gulps of air, "you have made an enemy. I would not take me so lightly!"

Coutre's lame warning, in light of their upcoming mission, prodded the Jabali into an uncharacteristic smile.

"What does it matter how I take you? Do your job, Frenchman. If there is anything left of me tomorrow, you may avenge your wounded pride."

## Wolf Island

With the previous evening in mind, the guest list for the pending dinner party aboard the president's houseboat had been pared from seven to only four persons. Joining the president would be Mike, the vice president, Robin, and Sean.

The president hoped that the presence of another individual outside of the volcanic triangle that had so recently erupted would have a calming influence on the vice president. All necessary personnel were advised that Sidney was to be served alcoholic beverages at half-strength or less.

A customary bottle of the president's favorite wine would not compliment tonight's dinner. Diminutive by world standards, the president's sixty-two foot houseboat was his most treasured possession. Its size and design were perfectly fitted to the unusual topography of the area. Hundreds of islands, strewn haphazardly across Boulder Lake, created thousands of narrow channels that would prevent a larger boat from passing.

The chief executive's craft, christened *The Deficit,* was plush, yet unpretentious, a reflection of the owner's personal taste. "Comfortable" and "appropriate" were words the president liked to use in describing this, his most expensive toy. With a mischievous twinkle in his eye, he would often tell members of the press that he had spent the weekend "Working on *The Deficit.*"

No presidential journey, however short or remote, was ever simple. James Atwater could barely remember the last time he just picked up his hat, walked outside, and headed toward a destination of his own choosing.

In the beginning, the constant presence of the Secret Service was gourmet food for a hungry ego. Few men on earth could boast such dogged attention and concern. His every move was planned, guarded, and watched closely.

Soon after his election, the human cloak of protection that followed him everywhere began to wear on his nerves. It didn't take him long to realize that he had irrevocably lost the very thing he cherished and championed – his personal freedom. He was isolated and unable to move without extensive planning involving dozens, sometimes hundreds of people. Despite his effort, he grew more and more reclusive by the day. He was trapped.

"The most powerful man on earth," as he was frequently referred to by the world press, had a very short leash. For the evening's planned excursion, two Navy crewman were charged with safely navigating the president's flat-bottomed craft around and through the tranquil waters off Wolf Island.

Over one hundred security personnel from various agencies coordinated by the Secret Service had spent the latter portion of the day scouring small islands and any area along the president's anticipated route that might offer sanctuary to a potential assassin.

Six Secret Service agents were assigned to handle *The Deficit's* on-board security. One Navy cook would prepare the evening meal while two Navy stewards were given the task of tending to the personal needs of the president and his party. Lobster, a favorite dish of the chief executive, had been flown in from the East Coast especially for the occasion.

*The Deficit* would be escorted by two of the three Coast Guard patrol boats normally assigned to island duty. In addition to their regular crews, each boat would carry three agents armed with automatic weapons. It was their job to clear the water in the immediate vicinity of the presidential party. This would be no easy task.

By the end of the cruise, the boat and its famous owner would have accumulated a copious, possibly rowdy, collection of inquisitive onlookers. To further impede spontaneity, the entire extravaganza would be recorded in repetitive detail by the always predatory press corps and the probing eyes of countless cameras.

It was nearly 6:15 p.m. when *The Deficit* pulled away from the Wolf Island dock. Several hundred yards from shore, the president and his four guests assembled on the boat's spacious aft deck not far from the entrance to the boat's main cabin.

Casual dress was again the order of the day. The president, Sean, and Sidney wore shorts, sports shirts, and tennis shoes. Even Mike, was persuaded to abandon his traditional black wardrobe in favor of a pair of Bermudas, courtesy of Sean MacDougal. Robin, as usual, was striking in a blue and white polo T-shirt over blue cotton deck pants.

The tone of the conversation did nothing to betray the animosity that existed among the participants. Nearly every banal subject, associated with such occasions, was covered with agonizing thoroughness.

The only pre-dinner statement of note was delivered by the vice president.

"Robin and I have decided that we must return to Washington tomorrow. We both hate to leave. Hopefully, everyone will understand."

In keeping with the spirit of the evening, the president expressed his obligatory regret. Plans for an on-deck meal were unexpectedly canceled by the faint rumble of distant thunder and the sudden appearance of dark angry clouds on the western horizon.

At the request of the president, the elegant dinner table was moved to the interior of the boat's main cabin. The resulting commotion caused a slight delay in the meal. Two young stewards bore the brunt of the cook's wrath.

"When lobster is done, it is done!" roared the frustrated chef, "anything," he declared pompously, "served past that point, is a leftover!"

After what must have seemed like hours to the chef and seconds to the stewards, the move was completed. Red faced and frazzled, the senior of the two baby-faced Stewards made his announcement.

"Dinner, Mr. President, is served in the main cabin."

Everyone, but the president, was happy to escape the binoculared eyes of an ever-growing flock of onlookers. He couldn't help but wonder if it wasn't their presence that kept a temperate lid on Sidney's capricious behavior.

## Elbow Lake

The blood producing trench carved in Jean Balfour's skull by Ayesha's bullet, had finally clotted. For the first time since her capture, she had real hope. There now existed the possibility that she would survive her dreadful ordeal. The price of this new found optimism was exacted in the form of an inescapable responsibility. Just freeing herself wouldn't be enough. She had to do it in time to warn the president.

From overhearing bits and pieces of numerous conversations, Jean knew the attack would occur at 1:15 a.m. At that time, the helicopter used to ferry personnel to and from the island would be at its furthest point.

If the presidential party retired before 12:15 a.m., the raid was a definite go. If island activity didn't settle in until after that time, the attack would probably be postponed until the following night. Should that happen, Tabou and his people would return to Elbow Lake.

Weakened by days of confined terror and the loss of several pints of blood, Jean fought fatigue and pain as she strained to free herself. The flesh beneath her bindings had deteriorated from raw to bleeding. Every muscle in her body cried for relief.

It had been two hours since the random sounds of voices, car doors, and finally the rumble of tires were last heard. Since that time, Jean's furious efforts had accomplished nothing. Her bonds remained intact. Somehow, she needed to sever the ropes and free herself. Perhaps, she thought, a knife or sharp instrument was left in the main room or kitchen area of the cabin.

It was her best hope. There was only one way to find out. By violently rocking her body from side to side, she was able to tip herself and the chair to which she was bound to the floor.

With no way of cushioning her fall, Jean's right arm and shoulder crashed hard against the wooden planking. Several seconds passed before the pain subsided allowing her to open her tear-filled eyes.

By utilizing the limited movement of her right foot, she was able to push the chair and herself toward the doorway of her private hellhole. Inch by frustrating inch, she drug her body along the splintery surface. A persistence she wasn't sure she could maintain nudged her to the threshold of the narrow entry.

From her mouse-level vantage point, the main area of the cabin was clearly visible. She had no idea whether the single light bulb illuminated over the sink had been left on by accident or by Ayesha on purpose; she was only grateful for its assistance. Without it, she guessed she would be forced to wait until morning to search for something that might assist her in severing her ropes. By that time, she feared the loathsome men who captured her and killed her husband might return.

With her head pressed against the floor, she surveyed the littered room for any edged object or surface that might contribute to her liberation. There was nothing.

The kitchen table stood over eight feet away. Under the circumstances, eight feet was an intimidating distance. Determined to continue, she began to push herself through the heavily shadowed room toward the rusted chrome legs that supported the aging table. Her exact movements could be traced by the trail of blood and urine that snaked along the floor in the wake of her snail-like pace.

At last, she reached a point where her feet, still bound to the chair, could hook around one of the table's round metal legs. Maybe, just maybe, one of her captors had left a knife or sharp object on its surface. Her persistent thrashing and twisting caused the table to shake and jump.

A salt and pepper shaker crashed to the floor. More jostling produced a single spoon. Exhausted, she began to cry. Until then, it had never occurred to her that she might die tied to the chair. Through clenched teeth, she screamed. "*No!* I won't die like this!"

Her words were heard by the one person who needed them the most. Fueled by nothing more than self-determination, she renewed her efforts.

# Wolf Lake
## Aboard *The Deficit*

To the relief of everyone, the dinner aboard the president's houseboat was proceeding in the same cordial atmosphere that permeated earlier premeal chatter.

For reasons known only to himself, Sidney, on the outside, was the Sidney of old.

The appearance of the evening's entree furnished the chief executive and his guests with a welcome respite from their compulsory conversation. Everyone, except Robin, who poked at her lobster with half-hearted indifference, satisfied their hunger with unexpected enthusiasm.

Darkness brought with it an air of fragile optimism. Sidney had still not catered to his recent penchant for ugly outbursts. For some reason, he had declared an unspoken truce. There was no question in the president's mind that his vice president sensed a victory.

Threatened by inclement weather, *The Deficit* returned to the vicinity of Wolf Island. The remainder of the cruise would be spent fewer than one hundred yards from its rocky shore.

A little after 10 p.m. a continuous roll of thunder drove the houseboat and its prominent passengers to the nearby safety of the main dock. Strobe-like lightning hastened the president and his party past *Guard One* toward the path leading to the lodge.

Sporadic drops of wind-blown rain accelerated their pace from a brisk walk to a more appropriate jog. They covered the final fifty feet in an all-out sprint. Another few seconds and they would have been soaked.

# CHAPTER 10

## Somewhere on Boulder Lake

Only water stood between the President of the United States and the six individuals determined to take his life.

Both of Tabou's twenty-foot runabouts had been removed from their trailers and placed in the water at Parker's landing, a scant three miles east of Wolf Island.

Tabou, Ayesha, and Jaabir would occupy one boat, while Sharif, Coutre, and Arbash manned the remaining craft. The decision to launch before sunset went unchallenged.

None of the would-be assassins wanted to navigate the three miles to Wolf Island in total darkness. An early arrival also ensured an opportunity to observe any unforeseen changes in island security that could influence or possibly delay their attack.

Furthermore, they wanted absolute confirmation that their target remained on Wolf Island. The capricious nature of a president's chaotic schedule made his presence in any one location at a precise moment a risky proposition. The by-product of this strategy was a long anxious wait. A torrent of rain and the choppy waters, associated with a wind-driven storm only made matters worse.

## Guard Three

In the protective confines of Guard Three, the small guard house on the southeast tip of Wolf Island, Agent

Thomas Speck puzzled over the two boats that appeared as small blips on his marine radar.

"Some guys will do anything to catch a fish," Speck said shaking his head in disbelief.

Twelve years of government service had dulled the awareness of his complacent companion.

"Anybody stupid enough to sit in a boat on a night like this deserves whatever he gets," scoffed Agent Daniel Warren.

"Maybe we should call Vigil One. Kinda funny to have two boats out there like that," observed Speck.

"Fuck 'em. You want to call the shift commander and tell him there's two boats on the lake? Besides, they're outside the markers – that area's open to the public."

"In a storm like this? You can't call that normal!" Speck shot back.

"Half of these Scanda-hovians up here would trade their wives for a ten pound walleye."

Warren took a listless step away from the console and slumped into a nearby chair. With little or no enthusiasm, he grabbed a small stack of playing cards and resumed an already hopeless game of solitaire.

## Elbow Lake

A groan accompanied each movement of Jean Balfour's weary body. Every battered muscle and fiber of her being cried out for rest. She had managed to maneuver the chair into a position that balanced the entire weight of her body on her forehead and knees. An upright position was made impossible by the back of the chair.

Fear for her own life and that of the president propelled her on. Breathing heavily and drenched with perspiration, she struggled to raise her head far enough to pull with her teeth on a brass doorknob that would open one of the two doors beneath the kitchen sink. Her effort ended when she lost her balance and tipped awkwardly to the floor.

Her spill thrust the upper-half of her body against the base of an old-fashioneded cooking stove. Fatigue forced her to pause and regain her faculties.

With her face mashed against the cold metal, she was reminded of a bad cut that she had once suffered while cleaning the broiler of her own oven at home. Though the memory was unpleasant and strangely inappropriate, it proffered the possibility of an unexpected solution.

After turning her body on its left side, she began to work the chair toward a position that would allow her to position her feet in front of the lower oven. With that accomplished, she pushed against the rope that bound her right ankle to the leg of the chair and managed to hook the top side of her foot under the chrome handle that stretched the width of the drawer.

Mustering every ounce of available energy, she writhed and rocked until her entire body pulled slowly away from the stove. The pain generated by her desperate thrashing almost forced her abandon the effort. Blood mixed with sweat dripped from her face splattered the floor with irregular pools of rust colored liquid.

The drawer began to open; at first a crack, then an inch. Gradually, it extended half of its length. At last, she was able to touch the unfinished edge of the metal side rail with the large toe of her right foot. After several frustrating minutes, she was able to maneuver the chair so that the rope binding her right ankle rested against the bluish railing.

Buoyed by hope, she summoned the energy to establish a consistent to-and-fro motion against the sharp metal. She did not know how long could she sustain the effort, but she would give it her best shot.

To her complete surprise and relief, the binding gave way. It had only taken a half dozen strokes to free her right leg. After all of her misfortune, she had received a merciful break.

"Thank God!" she exclaimed.

With her right leg free, she was able to scoot her body and the chair across the floor with relative ease. Bolstered by her new found agility, she moved to within reaching distance of a drawer situated beneath the counter-top to the left of the sink.

With her toes, she pulled awkwardly at the handle. Familiar sounds made by metal objects rattling against the inside of the wooden drawer were encouraging. Amidst a loud crash, the contents spilled across the floor. A frantic examination of the immediate area revealed an assortment of forks, spoons, and table knives – but nothing sharp enough to cut her ropes.

One drawer remained, offering a second and what might be, her last chance. She pulled herself the necessary three feet and repeated the movements that had successfully unveiled the contents of the previous drawer.

This was the only unopened drawer in the room – it had to be this one. Utensils, including a half dozen kitchen knives, rained down on the linoleum surface. Jean screamed

"Yes! My God, yes."

She would live, she told herself, and with God's help, save the president's life.

Thoughts of freedom provided a much-needed shot of adrenaline. Within a few frenetic minutes, she managed to cut the nylon rope binding her right hand, guaranteeing her release.

The remaining bonds were quickly severed. Exhausted, she struggled to her feet. A small mirror, affixed to the inside of an open cupboard door scared the hell out of her. The face in the reflection, covered by a sheath of crusted blood, surely couldn't be hers, but it was.

If the old-fashioned alarm clock left on the kitchen counter was correct, it was nearly 11 p.m. In a little more than two hours, it could all be over. There was no time, she thought to herself, to pine over her own condition.

Like many of the cabins in the area, built as vacation hideaways, this one had no telephone. A hasty search of the cupboards turned up a half-empty box of wooden stick matches.

Without hesitation, she walked to the nearest window, lit one of the matches and held it a fraction of an inch from the ragged hem of one of the badly faded curtains. The dry cotton fabric ignited easily. Within seconds, the entire north wall of the building was engulfed in floor to ceiling flames.

Goaded by a new and constant companion – fear, she grabbed one of the large knifes from the kitchen floor. After four days of vulnerability, it felt good to hold a weapon. Any innocence that she once had was gone. She found herself blitzed by vengeful yearnings, that a week ago, she was not capable of imagining. She would never be a victim again – not without a fight.

A final survey of the cabin's smoke-filled interior confirmed that her tormentors had left nothing that might assist her in escaping or reaching the outside world. Heat from the spreading fire finally pushed her into the cool black night.

Along her walk toward the road, she could see flames shooting from beneath the eves of her wooden prison. She felt no regret over the loss. Her motive for setting the fire, however, was spurned by more than personal satisfaction. With a little luck, the blaze might attract a nearby resident, or less likely, a passing motorist. She knew there was only one road to the cabin, so if anyone responded to the fire, they were bound to pass her.

A heavily clouded sky and lack of reflected light from nearby cities or buildings wrapped the surrounding landscape in a jet-black shroud that few city dwellers could imagine. Walking or forward movement of any kind was extremely perilous. The now-distant fire, obscured by brush and trees, was of little or no assistance.

Jean stumbled along the road's uneven gravel surface at a beggar's pace. In frustration, she lit one of the matches she had found at the cabin. It was a mistake. Light from the puny flame was swallowed by the night like a black hole. Worse yet, her night vision, what there was of it, was completely destroyed. Given no other option, and with regret, she blew out the match and continued her precarious journey.

Just staying on the road was a chore. Small rocks, muddy ruts, and low-hanging branches were all discovered the hard way. Time after time, she stumbled to her knees. Each painful fall strengthened her resolve. She would not be stopped – not now – not ever – not until she reached help. Two weeks ago, a night trek through unknown wilderness would have been horrifying. But considering the animals she had just left, the creatures of the forest didn't seem scary at all.

## Wolf Island
## Main Lodge

The winds had calmed and the lightning passed, leaving the rain-soaked island under a light but steady mist. The tone of the evening, established earlier on the houseboat, was carried over to the lodge. Everyone, especially Sidney, remained careful to say nothing that might provoke an incident.

A day of fishing and fresh air had taken a toll on the president and his guests. In rapid succession, they retired to their quarters. Sean, half asleep, remained with the president out of fear that his departure might furnish Sidney with another opportunity to make an ass of himself. To the bleary-eyed Irishman's relief, the vice president, with Robin at his side, was walking toward the door. Their goodbyes were thankfully short.

After watching Robin, Sidney, and Agent Pinder disappear into the darkness, the president retreated to the comfort of his favorite recliner.

"Thanks, Sean. I appreciate that you stayed up."

Sean stood, "Sidney wouldn't have said shit if he'd had a mouthful. Talk about a Jekyll and Hyde personality."

"We got through it. That's what counts," reminded the president. "Do you think he actually believes he's got a shot at the presidency?"

Sean shuffled to the base of the carpeted stairway that would take him to his second floor bedroom. An impish smile infiltrated his fatigued expression.

"As my old pappy used to say 'The best way to make a politician see the light is to make him feel the heat.' By now, Sidney should realize that his ass is on fire."

"I hope you're right."

With his back to the president, Sean began a slow climb up the wooden hill. A final gesture of futility summed up his feelings.

"Whatever happens, Jimmy ... Fuck him!"

## Guest Cabin

A gentle rain tapped a lonely ballad against Robin's bedroom window. Sounds of the passing storm perfectly complimented her disconsolate mood. In anticipation of a chilly North Woods night, she removed a pair of heavy cotton pajamas purchased specifically for the occasion from the bureau drawer. Only her body was occupying this space and time; her mind and soul rested several hundred feet away with her lover.

A glimpse of her own forlorn expression in the mirror above the dresser made her realize how ungrateful she had been. After all, she reminded herself, she should be thankful for what she had. It was sinful to sulk when she had been blessed in so many ways.

With her toothbrush in hand, she walked toward the bathroom. Halfway down the hall, Sidney stepped through a connecting door to block her path. His aggressive behavior was somewhat surprising since he had all but ignored her over the past twenty-four hours. No doubt the encounter was planned. She could only wonder how long he had been waiting to make his big move.

"How many times have you fucked him?" he asked. From the pissy-tone of his voice, Robin knew that Sidney had undergone one of his nefarious mood changes. The prospect of another verbal fencing match forced her to make a benign, almost cordial, reply.

"Let's not torture ourselves, Sidney."

"Is he good? Has he got a big one?"

With a maximum effort, she managed to suppress her revulsion for his line of questioning, "Forget it and go to bed."

Sidney pointed to the main bedroom, "Our bed is in there."

"Don't make me laugh," she said, scornful of his offer, "That's one place I'll never go."

"Don't be so sure."

Upset and unwilling to engage in a fight that she had promised herself she would avoid, Robin turned away from her abusive husband and invoked a hasty retreat. By closing her bedroom door with a resounding slam, she made her final statement of the evening.

To hell with brushing her teeth – she decided to put it off until morning. Anything to avoid another ugly confrontation with her prick of a husband. All she wanted now was a peaceful night of sleep.

The bedspread bearing the Presidential Seal was just too much. She reminded herself to tease the president about it the next time they were together.

After unfurling the heavy quilt, folded neatly and left atop an elegant chiffonier situated against the far wall, she snuggled her tired body into the nurturing expanse of the queen size bed. The damp coolness of the sheets made her appreciative of the cotton pajamas.

Her fingers were only inches from the toggle switch on the bedside lamp when the door of her room crashed open against the adjoining pine wall. Her unsuspecting eyes were greeted with a shocking sight.

Sidney was standing in the doorway stark naked with an erection. Her impulse to laugh was stifled by the thought of what she feared he was about to try.

"What are you doing, Sidney?" she asked.

"You probably wouldn't know. It's been so long," he said, sporting a grim no-nonsense look that evidenced his intention to use the unsheathed weapon that was bobbing between his legs. It took him only a second to cover the short distance to his wife's bed.

"Keep away from me!" she warned.

"Or you'll what?" he taunted. "Isn't this what you've been complaining about? I'm your husband. It's time for me to exercise my conjugal rights!"

By the time she overcame her initial shock and realized that he could not be dissuaded, it was too late. Her attempt to stand was countered with a hard shove that pinned her shoulders to the mattress. Before she could rebound, Sidney threw his one hundred and seventy pound frame on top of her slender body.

Sitting astride her waist, he ripped open the front of her cotton pajamas with a single jerk. Small white buttons flew through the air allowing both of her breasts to spill into full view.

"Stop it, Sidney! Don't do this!" she pleaded.

Her efforts to kick him were thwarted by his superior position. Shifting his weight from her hips down to her thighs, he was able to gain access to the top of her pajama bottoms.

Despite her frenzied resistance, he managed to slide the elastic waist band over her hips. The sight of dark pubic hair accelerated his effort. A frantic grab for his testicles resulted in a sharp backhand to the face.

"Not this time, bitch!" he growled.

The blow stunned her, providing Sidney with enough time to complete the removal of her clothing. She could feel his hardness jab between her closed legs.

"Don't do this, Sidney!" she screamed, "Please don't!"

Robin was losing the battle, and she knew it. Fear of penetration forced the panic-stricken beauty to a last resort. Her desperate cries for assistance echoed through the cabin.

"Help me!" she pleaded. "Help!"

Unable to pry her thighs apart and cover her mouth at the same time, Sidney took the chance that her calls for intervention would go unheard or unheeded. He was wrong. His wife's frantic screams were gaining a quick audience. Both the agent at the door and one of the agents assigned to walking the grounds were responding.

On the deck in front of the cabin, the two agents agonized over a difficult decision – a decision that had to be made now.

"Christ, Tom! What should we do?" Sauer asked.

"Punt," Pinder replied, "Let the shift commander make the call."

Pinder hit the call button on his field radio.

"Pinder to Vigil One, do you copy?"

Shift Commander Burke immediately answered his call.

"I copy Pinder. What have you got?"

"There are screams for help coming from Guest Two. Female, probably Blue Bird. Should we go in?"

A long pause prefaced Burke's reply. He knew, as did all the agents assigned to the "Royal Guard," as they often referred to it, the likelihood that this was a simple domestic quarrel. But still, he had to be sure.

"Okay, go in. Make sure they're only killing each other."

"Ten-four."

"What if it's personal? What if they're just fucking or something crazy? What if the screaming is just foreplay?" asked Sauer excitedly.

"We've got to go in, goddamn it! Give me the keys!" Pinder demanded.

Urged on by Robin's continued cries, the agents piled through the door. In the bedroom, Sidney had managed to pry his wife's legs apart. Agent Sauer entered the room just as the vice president was poised to make a penetrating thrust with his unprotected penis. The sudden presence of the two intruders diverted Sidney's attention in mid-stroke.

"Get out! Get out! Leave us alone!" he snarled.

Robin wasn't about to let the agents leave. In spite of her embarrassing position, spread-eagle and naked, the beautiful blonde made her own plea.

"Get him off me! Please! He's hurting me!"

The agents were stupefied. Robin's involvement with the president and the general contempt every agent felt for the always abusive Sidney Holdridge, were the only things preventing Agents Pinder and Sauer from leaving the room.

This appeared to be a no-win situation that might cost both men their jobs. Sauer asked for help from the only person that could offer a solution.

"Look, Mr. Vice President, I don't want to cause any trouble. But do you think you could let your wife get up so the two of you could talk this out?"

Sidney, deflated in more ways than one, released his wife's legs and stomped out of the room in nothing short of a rage.

"I'll have your fucking jobs for this!" he shouted.

After covering herself, Robin slung her bare feet over the edge of the bed.

"Thank you. Please don't leave without me. I can't stay here tonight."

Clad in a plaid robe and wearing a red face, Sidney reappeared.

"Get out! You fuck-ups are only hours away from the unemployment line! How dare you invade my private quarters!"

Sidney's brash behavior worked against him. If what he said were true, the agents reasoned, it didn't matter anyway.

"We'll wait until Mrs. Holdridge is ready to leave," Pinder replied.

Once her defenders had left the room, Robin began dressing. With little regard for the agent's protective presence, Sidney stalked back toward the bedroom. He looked Sauer directly in the eye as he passed. Neither agent spoke or dared to interfere with the vice president's pugnacious advance. In defiance of what Sidney considered unwarranted interference, he stormed into the room. Robin's only concern was her protection.

"Are you men still here?" she shouted.

"Yes, Mrs. Holdridge!" Pinder assured her.

Sidney punctuated his belligerence by slamming the overworked bedroom door closed with as much force as he could generate. The resulting crash shook the entire cabin and, in his own mind, affirmed his right to privacy. Despite the fact that she was dressing, Robin made every effort to ignore her husband's hostile presence.

"Where do you think you're going?" he scoffed.

"Away from you as fast as I can."

"You're pulling the trigger on your boyfriend's presidency. It'll be over. The press will eat you two alive."

"You're part of the administration, Sidney. If you think you have a chance to be president, you'd better keep your mouth shut."

Sidney smiled a strange smile.

"You're a bum fuck anyway!"

Robin acted as if she didn't hear him, so he leaned closer.

"I've described your so-called love making to some of our mutual friends – we all had a good laugh."

Two years ago, when her confidence was all but destroyed by her inability to maintain a successful marriage, Sidney's taunts would have been devastating. But now, she could only pity him.

Over the past few days, Robin had discovered more about Sidney Holdridge than she had learned in the course of her ten year marriage. For the first time, she could see him for the vile person that he was. His whining petulance, always lingering just beneath the surface, had finally surfaced. Throughout their relationship he had never placed his brutal personality and loathsome depravity on such prominent display. From this moment on, she silently vowed, she would never spend another moment in his company.

By puffing out his chest and positioning himself between Robin and the door, Sidney made a lame attempt to block her exit. It took a mere sidestep to evade his half-hearted effort. With both agents only a few feet away, she turned to her husband.

"You deplorable bastard, if I ever see you again, I hope it's in a court."

Accompanied by Agents Sauer and Pinder, she left the cabin with the certain knowledge that she had turned an important corner in her life. No one near the building or on the grounds could escape the licentious nature of Sidney's parting shrieks.

"Go ahead! Sleep with Atwater! Fuck his brains out! You're a tramp! You'd fuck anybody! I'll have the last laugh," he warned.

Inside the main lodge, the president had yet to fall asleep. Sidney's muted cries, faint as they were, brought the chief executive to his feet. His mind raced through the possibilities. Was Robin all right, or had Sidney lost it completely and tried to injure or even kill her?

Propelled by fear, he rushed down the stairs to the living room where Robin and Agent Pinder were entering the front door.

"What's wrong?" asked the president.

Agent Pinder placed his head on the chopping block, "There was a problem with the vice president. It seems he ..."

Robin interrupted, sparing the embarrassed agent a difficult description.

"He was trying to rape me. Agent Pinder and ..."

She looked at Pinder for the name.

"... Agent Sauer," he injected.

"... Sauer heard my screams and saved me from something I vowed I'd never do with him."

The presence of a third party didn't stop the president from moving to Robin's side.

"Are you all right?" he asked, tipping her head to one side so he could see the small abrasion on the left side of her cheek.

"Yes," she whispered.

Emotions, held in check throughout the tumultuous events of the past two days, were suddenly unleashed. Robin reached for her lover's sheltering embrace. Tears began to fill her beautiful green eyes.

"I was so scared," she sobbed.

"He'll never have another chance to hurt you. I'll see to that."

"I love you so much, Jim."

"I love you, too," he replied, "I'll always love you."

With Robin wrapped in his arms, the president turned his attention to Agent Pinder.

"Some things are hard to explain. I know you don't understand, but someday you will. I can only thank you for what you've done."

The agent was stupefied by the president's unexpected candor. Presidents didn't make explanations to agents.

"Yes, Mr. President. I ... well, I'm glad we could help. I hope ... I hope everything works out. You two make a nice couple."

The statement rang in Pinder's ears like a church bell. Almost before the words had passed his lips, he regretted his all too colloquial observation. He had been too candid, too wordy, too stupid; he tried to mend his impulsive outburst.

"I didn't mean anything by ..."

The president, sensing Pinder's dilemma, interrupted.

"I know, and you're right, I think we make a nice couple, too."

Both men smiled before the president put a merciful end to a most unusual conversation.

"Good night, and thanks again."


### Elbow Lake


The faint outline of a building several hundred feet from the road enlivened Jean Balfour's sluggish pace to a risky trot. She had no idea how long it had been since she left her captor's cabin. An hour, she guessed, maybe a little less – hopefully not more. If it had been an hour, she would have only sixty minutes in which to warn the president of

288

the pending attack. Someone had to be in this cabin … they just had to be.

Jean's reckless gait caused her to stray from the relative safety of the narrow driveway. Her unexpected deviation exacted a painful price. A broken branch, extending from the trunk of a twisted oak, punctured the soft tissue near the outside corner of her left eye, dropping the bedraggled woman to her bruised knees.

Eyes that had become accustomed to frequent crying, again wept. A fresh stream of red blood saturated the crusted veil left by Ayesha's bullet.

From somewhere deep inside, Jean found humor in her pathetic condition – she could only imagine what she must look like. Amidst laughter and tears, she stumbled to her feet, cleared her senses and continued her obstacle ridden journey toward the building.

Encouraged by the faint smell of kerosene, Jean felt her way along the side of the building until she found a side entrance. Knuckles were quickly abandoned in favor of closed fists. Her vigorous pounding peppered the door's white surface with tiny drops of blood.

A full minute passed before she was finally convinced that no one was going to answer her call. The realization that she might be forced to resume her harrowing journey and return to the darkness was dreadful. Time was slipping away. How far would it be to the next cabin and even when she found it … would there be anyone there to help?

In despair, she determined that she would force her way into the building. The slim chance that there might be a telephone inside was enough to justify the break-in.

To eliminate the obvious, she jiggled the doorknob. As she expected, the door was locked. In her weakened condition, forceful entry wasn't an option. Using her hands as eyes, she groped her way along the outside of the cabin until she came to the smooth texture of glass.

From her recent experience, she knew that finding a rock would be an easy task. With that thought in mind, she began to move away from the building.

A few steps from the house, she was blinded by a burst of light. The sudden illumination startled her so badly that she let out an involuntary yelp.

Bathed in the yellowish wash of a two-bulb fixture attached to the rear of the cabin, she whirled toward the sound of an opening door. A diminutive male figure wearing a faded blue robe over a pair of cream colored long johns stepped cautiously into the light.

"What's goin' on?" an elderly voice inquired.

Jean, forgetting for an instant that she looked like Bigfoot, bolted for the cabin. Her headlong charge forced the cabin's eighty-two year old occupant into a hasty retreat. Without further conversation, the old man slammed the door.

"Please let me in! I need help!" she pleaded.

The door reopened a crack.

"Ya' just stay back there. Hear?" he warned.

"I will! I will! Please listen," she begged.

The old man opened the door far enough to allow a brief inspection.

"Ya' sure 'nough sound like a woman."

" I am. I've been hurt."

To be this man's age and this impetuous would be an oxymoron. Through spectacles that could have been handed down from Ben Franklin, the old gentleman gave the suspicious figure standing outside his cabin a careful head-to-toe inspection. Guided more by compassion than common sense, he motioned her to step forward.

"Elwood Baysinger's the name – come on in. Judas Priest!" he groused. "I never seen such a mess. Ya' look like somethin' the cat drug in."

Grateful for the offer, Jean entered the cabin. It had been days since she felt the security of a non-hostile environment.

Spartan as it was, the antiquated kitchen was tidy and virtually spotless. From the conspicuous absence of a woman's touch, she surmised that her elderly mentor probably lived by himself.

"What's yer name?" he asked.

"Jean ... do you have a phone?"

"Do I look crazy?" Elwood said indignantly. "I'm at a lake, fishin'. What the heck would I want a phone fer?"

"We need to call the authorities. Some men are going to try and kill the president tonight. We've got to warn him."

"Ya' took a pretty good shot in the head there, Dearie. Ya' better sit yerself down over there on the chair."

She had just given the old man the most important information of his life and he wanted her to sit down. There was no time to explain; it had to be late. She scanned the room for a clock.

"What time is it?" she asked.

"Time fer sleepin'," he replied dryly before motioning to a clock on the far wall near the door. It was 12:10 a.m. Jean was incensed.

"I've got to get to a phone. They're going to kill the president. Please!"

It was obvious that her appeal was falling on deaf ears. Elwood Baysinger wasn't buying the ravings of a late night intruder who he wasn't even sure was a woman.

Jean headed for the door.

"I can't wait for you. I need help."

"Hold on, Dearie! Don't get yer britches in a bundle! I'll take ya' to a phone." he said, resigned to their circumstance. "You need a doctor."

Mumbling to himself, the old man tottered toward what she surmised, was his bedroom.

Perhaps another plea would hasten his faltering pace, "Please hurry!"

## Wolf Island
## Main Lodge

The president slipped Robin into one of the five upstairs bedrooms in the main lodge. Secure in the warmth of a goose down quilt, she watched as he tucked her in with the care and attention of a doting parent. When he was finished, he sat next to her on the edge of the bed, placing the fingertips of his right hand against her soft cheek.

"You can't go back – not after what's happened tonight."

"I'll never go back. It was scary. I couldn't fight him off."

"I'm afraid the fuse has been lit."

"I'm sorry."

"It's not your fault. I think we both knew it would come to this."

"There are going to be a lot of questions."

"We can't let them overwhelm us. We'll either manage the situation, or it will manage us."

"What about tomorrow morning? There's a good chance that Kincaid and Harper will know that I've slept here … away from Sidney."

"You two have had a fight. We'll go with that until we see what direction this thing is going to take."

"I love you."

"And I love you. It's almost 12:30. We should get some sleep."

"I wish you could crawl in here with me," Robin made a powerful argument by holding open the covers.

The pair of heavy cotton pajamas that he had given her, only served to enhance her sexual appeal. To their common delight, he made an appreciative survey of the lush terrain.

"I'd like that," he said, finishing his inspection at her beautiful green eyes. "Soon," he assured her, "we'll be together soon."

With Doc Harper, Ralph Kincaid, Mike, and Sean all sleeping in rooms adjacent to Robin's, commonsense left the president with no alternative, he would be forced to return to his own bedroom. Their parting embrace, however passionate, seemed woefully inadequate.

# Baysinger's Cabin

Elwood Baysinger backed his 1988 four-door Reliant the length of his driveway to the gravel road. The old gentleman's deliberate manner and sluggish pace frustrated his already frazzled passenger. Jean could barely restrain herself as he continued to waste precious seconds shifting from reverse to drive.

"Please hurry!" she begged.

"I said that all my life, Dearie. Now look at me. I hurried myself right along to age eighty-two."

The speedometer on Elwood's car never reached thirty miles an hour as he dawdled along the bumpy road toward civilization and a much needed telephone. His two hand death-clutch hold on the steering wheel told Jean that he was probably zipping along ten miles an hour faster than he had ever traveled this road before.

Five minutes passed before a weathered sign announced the upcoming intersection with State Highway 53. Following an agonizingly slow stop, Elwood turned north toward Orr, Minnesota. The resort town of 265 people was at least fifteen minutes away.

The glow of a distant sign advertising the services of Toby's Quick-Mart caught Jean's attention.

"Pull in!" she pleaded. "We can stop here!"

"Wouldn't do no good, Dearie. Place is closed."

"Just stop!" she begged.

To humor his headstrong passenger, Elwood turned from the road, pulled across the gravel driveway, and stopped in front of the Quick-Mart's darkened gas pumps.

"Now what?" he asked. "Nobody goin' to do nothin'. Place ain't open."

Jean exited the car, grabbed a nearby trash barrel, and flung it through the plate glass window near the store's main entrance. The sound of breaking glass sent Elwood Baysinger into shock. He had no intention of becoming an accessory to a break-in or robbery. With the door on the passenger side of his car wide open, the old guy hit the accelerator. In a shower of gravel and dirt, he was gone.

"Come back! Come back!" Jean shouted.

Her cries were futile. She could only hope that he had gone to call the police. Perhaps she should have tried harder to explain, she thought. Anyway, it didn't matter now – time was running out.

Jean returned her attention to the Quick-Mart; the trash barrel had performed its task admirably. The huge piece of plate glass that stretched half-way across the front of the recently built structure had completely disintegrated. Gaining entrance would be no problem.

Wary of unseen chards of glass, she stepped through the window opening into the interior of the building. With the light from one of the stick matches that she had taken from her captor's cabin, she discovered a telephone on the wall next to the front door. Her spirits were tempered by the fact that the phone was a pay phone requiring twenty-five cents to operate.

Common sense directed her to the main counter where she hoped to find a cash register and some much-needed change. To her relief, a half dozen dimes and nickels had been left by a wary owner who had anticipated the possibility of surrendering a few coins to an intruder in lieu of having his cash register smashed. With jittery fingers, she removed the coins and returned to the phone.

After depositing twenty-five cents, she pushed zero. A male operator, who sounded as if he had better things to do, answered her call.

"AT&T. This is the operator. May I help you please?"

"Thank God! I need to contact the president's summer residence?"

"The president?" he questioned.

Jean was crazy with frustration.

"We've only got one! Our president – James Atwater! Do you have a number?"

"You'll have to call information. That's 1-612-555-1212."

To avoid further inquiry, the man hung up.

Until now, Jean had not considered the intricacies of actually warning the president or those around him that his life was in imminent danger. Frustrated and shaking, she retrieved her money from the coin return and redeposited it. One of the dimes dropped into the return bucket and required reinsertion.

At the first sound of a dial tone, she frantically punched in the seven digit number that would connect her with the information operator. As she had done so often the past ten days, she prayed to God for help.

After four agonizing rings, a slightly more enthusiastic voice acknowledged her call. She realized that her previous request for a number that would connect her to the president's summer residence had been foolish. This time, she elected to contact a more appropriate authority through which she could relay her crucial warning.

"This is an emergency. I need to contact the St. Louis County Sheriff's Department."

## On Boulder Lake

The low pressure system that produced the evening's earlier storm had passed, leaving in its wake, clear air and cooler temperatures. The cloud line was directly overhead – to the west, stars, to the east, black ominous clouds. The water's glossy veneer reflected a welcome calm that had settled over the lake.

Absence of cloud cover forced Musa Abu Tabou to readjust the highly sensitive night-vision scope atop his Walther sniper rifle. This third-generation device was capable of multiplying available light nearly 70,000 times. Images of both structures and agents appeared in detail as the Jabali scanned the unlit areas to either side of the main dock.

Over the past hour, both Sharif and Tabou had allowed their boats to drift within six hundred yards of the jagged shoreline. It had been three minutes since *Patrol Boat Two*, cruising at its usual three knots, lumbered past Tabou's position. As before, the continued presence of the Jabali and his comrades *fishing* just outside the marker buoys, went unchallenged.

The island was quiet. Blackened buildings and a general lack of activity had persuaded Tabou to remove the microphone of his boat's CB radio from its metal clip. In a hushed growl, he transmitted a brief message to Sharif's boat anchored barely a hundred feet away.

"ig-Is-wid GA-meh," Tabou uttered the Arab code name for he and his group. The words translated to *The Black Mosque*.

The mission was go.

Sharif acknowledged his reception and approval by repeating the name, "ig-Is-wid GA-meh."

In the wake of Sharif's confirming reply, both radios were turned off and would remain so for the duration of the attack. The wheels had been set in motion – nothing short of a catastrophe could stop the inevitable.

Tabou had waited for this moment all of his life. He had always known that he would be the one – the Arab who his Jewish enemies and their American friends would never forget.

Pictures and stories of tonight's attack would rally the Muslim world for generations to come. The Western World, always disrespectful of Arab concerns, would witness the birth of a new animal. A ferocious beast, capable of lashing out against Zionist domination and capable of killing its enemies.Finally, the Jabali could fulfill his destiny.

Overcome by the promise of paradise and his own fame, he grabbed Jaabir by the arm and jerked him around so that they stood face-to-face.

"Allah is with us! Our time is now. Centuries of oppression will be avenged on this day ... in this place. Our surprise is total – we will not fail!"

After bowing her head, Ayesha whispered a prayer to a God unfamiliar to many Christians. Her faith and commitment to her people was deeply rooted in the past. She knew that her family, despite their grieving, would be proud. Her father, above all others, would appreciate his daughter's courage and daring. He would love her, and that would be more than enough to justify her sacrifice.

The waiting was over. From this moment on, every move had been planned and rehearsed many times – any deviation from their timetable would be disastrous.

Both of the 415 horse power inboard motors that would propel Tabou and his cohorts into the dark side of history, were ignited. To minimize the loud rumble of their huge eight cylinder engines, they accelerated slowly.

A basic outfit, consisting of a black wet suit with attached hood and gloves was common to all. Everyone but Arbash and Coutre wore ballistic jackets that could thwart the effectiveness of small arms fire and even shrapnel under the right conditions. Aluminum tanks, holding 80 cubic feet of air, were strapped to the backs of Arbash, Jaabir, and Coutre. Each individual carried as many grenades and clips of ammunition as his or her strength would allow.

A half mile from the island, Sharif executed a slow turn to the north. In a large sweeping circle he steered to the far side of the island. One hundred yards from the warning markers, he cut his engine.

Aided by binoculars, Sharif watched *Patrol One* approach the furthest point of its run. It turned, as he knew it would, repeating an oft-traveled endless loop to the other end of the island. By climbing over the back seat and stepping onto the transom, the Syrian was able to reach the rope starter on the nine horse trolling motor that he and his confederates had jerry-rigged to the stern of the boat.

Dwarfed by its inboard brother, the tiny motor started on the second pull.

In a move that any fisherman might make, Sharif trolled quietly toward the shore of Wolf Island. Fifty yards from the warning buoys, Coutre adjusted his mask and began the flow of compressed air through his regulator. *Patrol One* was now half the length of the island away.

Arbash handed the Frenchman a shoe-box sized package. Coutre crammed the parcel into the tight confines of a nearly full duffel bag. He then placed the bag into a black net satchel commonly used by divers for treasure and souvenir hunting.

For the Frenchman, it would transport explosives, tools, an Uzi machine gun wrapped in plastic and a dozen clips of ammunition packed in a clear watertight container. Arbash spoke as Coutre prepared to enter the water.

"Don't fuck up, Frenchman!"

Coutre removed his mouth piece.

"Do not worry. I have no Arab blood in my veins"

He knew that his reply would anger the Palestinian, "You fuck ..."

By falling backward, over the side of the boat, he robbed his antagonist of an opportunity to respond. Arbash was forced to console himself with the thought that the insolent Frenchman was not a believer and could never join him in whatever afterlife existed.

The moment Coutre slipped from sight, Sharif applied pressure to the handle of the trolling motor and steered his boat away from the island. Winter ice had melted from the lakes surface just six weeks ago. Thick vegetation that would hamper clarity had limited growing opportunities in the fifty eight degree water. Consequently, underwater visibility was excellent – approximately thirty feet.

On the east, or lodge side of the island, Jaabir had followed a routine identical to that of Coutre. Dressed in scuba gear, he had been positioned by Tabou near the turn-around point of *Patrol Two*.

Five minutes after he entered the water, Coutre reached his destination and swam to the surface. He could easily identify the outline of *Patrol One* near the far end of the island. Before removing his flashlight, secured in a sheath attached to his belt, he dipped below the water's surface.

After disencumbering the C-3 plastic explosive from the duffel bag in the net satchel, he set the digital timer in accordance with the divers watch strapped to his wrist. It must explode at precisely 1:15 a.m.

Sharif's boat made another wide circle, this time, approaching the south side of the island where Arbash assumed the responsibility of intercepting Patrol Three. Tabou's men, Coutre, Jaabir, and Arbash, were all in position. Now, all they could do was await the return of their targets.

The steady drone of *Patrol One's* engines grew louder and louder. At two hundred yards, Coutre avoided possible radar contact by diving to the lake's rocky bottom. There, only twenty feet below the surface, he waited.

Several minutes passed before the black shadow of *Patrol One* made its calculated appearance. The lumbering vessel passed directly overhead then began a predictable swing. Careful to avoid the boats two propellers, the Frenchman darted for the bow and attached the large suction cup side of the C-3 explosive to the smooth metal hull.

With his goal accomplished, Coutre returned swiftly to the bottom of the lake. From the pitch of the engine, he could tell that the boat was maintaining its speed. This meant that the crew had not heard, or more likely ignored, the thud of rubber on aluminum. Their reaction was expected since logs and branches, floating on or just below the water's surface, were often encountered, particularly in the spring of the year.

After a short precautionary wait, Coutre surfaced into the bluish-white light of the newly exposed moon. In the distance, he could see his unsuspecting victims chug along their repetitious route toward certain death.

Even in its second quarter, the lunar reflection was sufficient to create a much more manageable condition. Tabou and his comrades would not find it necessary to use night scopes, as they had planned. The Frenchman knew this would further enhance their chances of success.

### Toby's Quick-Mart
### Highway 53

In response to a silent alarm phoned into the sheriff's office by a security company's unmanned computer, Deputy Dan Tate pulled into the Quick-Mart's driveway confident that his presence was little more than a formality. The last time, it was the fan from an air conditioner that set off the store's improperly tuned motion detector; the time before, a new employee, unfamiliar with closing procedures was responsible for tripping the alarm – it was always something.

It took the rookie deputy several seconds to recognize that the tiny pin-points of light twinkling in the reflection of his squad's high beams were actually bits of broken glass scattered across the concrete beneath the store's missing front window.

The sudden realization that the Quick-Mart had actually been vandalized, and most probably been entered, prompted him to stomp on his brakes, forcing the squad car to skid to a noisy standstill.

With his sidearm drawn, the young officer stepped into the pulsing red light emitting from the beacons atop the roof of his own vehicle. A billowing cloud of dust, created by his abrupt stop, drifted toward the building, convincing him to take a precautionary pause.

Before the air could clear, Jean Balfour emerged from the shadows. Elated by the sight of the squad car, she attempted to run. Her effort, on injured legs, gave her the appearance of a female Frankenstein. The sight of a long-haired figure dressed in tattered clothing and covered with dried blood while dragging its left leg as it ran from a crime scene did little to settle the rookie's jittery nerves.

In a near panic, he reached through the window of his car, fumbled for the microphone, and with a flick of his finger toggled the switch on his radio from RADIO to P.A.

"Halt! Stop right there!"

His voice, amplified to an ear-splitting level, stopped Jean in her tracks.

"Put your hands in the air!" he commanded.

With outstretched arms, she begged, "Please! We've got to hurry! I'm the one who called!"

With his gun pointed at the "thing" standing before him, Tate approached with caution.

"What the hell's going on here?" he demanded to know.

"I'm Jean Balfour. The one I think you've been searching for. I've been held captive. My husband's been killed, and they're going to kill the president."

Soothed by the woman's sincerity and the fact she didn't appear to be armed, the young deputy holstered his gun.

"Keep your hands up," he cautioned.

Sensitive to the fact that he was dealing with a woman, Tate gave his bedraggled prisoner a cursory pat-down search. After satisfying himself that she wasn't armed, he continued.

" Okay ma'am. What's going on here?"

"You must believe me," she pleaded, "there's no time."

"Believe what?" Tate asked.

"They're going to kill the president."

"Who's going to kill the president?" he asked.

"There are six of them. They've already killed my husband. They've been staying in a cabin on Elbow Lake. Most of them are Arabs. They're going to kill the president … tonight!"

Tate would have normally chalked off the injured woman's babblings as bunk, but something in the back of his mind conjured up the memory of two fellow-deputies joking about some "A-rabs", as they put it, who didn't seem to belong up here. If she was right …

He ran to his patrol car radio.

"Where are you going?" she shouted.

"I'm going to call my dispatcher. When is this supposed to happen?"

"At 1:15 a.m."

He checked his watch; they still had time – it was 12:46.

Jean dragged herself to the side of the squad car and draped the upper half of her body across the warm hood. The dispatcher and Tate's immediate superior, Sargent James Calley, quickly answered the officer's call.

"I'm 10-20 at Toby's Quick-Mart on Highway 53. I've got a subject here, a white female, who claims she's the Balfour woman who we've been looking for. The subject further states that she's been held by so-called Arabs who intend to kill the president, tonight. Over."

"Sounds like you've got a 10-51 on your hands. Have you checked her? Over."

"She doesn't have a car and she's injured ... she doesn't seem drunk. Over," Tate replied.

"Come on 23," Calley prodded, "you hear a story like that and you think you're dealing with a sober individual ? Give the subject a breathalyzer test. Over."

The Sargent's skepticism angered Tate.

"She says it's going to happen at 1:15. It's 12:46 now. Over."

"I'm not making any calls until you give the subject the test. Over."

Tate looked at the injured woman clinging to the hood of his car.

"You heard him. I'm sorry. But, it'll just take a minute. Can you do it?"

She nodded her head in the affirmative. The army-green ammo box on the floor of the squad car in front of the back seat produced a crystal filled glass tube. Tate held the small cylinder in front of Jean's mouth.

"Take a deep breath, then place your lips on the red plastic portion of the tube and blow as hard as you can," he instructed.

To avoid further delays, Jean did as she was asked without comment. Tate waited a few seconds, then examined the crystals. They remained unchanged.

"I knew it! goddamn it!"

He ripped the microphone from its hanger and once again called his dispatcher. Time had done little to temper the condescension in Calley's voice.

"Dispatch, 23. What have you got? Over."

"She's sober as a judge. Call somebody. Over."

"It's probably drugs. 10-19 the subject. Over," ordered Calley.

"I'll bring her in. Are you going to call? Over,"

"I'll call somebody. Just make sure you 10-19 the subject ... now!"

"Roger, dispatch. Over."

Again, Jean's frustration surfaced.

"He doesn't sound as if he understands. Why won't anyone listen?"

The young deputy shook his head.

"I don't know ma'am. He said he'd call. There's not much we can do standing out here."

Jean felt as bad as she looked. Tate grasped a spot on her right arm that wasn't covered by blood and urged her to stand.

"You need medical attention, ma'am."

The deputy's voice revealed a compassionate nature that Jean had not encountered for a long time. She reached for the welcome support of the young man's outstretched hand. His unexpected kindness had touched her.

"Come on," he said tenderly.

With care, he escorted her to the passenger side of his car.

"Get in. We're about forty-five minutes from the office. It's right across the street from the hospital."

Jean, hampered by a variety of cuts and bruises, eased into the front seat of the squad car. Terror and anguish had taken its toll. Would her efforts be enough, she wondered. And then there was the girl, Ayesha. Would the young Iranian's act of kindness cost her *her* life?

For the first time in two weeks, Jean was able to think beyond the moment and survival. Thoughts of the future spurned a profound sense of loss. Martin was gone. He wouldn't be there when she walked through the door of their home. All the plans, the loving, the whole thing seemed like such a waste. Worse still, if the president loses his life, the death of her husband and her own efforts would all be in vain.

## Wolf Island

Coutre, Arbash, and Jaabir had performed their tasks admirably. Each of the three Coast Guard patrol boats were unknowingly carrying ten pounds of C-3 plastic explosive somewhere on their hulls.

Moving beneath the water's surface, Coutre had worked his way to the east side of the island. There, he joined Jaabir. Arbash had been picked up by Sharif midway between shore and the island's southernmost point.

After many hours of observation, it had been decided that the small guard posts, situated to the far end and middle of the island, would be left alone. Through the woods, at night, it would take the two men manning the closest post at least five minutes to reach the main lodge. By then, it would be over.

Present concerns centered on the agents in the immediate vicinity of the lodge. Intelligence extracted from a variety of international sources had provided the mission planners with accurate numbers. There were two agents in the guard house near the dock – five were randomly patrolling the grounds, one outside the main lodge and one outside Sidney's guest cabin door.

Not included in their intelligence were three agents accompanied by German Shepherd dogs. Tabou spotted them as they walked along the island's irregular perimeter.

The only structure on the island that Tabou had never seen was the Communications Building. Hidden by trees, it remained the unknown factor. From detailed intelligence provided by their sponsors, he knew at least three individuals were regularly assigned to the building – the Secret Service shift commander, a military communications officer, and the president's personal military attaché.

These men were transported to and from the mainland by helicopter. The fact that the landing pad was immediately adjacent to the communications building made a numerical assessment nearly impossible. If the three men inside abandoned their posts to enter the fray, they would simply have to be handled. There was no other option. Surprise was their one indispensable weapon. Without it, they would have no chance.

Both Tabou and Sharif allowed their Z-275s to drift silently toward the area where they had *fished* so often on previous visits. Floating a mere six hundred yards from the main dock, they were prepared to strike.

At precisely 0114 hours, they would open their throttles and head straight for shore. With their huge 415 horse engines on the Z-275 Davantis, the distance between the markers and the island could be covered in a meager fifteen seconds. There would be no time for the island's defenders to react. Before they could fathom the improbable raid, it would be too late.

The attack would be straight-on the last thing the Secret Service would expect. In over two hundred years, no president had ever faced a frontal assault by well-equipped, well-trained individuals. Armed incursion by foreign troops had no precedent in American history. Consequently, and perhaps naively, the protection afforded the President of the United States was geared toward the lone gunman, the disturbed individual who would shoot from afar or thrust a small pistol through a sea of otherwise smiling faces.

# CHAPTER ELEVEN

## Boulder Lake
## 1:13:30 A.M.

One minute remained. Coutre and Jaabir had evaded numerous alarm systems to reach a predetermined point of concealment under the main dock, barely twelve feet from shore. With only enough room to breathe between the water and the dock's wooden slats, they waited. A single quartz light atop a ten foot four-by-four attached to Guard One, illuminated the immediate area in a sixty yard circle.

With practiced precision, Tabou and Sharif affixed the Soviet-made Degtyarev heavy machine guns to the pod supports attached to the decks of their respective boats.

### On the Shore of Boulder Lake

The small army of press assigned to the president formed an electronic camper city on the mainland only a half-mile from Wolf Island. While elaborate trailers and top-of-the-line Winnebago travel homes satisfied the minimal needs of the more notable among the group, technicians, cameramen and the like were forced to ferret out sleeping accommodations in everything from pup-tents to the cramped confines of a rented car.

Unable to sleep, Henry Saperstein decided to trade the smelly drone of electric generators for the relative tranquility of the lake. After donning some essential clothing and a light jacket, he left his rented camper and wove his way through a labyrinth of portable satellite dishes and makeshift sleeping accommodations.

Upon arriving at the dock he made a quick survey of the small flotilla affixed to the posts of the aging platform. most of the boats were rented from eager residents who were anxious to rub elbows with the familiar faces associated with the various news organizations.

This wild country, so different from his home in Virginia, fascinated him. Maybe … just maybe … he thought to himself, he might like to retire in an area like this. He doubted that his wife would go along with the idea, but still, he'd mention it when he returned. For now, he would simply enjoy the serenity of his remote surroundings.

Moonlight revealed a familiar figure of an old acquaintance standing at the end of the dock. Ferrington "Cuz" Cousins was a Texan. His trademark Stetson hat made his already intimidating six feet four inch frame appear enormous. Over the years, Henry had worked with the affable freelance photographer on several different projects.

"Hey Cuz. I didn't know you were up here."

"Henry!" exclaimed Cousins, "how the hell are you?"

Henry beamed. "I'm in pretty good shape for the shape I'm in."

"What lures a *Post* columnist out of Washington to a snooze job like this? How fucking many ways can you describe that rock pile over there?"

"I'm working on a feature," Henry answered, eager to change the topic. "What brings *you* to the Great North Woods?"

"I'm beginning to wonder. I've only been here a couple of days and I'm already going stir crazy. I feel like I'm trapped in a sensory deprivation experiment."

## Wolf Island

Inside Guard One, Agents "Tip" Farrel and Chuck Parry were fighting an old enemy – boredom.

"Politicians are like movie stars – they get into it so they can get laid. I guess this president 's no different than the rest," suggested Parry.

"The public wouldn't believe who's plugged who in the White House over the years. I've heard some of the older guys talk," added Farrel.

"Yeah, I've heard the stories. At least Atwater's only had one."

"But look at the one he's *had*! The V.P's wife!" laughed Farrel.

"Blue Bird's a lucky girl. How many women get to be the first and second lady at the same time?"

Farrel groaned at his partner's corny sense of humor then opened the door and stepped into the still night air. Except for the humidity that hovered around ninety percent, traces of the evening's earlier storm had all but vanished. In search of seclusion and a more aesthetic view, he ambled toward the lake.

The early morning hour, coupled with the inherent tedium of his chosen profession, nudged the young agent into a brief cognitive lull. Thoughts of his home back in D.C. made him crave the company of his beautiful new bride. Much to his regret, he had spent nearly half of their four-month marriage on assignment away from her and away from their new house.

It was at this time of night when it was quiet, and he was alone that he frequently found himself immersed in sensuous images of her lovely body. Fantasies, inspired by their newfound intimacy were an agreeable diversion. He allowed his prurient thoughts to wander as he stared across the inky expanse of water that stretched from the island's shore to the far side of Boulder Lake.

The distinctive wail of a distant loon, underscored by the repetitious proclamations of a thousand night creatures filled his ears with a haunting melody that only served as a lonely reminder of where he was and where he couldn't be.

With the exception of Robin, the president and all of his guests were sound asleep. The incident with Sidney was so personal and terrifying that it had left Robin emotionally wired. Her efforts to unwind were thwarted by a variety of fears – both real and imagined.

## 1:14:30 A.M.

The time had come. The two Z-275 Davantis surged from the water with a thunderous roar. A mere seventy-five yards separated the speeding craft from the shore as they charged toward Wolf Island.

It took Patrol Two, at the far end of its run, several seconds to hear, identify, and react to the noisy incursion. Second Class Petty Officer Spivey couldn't believe his eyes.

"What the hell is that?"

313

Lieutenant Donnerelli grabbed a pair of binoculars and did his best to locate the source of the sudden commotion.

"Those assholes are headed for the island!" he exclaimed.

At the sound of the powerful engines echoing across the lake, the cigarette in Agent Farrel's mouth dropped to the dock. Fantasies of a newlywed were replaced by the protective instincts of a Secret Service Agent. He could not imagine what was happening. It took him only a fraction of a second to locate the rooster tail of white water that was vaulting high behind the onrushing craft. It was obvious that the Davantis were moving at a tremendous speed. How could they have ignored the marker buoys? They must be crazy, he thought, or maybe lost or more probably … drunk.

Their destination was clear.

"No! No!" he muttered.

They were charging directly toward the main dock. Did these rummies with a couple of juiced-up boats think they could penetrate the Coast Guard and a full contingent of Secret Service agents?

His mouth dropped open. Where *was* the Coast Guard?

"Shit." he exclaimed under his breath, "they're at the far end of their run!"

The sudden realization that his future, and possibly his life, might hinge on his conduct over the next few moments gave Farrel a rush that any street cop could appreciate. He had to be sure. In his struggle to believe the unbelievable, he took a few steps forward. Both boats were fewer than one hundred and fifty feet from the dock.

He was right, for Christ's sake, this was it!

314

As Farrel turned toward Guard One, a disturbance in the water a few feet from shore demanded a parting glance. It took him a long second to comprehend what his eyes were telling him. The featureless outline of a human figure half emerged in water appeared a few feet from the south side of the dock.

A sudden burst of machine gun fire resolved the question of reality. Six of Pierre Coutre's 9 mm bullets pierced the young agent's chest puncturing both lungs and his heart. The ballistic vest that he promised his bride he would always wear might as well have been made of cardboard. It was no match for full metal jackets. Agent Farrell was dead before he hit the edge of the dock and rolled into the water.

Inside the main lodge, Robin was the only person in the cabin yet to fall asleep. Her restless movements were stilled by a strange noise. Suddenly, and inexplicably, she was afraid. But why? At first, she couldn't pin down the source of the disturbance. Then it hit her. Robin's conclusion brought her to an upright position. She had watched enough violence in the movies and on television to recognize the deadly sound of machine gun fire.

Jaabir, water still dripping from his wet suit, stood across from the Frenchman with an RPG-7 rocket launcher resting on his shoulder. Used primarily as an antitank weapon, the RPG-7 was able to penetrate up to 300 mm of tempered steel.

The lightly armored walls of Guard One, designed to house an agent, and at worst, protect him from small arms fire offered little resistance to the onrushing rocket. With a resounding explosion, the small building and its lone occupant, Agent Parry, were blown to pieces.

Amidst falling debris and distant screams of stunned agents, Coutre and Jaabir sought concealment in opposite directions away from the main dock. The Wolf Island shoreline, rugged and uneven, provided a wealth of suitable cover. A small grove of birch trees hid the Frenchman while Jaabir found refuge among the partially submerged boulders that dominated the shoreline fifteen yards north of the dock.

Agent and Shift Commander Ted Burke was manning the FIB, or fire and intruder board, in Communications Control. He sat mesmerized by his surface radar and the two fast-moving blips that were approaching the island.

A distant explosion and a change in the screen on monitor twenty-one labeled GUARD ONE forced him to redirect his attention. The screen was awash with white light too bright for a pole-mounted camera fitted with a light sensitive nuvacon tube to define.

A half-dozen red lights on the FIB began pulsing in matched cadence. Each of the six warning lights were relayed from the console in Guard One. Almost immediately, two additional intruder lights began blinking in response to unmanned alarms in the vicinity of the shoreline near the main dock.

A quick check of monitors eight and nine uncovered a startling sight. An agent's body, partially obscured by debris, was floating in the water on the lake side of Guard One.

With his eyes glued to the surveillance monitors, Burke acknowledged the obvious to Duane "Dewey" Edwards, the

Navy Communications Officer seated on the other side of the room.

"Christ, Dewey! We're under some kind of attack!"

While Burke tried to contact the helicopter that was ferrying agents back to their sleeping quarters on the mainland, Edwards, who had been watching the incredible sequence of events unfold, turned his attention to his own console.

His hands shook as he grabbed the phone and hurriedly punched in one of three numbers taped to the inside of the handset. A regular army unit placed on alert for the president's visit was stationed in Duluth nearly fifty miles away.

The practicality of the call was questionable, but still it had to be made. The young corporal answering the phone was cut short by Edwards' urgent interruption.

"This is mother one. The grass is blue! I repeat The grass is blue!"

"Are you sure?" asked the doubting nineteen-year old.

The ridiculous question prompted Edwards to abandon any pretense of civility. He yelled into the phone's mouthpiece.

"I'm sure! Initiate a response!"

"Yes sir! Just one moment, sir."

After a brief pause, an older voice resumed the conversation.

"This is Captain Gertz. May I have confirmation?"

"Zebra Boy," Edwards replied without hesitation. Authorization?"

"Tiger Bandit."

"Degree?"

"Nine Lincoln."

"We're on our way," replied Gertz.

The president's Attaché Officer Maurice Billings moved to Burke's side.

"How long before we can get the chopper back?"

"They've just unloaded. They're on the ground. They've got to get everybody back ... Shit ... I'd guess eight to ten minutes minimum."

"Will that be soon enough?" asked Billings.

The expression on Burke's face was less than reassuring. At this point, he could only assume two things about their attackers – they were well-armed and they wanted to kill the President of the United States.

His open call for information was acknowledged by Agent Tollis, who was patrolling the grounds at the time of the attack. He ran as he spoke into his field radio.

"Tollis here, gunshots, automatic weapons from the area where two boats are grinding against the rocks, West of the dock ..."

Tabou and Sharif cut their respective engines, allowing momentum to carry their boats to opposite sides of the main dock. Twenty feet from shore, they ran aground. Despite a last second effort to brace themselves, the abrupt stop hurled Ayesha and Arbash to the decks of their respective boats. Unscathed by their unexpected tumble, they scrambled to their feet and pivoted the Degtyarev machine guns toward the island.

With indiscriminate fervor, they systematically riddled everything in their path. 12.7mm bullets, capable of piercing light armor, easily cut through boats, dock posts, deck chairs, and small trees. Even the meager remains of the boat house was destroyed by the collective wrath of the thundering Russian guns.

Since the destruction of Guard One, which supported surface radar directed to the east side of the island, Burke was virtually blind. Agent Pallen, assigned to the president, broke in.

"This is Pallen, I'm headed toward Blue Boy! It sounds as if all hell's breaking loose out there!"

"Guards Two and Three, hold your positions," ordered Burke. "Canine teams and rovers to the main lodge area. Pinder stay close to Red Dog. Perez, Tollis, Dunlavey, Sauer, LaCourse ... Do your jobs!"

## 1:15 A.M.

Patrol Two swung toward the island in belated response to the startling assault that had already reached shore. Four hundred yards from his destination, Lieutenant Donnerelli, who had shirked his duty for fear that his next water command might be "The Admiral's Aquarium," and his three man crew, died in a ferocious explosion generated by the C-3 fastened to the hull of their boat. Scraps of aluminum and parts of four bodies fell like rain to the water's surface. There was nothing left to sink.

Scant seconds separated the demise of all three patrol boats. The concussions from the explosions rocked the landscape and everyone within a four mile radius of the island.

# On the Shore of Boulder Lake

A burst of gunfire, followed rapidly by four mammoth explosions left Henry Saperstein in openmouthed astonishment.

"Jesus Christ!" he yelled at Cousins. "What's going on out there?"

"Shit must be hitting the fan!" declared Cousins.

"Somebody's attacking Atwater," Henry cried, "let's go!"

Henry ran to the end of the dock and jumped into a boat with an outboard motor that wouldn't require a key to start. Cousins followed.

"How'd you know this one was mine?" asked Cousins.

"I didn't, but since you're here, I won't have to steal it."

Cousins pushed passed Henry and grabbed the rope starter atop the boat's fifteen horse motor. He started the engine with a single pull.

"Sit down Henry!" Cousins called out, "and hold on!"

With Henry's butt a few inches from the seat, the boat lurched forward. In a few short seconds they were headed across the inky water toward an unknown gun fight

The disintegration of Guard One had rousted the president from a sound sleep. Agent Pallen, gun in hand, pounded up the carpeted stairs to the second floor of the lodge, shouting as he climbed.

"Mr. President! Mr. President!"

Dressed only in pajama bottoms, the president opened his bedroom door.

"I'm all right," he assured the agent.

Out of breath, Pallen made a quick survey of faces. Sean, Don Kincaid, Ralph Harper, Mike Atwater, and Robin had all stepped into the hall. Everyone, but the president seemed confused. Robin's presence, in a robe, did little to mollify the situation since neither Kincaid nor Harper had any previous knowledge of her affair with their boss.

In a controlled voice, the president questioned Agent Pallen.

"We're under attack, right ?" asked the president.

"Yes sir, I think so. It's pretty crazy on the radio."

"Is this an attack on me, or is this a conspiracy? Do we know whether Washington or any other part of the country is involved?" asked the president.

"I don't know, Mr. President," the agent responded.

allen spoke into the mouthpiece of his field radio, "Vigil One, this is Pallen!"

"Go ahead, Pallen," Burke replied.

"I'm in the Castle with POTUS! So far, everyone's secure!"

"Agent, let me have the radio!" ordered the president.

In violation of standing orders, Pallen handed the radio to the president.

"To whom am I speaking," the president asked Pallen.

"Shift Commander Burke, sir."

"This is the president, Agent Burke. I must know if this is a general attack on the United States or does it appear that this is a decapitation attack?"

"I have no outside information, Mr. President. I'll put you on with Edwards, your communications officer."

"Mr. President. This is Captain Edwards. Our lines are all functional. The indicators are negative. So far, this seems to be your show, sir ... just you."

"Thank you Captain, keep me posted."

"Yes, Mr. President,"

"Pallen!" Burke snapped, prompting the president to relinquish control of the radio. "Don't move! Stay with POTUS!"

Agent Pallen knew that from the moment the first shot was fired, he was in charge of the president's immediate safety. The chief executive was his responsibility, and his alone. Procedures for such an attack had been established long ago. In training, they called it *The common sense defense.* In the event of a sustained attack, he was to transport the president to the safest haven possible and wait for help. In fact, the training he had received at Beltsville, Maryland rarely touched on the possibility of a full frontal assault that included rockets, missiles, and a determined force of well-armed unknown assailants.

Unlike the White House or Camp David, there was no "safe" area on Wolf Island. The whole complex was built on one big rock. Any mention of a radical renovation to his "home" was always met with strong resistance from the chief executive. Even the infamous helicopter pad was only agreed to on the condition that the plan for an underground safe area be abandoned.

With little regard for their protests, Pallen herded his charges into a middle bedroom, limiting their exposure to a single outside wall. Surely, he thought, the fight would never reach the main lodge.

Agents Tollis and LaCourse dashed through the trees toward the vicinity of the main dock. Earthshaking explosions, punctuated by the deadly rattle of heavy machine gun fire, did nothing to bolster their confidence in the effect that their 9 mm Uzis would have on the situation.

They were barely fifty yards from the fragmented remains of Guard one when a bullet from Ayesha penetrated Tollis's throat, severing his spinal cord. Caught in full stride, his body tumbled to a lifeless heap at the bottom of a gentle slope leading from the lake.

LaCourse hit the ground firing. From his position and distance to the target, the Uzi was far from an ideal weapon. Both of the big Degtyarev guns turned their undivided attention to the muzzle flash of LaCourse's machine gun.

A torrent of well-directed fire rained hell on the overmatched agent. The small tree that he looked to for protection barely slowed the chunk of lead that blew his head apart. Two more bullets tore through his lifeless body before the firing stopped.

In the guest cabin, Agent Pinder found the vice president sitting on the corner of his bed. He was surprisingly calm.

"Trouble in paradise?" asked Sidney.

"We don't know what we're up against. We've got to limit our exposure and trust in the men outside. I'll stay with you."

"Big fucking deal!" Holdridge mocked. "I'm stuck out here on this rock and all I've got between myself and an assassin is you?"

The vice president's remark reminded Pinder of how much he loathed the bastard whom he was sworn to defend. He turned away and barked into the tiny microphone of his headset.

"This is Pinder! Anybody know what the hell's going on?"

"It's a fucking masa ..." Agent Dunlavey's reply was cut short by Shift Commander Burke.

"This is Vigil One. We're under attack! Stay with Red Dog and stay off the air unless you've got something to contribute!"

Sidney clapped his hands together.

"We'll see how you boys do against someone who's carrying more than a hard-on!"

Even under conditions that threatened his own life, Sidney continued to rail against his protectors. Again, it took every ounce of Pinder's willpower to stifle his retort. He looked at the vice president with contempt, shuddering at the thought of risking his life for someone who deserved so little respect. But as he had done so often, he reminded himself that it was the office, not the man, who he was protecting.

## On the Shore of Boulder Lake

The battle on Wolf Island ignited a panic among half-dressed, bleary-eyed reporters, photographers and technicians. Everywhere, men screamed at other men. Shouts of *grab the tape, Where are the batteries?,* and *What the hell's happening?* roused the thirty-five vehicle encampment to a state approaching panic. One could only imagine the professional fate of the poor bastards who had sneaked away from the rigors of a predictable presidential visit to partake in the rowdy nightlife of Virginia, Minnesota nearly thirty miles away.

Corey Kamen, Henry Saperstein's photographer, raced down the dock with his shirt unbuttoned carrying his beloved Nikon. The first two boats he passed were already occupied – He vaulted into the third as if he owned it.

## 1:16 A.M.

Tabou and Sharif each stepped ashore carrying RPG-7 rocket launchers. With surgical precision, they directed their fire toward the closest possible areas of concealment. One by one, the projectiles pounded into the surrounding structures. The boat house, already collapsing from machine gun fire and the original two-bedroom cabin were the first to go. Even the small building used to clean fish was quickly reduced to rubble. Fires from the resulting destruction illuminated the entire area.

Inside Vigil One, Shift Commander Burke watched in utter consternation as the attack progressed. From what he could see, his well-trained, but overmatched agents would soon be overwhelmed.

The sudden havoc created by the insurgents in a matter of seconds appeared devastating. A hundred talked about precautions that were never implemented flashed through his mind. The environment, inconvenience, money, there was always a reason. No one, he was sure, ever thought that this could happen – not here, not against this president.

Nearly half of the two hundred warning lights on the FIB were now flashing.

Agent Ellis, accompanied by his four year-old German Shepherd, Prince, approached the dock from the north side of the island. Love for his dog prompted the agent to keep the beautiful animal close to his side. He was determined not to release his friend unless it was absolutely necessary.

Jaabir, caught up in the fiery display to his left, didn't catch sight of the approaching agent until it was too late. One of three rapidly fired shots struck the Libyan in the right side of his abdomen. The resulting impact flung his lanky body against a large boulder where he quickly returned fire.

Five bullets from his Finnish M82 machine gun caught the oncoming agent in full stride. With his legs shot out from under him, Ellis lost the grip on his German Shepherd and tumbled forward.

Jaabir fired wildly at the sight of the charging animal. In a fraction of a second, one hundred and twenty pounds of snarling fury enveloped the screaming Libyan in a blanket of fur and hot spit. Instinct, honed by years of evolution, directed the dog's long white teeth to the soft flesh covering Jaabir's throat. Flailing arms and a muted cry for help only served to tighten the animal's powerful grip. A sudden shake of the beast's frenzied head severed Jaabir's brachial artery initiating a gush of blood from between the dog's clenched teeth.

Sensing no further resistance, the German Shepherd repositioned his bite and tore a mouthful of whiskered flesh from his victim's throat. The Libyan's body dropped to the ground like a discarded rag doll. In the mud of Wolf Island, Jaabir died.

The dog stood motionless as he watched the throatless body for any sign of life. Satisfied that his victim posed no further threat, he let a baseball-size chunk of bloodied tissue drop to the wet rocks then returned meekly to his fallen master's side.

The president, Mike, and Pallen peered through an upstairs window at the surrounding fires and ongoing destruction. A nightmarish backdrop of shouted observations, underscored by sporadic gunfire, was supplied by the agent's field radio.

A rocket, fired by Tabou, snuck through the trees and pounded into the far corner of the main lodge. The resulting concussion knocked almost everyone, including the president, to the floor. Every board in the two-story structure shuddered at the ear-shattering force of the explosion.

Shaken by the blast, the president, Mike and Pallen returned to the bedroom where the remainder of their party was sequestered. The president grabbed Pallen by the arm.

"Agent, I've got two guns in my bedroom. I want to get them."

"You should stay here, Mr. President."

"I'm not going out with a whimper, agent. I want a gun!"

Pallen was caught between the book and a hard place, "Sir, I don't know if ..."

The president was unruffled and adamant in his demand.

"I want a chance. I can help. Let's go!"

The president's offer seemed sensible, and under the circumstances, couldn't be refused.

Suddenly, everything was dark. One of the explosions had knocked out the transformer through which electricity to every structure on the island was funneled. Only Communications Control, which housed its own backup generator, was comparatively unaffected by the blast. From this point on, the island's defenders would be forced to operate in relative darkness.

Using his flashlight, Pallen led the president and his guests toward the master bedroom at the end of the hall. Subsequent to loading the twelve gauge shotgun that he always kept in his closet, the president nodded toward the end-table next to his bed.

"Sean, in there, there's a pistol."

"Thank God!" exclaimed the Irishman.

"... and Mike," the president continued, "If you're interested, check the other side of the closet. I think there's a .22 caliber rifle in the corner. There should be some ammunition on the floor next to it."

### 1:17 A.M.

Agents Warren and Speck, in Guard Three, watched while an unfathomable drama played out before their eyes. From across the bay, they could see numerous explosions and hear sporadic bursts of machine gun fire.

Protocol established for this scenario dictated that they hold their position. The directness and intensity of the attack made such an order seem foolish. If the president's life was lost, what value would additional observations

328

from their position provide? Agent Warren expressed his anguish.

"Jesus Christ! We've got to get over there!"

"Our orders are to hold our position," reminded Speck, the junior of the two agents.

"Fuck that! This isn't Lee Harvey Oswald or Sirhan Sirhan – we're not looking at some hit and run deal. They need us! Shit … look!"

Warren gestured to the warlike conditions on the other side of the island.

"I don't know, man! I don't know! We've got no boat and we're seven or eight minutes from there by foot."

"Fuck it! I'm not going to guard this building and let the president die."

Warren grabbed his radio, "Guard Three to Vigil One."

"Go ahead, Vigil One!" Burke answered.

"We're coming over! This is bullshit! They're dying over there – they need us!"

Burke pondered the agent's words. From the battering his men were taking, it seemed more than likely that Warren was right.

"Yeah! Get your asses in gear! As shift commander, I'll take the responsibility. Manville, Harris, are you listening?"

"Yes! And we feel the same way," added Harris.

"All of you, go ahead. It's my call," Burke demanded.

There was no hesitation in Harris' reply.

"We're on our way."

Agents Manville and Harris, in Guard Two, were at least three minutes closer to the cabin side of the island than Agents Warren and Speck. Uzis in hand, they ran through the darkness.

Tabou, Sharif, and Ayesha began their advance up the hill toward the main lodge. As planned, Coutre and Arbash broke left toward the vice president 's cabin.

Agent Sauer, wounded earlier by shrapnel from one of Sharif's rockets, sat on the ground with his back propped up against the trunk of a birch tree. Both of his legs were numb and useless. What remained of his shredded left arm dangled from his shoulder and made him sick to his own stomach.

Despite his injuries, he remained alert and determined to do his job. Forty yards away, three figures silhouetted by the orange glow of a burning building emerged from below the hill.

With his good arm, Sauer raised his Uzi and fired a burst of 9 mm bullets. Tabou, cursing as he fell, rolled to the questionable protection of a nearby tree. Like most of the birch trees in the immediate vicinity, this one was a skimpy six inches in diameter. Sharif and Ayesha saturated the probable area of attack with a dense spray of machine gun fire.

Their miscalculation resulted in a lethal response from the wounded agent. Ayesha toppled to the ground. The brain that had served her so well dripped in stringy gobs from the surrounding foliage; most of the back of her head was gone. The big brown eyes that saw every injustice to her sex and her country remained open.

Sharif did not make the same mistake twice. The flash from Sauer's gun had divulged his unprotected position. The Syrian emptied what remained of his forty-shot clip into Sauer's already injured body. Tabou, blood oozing from his left side, struggled back to his feet and glanced toward Ayesha's lifeless remains. Sharif also looked at the girl and then turned to his Jabali companion.

"Good thing Coutre isn't with us now," he smirked.

"What do you mean?" asked Tabou.

"He'd try to fuck her."

Sharif smiled while an emotionless Tabou, in obvious pain, resumed his march toward the main lodge. The blood that streamed down the leg of his neoprene wet suit did little if anything to slow his pace.

From the second story window at the end of the hall, the president, Sean, and Pallen surveyed the destruction. Fear of another rocket, coupled with the limited range of their own weapons, kept them from firing. They would be forced to wait until their attackers closed in. At least, they weren't totally defenseless.

In Vigil One, Captain Edwards had completed his list of mandatory telephone calls. Everyone who needed to know knew the president was under attack. There was nothing more he could do. Agent Burke, who had also notified his superiors within the agency of the ongoing attack, called Pallen on the radio.

"Vigil One to Pallen."

"Pallen here."

"I'm on my way!"

"Good, we'll look for you,"

Burke turned to Communications officer Edwards and the president 's Military Attaché Billings.

"What about you guys?"

"S.O.P. doesn't seem to apply. I'm with you," declared Edwards.

"Me too," added Billings.

After walking to the arms cabinet, the three men scrounged through a skimpy assortment of available weapons. With a full complement of agents on duty, only two Uzis remained in the steel cabinet. Billings would have to make do with an out-of-place M16 rifle. In haste, the trio grabbed several grenades and the ammunition appropriate to their respective weapons.

Corey Kamen was frantic. The motor of the boat he had chosen wouldn't start. In fact, the engines on the two boats tied next to his, weren't starting either. Curses and screams may have vented anger but they offered no solutions. As more people arrived, it became apparent that the motors on every boat tied to the dock, were inoperable.

Unwilling to accept the fact that he was going to miss the opportunity of a lifetime, he abandoned his effort and ran to shore as fast as his out-of-condition legs would carry him. The row of five cabins that he had seen earlier in the evening couldn't be more than a half-mile away. He didn't remember anything specific, but cabins almost always have docks and docks have boats.

His lungs were unable to support the pace that the bright moonlight encouraged. Sucking air in huge gulps, he ran west along the shore. Nothing was going to keep him away from Wolf Island.

After sloshing through a swampy finger-shaped protrusion referred to as 'Frog Point' by the locals, he caught a glimpse of the first cabin – and yes, there was a boat tied in front.

As he approached the dock, he heard a man yell, "Stop! Where do you think you're going?"

The voice was coming from inside the cabin, probably through an open window.

There was no question that he would *borrow* the boat and worry about the ramifications later. To his relief, the key of the well-kept craft was left in the ignition. The knot that secured the boat, however, was frustratingly complex.

"The bastard must've been in the Navy," he muttered as his fingers tugged frantically at the spaghetti-like maze. Once the puzzle was solved, he plopped into a cushioned chair behind the boat's sparsely appointed console.

A half-turn of the key started the engine. Thank God for little favors, he thought.

The voice from the cabin was suddenly closer and easily heard over the throaty rumble of the motor.

"You son-of-a-bitch," the shirtless man hollered as he pounded down the dock, "Stop!"

Kamen reversed the prop on the boat's sixty horse motor, backing it away from the dock. With the craft's enraged owner only thirty feet away, he hit the throttle.

When the boat lunged forward, it scooped out a huge divot in the lake's surface – most of which descended on the irate man standing at the end of the dock soaking him. Kamen and his commandeered transportation thundered into the night.

# CHAPTER TWELVE

## 1:18 A.M.

Coutre and Arbash picked their way through the trees along either side of the path leading to the deck of the vice president's cabin. Agent 'Mandy' Dunlavey, one of the agents assigned to patrolling the grounds had positioned himself to the rear corner of the building.

He watched as the foreboding shadows advanced. The area surrounding the guest cabin, like the rest of the island, was peppered with young birch trees six to ten inches thick at their trunks. While beautiful to look at, they provided an aggressor with an intermittent wall of extra protection. One second Dunlavey's targets would appear to be in the open, the next second they were obscured by one or more of the trees.

When the black-clad intruders neared the steps leading to the deck, the young agent knew that he had to make a decision. Resigned to the fact that he would be forced to reveal his location without the promise of a clear-cut kill shot, he opened fire.

One of his bullets slipped through the trees and struck Arbash in the throat. The Palestinian, whose father was branded a "nebbish" by his Jewish oppressors, slumped to the ground with a severed spinal cord. He fell without so much as a whimper.

Another one of Dunleavy's rounds grazed the left cheek of the Frenchman who had attempted to escape the agent's deadly barrage by pinning his slender body to a birch tree. With blood dripping from his chin, Coutre listened to his cohort's body begin to convulse. When the thrashing finally stopped, a chilling death rattle left no doubt whether Arbash was dead.

Intent on avoiding a head-on fire fight, Dunlavey ran the length of the forty foot cabin as fast as his thirty-five year old legs could carry him. When he reached the far corner of the building, he turned and dashed toward the front deck. He hoped to regain the element of surprise from this new vantage point.

Coutre had the same idea. They both reached the front corner of the cabin at exactly the same moment. Neither man had time to avoid an inevitable collision; bodies and guns smashed together then careened into a large bed of multi-colored flowers in full bloom. Only a few inches and a dozen petunias separated the stunned combatants.

A split-second of mutual indecision was broken by the impact of the Frenchman's gun against the agent's mouth. The savage blow fractured Dunlavey's jaw, rendering him unconscious. At point-blank range, Coutre fired his Uzi into the face of his young adversary.

Before leaving the gruesome scene, and almost as an afterthought, he spit into the gooey mess that only seconds before was a living man. A man who had dared to draw blood from Pierre Coutre. With the neoprene sleeve of his wet suit, the Frenchman wiped the red liquid from his chin and stalked toward the wooden steps that would lead him to the vice president.

The presidential party stood at the top of the stairway leading to the ground floor of the main lodge. Robin nudged her way past Don Kincaid and Doc Harper to be with her lover. From her firm grip around his left arm, the president knew that she was scared.

"What do you think?" she asked.

The president peered down the darkened stairway as he whispered, "I don't know. These bastards seem well equipped."

"However it turns out. I'm glad we were together," she said quietly, but loud enough for everyone in the group to hear.

"So am I," he replied, never taking his eyes off the visible area at the foot of the stairs.

Behind them, Kincaid and Harper stood in stunned disbelief. The astounding admission of a relationship, between the president and the vice president 's wife was nearly as shocking as the attack itself. They could only wonder if this whole scene wasn't some sort of twisted nightmare.

Pallen, kneeling in front of Robin and the president, stood.

"We've got too many people here. Everyone should move down the hall toward the far bedroom."

Agents Harris and Manville from Guard Two had covered nearly one third of the necessary distance to the main lodge. Flashlights helped, but at a run they were pitifully inadequate.

Branches and rocks, shrouded in darkness, sent the frantic agents sprawling on several occasions. Fueled with adrenaline, they ignored the hazards and charged toward the menacing chatter of recurrent gunfire.

Without warning, something grabbed Harris by the ankle, tripping him brutally to the ground. A vicious ball of hot breath and sharp teeth ripped at the calf of the stunned agent's right leg. His screams and the efforts of Manville to ward off the attack were mercifully halted by the animal's confused handler.

Agent Bussard's effort to curb his German Shepherd's fierce attack fell short by several seconds. With shark-like efficiency, the dog had torn a jagged chunk of flesh from the back of Harris' leg just above the ankle. The injured agent writhed in agony.

"Holy Jesus! What the fuck are you guys doing here?" Bussard demanded to know.

Harris, out of breath and in severe pain, was barely coherent.

"Bussard, you dumb fuck!" he screamed.

"I was patrolling the far shore when the shit hit the fan. I thought you guys were insurgents. In a code three situation, you assholes are supposed to stay put, remember?"

In pain and very pissed, Harris continued to fume, "Don't you listen to your fucking radio?"

"My goddamn radio must've hooked on a branch or something! I lost it right after the first shots were fired!"

Manville had no time for a shit-throwing contest; he laid it on the line.

"Fuck it, you're out of it, Harris. We've got to go. Come on Bussard, let's hit it!"

The two agents, led by the German Shepherd, resumed their obstacle ridden course. Harris, bleeding profusely, was left to fend for himself.

Gunfire stopped Tabou and Sharif thirty yards short of the steps leading to the deck of the main lodge. Agent Miguel Perez had taken a position in the narrow crawl space beneath the northeast corner of the building. Errant shots from his Uzi slammed harmlessly into the surrounding trees.

Tabou's return fire was equally ineffectual. Sharif pulled the pin on one of his four remaining grenades and slung it toward Perez. The deck overhang made it impossible for the Syrian to place the proper trajectory on his throw. The resulting toss bounced off the facing of the deck and exploded far short of its mark. Perez continued to pepper the area with bursts of gunfire.

Valuable time was being wasted. Sharif removed the disposable rocket launcher from the carrier slung over his shoulder. The deadly weapon was perfectly suited to their circumstance. With a portentous hiss, the German-made rocket slithered beneath the building toward the helpless agent. Perez had no chance for survival. The resulting explosion tore upward through the oak floorboards into the far corner of the president's living room. The threat to Tabou and Sharif was eliminated, but an irreplaceable asset had been expended.

□□□□□□

Debris from Patrol Two littered the water around the boat transporting Henry Saperstein and Ferrington Cousins toward the war on Wolf Island. Details were Henry's business. Explosion by explosion, he attempted to chronicle the astonishing assault on the President of the United States.

Despite his intense curiosity, Henry feared that Cousins had positioned their boat too close to the action.

"Back off Cuz. You can't write history if you're dead."

"That's true, Henry."

With one hand steering the boat, Cousins reached into a duffel bag at his feet, withdrew a pistol and shot Henry Saperstein to death.

Ferrington Cousins, code name Parker, was in no mood for company.

## 1:19 A.M.

With a spray of machine gun fire, Coutre shattered the glass door entrance to the guest cabin. He walked into the building, bolstered by a newfound confidence.

Rather than remind him of his own mortality, his recent brush with death had endowed him with an aura of omnipotence. Destiny was his ally: fate his unwavering companion. On this day, at this time, in this place, he was invincible – no one could stop him.

Orange light from nearby fires furnished the interior of the cabin with an eerie irregular source of illumination. The Frenchman never faltered as he walked directly through the living room to the door of the main bedroom.

Inside, Agent Pinder listened to the approach of Coutre's footsteps – they stopped. His best guess placed the intruder directly in front of the door, but he couldn't be sure. There was no way he would risk revealing his position by firing at a questionable target who could, however improbable, be one of his fellow agents.

He had placed Sidney directly behind him. They would have to kill him to get to the vice president. If they did, he knew that he wouldn't go alone.

His Uzi was pointed at the only entrance through which an intruder could pass; he would get at least one of them. Despite the cool temperature, his face was dripping with perspiration. The wait seemed interminable.

Coutre, standing to one side of the door, reached for the knob, turned it, and pushed it open – all remained quiet.

The Frenchman waited several seconds before hurling himself through the doorway and into the room. Two shots rang out leaving Pinder's body motionless on the hardwood floor. Two small holes pierced the center of his government-issued jacket.

Sidney, pistol in hand, stood over the fallen agent.

"Is it finished?" he asked Coutre.

The Frenchman lowered his weapon.

"It is being taken care of as we speak, Mr. President."

"A rocket narrowly missed this building," Sidney said indignantly. "You could have killed me."

"Shit happens," Coutre shrugged as if he couldn't care less. "Let's get this over with."

Agitated and in a hurry, Sidney spoke.

"Here." He pointed to a fleshy area on the outside of his right thigh, "put the bullet here, and be careful," he warned.

"If it were up to me," Coutre pushed his forefinger into the vice president's chest, "you know where I'd put it."

"It's not up to you," Sidney said with an air of smugness. "Kabazi doesn't want me dead. We've got a long-term deal."

Coutre placed the muzzle of his gun several inches from the vice president 's leg. Sidney shook with fear and screamed, "Now! Do it now!"

The Frenchman lingered a few seconds, savoring his victim's anguish. Finally, he pulled the trigger.

A single bullet plowed a bloody, but relatively harmless, path through the soft flesh just below Sidney's hip. He clutched his leg and shook violently.

Coutre made no attempt to conceal his pleasure, "Too bad. I'll bet that hurts like hell."

Sidney was so traumatized by his wound that he had not heard a word the Frenchman said.

"Oh God! It hurts! It wasn't supposed to be like this!" he screamed.

□□□□□□

Tabou and Sharif had just stepped inside the door of the main lodge when the sudden clamor of approaching footsteps froze them in their tracks. Blake, Edwards, and Billings had entered the cabin through the kitchen and were pounding down an unlit hallway toward the stairs leading to the second floor. In his haste, Blake had forgotten that the second floor could be reached via a seldom used back stairway, only a few feet from the entrance through which the trio had passed.

Burke heard an object skip across the ceramic tile. He first concluded that, in the darkness, Edwards or Billings had inadvertently kicked one of the two stainless steel dog dishes that were kept just inside the rear door – but no, that wasn't it. It just didn't sound right. The beam of his flashlight picked up Tabou's grenade a fraction of a second before it exploded.

Only Billings lived long enough to see the muzzle of Sharif's AK-47 cast a sparkler-like light through what remained of the smoke-filled hallway. The Syrian's bullets perforated the lifeless remains of Burke and Edwards then worked their way toward the president's young military attaché.

With his weapon torn from his hand by the concussion of the grenade and his legs pinned under Edwards' perforated torso, Billings was unable to defend himself. A smoldering pile of blood-soaked flesh twisted into a collage of grotesque positions was all that remained of three brave men.

□□□□□□

In the deserted confines of Communications Control, the phone continued to ring. The call from Sargent James Calley, the St. Louis County Sheriff's Dispatcher, would never be answered. His belated warning was seven minutes too late.

### 1:20 A.M.

With sweat pouring down his ashen face and both hands clutched tightly around his leg, just above the deceitful wound created by Coutre's Uzi, Sidney sat on the edge of his bed.

"Who else knows about this?" he asked through clenched teeth.

"Only one other in our group. You would be of no value if the world were to learn of your deception."

"Why you?" asked Sidney.

"I'm the best, and I've been paid not to kill you. The others wouldn't have cared about the money; they would have killed you anyway. Kabazi knows his people."

Despite the two bullets from the vice president's pistol, Agent Pinder was still alive. His ballistic vest had done its job against Sidney's unclad .38 caliber bullets. The force of the shots, however, had rendered him unconscious for several seconds, but not long enough to prevent him from hearing of the vice president's participation in the assassination.

Without moving, Pinder could see that his unfired Uzi was positioned only inches from his right hand. He knew that he had to make his move before someone got the bright idea to check and see if he was dead. With a little luck, which he hadn't had so far, he would get off the first shot.

Since he was standing in the open, Coutre would be an easy mark. Sidney, on the other hand, was seated and partially obscured from his vision by the foot board of the bed. There was no doubt who his target would be. The man he was about to give his life for was a traitor. He, above all others, could not be allowed to benefit from his betrayal.

Driven by the belief that he was all that stood between his country and an assassin's treachery, Agent Pinder reached for the Uzi. An immediate and unexpected pain engulfed his entire right side, forcing an involuntary groan. The Frenchman's reaction was swift, but not swift enough. Pinder's first shot was deflected by the walnut bedpost. His second round struck Sidney Holdridge square in the chest. There would be no third bullet.

Coutre saturated the agent's upper body with a volley of gunfire that penetrated his ballistic vest with ease. Thomas Pinder died, never realizing the magnitude of his accomplishment. An ever-widening pool of blood rapidly encircled his body.

One look told the Frenchman that the American Vice President, who had traded his country and his honor for the presidency, was dead. Confronted with his inexcusable failure to achieve one of the mission's prime objectives, Coutre pushed Sidney's quivering body to the floor with an angry shove.

He didn't give a shit about Holdridge. His concerns centered on the money he was yet to receive. That was the problem with contingency contracts. If something went wrong, you were fucked. It was a silly mistake, he thought. He knew that he should have checked the agent's body when he entered the room.

Footsteps outside the door jolted the Frenchman out of a rare moment of self-reproach. Whirling toward the noise, he caught a fleeting glimpse of an air-born German Shepherd.

The attacking dog, fangs bared, was only inches from the barrel of his Uzi when he pulled the trigger. The substantial weight of the animal's falling carcass knocked him backward against the bed.

More noise ... footsteps ... someone was just outside the bedroom door. After scrambling to his feet, he placed his arms in front of his face then turned and dove through the bedroom window.

If the recent rain had not softened the ground, the Frenchman's awkward landing, on his right shoulder, could have been much worse. From the moment he thumped onto the wet grass, he found himself embroiled in a frantic fight to free himself from the blue curtain that ensnared the upper portion of his body, entangling his arms as well as his life sustaining Uzi.

His timing was perfect. The vague outline of Agent Philip Kanzowski, framed by the newly created opening, was allowed only a fraction of a second to regret his reckless pursuit. The face and chest of the over-zealous dog handler were immediately saturated with a lethal volley of hastily directed machine gun fire.

□□□□□□

The president and Pallen were crouched at the top of the stairs listening to the rustle of clothing and the faint sound of footsteps on the floor beneath them. Under protest, Robin and Sean had joined Mike, Kincaid, and Harper in the debatable safety of a bedroom at the far end of the hall.

"Could that be Burke?" whispered the president.

Pallen shook his head. From the landing at the base of the steps leading to the second floor, Tabou and Sharif laid down a precautionary barrage of gunfire. Both of their machine guns emptied simultaneously.

When the president and Pallen heard empty ammunition clips strike the hardwood floor, they seized the initiative and fired into the darkness toward the base of the stairs. One of Pallen's blindly fired shots shattered the joint of Tabou's left elbow causing him to cry out in excruciating pain.

"One of them isn't feeling very good," whispered Pallen.

Sharif removed his second grenade from its hanger, pulled the pin, and tossed it to the top of the stairs. The president, recognizing the sound of a grenade being armed, dived through an adjacent doorway into the bedroom where he had initially placed Robin.

Pallen, lying flat on the floor, on the other side of the stairs, found himself trapped with nowhere to escape. The grenade landed behind him, hurling his body forward, head-over-heels down the carpeted steps.

Covered with plaster, the president groped his way through the rubble and ran down the hall toward the bedroom where his guests waited in a near panic. He knew that his shotgun was no match for grenades. The second he opened the door, Robin flew into his arms.

"Are you all right?" she cried out.

Her question went unanswered. The president knew what had to be done.

"We can't stay here. If we allow ourselves to be trapped in one of these rooms, one blast could kill us all."

"Where to?" Sean asked.

"The back stairs. Let's go."

Mike grabbed the president by his arm.

"Jim. I'm going to stay here. I'll watch the hall and keep them off you while you try to get out of here."

"No way, little brother."

"It doesn't matter," Mike said solemnly, "and you know what I mean by that."

"It does matter. You're going with us."

## 1:21 P.M.

Corey Kamen pulled his boat into one of the storage slips situated fifty yards south of the main dock. Eager to document the unprecedented attack for an anxious world, he walked ashore and followed a grassy path that would lead him to the fragmented remains of Guard One.

The devastation on the island was sobering. From the totality of the destruction, he wondered if anyone would survive.

A limited supply of film necessitated a change in the *shoot everything in sight and sort it out later* philosophy, with which he normally approached an ongoing event. With little regard for the gunshots and explosions that he had heard over the past few minutes, he focused the splintered remains of Guard One in his Nikon's viewfinder.

After taking several more pictures, including a grim shot of Agent Farrel's dead body, he proceeded up the hill toward the lodge. Startled by more gunfire, he altered his course and headed in the general direction of the guest cabin away from imminent danger.

The body of Agent Tollis, with his head attached to his shoulders by a piece of flesh no larger than two inches square, was easy to find against the well-manicured lawn upon which it had come to rest.

Kamen was the consummate professional, keenly aware of the historical importance of each photograph. He felt a genuine responsibility for documenting the horror of the unprecedented attack. It was his pictures that would illustrate tomorrow's headlines.

Fifty feet from the ravaged guest cabin, his attention was diverted by a sharp snap, like a breaking stick. The movement, so close, startled him. He turned to find Coutre, gun in hand, standing only a few feet behind him.

"I'm with the press," Kamen blurted out.

"So what?" asked Coutre, who didn't sound as if he wanted an answer.

The veteran photographer knew what was coming next, but he couldn't stop it. He had only taken a step when the Frenchman opened fire. With bullets ripping through his flesh, Corey Kamen involuntarily tripped the chrome plated shutter release on his camera. He had taken what would become his most famous picture – it would also be his last.

□□□□□□

They were only seconds from death, and the president knew it. He herded his small band down the darkened hallway. Mike, trailing the group, took advantage of the confusion. A few feet short of the stairs, he stopped and watched his brother's entourage disappear into the darkness.

"Move! Move!" the president urged in a commanding whisper.

With Robin's hand clutched in his own, they descended the stairs and groped through what remained of the darkened first floor hallway. The mangled bodies of Burke, Edwards, and Billings couldn't be avoided.

Stumbling through the carnage, Robin lost her balance. To avoid falling, she inadvertently thrust her left hand into the perforated chest of Agent Burke.

Even in the darkness she recognized the warm pulpy flesh for what it was. The president managed to cover her mouth in mid-scream.

"We've got to be quiet," he cautioned, "or we won't get through this."

Something was wrong. The president searched the dimly lit faces of those around him.

"Where's Mike?" he asked, unwilling to accept the obvious.

Sean grabbed the president's arm as he bolted for the stairs.

"Jimmy!" he whispered, "he wanted it this way. Let him be a hero."

The feeble crack of Mike's small bore rifle, followed by the immediate rattle of heavy caliber machine gun fire, eliminated any decision that the president had to make. James Atwater winced as if he had been shot himself.

"Oh God!" he exclaimed, "Mike's gone."

Sean wrapped his arm around the president's shoulder. "I loved him too, Jimmy. But we're all going to be gone if we don't keep going."

"Wait," cautioned the president.

For the first time since the attack began, there was silence from both inside and outside the lodge. Only the distant barks of the president's two golden retrievers could be heard.

"I wonder if there's anyone left?" whispered Sean.

"We know there's at least one," answered the president.

Neither man had any knowledge of what was going on beyond their immediate circumstance. Were men armed with automatic weapons waiting for them outside? Or, had the combatants killed each other off, leaving only one or two assassins in pursuit? One thing was for sure. They couldn't stay where they were.

"Let's go!" whispered the president.

A right turn placed them in the kitchen which connected through a door on the far wall with the main dining room. It was there, through the dining room's floor to ceiling windows, that the president expected to assess their situation. If they saw little or no activity, they would split up and make a break for the surrounding woods. This would further fragment what remained of their attackers. Help couldn't be far away.

□□□□□□

The cook and both Navy stewards had moved from their downstairs sleeping quarters to the kitchen. Except for some cooking knives, they were both unarmed. As the presidential party entered the room, the frightened trio revealed themselves.

The forty-five year old chef was well beyond terrified.

"Don't shoot! Mother of God! What is happening?" he screamed, while his Navy companions, little more than teenagers, retained their composure.

The chief executive lowered his gun.

"We're under attack. Come with us," he commanded.

Footsteps, crashing down the stairs at the end of the hall, were closing the gap. A party of eight was not likely to outrun a single pursuer – they would have to deal with him.

The president found himself caught on the wrong end of the line. He had led the group into the kitchen which placed him furthest from the door through which their pursuer must pass.

"Get down!" the president ordered.

With a clear line of fire, he brought the shotgun to his shoulder. The man who had killed his brother stopped short of the door.

A moment of silence was interrupted by the clatter of another grenade skipping across the tiled surface of the kitchen floor. Trapped in the room's tight confines, there was no place to hide, no time to run. The blast was devastating.

Press Secretary Kincaid, the cook, and one of the stewards were killed instantly. The second steward, peppered with shrapnel, shrieked in agony.

Before the smoke cleared, machine gun fire engulfed the stunned survivors. One of the 7.62 mm bullets ripped into Doc Harper's chest severing his subclavian artery.

Blood and flesh sprayed across Robin and the president. With no other option, the remnants of the president's small band made a mad dash for the dining room. Sean, trailing Robin, turned and fired his revolver into the smoke. His shots were returned tenfold.

A randomly fired bullet penetrated the Irishman's right side, through the lower rib cage. The impact of the projectile threw him against the back of Robin's legs which caused her to stumble to the hardwood floor. Sharif, gun blazing, continued to plunder through the debris and smoke.

A single shot from the president's twelve-gauge tore into the Syrian's pudgy face. All two hundred and sixty pounds of Sharif's fury collapsed just inside the kitchen door.

His much ridiculed prediction was suddenly a fact. He would not walk away from this mission alive.

□□□□□□

Even from a distance of two miles, it appeared to Dooley Johnston that the whole north end of Wolf Island was on fire. He was scared. Every instinct he possessed urged him to turn his plane around and go home. But he knew what they would do to him if he backed out or faltered. No matter how badly he wanted out, he was committed, and nothing was going to change it.

When he crossed the Boulder Lake shoreline, he dropped from just above the trees to a few feet above the water. They might get him, but it wouldn't be because of radar. Three hundred yards from the island, cursing his predicament and the man with the white Stetson hat who hired him, he landed his plane.

### 1:22 A.M.

With Henry Saperstein's blood soaked body still crumpled up in the bow of his aluminum Starcraft,

Ferrington Cousins turned off the boat's motor and allowed it to drift. From his position, fifty yards east of the main dock, he could evaluate the progress of the assault without revealing himself as one of the participants.

He wouldn't enter the fray unless it was absolutely necessary. That was not his job. He was merely the backup – Kabazi's insurance ticket.

If he received a confirming signal within the next two minutes, he would go ashore with his camera and stash the pistol that he used to kill Henry somewhere in the vicinity of the dock. It was too bad that Henry had lost his life in their 'heroic' attempt to reach shore early in the confrontation. He smiled to himself as he envisioned an adoring world praising his courage, never suspecting his role in the brutal attack.

□□□□□□

Urged on by the president, Robin rose to her feet. Out of the corner of her eye, she saw the vague outline of a man. He was standing behind them in the double doorway leading to the living room.

The pistol in Musa Abu Tabou's right hand was pointed squarely at the president 's back. Robin willingly stepped between the gun and the man she loved. The president, unaware of Tabou's presence, had turned to aid his fallen friend, Sean.

The pistol barked a single shot. Robin gasped as the bullet smashed its way into the flesh above her left breast. The president whirled toward the source of the gunfire and pulled the trigger on his model 12 Winchester. Robin's falling body struck the barrel of his gun, forcing a missed shot.

Tabou's second shot hurled the president to the dining room floor. The most basic of instincts forced his hands into the warm liquid that streamed from his lower abdomen.

The bullet had passed through the ilium, forcing bone and cotton fabric through a dime-size exit hole in his lower back about three inches from his spine.

Half walking, half staggering, Tabou advanced to the side of the fallen president. The sight of the most famous man in the world, helpless at his feet, brought the faintest of smiles to the Jabali's tortured expression.

He was about to do what no one of his kind had ever done. Decades of Arab defeat and humiliation would end here.

This was the moment he had waited for – the hunter had cornered his elusive prey … it was over. He pointed his pistol at the president's brain.

□□□□□□

Manville, the agent from Guard Two, and Bussard, the dog handler, fired their weapons through the broken dining room window. They didn't stop until the black-clad figure standing in the middle of the dining room was on the floor.

A dozen shots found their mark. The heart, that many thought he never had, was no longer beating. Musa Abu Tabou, the world's most hunted terrorist and elusive killer, was dead.

It had been nearly eight minutes since the attack began. Three minutes longer than the Jabali had planned. His miscalculation was fatal.

With smoke still curling from Manville's Uzi, a two second machine gun burst from somewhere behind he and Harris, stilled them forever. In their haste to reach the president, the two agents had missed Coutre, the man who had killed them.

The Frenchman jammed a forty round clip into his Uzi, and with no time to waste, he vaulted through the opening created by the shattered picture window. Once inside the dining room, the cocky Frenchman easily identified his target. James Atwater was slipping in and out of consciousness as he laid stretched out before Coutre.

A pitiless sneer eclipsed the cruel features of Coutre's blood-streaked face. The dagger, that had stilled so many hearts, was clutched firmly in his right hand. He wanted this one to be personal.

"Mr. President, what a pleasure. I just left your vice president – not much of a man. How about you?"

To avoid the blunder that felled Tabou, Coutre restrained his exuberance long enough to make a precautionary examination of the area in and around the exterior of the cabin – there was no one.

Delighted by the fact that he alone had survived, he knelt at the president's side and placed the blade of his knife a few inches from the chief executive's throat.

Nine lives had succumb to his cunning in the last eight minutes. The killing was addicting, he loved it. " Him," Coutre nodded toward Tabou, "he hated you, me – I just want to watch you die."

The president, dazed and unable to move, refused to enhance his assassins accomplishment by begging. He remained motionless and quiet.

A familiar glaze spilled over the Frenchman's eyes. Again, the animal that was Coutre, was loose.

"Time to die!" he declared, relishing the effect those words always had on his victims.

Coutre was right. Robin emptied all four shots remaining in Sean's pistol into the middle of the Frenchman's lower chest and stomach.

A look of total astonishment replaced the sneer that usually mirrored his contemptuous nature. In his arrogance, he had refused to wear the ballistic vest that would have saved his life. His own demise was a possibility that he had never considered. Stumbling over Tabou's dead body, the Frenchman fell. His heart stopped pumping before he hit the floor.

An eerie quiet settled over the island. Robin, with her head resting on the arm of a fallen chair, lay in a darkened area of the dining room. She felt like crying, but there were no tears. The suffocating protection that she had always resented was now gone.

If an assassin remained alive, he or she would have a free pass. The president was helpless, and she had no weapon with which to defend them.

Emptied of its contents, she allowed her hand, holding the Smith and Wesson, to sink slowly to the floor. The excruciating pain in her shattered shoulder didn't prevent her from crawling through a pool of someone's blood to reach the president's side.

She could see that he was bleeding profusely. If it was not stopped, or at least slowed, he would not survive. With Coutre's black dagger, she cut a piece of fabric from his pajamas. Then, mustering all of her courage, stuffed the wad of cotton into the mushy hole left by Tabou's bullet. Her effort along with the resulting pressure rallied the president to a dim consciousness.

The pain of Robin's own wound was beginning to escalate. A whispered question brought her closer to her lover's lips.

"Are you okay?" he asked.

"Neither one of us is in great shape," she replied.

"Where are you hit?"

"Shoulder."

"Is everyone dead?" he asked.

"Seems like it. I don't hear anyone."

After a brief silence, the president lapsed into unconsciousness. It wasn't long before Robin was also forced to let go, passing out, and away from the intolerable pain.

□□□□□□

The anticipated signal that would indicate the president was dead had not been made. "

Fuck!" Cousins muttered, accepting the fact that he would be required to go ashore and possibly finish the job himself.

Because the destruction seemed total, and there appeared to be no one alive, he was tempted to assume the assassination had been carried out and head for Canada in

Johnston's Cessna. But if the president was alive, Kabazi would never stop. Life as he knew it would be over. Even the Mafia couldn't match the Jabali's reputation for revenge – this attack was certainly proof of that.

With a flashlight from his duffel bag, he gave the plane and it's nervous pilot a prearranged signal. Since he was the one who had made the original deal with Johnston, he was able to make certain that this portion of the operation was crystal clear.

If he had to go in, the plane was to wait offshore as long as it took or until it was fired upon. Once Dooley accepted the money, and there was no turning back, Cousins let him know, that if he didn't survive, the coward who had abandoned him would be dealt with accordingly. This gave his backwoods pilot a rooting interest that Cousins found comforting.

The instant his aluminum hull thudded against the wood dock, Cousins jumped to the slated walkway and ran toward the lodge. Behind him, his boat continued to idle toward shore. The smell of man-made explosives saturated the island like a London fog. Fire, debris, broken trees, bodies – death was everywhere.

When his lungs felt as if they would explode and his legs began to slow, adrenaline took over, propelling him up the path toward the front of the building. His sedentary lifestyle demanded recognition – a few yards from the lodge, he was forced to stop.

Gasping for air, he doubled over, placing his hands on his knees. When he looked up to survey his circumstance, he could see two bodies no more than thirty feet away. If he didn't want to join them, he thought to himself, he'd better keep going.

Halfway up the steps, leading to the deck, he froze like a statue. His own wheezing left doubt, but he thought that he had heard a voice.

Drenched in perspiration, he sought concealment at the top of the steps behind a pile of debris near the main entrance. Peering over a large chunk of side wall with the insulation still attached, he watched Agents Speck and Warren arrive from the far end of the island.

"Son of a bitch," he muttered.

☐☐☐☐☐☐

Warren, trailing his younger friend by a dozen yards, stopped near the guest cabin and yelled.

"I'll check it!"

Speck stopped running long enough to look back at his partner.

"I'll go ahead and see if the president's alive."

He had taken only a few steps, when he encountered his first body. From the camera around the victims neck and his casual dress, he correctly surmised that a photographer had gotten too close – too soon. He didn't stop to find out. There were only two people that mattered, and he knew Warren was checking on one of them.

Every building north of the guest cabin, except for the president's residence, was either flattened or burning. With his objective looming in front of him, despite his excellent conditioning, exhaustion was forcing him to slow his pace.

He viewed the bullet-riddled bodies of Agents Manville and Bussard as an ominous precursor to what he would find inside. Bussard's German Shepherd, like his master, was lying dead in the grass.

The bloodbath that had taken place on Wolf Island didn't seem possible. He wondered if nearly everyone he knew was dead.

Anxious to find out if the assassins were successful in their quest, he entered the cabin through the opening which Coutre had used only a few moments earlier.

Even in near darkness, there was no mistaking the litter of contorted bodies strewn between the kitchen and dining room. He couldn't be sure but – yes, it was the body of Robin Holdridge, and next to her was the president. The dark blotch on the chief executive's stomach couldn't be anything but blood.

"Mr. President!" he called out, stepping over Coutre and Tabou before dropping to his knees at the president's side.

From his appearance, the agent couldn't tell whether he was unconscious or dead. By placing the three middle fingers of his right hand on the president's throat, he was able to find a pulse – he was alive.

Wary of a remaining assassin, the cautious agent positioned his Uzi in a way that would allow him immediate access should it be required. Using the patch of cloth that Robin had cut from the president's pajamas, he applied pressure to the chief executive's ugly wound.

While Speck was administering first-aid, Cousins had moved quietly inside the lodge through an open front door. He crouched behind a sofa in direct line with the dining room.

The bodies of Tabou and Coutre blocked his view of the president. Even Speck, though visible, was a poor target. He was crouched over the president at least sixty feet away in poor light that just wasn't good enough for a reliable kill shot.

If that fucking agent had just been thirty seconds slower, it would have all been over, he thought to himself. As it was, he'd have to kill him.

After pocketing his Beretta, Cousins stood, making sure that his movements were loud enough to sound like a man with nothing to hide.

"Press!" he yelled.

Speck grabbed his Uzi. "Stay back!"

"I'm with the press!"

All Cousins needed was time to get close. Ignorance was always a good stall. The 'good guys' were at a disadvantage in a situation like this – they had to make sure before they pulled the trigger before the other person.

Speck was twenty feet inside the dining room. If he could make it to the doorway, he figured that would be close enough.

"Stop! and don't come any closer."

Ten feet from where he wanted to be, Cousins paused. The area outside the dining room was windowless and dark.

He knew that the agent couldn't be seeing more than a silhouette.

"I'm a reporter for the *Post*. Let me observe the scene. I'll stay back."

"No! I don't know who you are. Don't move."

"I'm an American. I represent the people," Cousins continued to shuffle forward.

"Bullshit! You stay where you are until I get more help."

Three more feet. That's all he needed. He had to keep the agent talking.

"The American people are going to read about this in tomorrow's paper."

"Fuck 'em!" shouted Speck. "Stop!"

It was now or never. Cousins slowly removed the pistol from his pocket and pointed it at Speck. There was no reaction from the agent because he knew his victim couldn't see the weapon.

"The V.P.'s dead!" yelled Warren from just outside the dining room.

"Christ" Cousins thought, "I'll have to take them both."

Distant sounds of outboard motors and frantic shouts left him with no choice. He fired his pistol at Speck, who immediately slumped forward, covering the upper half of the president's body.

The agent's weapon clattered to the floor. Cousins whirled toward Warren who had reacted quickly, concealing ninety percent of his body behind the window casing.

Cousin's second and third shots missed their mark. The agent responded with a spray of 9mm bullets, one of which struck the assassin on the inside of his upper left arm, just missing a main artery. The impacting lead spun him sideways and dropped him to the floor. In that instant, his objective was reduced to pure survival.

In great pain he stumbled through the hall to the living room. He couldn't escape through the front door without exposing himself to the man who had just shot him.

The gaping hole in the floor, created earlier by Sharif's rocket, offered an opportunity. He jumped into the ink black opening uncertain of what he would find.

His head smacked against the remnants of a splintered floor joist as he tumbled painfully into a shallow crater left by the explosion. Fear of death did little to ease his pain, but it kept him moving. In a matter of seconds, he managed to drag himself to the north end of the building.

With his lifeless left arm dangling at his side, he launched a headlong run for the lake.

□□□□□□

Warren moved into the dining room and knelt next to the stricken president. He could hear the assassin retreat through the trees, but he would not give chase. Others could do that. The president was now his only responsibility.

Speck was dead. The bullet had passed through his lower neck just an inch above the vest that might have saved his life. There was no time to grieve. Never wavering for a second, he shoved his friend's body to the side, allowing him to make an assessment of the president's condition.

□□□□□

When Cousins neared shore, he turned south. With the dock at least two hundred feet away, he was not sure if he could make it. Despite the fact that blood ran down his arm and off his fingers in a steady stream, there was no time for a tourniquet – in a matter of seconds he knew that all avenues of escape would be cut off. Out on the lake, several boats were already approaching the dock.

Not far from Guard One, he could see that his outboard motor was still running, pushing the bow of the Starcraft against the rocks. Rubbery legs navigating uneven ground resulted in a head-over-heels tumble twenty yards from the dock.

The wet ground softened his fall but painted him with long streaks of black mud. Added to the sweat and blood that was pouring from his body, he took on the persona of a wild animal.

He had never thought of his role as anything more than that of a backup. Now, he found himself the only surviving perpetrator of a massacre. They would never take him alive. He would do anything to escape.

After sloshing across the rocks, he rolled his body into the stern of the boat and frantically reversed the thrust of the motor's propeller. His weight was lifting the bow of the boat just enough to facilitate his escape from shallow water. When he reached the end of the dock, he heard a voice – it was close.

"Cuz! What's going on. You hurt?"

Cousins turned around and shot the man who had called his name in the face. In the split-second that it took him to fall, he recognized his victim as an old acquaintance from CBS News.

The young man steering the boat, probably a local pressed into service, couldn't have been more than sixteen years old. Cousins didn't give a fuck who it was. Two hastily directed shots put the kid on the floor of the boat. Either of the bullets that ripped through his high school letter jacket would have been enough to kill him. With the boy dead, the pilotless craft careened into the dock then lurched sideways where the motor could push it west out into the lake.

Clear of the dock, Cousins shifted the outboard into a forward mode then gave it full throttle, swinging the small craft into a tight one hundred and eighty degree about-face. With the bow of his boat pointed in the general direction of Johnston's Cessna, he sped forward.

His chosen route was forcing him to pass near a second boat. He guessed that the three men navigating the tiny craft were probably reporters.

They sat, watching his approach with glazed eyes, not sure whether they should duck or take notes. All he needed, he thought to himself, was a few heroes shadowing his escape.

He pointed the Beretta at the boat and continued to pull the trigger until it was empty. Of the seven shots he fired, three found flesh. The boat and its occupants would not be following anyone.

Warren could hear gun shots and the screams of men near the dock. From the sound of the motor that revved up and away from the island, he guessed that the assassin he had fired upon was escaping.

He cursed his decision to let the man go, but he knew that he had done the right thing. Thoughts of the press dissecting the scene with cameras summoned Warren's protective instinct.

He knew why Robin Holdridge, clad in pajamas, had her head on the president's arm and so would every other agent, but that's where it would end.

He could see she was breathing, so he ran his fingertips along her cheek with the hope of rousing her to consciousness. His touch and her vulnerability engendered a feeling of closeness.

He had watched Robin Holdridge with a teenager's fascination for the past six years. She was undoubtedly the most beautiful woman he had ever seen. More than once, he had fantasized that he was with her.

When her eyes opened and she stared up at him, he wanted nothing more than to help and protect her.

"How is the president?" she asked in a whisper.

"I'm not sure, Mrs. Ho... Robin." The sound of her first name on his own lips seemed strange but appropriate. "The press will be here. I think we should move you."

It took Robin's mind, crowded with thoughts of survival, a few seconds to comprehend the motivation behind his request.

"You're right," she said.

As gently as he could, he gathered her in his arms and walked her to the kitchen. She nestled her head against his shoulder as he walked.

"I'm going to lay you down here, among the others. I think it's the only way."

He placed her on the floor, gently turning her head so that he could look directly into her eyes.

"An agent brought you over here after the attack began. I don't think you remember anything else, do you?"

Robin looked up at him, managing a partial smile.

"No, I don't ... and thanks."

□□□□□□

Cousins pulled his boat alongside Johnston's float plane and killed the motor. Extreme loss of blood was overcoming the initial rush of adrenalin that had allowed him to escape. Suddenly, he was fighting for his very life.

Dooley opened the door and stepped out on the float as close to the Starcraft as he could stand and still maintain his grip on the plane's strut.

He was wild-eyed and barely coherent.

"Holy fuck, Parker! I god damn near left you. What took you so long."

Cousins lifted his head.

"Help me in," he groaned, "and let's get out of here."

"Holy fuck! Holy fuck!" Johnston kept repeating while he attempted to hold the boat next to the plane and assist his floundering passenger at the same time.

"Get hold of yourself, man," said Cousins.

Johnston was near tears.

"I never should have done this! They're gonna kill us. We're gonna die."

As he stood, Cousins grabbed his Beretta from the bottom of the boat. He knew it was empty, but that didn't matter. He pressed the barrel into Dooley's stomach.

"Look, you dumb fuck," he growled, "stop acting like a pussy and get this mother fucker in the air."

□□□□□□

At the main dock, a boat transporting two newspaper reporters and a broadcast team rammed it's bow into the rocks. The awestruck newsmen, led by ABC's White House beat reporter, Bob Wood, waded silently from the boat to shore.

Along their walk toward the main lodge, the reality of the ferocious attack was driven home with graphic detail. The fact that this savage battle had taken place in the heart of America was inconceivable.

First, there was Farrel and the splintered remains of Guard One. Then, at the base of the hill, they found the bloody bodies of Agents Tollis and LaCourse.

Farther up the path, laid the girl, Ayesha. From grisly scene to grisly scene, their Ikegami television camera recorded it all.

Hushed by the significance of their ponderous march, the stunned journalists approached the main lodge. Wood, expecting the worst, was the first man to enter the interior of the ravaged building.

Through the dining room door, he spotted Agent Warren kneeling over the president. The agent's Uzi was pointed in his direction.

"Is the president alive?" asked Wood.

"Yes, stop! Don't touch anything," said Warren.

Wood and his cameraman continued to advance while the other reporters honored the agent's command.

"Stop! This area is off limits. Take pictures, but stay back."

Wood, known for his arrogance, turned to his cameraman and pointed toward the president.

"Get in there!" he ordered.

Warren stood while shifting the business end of his machine gun to the cameraman. His voice cracked with emotion.

"I'll drop you right where you fucking stand! I swear it. This is a crime scene. The president's hurt. He shouldn't have your cameras stuck in his face – he's not on display!"

Wood was fuming.

"It's our job! He doesn't belong to you."

"You're wrong," tears filled the agents eyes, "he belongs to me until I get help!"

Wood and his cameraman stopped in their tracks, convinced of the likelihood that the agent would make good on his threat.

The distinctive beat of a landing helicopter broke the tension. Wood held his ground, but he didn't advance.

□□□□□□

In the sixty minutes that followed, government agencies flowed across the island in numbers far beyond the dictates of necessity or reason.

The ensuing twenty-four hour period proved to be a forensic disaster. Interagency conflicts, coupled with deliberate manipulation of physical evidence, would confound and confuse investigators for years to come.

# *Epilogue*

An estimated three hundred thousand people lined the streets leading to Arlington Cemetery. The first car in the processional, a limousine carrying the president, was a minor attraction.

The popularity of president Inglehart, while high, paled in comparison to the love showered on James Atwater and his wife, Robin. The throngs that had gathered, belonged to them. The Atwaters had become America's Royal Family.

In a rare unanimous vote, Congress declared June tenth a day of remembrance. A day that would allow those who survived, and the nation, an opportunity to remember those who were forced to surrender their lives in what the press had dubbed *The Wolf Island Massacre*.

The unveiling of a solid marble cross, upon which the name of each victim was carved, would highlight the day's planned activities.

Fifty-three Americans were posthumously selected for this unprecedented honor. They included: Vice President Sidney Holdridge, the president's brother, Mike Atwater, Press Secretary Kincaid, eighteen Secret Service agents, twelve Coast Guardsmen, the president's physician, his military attaché, his communications officer, a Marine steward, a cook, and *Washington Post* photographer, Corey Kamen.

At James Atwater's insistence, the names of seven Coast Guardsmen from the *Cape Carol* were added along with the names of Henry Saperstein, Martin Balfour, Mike McLeany, the sixteen year old boy, who without his parents' consent, volunteered to transport a desperate reporter to Wolf Island, and three reporters from assorted national news organizations.

Over many objections, the final name carved at the foot of the national monument was that of seventeen-year-old teenage runaway, Tracy Parks. Her senseless death, used as a subterfuge, would not be forgotten.

Jim and Robin were riding in the second limousine, directly behind President Inglehart. As tempting as it was, the solemnity of the occasion prevented them from waving to the excited crowd.

Members of the press were having a field day. This was their first opportunity to view the Atwater's three-month-old daughter, Kelly Marie. Cradled in her mother's arms, she was the realization of a love that had endured and prospered, despite insurmountable odds.

The Atwaters had survived, in fact flourished, since their ordeal. In the wake of a difficult period of convalescence, Jim Atwater was feeling chipper and extremely pleased with his new life.

Robin's scar above her left breast had done nothing to diminish her beauty. The scars that surgery couldn't correct were deep inside. It had taken her many months to rationalize the traumatic two-week ordeal that began with the chatter of machine gun fire and ended in ten minutes of horror on Wolf Island. The terror of that night, including her episode with Sidney, would always remain with her.

Passengers in the third car included Jean Balfour, the recipient of the nation's highest civilian honor, The Presidential Medal of Freedom. Next to her sat Sean MacDougal, the president's indomitable friend. His recovery, a tribute to modern medicine and a stubborn Irish personality, was complete; at sixty-six years of age, he remained the picture of health. In refusing a position in President Inglehart's administration, Sean stated simply, "I want to go fishing."

Across from the Irishman sat the young Spanish-American, Paul Rojas. The former Marine corporal, steward to the president, and a wounded survivor of the assassination attempt, was now an appliance salesman for Sears Roebuck and Company.

At the insistence of former President Atwater, Agents Pallen, Harris and Warren, rode in the fourth limousine, taking their rightful places among the honored survivors. Terry Pallen, confined to a wheelchair, had refused early retirement and chosen to remain with the Treasury Department as a training supervisor.

Two months after the assassination attempt, the body of bush pilot, Dooley Johnston was pulled from Lake Audy in Riding Mountain National Park, Manitoba, Canada by Canadian authorities. Though his murder remained unsolved, it was widely held that Ferrington Cousins fired the shot that killed Holdridge. Johnston's plane, curiously, was never been recovered or accounted for.

Ferrington Cousins became the D.B. Cooper of his era. Even though the Texan's role in the assassination attempt was rapidly uncovered, he was never captured. Speculation over his fate became a national pastime. Conventional wisdom had it that the wily would-be assassin was alive, well, and very rich.

The death of Halim al-Kabazi three years ago occurred only a month after the attempt on President Atwater's life. It seemed the infamous Jabali leader was involved in a car accident on the outskirts of Khalid. The press called his death *a timely coincidence*. Subsequent reports hinted at foul play. Americans, barraged by a string of post-death literary resurrections, gave little credence to the unsubstantiated accusations.

After the "accident," relations with Jabal greatly improved. In a reconciling gesture, Jabali president, Muhammad Azzuz Talhi, assisted James Atwater and his fellow survivors in laying a wreath at the base of the monument.

In the course of their investigation, the CIA uncovered Sidney Holdridge's treacherous role in the attempted assassination of the president. After consulting with the chief executive, it was decided that preserving national pride and confidence was more important than the sordid details of the vice president's betrayal.

All documentation, including the details that pointed a finger at the vice president's probable killer, was sealed and hidden among the tons of material protected in the National Archive where they will remain sealed for a period of one hundred years.

Without breaking her vow of silence to the president, Jean Belfour's' recent book, *Hostage*, alluded to a veiled conspiracy. The name and office of the perpetrator, however, was conspicuously omitted. Conspiracy buffs had a field day speculating over who the traitor might be. Oddly enough, the name Sidney Holdridge, probably because he lost his life in the attack, was rarely mentioned.

*The Washington Post* expose chronicling the president's affair with his vice president's wife was never published. Ten ferocious minutes rendered the story of the decade unpublishable. It was indefinitely postponed. The subsequent marriage of James Atwater and Robin Holdridge made the whole scandal sound like so many sour grapes. Any mention of an illicit affair between the wounded president and 'America's sweetheart' would have been unthinkable.

Many people, including a score of influential congressmen, feel that the Secret Service failed in its responsibility. A long string of Congressional investigations prompted every involved agency to publish its own biased version of the event. Even a 3,200-page report issued by a blue ribbon bipartisan panel, published at the conclusion of an exhaustive eight-month investigation, proved itself a compelling target. Critics of government, along with bureaucratic watchdogs from every quarter, attacked the self-serving document as inaccurate and naive.

One fact emerged as indisputable – security surrounding the President of the United States was inadequate. In a modern world where human ingenuity has accelerated every facet of our existence, where missiles travel at 2,400 feet per second and small inexpensive scopes turn night into day, it is absurd to think that we can protect our chief executive with an elementary configuration of well-intentioned individuals carrying small arms.

In a country where 125,000,000 people own a firearm and 600,000 people are licensed to pilot an airplane, it is impossible to protect any public official from the wrath of an adversarial government or group willing to sacrifice themselves to the act.

When their limousine entered the cemetery, Jim Atwater returned the pacifier that had slipped from Kelly's hungry mouth. He then placed his hand on her tiny head and reminded himself of his good fortune. A glance into Robin's loving green eyes brought back that familiar jab in his chest, near the heart. James Atwater was indeed a very lucky man.

# Character List

| NAME | ROLE |
|------|------|
| Arbash, Muftah Al | Assassin – Palestinian |
| Atwater, Christie | President Atwater's child (deceased) |
| Atwater, James | President of the United States |
| Atwater, Megan | President Atwater's first wife (deceased) |
| Atwater, Michael | President's brother |
| Bainbridge, Charles | Appointments Secretary to POTUS |
| Baker, Roosevelt J. | Captain of the *Medgap* |
| Balfour, Jean | Hiker camping near Elbow Lake |
| Balfour, Martin | Hiker camping near Elbow Lake |
| Baysinger, Elwood | Elderly Cabin Owner in Elbow Lake |
| Benzley, William "Benzy" | President Atwater's personal valet |
| Bertrand, Thomas | Secretary of State |
| Billings, Maurice | Presidents' Military Attaché Officer |
| Blake, Matthew | Seaman on the *Cape Carol* |
| Bonilla, Miguel | Assassin – Cuban |
| Brock, Patricia | Lifelong Friend of Robin Holdridge |
| Burke, Ted | Secret Service Agent |
| Bussard | Secret Service Agent – Canine Squad |
| Calley | Dispatcher – St. Louis Co. Sheriff |
| Carelli, Tony | 1st Class Petty Officer on the *Cape Carol* |
| Cooper, David | Pilot – *Shadow Two* |
| Coutre, Pierre | Assassin – French |
| Devlin | Lieutenant – Communications Officer |
| Donnerelli | Lieutenant – Patrol Two |
| Dunlavey | Secret Service Agent |
| Edwards, Duane "Dewey" | Navy Communications Officer |
| Ellis | Secret Service Agent – Canine |
| Farrel, "Tip" | Secret Service Agent |
| Flaskerud, Rudy | Deputy – St. Louis Co Sheriff |
| Freeman, Constance | Reporter – *The Washington Post* |
| Gertz | Captain – Duluth MN Military Unit |
| Grant, Terrance | 2nd Class Petty Officer on the *Cape Carol* |
| Grey, Edward | Forensic Specialist – D.C. Police Dept. |
| Handelman, Matthew | Director of the CIA |
| Harris | Secret Service Agent |
| Harper, Dr. Ralph | President's Personal MD |
| Holdridge, Robin | Vice President's Wife |
| Holdridge, Sidney | Vice President of the United States |
| Inglehart, Michael | President of the United States – Successor to President Atwater |
| Jaabir, Mustafa Al | Assassin – Libyan |
| Kamem, Corey | Photographer – *The Washington Post* |
| Kanzowski, Philip | Secret Service Agent – Canine Squad |
| Kazner, Rudolph | Physician to Sidney and Robin Holdridge |
| Kincaid, Donald | Press Secretary |

| | |
|---|---|
| Kosio | Seaman aboard the *Medgap* |
| MacDougal, Sean | Presidential Aide and Long-time Friend of the President |
| Magrane, Tom | Executive Petty Officer of the *Medgap* |
| Manville | Secret Service Agent |
| McDaniel, Charles | Secret Service Agent |
| Mazlowski | Uniformed Cop - D.C. Police Department |
| Meyer, Fritz | General and Head of the "Operation Takeback" Planning Team |
| Murtaugh | President Atwater's Golden Retriever |
| O'Leary, Monsignor | Priest – St. John's Catholic Church |
| Osborne, Ted | Detective – D.C. Police Department |
| Overton, Harold "Whipper" | General/Chairman – Joint Chiefs of Staff |
| Pallen, Terry | Secret Service Agent |
| Parks, Tracy | Teenage Prostitute |
| Parry, Chuck | Secret Service Agent |
| Pasha, Zalman | Israeli Ambassador |
| Pasonivich, Timoth | Clerk – Royal Haven Motel |
| Perez, Miguel | Secret Service Agent |
| Pinder | Secret Service Agent |
| Pinkle, David | CIA Agent |
| Riggs | President Atwater's Golden Retriever |
| Rueds, The | Couple Blackmailing Sidney Holdridge |
| Russell, Willie "Slick" | Detective – D.C. Police Department |
| Saperstein, Henry | Reporter – *The Washington Post* |
| Sauer, Phil | Secret Service Agent |
| Sharif, Mohammed Al | Assassin – Syrian |
| Smith, Royal | Deputy – St. Louis Co. Sheriff |
| Solis, John | Secret Service Supervisor |
| Speck, Thomas | Secret Service Agent |
| Spivey | 2nd Class Petty Officer – Patrol Two |
| Stream, Douglas | Captain of the *Cape Carol* |
| Sukayna, Ayesha | Assassin - Iranian |
| Tabou, Musa Abu | Assassin Leader – Jabal |
| Tate, Dan | Deputy – St. Louis Co. Sheriff |
| Tollis, Wayne | Secret Service Agent |
| Tripp, Thomas | Chief Boatswain's Mate on the *Cape Carol* |
| Walsh, Clinton | Former Campaign Advisor for Sidney Holdridge |
| Warren, Daniel | Secret Service Agent |
| Wells, Herb | Assistant Secretary of State |
| White, Mitchell | Secretary of Defense |
| Wingate, James | Editor – *The Washington Post* |
| Wood, Bob | ABC News Television Reporter |

# *Bibliography*

Bamford, James. *The Puzzle Palace*. New York: Penguin Books USA Inc., 1983

Briggs, Carol. *Sport Diving*. Lerner Publications Company, 1982

Broughton, Jack. *Thud Ridge*. New York: Bantam Books, 1985

Carter, Rosalynn. *First Lady From Plains*. New York: Ballantine Books, 1985

Copeland, Paul. *The Land and People of Libya*. Paul W. Copeland, 1967

Gunston, Bill. *Warplanes of the Future*. London: Salamander Books Ltd., 1985

Jensen, Amy LaFollette. *The White House and it's Thirty Three Families*. New York: McGraw Hill, 1962

Long, Duncan. *Assault Pistols, Rifles and Submachine Guns*. New York: Citadel Press by Carol Publishing Group, 1991

Marolda, Edward. *Carrier Operations*. New York: Bantam Books

McCarthy, Dennis with Philip W. Smith. *Protecting the President*. New York: William Morrow and Company, Inc., 1985

Miller, David, and Foss, Christopher. *Modern Land Combat*. London: Salamander Books Ltd., 1987

Richardson, Doug. *Techniques and Equipment of Electronic Warfare*. London: Salamande Books Ltd., 1986

Thompson, Leroy. *The Rescuers*. New York: The Bantam Doubleday Dell Publishing Group, Inc., 1986

Wilson, Frank. *Special Agent*. New York: Holt Rinehard and Winston, 1965

Wolff, Perry. *A Tour of the White House with Mrs. John F. Kennedy*. Columbia Broadcasting System Inc., 1962

*The Encyclopedia of World Military Power*. London: Aerospace Publishing Ltd., 1986

*Israel A Country Study*. Washington: The American University, 1979

*The White House*. Washington: The White House Historical Association, 1962

73322730R00236

Made in the USA
San Bernardino, CA
04 April 2018